*Twin*Trouble

When twin sisters are involved
—anything can happen!

About Catherine George

"Catherine George brings readers a delightful tale of falling in love."
—*Romantic Times*

About *Heartless Pursuit*

"Ms Steele pens a touching love story with vivid characterizations, gripping scenes and a powerful conflict."
—*Romantic Times*

About *Charade of the Heart*

"Cathy Williams' precious mix of volatile emotion and steamy sensual tension makes this a treat to savor."
—*Romantic Times*

*Twin*Trouble

EVER SINCE EDEN
by
Catherine George

HEARTLESS PURSUIT
by
Jessica Steele

CHARADE OF THE HEART
by
Cathy Williams

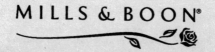

MILLS & BOON®

*MILLS & BOON and MILLS & BOON with the Rose Device
are registered trademarks of the publisher.
Harlequin Mills & Boon Limited,
Eton House, 18-24 Paradise Road, Richmond, Surrey, TW9 1SR*

TWIN TROUBLE
© by Harlequin Enterprises II B.V., 1998

Ever Since Eden, Heartless Pursuit and *Charade of the Heart* were first
published in separate, single volumes by Mills & Boon Limited.
Ever Since Eden in 1989, *Heartless Pursuit* in 1995
and *Charade of the Heart* in 1992.

Ever Since Eden © Catherine George 1989
Heartless Pursuit © Jessica Steele 1995
Charade of the Heart © Cathy Williams 1992

ISBN 0 263 81133 6

05-9810

*Printed and bound in Great Britain
by Caledonian Book Manufacturing Ltd, Glasgow*

Catherine George was born in Wales, and early on developed a passion for reading which eventually fuelled her compulsion to write. Marriage to an engineer led to nine years in Brazil, but on his later travels the education of her son and daughter kept her in the UK. And instead of constant reading to pass her lonely evenings she began to write the first of her romantic novels, which was accepted by Mills & Boon® in 1982. Since then, Catherine has written more than 45 novels and has currently had over 18 million copies of her books distributed worldwide. When not writing and reading she loves to cook, listen to opera, browse in antiques shops and walk the Labrador.

EVER SINCE EDEN

by

CATHERINE GEORGE

To Jacqui

CHAPTER ONE

THE MIDSUMMER moon shone, bright and obliging, just as if hired for the occasion. It silvered the grass and painted black pools of shadow under the trees in the gardens of Overbury Manor, while inside the old house chandeliers glittered down on a ballroom scene straight from a precocious child's fantasy. Masked characters from every fairy-tale ever read pranced and perspired to the heavy beat of the latest hit: Red Riding Hood and the Pied Piper, Snow White and a selection of Dwarfs, Hansel and Gretel, Jack and Jill, Goldilocks and innumerable Bears were all cavorting on the dance-floor, roaring at each other's antics, everyone having a wonderful time. The only exception seemed to be the lady who should, by right, have been enjoying the ball most.

A tall, brocaded Cinderella, with powdered ringlets and gilt satin mask, stood at bay near one of the long open windows, resentment in every line of her as she parried three men who hemmed her in like dogs snarling over a bone. As Prince Charming grew more proprietorial, and Sinbad and Robin Hood more predatory, a hint of desperation edged the smile the lady turned on her three admirers.

'By the way,' said Cinderella, inspired, 'how was the hundred-share index at close of trading today?'

No magic wand could have worked faster. In an instant the three men were deep in discussion of share prices and the world market, and not one of them even noticed when Cinderella drifted, retreating, until she could make her escape through the nearest window. Once on the terrace she lifted up her panniered skirts and raced down the shallow stone steps, threading her way swiftly through the knot garden, then on down an avenue of beeches until she found the opening she was looking for. With a swift look over her shoulder, she turned off on a narrow path which brought her to a copse of trees near an artificial lake, and with a sigh of relief she reached the sanctuary of a wrought-iron seat which was hidden, as remembered, by a thick screen of conifers.

She sank down on the seat and leaned back against the hard iron tracery, kicking off slippers sewn with beads to represent the necessary glass. As she gazed over the gleaming stretch of water she began to feel better, smiling as a ray of moonlight lit up the frivolous little gazebo on the far bank of the lake. As a child she had come here often to fêtes and garden parties. The gardens, particularly, had always been a favourite haunt, full of secret places for a child to play. She sighed. In some ways it had been a mistake to revisit the place tonight, to see it full of inebriated strangers. But Hugo had been very insistent. The ball was for charity, and a lot of useful people would be there. Useful to Hugo Barrington, he meant; contacts who could help him up the financial ladder he was climbing with such determination. Besides, as he had pointed out several times, the venue was Overbury Manor, hired out regularly these days for banquets and balls, and near enough to Clem's parents' home to make an overnight stay there at the weekend far more convenient than driving back to London after the ball.

Clem flicked at her elaborate skirts with distaste. She loathed this kind of costume affair. Her own idea of fancy dress was raiding the trunks in the attic at home to play Charades with her sisters, parading in Granny's flapper dresses, or fashioning weird and wonderful costumes from crêpe paper and faded artificial flowers. Her present outfit was stiff and uncomfortable, and she eased the bodice away from her heated skin, grateful for the cool night air coming off the water.

She smiled as she remembered the argument with Hugo over their choice of characters. He had been quite obstinate, obviously rather fancying himself as Prince Charming. And to be fair, she conceded, the style suited him well enough. The powdered wig concealed the slight thinning of his hair, and the velvet coat was flattering, but if she were honest his legs were a bit on the spindly side for silk stockings and knee-breeches. Her own plea to dress as Cinders in rags with soot on her face had been summarily quashed. Hugo wanted her as Cinderella dressed for the ball, the Princess Incognita herself, and had been unusually eager to lash out for once, paying a large, unspecified sum for the hire of the elaborate costumes he insisted were necessary. Clem wondered idly if he'd recoup his outlay in the contacts he expected to make. From her own point of view she felt she'd more than done her bit towards it. For two hours she'd smiled and chatted and charmed as Hugo wanted, playing her part dutifully right up to the point where Robin Hood and his chum had demanded dances with her. Then Sinbad's hands had been hot and damp, Robin Hood over-blunt with his opinions of her charms, and as far as Cinderella was concerned they could both jump in the lake. She smiled. It was a great idea, but on second thoughts no. She wanted the lake to herself. En route to her hiding place she had passed quite a few people strolling in the moonlight near the house, but happily no one had penetrated this far.

She yawned and settled herself more comfortably on the seat, her eyes dreamy as she gazed out over the water. The music from the ballroom was just faintly audible, sounding rather pleasant from this distance, but she had no intention of returning yet to the heat and noise inside. It was so much pleasanter to sit alone out here in the garden, enjoying the rare pleasure of a perfect summer night. The charity organisers were no doubt delirious with joy over their luck with the weather, particularly with a full moon thrown in as the crowning touch. It seemed a shame to waste it all indoors.

A twig cracked nearby and Clem waited, resigned. It had been only a matter of time before Hugo put in an appearance, of course, but to her dismay Clem realised she didn't want him to find her. Which was an unsettling thought, since until tonight she had been giving due consideration to the idea of marrying him one day. Which was the point at issue, of course. If he were the right man, she knew very well no consideration of any kind would come into it. Something her sisters had demonstrated very conclusively in their choice of husbands.

There was a slight rustle in the copse, and she frowned.

'Hugo?' she called uncertainly, peering through the darkness. 'Is that you?' She caught a glimpse of satin knee-breeches, brocaded coat, a wink of light from shoe-buckles, as a tall figure materialised in the shadows, a tricorne hat hiding his face as he made an elaborate leg from a distance.

'Alas,' he said, in an oddly muffled voice, 'I confess I'm not the fortunate Hugo. He of the red velvet coat and powdered wig, I presume? Your Prince Charming.' The intruder retreated to lean against a tree, his upper half hidden from her in the shadows.

Clem stayed where she was, wondering if she

should make a run for it, yet not in the least afraid. She eyed the figure in the shadows curiously, deciding no menace came from him, despite the aura of mystery.

'That's the one. Are you by any chance Prince Charming, too?'

'No, Highness. Mine is a different story.' There was a hint of laughter in the muffled voice. 'Unfortunately my partner was prevented from coming at the eleventh hour. So here I am—alone.'

Clem's eyes gleamed at him through the slits of her mask. 'Is that why you're out here in the garden instead of inside, dancing?'

'No. I find dancing difficult at the moment. Especially what passes for dancing among the young these days.'

'Are you so very old, then?'

'Centuries old, Highness!'

'Only two centuries, by your costume, sir.'

'And are you an expert on costume?'

'Interested, rather than expert.' Clem peered at the stranger, intrigued, wishing he'd come nearer. 'Do you know Overbury Manor?' she asked.

'Yes. My parents live in the district.' He laughed a little. 'But that's not why I'm here in the garden. I followed *you*, Highness. I'd been watching you from a vantage point behind a pillar on the other side of the ballroom, saw you fending off your three predators——'

'Two predators, one protector, to be exact.'

'From where I was standing the difference was indistinguishable. You had the air of a graceful doe keeping three rutting stags at bay. Then I saw you say something to them, and Abracadabra, your suitors were knee-deep in conversation with each other instead. How did you do it?'

Clem's mouth curved in a mischievous smile. 'Magic!'

'If you mean you're a bewitching creature, Cinderella, I'm in full agreement.'

She narrowed her eyes at this. 'It was all too easy. I said the magic words "share prices", and the spell was cast.'

The stable stock in the distance chimed midnight, and the man gave another muffled laugh.

'The witching hour. Time to unmask.'

'And time I went back to the ball,' said Clem briskly, searching for a slipper.

Before she could find it the man moved towards her and went down on one knee, his head bent as he rescued the slipper and slid it on her foot. She felt his fingers fleetingly on her instep, and caught her lower lip in her teeth, breathless as she gazed down on the satin-clad shoulders and black three-cornered hat. The desire to see the stranger's face was suddenly overpowering.

'Will you unmask if I do?' she asked.

'If you really want me to.' The tall man rose to his full height and removed his hat. Clem gasped, a hand to her throat as the moonlight revealed the stranger in every detail.

From his buckled shoes to the foaming lace of his cravat, her companion was the archetypal eighteenth-century exquisite. But from the throat upwards he wore the mask of some apocryphal cat-like beast, with slanting openings for his eyes to gleam through, and delicate, irrelevant tusks above the aperture which allowed his own white teeth to show through the dark silky hair which covered his entire face and head.

He swept her a bow. 'I *said* I came from a different tale, Highness. Mask or no mask, *you* can only be Beauty, while I—allow me to introduce myself—am the Beast.' And he straightened, laughing his hollow, muffled laugh inside his mask.

Clem stood up, shaking out her skirts as her heartbeat slowed gradually to normal. 'No doubt you took pleasure in that, Sir Beast. Do you enjoy frightening defenceless females?'

He stood very still, then shook his fantastic head. 'No, Highness, I've no stomach for it at all. Which, in part, is why I chose to wear the mask.'

'Are you so ugly, then?'

'Beauty lives in the eye of the beholder, so they say.' He shrugged. 'To my mother I'm not ugly. Others—others might think differently.'

Silence fell between them once more, as the two brocade-clad figures faced each other by the moonlit lake.

'In the story,' Clem heard herself say, 'a kiss changed the Beast into a mortal man.' And on impulse she reached up and kissed the place where the silky dark hair covered his cheek. She sensed the sudden rigidity in the stranger, and stepped back, her face warm behind the mask as she gestured towards him in appeal. She watched, expectant, as two slim hands went up in what seemed like slow motion, the lace ruffles at his wrists falling back as he loosened the mask at the throat. She held her breath, her curiosity almost outweighed by fear of what the mask might hide. Was he so ugly, or deformed, even? It was possible his reasons for hiding his face had been a lot stronger than a mere whim to assume the role of Beast for a fancy-dress ball.

She waited in silence as he slowly peeled the mask upwards, to reveal an aggressive chin, a wide lower lip and a short, curving upper lip, a jutting nose and high, sharply chiselled cheekbones—but only one visible eye. The other was hidden by a black patch. And as the mask came off the man shook back his hair and moved deliberately so that the cruel white light fell on one half of his face, showing up an angry scar which began just above the jawline and travelled upwards, disappearing under the eye-patch to re-emerge on its journey to his hairline.

Clem's reactions were mixed, but the strongest was relief, and she gazed very steadily at the face of the stranger, aware of a strong feeling of recognition, certain she had met him before. 'You've been hurt,' she said with compassion. 'Is that why you wore the mask?'

His smile matched the mockery in his voice. 'Because of my vanity, you mean.'

'No. I think you're probably over-conscious of the scar. You needn't be.' She tilted her head to one side, assessing him dispassionately. 'And the patch is rather romantic, I think.'

'What's underneath it isn't.'

'Have you lost your eye?'

'No. Somehow or other it survived. I'm assured I'll even be able to use it again in time.'

'Was it an accident?'

'Yes.' He ran his hand impatiently through his hair. 'Let's not talk about it, please. Instead, Highness, I think you should repay the compliment. It's time you played fair and let me see what lies beneath *your* mask.'

Clem swept him a curtsy and did as he asked, smiling up at him as her mask dangled by its ribbons from her hand. 'Better?'

He looked at her for several moments in silence, then smiled a strange, slow smile. 'I was mistaken. It would have been much more like fair play if you'd kept the mask on. You're very beautiful, Highness.'

'Moonlight is kind.'

'Then God help me when we meet in daylight —one way and another.' His face looked haggard suddenly, then he took one of her hands and raised it to his lips, the single penetrating glance meeting hers over it. 'Do you want to go in now?'

Clem did not. She wanted nothing more than to stay exactly where she was. 'Do you?' she parried.

His fingers tightened on hers. 'If a man finds he's strayed into a fairy-tale, complete with beautiful princess in the moonlight, is he likely to want it to end?'

'In that case I suggest we sit here for a while.' She resumed her seat on the iron bench, patting the place beside her. 'Let's watch the moonlight move over the lake and pretend we're old friends who do this sort of thing all the time.'

He sat down beside her with alacrity, and stretched out legs which were very much suited to silk stockings and satin knee-breeches. Not spindly at all, Clem noted with approval. Her companion was on the thin side, possibly, but muscular and fairly tall. Quite a few inches taller than herself, which was by no means common. Most men met her eye to eye, or fell short. Hugo was a fraction taller, it was true, but not much.

'Since we're old friends,' said the man abruptly, 'we should have no trouble in finding things to talk about. What subjects would please you, Highness?'

'Ourselves?'

'Right. You start.' Very gently he took possession of her hand, then leaned back, looking down at her with an encouraging smile.

Clem smiled back and obediently gave him a few basic details, telling him she designed and made clothes in partnership with a friend from art school days, had two sisters and one brother, came originally from a village near Monmouth, and currently shared a small terraced house in Putney with two other girls. 'There,' she concluded. 'One potted history. Now it's your turn.'

'Not so fast! You haven't told me your name.' His eye gleamed down at her. 'Unless you prefer to remain as Princess Incognita?'

'Since it wasn't my idea in the first place, certainly not. My name's Vaughan—Clemency Vaughan.'

'Clemency!' He laughed, a husky, infectious sound she responded to instinctively. 'And *are* you merciful, Miss Vaughan?'

'I hope I would be if necessary.'

'And this Hugo—Prince Charming back there.' He raised the hand he held to peer at her fingers. 'No badge of ownership yet. Will you allow him to buy you one?'

'If you mean a ring, I don't regard one as a badge of ownership,' she said. 'If ever a man *does* put a ring on my finger, it will be as a token of partnership, Sir Beast.'

'Ah! A latter-day Cinderella. I apologise, and agree wholeheartedly.' He hesitated. 'Do you require chapter and verse from me now, Clemency?'

She shrugged. 'Only as much as you wish. Or you can preserve your anonymity altogether, if you prefer. I don't suppose we'll meet again.'

'Why shouldn't we? Unless you find this face of mine a bit hard to take, of course.' His voice was so carefully expressionless, Clem experienced a sudden impulse to kiss his scar, tell him it didn't matter in the least to her, or to anyone else worth knowing.

'As I said before,' she stated matter-of-factly, 'the

patch *and* the scar are probably assets, where my sex is concerned. Females are usually bowled over by the piratical look.'

'Some, possibly.' He raised her hand to his lips again. 'Allow me to tell you what a very lovely lady you are,. Clemency Vaughan. In more ways than just that beautiful face.'

Clem was glad of the neutralising moonlight, as colour rushed to her face. 'Why, thank you, kind sir. But I can't just go on calling you "sir". Won't you tell me *your* name? Or is it classified information?'

'No, very ordinary. Wood—Nicholas. Nick to my friends.'

She frowned as she sensed tension again in the man beside her. 'Sounds familiar, ' she said slowly, then turned to him, smiling. 'The people who organised the ball! Hugo said their name was Wood.'

He laughed, relaxed again. 'True. Otherwise wild horses wouldn't have dragged me here. My aunt is a small but very overpowering lady, and passionately devoted to charitable concerns, so here I am as commanded, but without Miss Melanie Wood in tow. My sister,' he added, shaking his head. 'Eighteen and a handful.'

'So why didn't she turn up?'

'It was a matter of costume. My scar and I are not what you might call used to each other yet, so my attendance was conditional on a suitable disguise, thus Mel as Beauty and me as the Beast.'

'What happened?'

'I was rash enough to leave hiring the costumes

to her, the little monkey. Mine arrived as planned, but when Miss Melanie put in an appearance my father almost had a stroke. She'd changed her mind, she said. It was too hot for all that brocade.' Nicholas Wood laughed. 'She tripped downstairs in her version of the Little Mermaid, which meant a skin-tight gold tail, long blonde wig and a few pearls scattered strategically over her top half. My mother took one look and sent her up to her room mid-tantrum, and I, bloody fool that I am, obediently came on alone.'

'Are you sorry you did?' Clem flushed hotly the moment the words left her mouth, certain he'd think she was angling for a compliment.

'Don't be embarrassed. I know what you meant.' His intuition surprised her. 'And how could I be sorry? If we never meet again, Highness, I shall have this interlude to look back on.' He put a finger under her chin and turned her face towards him, his wide mouth turning up irresistibly at the corners. 'May I ask a final boon before Prince Charming comes after you in hot pursuit?'

'What is it?'

'Since I took off my disguise at your request—very reluctantly, I may add—will you return the compliment and let me see you without your wig?'

Clem's eyes opened wide, then she began to laugh as she shook her head. 'Sorry, can't be done. It may look like horsehair to you, Nicholas Wood, but it's mine, every last hair of it thick with powder because I wouldn't *wear* a wig.'

He caught a ringlet in either hand and pulled gently, bringing her face close to his. He breathed in sharply. 'A man can only take so much,' he muttered huskily, and kissed her.

Clem sat very still for a moment, taken by surprise, then she melted willingly into arms that closed about her in welcome, and her own arms went up around his neck. Their lips parted in unison as he held her so tightly against him that she could feel him trembling a little, his heartbeat thudding against her own, affecting her in a way she had never experienced before. At his touch, the feeling of recognition surged back again, along with a multitude of others clamouring inside her. She was sure she had never met this man before, yet she felt she knew him just the same, knew the touch of his hands and mouth, the feel of his body against hers as she experienced at last, for the very first time, the true heat of an answering flame in her own blood. She pulled away from him a little, her eyes glittering into his.

'I had no idea!' she said, in a strange, stifled voice, and held up her mouth again, and Nicholas Wood took it with a helpless groan, crushing her to him as he kissed her in a way she responded to with delight. Clem freed her mouth at last, but only to move her lips with exquisite care over the scar, pulling down his head so she could follow the raised ridge of it up into his thick black hair.

Suddenly an angry voice shattered their idyll. Clem jumped away guiltily, her hand to her mouth as Hugo's voice sounded in the distance, shouting her name.

'I must go,' she gasped, and held up her face for one last kiss.

Nicholas Wood held her fast for a moment, staring down grimly into her upturned face. 'Prince Charming—is he important?'

'No.' Her eyes widened as the truth of it struck her. 'No, he's not. But I don't want him to spoil this—'

'Give me your telephone number.'

'Will you remember it?' she asked anxiously, and he nodded, repeating it after her until he was satisfied he knew it.

'I'll ring you soon. Very soon.' He kissed her again, fiercely, then let her go. Clem gathered up her skirt to run in the direction of Hugo's voice, gave the tall, dark figure in the shadows a last smile over her shoulder and forced herself to leave him standing there alone, watching her out of sight.

'Where in God's name have you been?' demanded Hugo as she glided into view through the line of beeches. 'I was ready to ring the police!'

'I've been sitting by the lake, looking at the moonlight on the water,' said Clem, unrepentant. 'It was stifling in the ballroom, and you were so immersed in the Stock Market I decided to take a stroll in the fresh air.'

Hugo was deeply affronted, and insisted she stayed on at the dance for an hour longer than intended by way of reparation, then spent the entire journey to her parents' home telling her how irresponsibly she'd behaved, and how embarrassing it had been to make excuses to his friends for her disappearance. None of it had the least effect on his companion. She sat beside him in dreamy silence all the way home, deaf to his complaints, all her attention turned inward on the picture in her mind of Beauty and the Beast beside a moonlit lake, and of those few startlingly passionate kisses which made her heart thump at the mere memory of them, and left her on fire for more. When Hugo drew up outside the Vaughan home in Llanhowell it was two in the morning and the house was quiet, but lights were on in the kitchen for the latecomers' return.

A thermos of coffee and a plate of sandwiches waited for them on the table, and Clem gestured towards them politely, smothering a yawn.

'Do help yourself, Hugo, if you want. I won't keep you company—I'm for bed.'

'Have you nothing to say by way of apology?' he demanded, looking faintly ridiculous as he bristled in his velvet jacket and knee-breeches, which looked odd now he'd discarded the wig and wore his usual black lace-ups instead of the silver buckles of Prince Charming.

Clem fought back laughter in favour of smiling penitence, but it was difficult when excitement blazed inside her like a forest fire.

'I apologise for worrying you, Hugo, but I was perfectly safe. I know the garden at Overbury Manor almost as well as the one out there.' She gestured towards the window. 'I lost track of the time, that's all. I'm sorry.'

Hugo munched on a sandwich, looking irritable. 'It looked so bad to the others, Clemency. Surely you realise that!'

She looked hard at him. 'Was that all that mattered to you?'

He had the grace to look uncomfortable. 'No, no, of course not. But you just don't seem to realise anything could have happened to you out there in the dark on your own.'

Something had, she thought, hugging her secret to herself. She smiled at him with a radiance he eyed with suspicion.

'But nothing bad *could* have happened to me out there, Hugo. We were fairy-tale characters, remember. Fairy-tales always have happy endings.'

Hugo looked unappeased. 'I only hope you didn't spoil that dress.'

Clem swept him an ironic obeisance, then revolved in front of him slowly, holding out her rose brocade skirts. 'I don't think so. All present and correct—or pure and unspotted, whichever you prefer.' She glided over to the door, then turned and smiled at him mischievously. 'By the way, I'm so glad you vetoed my idea of a sooty Cinders.'

He frowned at her suspiciously. 'Really? Why?'

'If I *had* been in rags with a dirty face I would have been in quite the wrong fairy-tale after all, as things turned out.' She remembered something. 'By the way, I'd like to make a start back for town straight after breakfast, if it's all right with you.'

'But I thought we were staying to lunch!' Hugo

looked more aggrieved than ever.

Clem shook her head. 'I have to get back. I'm expecting a very important phone-call later in the day.'

'One of Lady Robina's friends with an order, I suppose.' He shrugged huffily, and poured himself a cup of coffee.

'No, nothing at all like that. No business involved, just pleasure.' She grinned at his incensed glare, and floated up to bed to lie for hours thinking how she had very nearly missed meeting Nicholas Wood beside the lake at Overbury Manor. If she'd followed her own inclination and refused to give in to Hugo's demands about attending the charity ball, she might have gone through life never knowing what it was like to fall in love. Her eyes opened wide in the darkness at the thought. Were a few stolen moments in the moonlight all it took to fall in love? It hardly seemed probable. She was twenty-eight years old, she reminded herself, not an impressionable teenager, old enough to know that what seemed like gilt in the moonlight might rub off the gingerbread all too quickly when she met her fairy-tale lover in the prosaic light of everyday. *If* she met him. How could she be certain Nicholas would remember her number, or ring her even if he did? But none of her arguments did anything at all to reduce the shining certainty that tonight had been the most momentous occasion of her life. Clem fell asleep at last, serene in the belief that not only was Nicholas Wood the mate she'd been waiting for all her life, but that, by some miracle, his feelings for her were exactly the same.

CHAPTER TWO

THE JOURNEY to London next day was not the pleasantest one Clem had ever made. It rained all the way along the M4, Hugo was in a very sour mood, and Clem too taken up with her own thoughts to try to sweeten his temper as she would have done on most other occasions. The sun reappeared as they reached the Hammersmith fly-over, and by the time Hugo stopped the car in the quiet little terrace in Putney midsummer was in full swing again. Clem's spirits soared as she jumped out of the black BMW.

'Thank you, Hugo,' she said, and hoisted her overnight case from the back seat. 'Don't get out—I can manage.'

Hugo stared at her in affront. 'Aren't you going to ask me in?'

'Not this time, if you don't mind. The girls may not even be decent yet, and I don't suppose there's much in the house to eat.'

'Then let's go somewhere for lunch,' he said promptly.

Clem shook her head. 'Not today.' She eyed him for a moment, thinking it over, then changed her mind. 'On the other hand, perhaps it might be as well. Let me just dash in the house for a moment—wait there, I won't be long.'

She flew up the path past the tiny patch of lawn
and the rowan tree, her fingers unsteady as she put
her key in the door. One of her fellow tenants,
Emma Reeves, stood in the kitchen in a sketchy top
and shorts, stirring something in a saucepan. She
smiled warmly in greeting at Clem, then peered
round her suspiciously.

'Hi! Hugo isn't with you, I hope?'

'No, he's out in the car. Why? Any phone calls?'

Emma tut-tutted. 'What *have* you been up to,
Clemency Vaughan? As a matter of fact, yes.
Someone with a dark brown voice, name of Nick.
Said he'd ring back about six.'

Clem threw her arms round Emma's sturdy little
person and hugged her so hard the other girl
begged for mercy. 'Thanks, Em. That's just what I
wanted to hear! I'm off down to the Drummond on
the corner of the High Street for something to eat
with Hugo——' She looked at her watch. 'Should
be home by two at the latest, just in case Nick rings
again before I'm back.'

Emma whistled. 'Is he likely to?'

'No idea—but I'm not taking any chances.'

'If you're that anxious, why don't you share this
rather peculiar risotto with me and just tell Hugo to
push off?'

Clem shook her head. 'Don't tempt me! But I'd
better have a talk with Hugo before—well, before.'

Emma's eyes glistened with curiosity, then she
laughed as an impatient toot sounded on the
BMW's horn outside. 'Off you go, then. I'll keep
this mysterious Nick on the boil if he rings before

you're back.'

Clem found it very difficult to embark on the conversation she had decided was necessary as far as Hugo was concerned. It was by no means the first time she'd let a man down gently, but with Hugo the reason was vastly different from all the other times, and she felt guilty. Until the evening before, she had been more or less contemplating marriage with Hugo Barrington, and had an idea he was fully aware of the fact. Yet it had taken only a few brief moments with the unknown Nicholas Wood to make the idea unthinkable. Even if she never saw Nick again it would make no difference now. Just meeting him had rendered a relationship with anyone else out of the question.

She knew in her heart of hearts that her reason for encouraging Hugo had been her feeling that time was passing, that she was twenty-eight, and high time she settled down if she wanted a home and children. As she did. And Hugo seemed like solid husband material: ambitious, suitable, even comfortably off financially. But now everything was changed. And, after a few mouthfuls of a salad she didn't want, Clem began, with care, to let Hugo know there was no point in going on with their relationship. He almost choked on a mouthful of pasta, his face flushing hectically under his smooth sandy hair as he stared at her.

'*What*? You don't know what you're saying!'

She swallowed some wine, feeling wretched. 'A clean break is better, Hugo, than letting you think——'

'Letting me think what?' he interrupted swiftly, his lips thinning. 'I've never asked you to marry me.'

'True. But lately you seem to have taken it for granted we were moving towards *some* kind of permanent relationship.'

Hugo had himself well in hand almost at once. He refilled his wineglass and sat back, smiling at her loftily. 'Well, yes, I'll admit I had toyed with the idea of asking you to move in with me. But marriage—that's a different kettle of fish. I'd have to be very sure any bride I chose was eligible in every way; well-connected socially. Nothing against your family, of course,' he added hastily, 'but a doctor with a country practice can hardly be termed a useful connection in my line of business.'

Clem's eyes narrowed to a cold sapphire glitter. 'How upsetting for my father to find he falls short of your requirements as a social connection! Not that it matters, of course, since the question doesn't arise.' She thrust her glass at him. 'I think I'll have a little more wine, then we can go our separate ways—in peace.'

Hugo looked a little shamefaced. 'Your problem, Clem,' he said sulkily, 'is that all the warmth is on the outside, on that beautiful exterior of yours. Inside you're cold.'

After the events of the night before, Clem knew beyond any doubt he was mistaken. 'You're entitled to your opinion, of course. But you're quite wrong, as it happens.'

'I suppose you're referring to the chap you lived

with once.'

Her eyes fell to hide the guilty surprise in them. She had actually forgotten Evan. Evan Rees, the graphic designer she'd first met in college, the one who had persuaded her to share the house in Putney with him at a very vulnerable time in her life. Wild, talented Evan, with his passion for mountains, had climbed one too many and fallen to his death on the anniversary of their first year together. But that was a long time ago. It seemed like light years away. And a lot of water had flowed under Putney Bridge since then.

'He's the reason really, isn't he?' demanded Hugo, leaning forward. 'Just because you got hurt once, you fight shy of letting yourself get involved again.'

It seemed wisest to allow him to labour under his quite mistaken delusion; kinder than telling him she'd met someone else. At the mere thought of the someone else in question Clem's heart beat faster, and she got to her feet, unable to sit still any longer. Hugo rose with her, but she shook her head.

'Please, stay and finish your lunch. I'll make my own way back.'

He looked at her glumly, then shrugged. 'If that's what you want.'

'It is, Hugo.' Clem held out a hand, and after a moment, reluctantly, he took it. 'No hard feelings?'

To his credit, he managed a smile. 'You ask a lot, Clem. But—well, all right. No hard feelings. Perhaps we might have lunch together one day.'

'Yes, let's.' She leaned forward and kissed his

cheek. 'And thank you for taking me to the ball last night, Hugo. I wouldn't have missed it for the world.'

His eyebrows rose. 'While I, Cinderella, have a feeling the entire evening was a colossal mistake on my part.'

She patted his cheek, smiling, and with a last goodbye made for the door, oblivious of the usual swivelling male heads as she passed on her way out of Hugo Barrington's life.

When she got home she found Emma out in the small back garden, surrounded by the Sunday papers as she lay mopping up the sun.

'No, he hasn't rung,' she said, grinning, before Clem could say a word. 'The telephone has remained quite, quite mute. He *did* say six, you know.'

Clem smiled sheepishly. 'Just checking. Where's Jane?'

'Staying overnight with the future in-laws.' Emma stretched luxuriously. 'Get your clothes off and come and join me—this sun's gorgeous. Besides, I think I merit a blow-by-blow account of what actually went on last night, Cinderella.'

'You'll never believe it!' Clem laughed, and ran upstairs to change, reappearing presently in a faded blue running vest and striped shorts, her hair tied up on top of her head. While she smeared herself liberally with suntan cream she gave Emma most of the details of the ball, going on at length about the meeting with Nick in the moonlight, but omitting any mention of the kisses, which proved too private to share with anyone.

Emma's eyes goggled at the point where Clem's intruder in her hidden retreat proved to be the fairy-tale Beast. 'You're kidding!'

Clem assured her she was not.

'But didn't he scare you to death out there on your own?'

'No. I was a bit startled at first, but not really frightened. I knew from the first he meant me no harm.'

'No—well, I mean, if someone had assault or rape in mind, I suppose they'd hardly get themselves up in fancy dress to do it. A mask, yes, but not lace and knee-breeches and so on.' Emma shook her head and sighed. 'And to think *my* Saturday night was spent at the cinema, watching Woody Allen with Hamish.'

'And very nice, too!' Clem lay flat on her back with her face to the sun, and finished her story in response to her friend's urging.

There was silence afterwards, then Emma said slowly, 'So on the strength of a few minutes in the moonlight with a man you've never met before in your life you've broken off with Hugo Barrington, boy wonder of the City.' She chuckled. 'And there I was, afraid you were actually working up to marrying him one day!'

'Afraid?'

'Yes. Now it's all over, I can say I'm sure it would never have worked, Clem. A bit lacking in the humour department, our Hugo.'

'I suppose you're right,' said Clem, thinking it over. She sighed. 'Poor Hugo! He turned a bit nasty at first, but by the time we parted he was being rather sporting.' Suddenly she leapt to her feet as the telephone rang, and tore into the house, out of breath as she grabbed the receiver.

'It's only me,' said her mother. 'Your father tends to be restless until he knows you're back safely.'

'Mother, I'm sorry!' said Clem, stricken. 'No excuse—I just forgot. My mind was rather full of having told Hugo we should go our separate ways.'

'So that's why you were so abstracted this morning. I wondered why you wouldn't stay for lunch.' Angharad Vaughan sounded amused. 'And what was wrong with Hugo, then? He's lasted longer than some.'

'Nothing, really. The fault's with me, I suppose.'

'Not as far as your loving mother's concerned, Clemency Vaughan. You just haven't found the right man yet, that's all.'

It seemed precipitate to announce that she was sure she had, so Clem just laughed and asked if the usual Sunday hotline had been busy with calls from her sisters, and learned that Kit's two small sons had German measles, and Charity was proud to announce she was pregnant for the third time.

'I had a feeling she was. Isn't it a bit soon?'

Mrs Vaughan laughed. 'Luiza's three, Dolly's five, and Charity feels it's high time she gave her husband a son.'

'How about Penry? He hasn't been round lately.'

'Cutting a swathe through the nurses at the hospital—as usual.'

Clem went back to the garden and stretched out again. 'It was only Mother,' she said, sighing.

'It's not four yet, dummy. The man said six.' Emma eyed the tense, graceful figure lying beside her. 'I've never seen you like this before. You're like a cat on hot bricks.'

Clem agreed ruefully, and did her best to relax, applying herself to the Sunday papers and making as intelligent an attempt at conversation as possible for someone whose mind was in a frenzy of anticipation at the thought of the expected phone call. When Emma went indoors to make tea, Clem gave up all pretence at doing anything but daydreaming about the night before as the sun poured down on the sheltered square of lawn. Nature had been generous, giving her an olive-tinted skin which tanned easily, and she lay motionless, acquiring a deeper shade of gold as the afternoon wore on, all her concentration on the hope of hearing that deep, clear-cut voice again. Tea had been drunk, Emma had wandered off for a bath, and still there was an hour to be lived through until six. Clem was amazed at herself. She knew she was behaving like a schoolgirl with a first crush, but no amount of self-derision had the slightest effect. As the minutes ticked by her nerves frankly jangled, until the tension inside her became almost unbearable.

Just before five-thirty the telephone rang, and she flew to answer it, her hand shaking as she picked up the receiver.

'Hello,' she said huskily, and sagged against the

wall as she heard the longed-for voice.

'Clemency?'

'Yes.'

'Nick. I know I told your friend I'd ring at six, but I just couldn't hang on any longer.'

'I'm glad. Neither could I.' She heard him breathe in sharply.

'What's your address?' he demanded.

She told him and he chuckled, the sound of his unconcealed delight raising goose-bumps along her spine. 'If I come round in half an hour would you come out with me for a meal? Please?'

Clem's eyes opened wide. 'Half an hour! Why, where are you?'

'Parson's Green.'

She laughed unsteadily. 'You mean we're almost neighbours?'

'Amazing, isn't it? Well, will you come?'

'Hold on.' She put a hand over the receiver as Emma came down the stairs in one of her prettiest dresses. 'Are you going out, Em?'

'I told you. *Twice*,' said Emma severely. 'Hamish is taking me to a party in Maidenhead. I knew you weren't paying attention.'

Clem pulled a face. 'Sorry. When will you be back?'

Emma grinned. 'Late—very late, if you like. And did you take in the fact that Jane isn't coming back at all tonight? She's going straight to the office in the morning from Guildford.'

Clem blew an ecstatic kiss at her friend, then took her hand from the mouthpiece. 'Hello? Nick?'

'I thought you'd rung off.'

'No fear. Could you make it an hour?'

'If I must. But not a second more.'

Clem put down the telephone in a daze of delight, her face flushed and radiant.

'Wow!' said Emma in awe. 'This man must be something. That *was* him, I imagine.'

'Yes!' Clem seized her friend and did a war-dance round the cramped little hall. 'Would you believe it, Em, he lives in Parsons's Green, and he'll be here in an hour——Oh God, I'm a mess, what can I wear? And just look at my hair——'

'Calm down!' Emma rubbed an elbow irritably. 'You've bumped me into the banisters, you idiot. Honestly, Clem, I've never seen you like this before.'

'I've never been like this before.' Clem took a deep, steadying breath. 'I've just *got* to get myself together.'

Emma hauled her into the kitchen and opened the refrigerator. 'I assume you want to feed this man here. Look, there's half a cold chicken I roasted yesterday, some salad greens, cheese. And you can open this wine Hamish brought me last night.'

'Em, you're a miracle!'

'I know. Now, for pity's sake go and stand under a cold shower and recite your twelve times table until you're sane. Works wonders.'

They both jumped at the thunderous knock at the front door.

'I don't know why Hamish can't ring the bell like everyone else,' said Emma, resigned, and patted

Clem on the cheek. 'I'll go straight off, love, otherwise he's quite likely to insist on waiting to see if this Nick of yours merits the Hamish Munroe gold seal of approval.'

Clem raced upstairs before the door closed behind Emma, lingering only long enough under the shower to rinse the last traces of the previous night's powder from her hair. She dried the springy curls at frantic speed while she decided what to wear, worried that Nick would probably find her everyday clothes a bit of a let-down after her fancy-dress finery. Her taste was fairly conservative, and ran to fine materials she made up herself in the plain styles she preferred, and after much indecision she finally stayed with a beautifully cut lawn dress, printed in shades of kingfisher and indigo which accentuated the tan of her bare arms and throat, the skirt cut to float gracefully as she moved.

After applying a minimum of make-up to her face, Clem thrust her fingers through her still damp hair and ran downstairs to set the table. The small dining-room was separated by an archway from the bay-windowed 'parlour', as Emma liked to call it, and Clem spread the best linen cloth on the table, and ran into the garden for a handful of buds from the Iceberg roses just coming into bloom. Arranged in a small crystal jug, they added a festive touch to the everyday cutlery and wineglasses, and, feeling this was an extra-special occasion, she rummaged for a pair of unused candles in the kitchen drawer, and put them on a couple of Coalport saucers kept for use as ashtrays.

At top speed she carved chicken and washed lettuce and radicchio, then whisked up some French dressing, quite amazed by her own efficiency in the circumstances, since her hands were obliged to work in conjuction with a mind inclined to wander every other minute to matters far less mundane than mere food.

When the doorbell rang at exactly the appointed time, Clem froze for a second, then breathed in deeply and ran to open the door, smiling in radiant welcome at the tall figure silhouetted against the evening sun.

'My God,' said Nicholas Wood, his voice husky with awe. 'Are you real?'

'Pinch me and see for yourself,' she said happily, suddenly in command of herself for the first time in hours. She beckoned him inside with ceremony. 'Welcome to my humble abode, sir.'

Nick followed her into the hall and closed the door, standing with his back against it as he looked at her in silence, his eyes travelling from her bare, sandalled feet to the unruly mane of ash-fair hair.

Clem returned the look with interest, wondering why a plain white shirt and cream cotton trousers managed to make her visitor even more attractive than the brocade and lace of the night before.

'The moonlight didn't do you justice, Clemency Vaughan,' said Nick at last. 'You're tanned! I didn't think of you as a golden girl. Last night you were all silver and moonbeams. Today you're different.'

'So are you,' she said, then could have kicked herself as the smile vanished from his watchful face. 'I think I prefer you in everyday clothes, Mr Wood,' she added deliberately.

The single visible eye looked quizzical. 'Even without the mask?'

'Especially without the mask.'

He smiled again, and Clem relaxed.

'Perhaps we should introduce ourselves in the more usual way, if it's not a bit late in the day.' She held out her hand with mock formality. 'Good evening, Mr Wood. I'm so glad to meet you.'

'It's so kind of you to let me come.' Nick took her hand in his and held it tightly. 'Could it be fate that we live so near each other, Clemency?'

'It would have been more difficult if you'd been in Huddersfield, or Edinburgh, certainly, but not insurmountable.' She laughed breathlessly, her pulse accelerating at the touch of his hand. 'Won't you come into my parlour?'

'With pleasure!' He followed her into the sunlit room, limping slightly, she noticed with a pang. And in the bright light he looked even more haggard than the night before. His face was tanned to a brown much darker than her own, but it was thin and hollow-cheeked, with a smudge of fatigue below the one visible eye, which was a warm wine-brown, with a questioning look in the depths as he bore her scrutiny uneasily.

'They say the scar will never go completely,' he said at last.

'Do you mind?'

'Not for myself.'

'It makes no difference to me either,' she assured

him. 'I didn't know you without it, so for me you are as you are.'

'Warts and all?'

'Ah, but you're much handsomer than Oliver Cromwell.'

Nick laughed. 'Which wouldn't be difficult. While you must be bored with remarks about that beautiful face of yours.'

'Not bored, exactly. But so few people bother to find out there's more to me than just the way I look.'

'Which merely proves how unfair life can be.' He took possession of her hand again. 'Don't your women friends resent how generous Mother Nature's been to you, Clemency?'

'None that matter.' She felt mesmerised by the single, searching eye, burningly aware that for the past minute or two they had both been talking to disguise the current flowing between them like an electric charge that dried her mouth. She watched the skin grown taut over Nick's cheekbones and the small silence grew, and lengthened, and neither seemed able to look away, until at last Nick blinked, and swallowed hard.

'Where are they?' he asked.

She gazed at him blankly. 'Who?'

'The friends who live here with you.'

'Out,' she whispered.

Nick thrust a hand through his hair. 'Then we'd better get out of here. Now. Where—where would you like to eat?'

Clem ignored a persistent inner voice which counselled caution. 'I thought you might like to have supper here.' As she moved closer, she could see he was trembling, and raised a hand to touch his face, alarmed. 'Nick, are you ill?'

He shook his head, teeth clenched. 'No,' he said through them. 'Not ill.'

The trembling communicated itself to Clem; then, after only a moment's hesitation, she slid her arms round his waist and leaned her face against his chest, listening, shaken, to the thunder of his heartbeat. 'Tell me what's wrong,' she pleaded.

'Nothing's wrong,' he said in a tortured voice. 'In fact, nothing's ever felt so right before, but it may surprise you to know, Clemency Vaughan, that it's not my practice to fall on a girl within minutes of meeting her. On the other hand, if you don't move away right now my powers of self-control are in deep trouble.'

'Oh, is that all?' she said in relief, and held up her face. 'Then please kiss me, Nicholas Wood, because it's all I've been able to think about since last night.'

With a sound somewhere between a sigh and a groan, Nick did as she asked, wrapping his arms round her as his hungry mouth met hers. And this time, even without fantastic costumes and moonlit setting, the magic was even stronger than before. He pulled her to the couch and sat down with her on his lap, his lips both demanding and tender on hers, and Clem gave herself up to his embrace without reserve, exulting in the fire running through her veins. When neither could breathe, Nick took his mouth from hers, but only to kiss her nose, her eyes, her ears, until he returned to her parted, questing lips again, the tip of his tongue touching hers, then sliding deeper within to learn the contours of her mouth, as her arms slid round his neck to hold him closer. Time passed unnoticed, until at long last he raised his head and looked at her with a gleam in his undamaged eye.

'Have you any idea how much better I feel now?' he said huskily. 'I'm not sure I could have survived much longer without kissing you.'

'I know exactly how much, because I feel the same.' There seemed no point in hiding it. Clem smiled up at him sheepishly. 'I was so afraid you wouldn't ring, you know.'

'Are you mad, woman? I rang before you even got back here this morning!'

'I know, but until then I was sure you'd forget my number, or—or change your mind.'

He scowled blackly in disbelief. 'How could you think that? Don't you ever look in the mirror? Believe me, I wrote your number down the first opportunity I got, and woke up with it on the tip of my tongue.' He looked relaxed as he grinned down at her, very different now from the tense man of a few minutes before.

Clem's eyes gleamed, iridescent with pleasure. 'Did you really?'

'Of course I did.' He settled her more comfortably against his shoulder. 'I lay awake most of the night just wondering about you. How a ravishing creature like you could still be unattached. Unless you're not?' he added, scowling again into her glowing face.

'Of course I am—completely now. I bade Hugo a fond farewell over lunch today.'

'At lunch? Before you even heard from me?'

'Yes.'

He smoothed her hair back from her forehead, looking dazed. 'What would you have done if I hadn't rung back?'

'Nothing. What could I have done? You didn't give me *your* telephone number, and I had no idea where you lived, so that would have been that. But having met you I knew I couldn't marry Hugo anyway. Whether I ever saw you again or not.' Clem looked up at him very steadily. 'The moment you held me in your arms and kissed me, I realised I'd never really responded like that to a man in my entire life.'

'Not even Hugo?'

'No. So I let him down as lightly as possible.'

Nick rubbed his cheek against hers and gave a long, unsteady sigh. 'If I'm dreaming all this, I hope to God I never wake up.' He chuckled suddenly. 'Tomorrow I'm going to send the biggest bouquet of flowers she's ever had in her life to my aunt Evelyn.'

Clem looked up, smiling. 'Because she insisted you go to the ball?'

'Exactly.' He shook with sudden laughter. 'Perhaps you didn't realise, my darling, which of those characters last night happened to be my aunt. She was the plump lady in spangles with a wand—the Fairy Godmother herself!'

CHAPTER THREE

IT WAS so late before they even began to think of eating that Clem found she was starving as they faced each other across the table. Nevertheless they talked non-stop as they demolished Emma's chicken and worked their way through the bread and cheese and wine. In response to Nick's demands to know all about her, Clem described Robina Crichton's studio in Pimlico, where she helped create special-occasion clothes for her partner's well-connected friends and relatives, told him her evenings were spent at the cinema or the theatre, that she liked reading and walking in the park when it was fine. Nick was such an attentive, absorbed listener, she found it very easy to talk about her hopes and her ambitions, and found it necessary to apply mental brakes after a while, wary of going into too much detail. Yet. She was almost afraid of this blazing new awareness of the man encouraging her to reveal herself to him. It was all so new, yet at the same time so familiar. Her feeling of *déjà vu* was so strong, she almost believed they had known each other before in another life.

'Enough about me,' she said at last, as they sat over coffee. 'Tell me about you. What do you do?'

Nick took her hand in his as he stretched his legs

out cautiously. 'I'm a journalist—or was. I've been out of action for a while.'

Clem reached to touch gentle fingertips to his face. 'Because of this?'

He nodded. 'Didn't dodge quickly enough in Beirut. Got caught by a ricochet.'

'Your leg, too?'

His face went blank. 'You noticed the limp?'

'Yes. Like I noticed you've got a mole near your left ear, and your two front teeth are slightly crooked. Everything about you is important.'

He caught her in his arms. 'I can't believe this, Clemency Vaughan. My experience of women hasn't prepared me for someone as open and candid as you.'

She flushed. 'You think I should be more restrained,' she said flatly. 'Hide my feelings and try to be mysterious and so on.'

Nick's teeth gleamed white in his dark face as he looked down at her with unashamed possessiveness. 'No, don't. Artifice is unnecessary in your case, sweetheart.' He shook her gently. 'All the same, I need to keep reminding myself that less than twenty-four hours ago I didn't know you existed. Yet now——' He paused, his arms tightening, 'now, Clemency, I feel that all the time we've spent apart until last night has been irrelevant, wasted.'

Clem shivered and slid her arms round his neck, rubbing her smooth gold cheek against his unscarred one. 'That's exactly the point. Why waste time on silly pretence? I've never felt like this before about a man in my life, but of course, if it embarrasses you for me to say so——'

Nick silenced her by kissing her swiftly, holding her with exquisite tenderness, as though she were porcelain and might break if he were rough. It was a long time before he released her. 'The feeling I have at this moment can best be described as awe,' he said at last. 'I never expected to find a woman who could make me feel so deeply within minutes of meeting her. Especially now, when I look like something out of a horror film.'

Clem glared at him. 'Will you stop talking like that? I don't care if you're a dead ringer for the Hunchback of Notre-Dame! It's what's deep inside you that calls to something deep inside *me*, Nicholas Wood, nothing at all to do with the way you look, and I hope nothing to do with the way I look, either. And if I'm breaking all the rules by putting all my cards on the table far too soon I'm sorry, but that's the way it is.'

'Sorry?' He pulled her on to his lap, cradling her against his shoulder. 'Clemency—my darling, beautiful girl—how could I be sorry? It's just that I can't believe my luck.'

She looked up at him anxiously. 'If you were in Beirut, you must be a foreign correspondent. Does that mean you'll have to go abroad again soon?'

He shook his head. 'I'm officially on the sick list at the moment, but actually I'm working on a book I've been commissioned to write.'

Her eyes lit up with admiration. 'Really? What sort of book?'

He grinned. 'Intrigue, action, love on the run, with Afghanistan as a backdrop. Everything about it is clear in my mind from beginning to end, except the woman in the story. I just couldn't bring her to life, somehow, see her face clearly. Until now.'

She eyed him uneasily. 'You don't mean——'

'I do.' Suddenly he tipped her off his lap and took her by the hand to stand her in front of the mirror over the fireplace. 'Look,' he whispered. 'There she is.'

Clemency gazed at their reflections as he put an arm round her shoulders and stood with his cheek touching her hair.

'See,' he said softly. 'Beauty and——'

'Don't say it!' she said sharply, then smiled at him in the mirror. 'I think we look rather good together.'

Inwardly she was more than a little disturbed by the change in herself. At first glance her hair and face looked the same as usual, but a second look showed eyes which shone with a new brilliance, a brighter light which glowed from within. Even to herself, used to her own face in the mirror, her eyes shone back from her reflection like lamps. In contrast to her tan, she told herself, but knew this was nonsense. The reason for the radiance was holding her in his arms. It was the emotion Nicholas Wood evoked inside her which made her glow against his darkness, everything about her a foil for his finely etched, bony good looks. His scar and the eye-patch were mere tokens of emphasis, adding to the charisma she'd responded to instinctively from the first moment he'd taken off the mask.

'I look different,' she said, and turned to face him. 'I *feel* so different, too; another person altogether from the Clemency Vaughan of this time yesterday. Are you a magician, Nicholas Wood? Because whatever spell I'm under has been cast by you.'

His jaw clenched as he held her away from him, and his gaze touched her like a caress as it roved over her flushed face and bare tanned shoulders. 'If you go on saying things like that, my darling, I won't be responsible for the consequences. It can't have escaped your notice that when you look at me with that extraordinary light in your eyes I go to pieces.' He looked at her hungrily. 'Will it shock you if I confess I want you so badly this minute I can't think straight?'

For answer Clem moved into his arms, offering her mouth to him, and he pulled her against him and kissed her savagely, his body vibrating with need against hers.

'It's too sudden, too soon,' he muttered hoarsely against her mouth, and she nodded blindly, her fingers busy with the buttons of his shirt.

'I know, I know, but does it matter?' She slid her hands over his bared chest.

'Clemency, for God's sake, I'm not sure I can——'

'Then don't try.'

Two wide blue eyes stared up in luminous trust into the single dark one holding hers with such anguish, then Clem took her lover by the hand and led him up to the bedroom at the back of the house and closed the door behind them. It was dusk, but there was light enough for her to see the taut expression on his face, and she drew him to the bed and put a hand to his cheek, running gentle fingertips along the scar, tracing the outline of his mouth.

'Will you believe me if I tell you, Nicholas Wood, that I've slept alone in that bed for more years than I care to remember? That I've never in my life asked a man to make love to me. As I'm now asking *you*.'

Nick sat down on the bed abruptly, as if his legs had given out from under him. 'I felt I had to wait,' he said unsteadily. 'Try not to rush things——'

'Why?' She stood before him, her fingers untying the ribbons which secured her dress at the waist. 'I'm twenty-eight, Nick.' She slid out of the dress and tossed it aside on a chair. 'Time's a-wasting.'

Dark colour rushed into his face at the sight of her golden-skinned body in its frivolous scraps of satin, then the colour receded slowly, leaving the scar prominent against his skin. Almost reverently he drew her down to him, and stretched out on the bed as he held her against him with a great, shuddering sigh, as though he'd come home.

'I thought it would be enough for now just to hold you in my arms like this,' he said, against her quivering mouth, 'but it isn't. I want more, my lovely one, I want all of you. And I'd better make something very clear before I lose what little reason I have left.'

'What is it?'

'If I take you now, Clemency Vaughan, I shall expect to keep you. All to myself.'

She wriggled closer. 'I think that can be arranged.'

Nick drew away from her and stripped off his clothes, and what remained of hers. He ran worshipping fingers over her cheek, her throat, and downward until he held her breasts cupped in his hands, and he bent his head to put his mouth to each rose-red nipple in turn. She gasped and clutched him to her, and he slid his thigh between hers, plaiting their limbs together so that they cleaved closer and closer, open mouth to open mouth, tongue to tongue and breast to breast, angles and planes to curves and hollows until no part of one was separate from the other as at last, in natural progression, his body merged with hers in the way man has claimed woman ever since the Garden of Eden.

'There was something I didn't tell you, Nick,' Clem said quietly, long afterwards, when her powers of speech had returned.

Nick tensed in her arms. 'What is it?'

'When I told you I sleep in this bed alone, I meant it. I do. But for a time, years ago, I shared it with Evan.'

He lay very still for a moment or two, then turned on his side, taking her with him, settling her carefully against his shoulder, so that all she could see of him in the summer dusk was his sharp-carved profile, rendered blank by the black silk patch.

'And who was Evan?' he asked very softly.

'I met him in college. He was all set to be a graphic designer, and I was going to paint master-pieces.'

There was a pause.

'Where is he now?'

'He went climbing in the Cairngorms and fell to his death in a blizzard. We'd been living together for a year. He was twenty-one. So was I.'

'Tragic.' Nick's voice was carefully neutral. 'Did you love him, Clemency?'

She stared at the ceiling, trying to choose her words with care. 'We were loving friends, I suppose. He was lucky enough to get a good job straight away, and shared this house with a friend who moved north after a while, so Evan asked me to share instead, and it seemed like a good idea. My sister had just got married and I felt a bit lost, and Evan Rees was familiar, lively company; a bit wild and a lot of fun, but with the accent of home in his voice. So I—I shared his bed occasionally and washed his shirts and paid him a peppercorn rent out of my pittance for the magazine which took me on as dogsbody.'

'But did you *love* him?'

'I was fond of him, but only in the way I feel for Penry.' Clem felt the muscular body stiffen against hers.

'And who the hell is Penry?' he demanded.

'My brother; surgeon in embryo, at present registrar at St Ed's and constant threat to the chastity of the nursing staff therein.'

Nick chuckled, to her great relief, and drew her closer. 'How about Prince Charming of last night? God, was it only last night? Where did *he* come into your scheme of things?'

Clem thought about it before answering, then decided the truth was best, telling him Hugo had seemed the type of man it seemed sensible to marry. 'My sisters already have two children apiece, and I felt I needed to get a move on if ever I hoped to do the same.'

'Can't help feeling sorry for the poor blighter.'

'He'll soon find someone else.'

'But not like you.' He turned her towards him. 'There *is* no one like you. Unique's the word. The mould was broken after you were made, Clemency Vaughan.'

'Nick——' she began, but his mouth silenced her and his hands slid to her breasts, then her thighs, and the talking was over suddenly as the loving began again. And this time Nick was no longer subject to his own urgency, and could take time to tease and dawdle and play, until she twisted and turned beneath his clever hands and resorted quite shamelessly to ploys which made him quench the fire he'd started.

It was midnight when he left. Only the arrival of the taxi he ordered tore them apart at the door as he kissed her over and over again before he could bring himself to say goodnight. And when he was gone Clem forced herself to wash dishes and tidy up as though this were any other normal evening of her life. She was sitting on a stool in the kitchen, staring into space as coffee cooled in a mug in front of her, when Emma arrived home.

One look at Clem brought Emma rushing to throw her arms round her fiercely. 'Didn't the swine turn up after all?'

Clem's dazed eyes opened wide. 'Oh, yes. But he wouldn't stay.'

Emma moved back, frowning. 'You mean to say he came, had a drink, then said cheerio?'

'No, no. He left about twelve.'

'*Twelve?*'

'Yes. I meant he wouldn't stay the night.'

Emma sat down suddenly on another stool. 'Dear me, how unsporting of him.' She shook her head in wonder. 'Clem, in all the time I've lived here you've never let a man upstairs except to go to the bathroom. Yet you tell me you actually *asked* this one to stay the night, the very first time you spend an evening together?'

'Yes. Want some coffee?'

'Yes. Black and strong, please. I'm in shock.'

Clem laughed. 'What's so shocking? Hamish stays the night with you, sometimes. And Don does with Jane.'

Emma took pains to point out that both gentlemen in question enjoyed fiancé status, and had known their future brides some considerable time before being granted the privilege in question. 'It seems to me,' she finished, 'that this Nick of yours had no idea what a unique offer yours actually was.'

Clem put a steaming mug down in front of Emma. 'Yes, he does. I made it quite clear that I sleep alone in it when I showed him the bed.'

Emma choked on a mouthful of hot coffee. 'You—showed him the bed?'

'Yes. And made love with him in it. More than once, to be precise.' Clem's face lit with a luminous, dreaming smile. 'It was utterly perfect.'

Emma stared in dismay at the vision before her. 'Oh, Clem, for heaven's sake, be careful!'

'Too late for that. I'm in love at long last and I've no intention of being careful. I want the same as my sisters. And in Nick I've found it, I know.' The certainty in her voice did nothing at all to reassure the troubled Emma, who looked deeply shaken by Clem's statement. 'I rang Robina after Nick left, by the way,' added Clem casually.

'After midnight?'

'Robina's a night-bird. Anyway, I told her it was an emergency. I haven't had any time off for ages, with all the stuff for Ascot and the Heyford-Stuart wedding, so I asked if she could manage if I took next week off, as well as my holiday in Spain later on.'

'I see. And this Nick—doesn't he have to work at something?'

Clem told Emma about his accident and the book he was writing, then patted her friend's cheek, told her not to worry, and went off to bed to stare through the window at the same full moon she had watched the night before, reflected in the lake at Overbury Manor. It was hard to believe it was a mere twenty-four hours or so since Nicholas Wood had first materialised out of the darkness and turned her world upside-down. Or right side up, she thought, with a smile, as she stretched luxuriously in the bed where just a short time ago she'd experienced her first true taste of paradise.

Clem woke early next morning to the sight of Emma's face at the foot of the bed.

'Phone,' said Emma tersely, and went off to the bathroom.

Clem dived out of bed and ran downstairs to snatch up the receiver.

'Good morning, Highness,' said Nick's voice in her ear.

'Good morning.'

'I trust you slept well?'

'Like a log.'

'Sacrilege! How can such a ravishing creature describe herself as a log?'

'I sew better than I write.'

He laughed. 'My idea was to catch you before you took off to *start* sewing today. Could you come to my place tonight, darling? I'm sure your friends are great girls, but for now I want you all to myself. I was in no condition to think of practicalities last night when I left.'

Clem slid slowly down the wall until she sat cross-legged on the floor. 'All right. What time shall I come?'

'How early can you make it?'

'Not until about ten.'

'*Ten*? For God's sake, Clemency——'

'Ten this morning, if you like. I've taken some time off.'

Nick let out an explosive sigh. 'Witch! Make it nine.'

'No—too much traffic.'

'Take a taxi. I'll pay.'

'I'll be there about ten,' she insisted. 'I need time to make myself——'

'Not more beautiful. Please! A poor guy can only take so much.'

'I was going to say presentable. See you later.' Clem put the phone down, grinning at Emma, who stepped over her in disapproval on her way through the hall to the kitchen.

'I assume that was Nick. Coffee?'

'Yes, to both.' Clem leapt to her feet and put some bread in the toaster. 'Want some scrambled eggs?'

'No. I'm worried.'

'Over me? Don't be. I was bound to fall in love just once before I die, you know. And you can't say you ever cared much for Hugo.'

Emma sipped her coffee, looking depressed. 'True. I just wish you weren't so—so sudden about it all. What's this man got that all the others haven't had?'

'No idea. But whatever it is I want it—all of it. For keeps.'

Emma groaned, and prepared to depart for the

firm of Roehampton solicitors where both she and
Jane worked as legal secretaries. 'It's too late to say
be good, Clem. But just to please me, do try hard to
be careful.'

Clem waved her off, laughing, then sat down to a
large breakfast and the unusual pleasure of lingering over the morning paper before making herself
as beautiful as possible for the delectation of one
Nicholas Wood.

The taxi put her down later outside a large
Victorian house in a quiet street in Parson's Green.
A separate entrance led to the top-floor flat, which
was occupied by a smart young couple in advertis-
ing, but the main front door was Nick's sole property, and gave access to the two lower storeys of
the house, which he occupied alone. As soon as
Clem rang the bell the door flew open and Nick
pulled her inside, kicking the door shut behind
them as he kissed her for some considerable time
before letting her say a word.

'Unbelievable,' he said when he let her go. He
looked her up and down, and shook his head.
'When I'm away from you I'm positive my memory
exaggerates. Then the moment I lay eyes on you
again I realise it hasn't even done you justice.'

'It's only window-dressing, Nick.' Clem
examined him in turn. He looked bright and
refreshed this morning, in a pale blue shirt and
faded jeans which hugged his narrow hips. 'You
look better today. Less haggard.'

'I've been given some quite miraculous therapy.'
He raised an eyebrow as bright colour flooded from

the neckline of her white shirt to the roots of her hair, and he shook his head, marvelling. 'Oh, Clemency, Clemency, you are something!'

She lifted her chin and stalked past him, demanding to see his part of the house, which was furnished for comfort rather than style, with lots of leather, and thin Eastern carpets, and books and records in such profusion that they dominated the entire living area.

'I sleep up there,' he said, jerking his head towards the stairs. 'I don't suppose you'd care to inspect?' He grinned as she shook her head primly. 'I wasn't suggesting we go to bed, darling.'

'Weren't you?' she challenged.

Nick's face took on a look that made her pulse race. 'I suppose I was, subconsciously,' he said slowly. 'To be brutally honest, I haven't been able to think of anything else since I left you last night. I still can't believe my luck in having you here with me right now. I lay awake last night trying to think of ways to get through the day until I could be with you again tonight, then, miracle of miracles, you're here. And God help me, I still can't think of anything else.'

Clem digested this in silence. 'I feel the same,' she said at last, smiling at him rather shakily. 'Though I'm certain I shouldn't admit it. But I don't think we should make love again until we've spent several hours doing other things. Ordinary things. We've started our story sort of in the middle, Nick. I feel we need to back-pedal a bit. Start at the beginning. Find out what else makes each other tick, besides the—the other thing.'

He nodded gravely, and reached out a hand to touch her cheek. 'Whatever you want. Now and always.'

Clemency's heart leapt at the 'always', and to hide it she went out with him to explore the small garden behind the house.

'It's too lovely a day to waste indoors, Nick. Let's have a picnic lunch out here, and sunbathe. I love the sun, and hardly ever have much chance to enjoy it. By the time I'm free at the weekend it's raining, more often than not.'

Nick applauded the suggestion, and dragged old deckchairs from a garden shed, and even a rusty old table they could use for their picnic. Afterwards they went shopping, and bought ham carved from the bone, great batons of crusty bread, lots of salad greens and fruit and several bottles of wine.

'Enough for a siege!' gasped Clemency as they reached the house.

'The idea of a siege sounds good—if it's just you and me holed up together.' He grinned as he opened the wine, then popped an expensive early strawberry between her lips as she washed lettuce. 'You know, Miss Vaughan, this is all a lot of fun. I like playing house with you.'

'Good. Peel those eggs, then. They should be done by now.'

Clem was in agreement with Nick. It *was* fun to eat out in the small garden with its moss-spattered patch of lawn. The houses around them were empty during the day, anyway, he told her, so she could sunbathe to her heart's content, secure from all eyes but his.

'Or eye!' he corrected solemnly.

She giggled. 'You sound like the little yellow god. Good thing your eye's not green.'

He regarded her contemplatively. 'It could be, if you make me jealous. I've never thought of myself as the jealous type before, but I rather fancy it might be different in your case.'

'You won't be put to the test, because I don't believe in playing silly games,' she assured him with energy.

They lay back in the old striped chairs, holding hands until it was too hot for comfort in their windless little retreat, and then went indoors to sit with long, cool drinks at hand while Clem demanded details of the places Nick had been and eye-witness accounts of all the exciting incidents in his career. He told her things which made her eyes open in astonishment, then soften with tears as he described his experiences from the time when he had started as a very green reporter in Cambodia, progressing to various other troubled parts of the globe, mainly in Africa and the Gulf of Hormuz.

'I wanted to go to the Falklands, but that didn't come off,' he said with regret.

Clem blenched at the mere idea of the danger he had obviously been exposed to, and eyed him questioningly across her glass. 'And now? Will you stay in this country from now on?'

'I might. It depends.'

'On what?'

'The incentives I get to stay here.'

'The book, you mean.'

Nick regarded her very intently. 'That, and other things.' He smiled. 'Now, what would you like to do this evening?'

Clem didn't mind what they did, as long as they did it together, and Nick took her out for a meal to a small Italian restaurant in the Fulham Road, a place where Nick was obviously well-known, since the proprietor came to the table to be introduced and brought his wife to meet Nick's 'lovely lady'. Afterwards Nick held her hand as they walked back through the hot summer streets, and when they reached the house Clem went to the telephone and rang Emma to say she was staying the night with Nick.

She put the phone down and turned to see Nick standing watching her, with a strange look on his tense face.

'You did want me to?' she said uncertainly, and he dived across the space between them, his mouth hungry on hers as he pulled her into his arms.

'Of course I want you to stay,' he muttered raggedly between kisses. 'I didn't know how the hell to ask!'

She laughed joyously and threaded her fingers through his untidy dark hair, her eyes alight with the warmth mounting inside her. 'I suppose I should have waited until I *was* asked!'

For answer Nick ran with her upstairs to his bedroom, which was large and shadowy, with windows he opened wide to the warm night. They stood together, arms round each other as they looked up at the familiar moon, and Clem shivered a little. He drew her down to sit on the bed, then went on his knees in front of her. He slid his arms round her waist and looked deep into her eyes, then kissed them shut and put his good cheek against hers, holding her with such tenderness she trembled.

'I never knew there was anyone in the world like you, my darling,' he whispered.

'Nick——'

'No, let me say my piece. I've been all over the world—hell-holes, beautiful places, I've lost count of them. But never, anywhere, have I laid eyes on anyone to compare with you.'

Clem shook her head, trying to break free. 'But Nick, please listen, there's something you should know——'

'I know *you* already. And if you're harbouring any dark secrets, they're in the past.' He turned her face up to his, suddenly rough. 'Unless there's some other man I should know about in the present?'

'There's no other man, Nick, I swear, but——'

'Then what else is there to know? Just kiss me, for God's sake. I've been good as gold all day and I want my reward.'

And helplessly Clem obeyed, forgetting everything as his lips met hers. By the time she was naked in his arms, nothing in the world mattered but the touch of his fingers playing harmonies on her skin and the feel of his mouth as it paid homage to every last inch of her, from her sunburned toes to the crown of her head.

And this time some of the initial diffidence had gone. They knew each other better now. Each had learned a little of what pleased the other, and took infinite pleasure in learning more. Soon Clem was fierce with need, and Nick fierce in his pride at assuaging it, until at last the storm was over and they were quiet in each other's arms, awestruck by the force of feeling each unleashed in the other.

They waited until the evening of the next day before going round to the house in Putney to collect some clothes for Clem, who made no bones about wanting to show Nick off to Emma and Jane.

'Show me off?' he said, scowling, and she laughed and kissed him.

'Yes. Because I want them to meet the man I—I met at the ball,' she said, and flushed as his eye fixed her with a bright, questioning look.

I must be mad, thought Clem wildly. She had almost said 'the man I love', and Nick looked dazed as though he suspected as much, but couldn't believe it. Neither could Clem. After a mere three days it seemed rash in the extreme to assume she actually loved this haggard stranger; that Nicholas Wood was all she'd ever dreamed of and would ever want, world without end. Yet it looked perilously like the truth. And Clem could tell Emma and Jane were in very little doubt about her feelings, either, when they were confronted with Nicholas Wood in person for the first time that night.

'So you're the famous Beast,' said Emma with characteristic bluntness. 'Haven't we met somewhere? You look familiar.'

'My God,' remonstrated Jane, 'that line went out with the Ark! Hello, Nicholas, I'm Jane Taylor, and pay no attention to my frank friend here. Em's famous for her sledgehammer approach.'

Nick laughed as he was directed to the most comfortable chair in the room, while both girls plied him with offers of coffee, brandy, food, cigarettes. 'Yes to the first, and no, thanks, to the rest. Clemency cooked a meal for me before we came.'

Clem flushed to the roots of her hair as her friends turned speculative eyes on her, and escaped upstairs to collect some clothes while the girls fussed over Nick. She was zipping a holdall when Emma joined her a few minutes later.

'Do you like him, Emma?' she said expectantly.

'Yes, I do. And I can certainly understand why.'

'Why what?'

Emma sat down on the bed, looking very serious. 'Why you've gone completely off your trolley about him.'

'Am I so transparent, then?'

'So much so, it's frightening, Clem.'

'Stop worrying!' Clem patted Emma's shoulder. 'I'm a big girl, love. By no means straight out of the egg.'

'That's what *is* worrying. You were stunning enough to look at before, God knows, but now——' Emma spread her hands. 'It dazzles me to look at you.'

Clem laughed, and gave a careless glance in the mirror. 'Nonsense! It's the same old me, I promise.

By the way, I'm staying for a couple of days at Nick's, then we're going down to Llanhowell for the weekend.'

Emma's eyebrows rose. 'Last weekend Hugo, this weekend Nick. Won't your parents be confused?'

'Not once they've met Nick.' Clem checked on her belongings. 'Right, let's go, before Jane gets too comfortable down there with my man.'

'Is that what he is?'

'I think so.' Clem's blue eyes shone with certainty as they met Emma's. 'In fact, I know he is. Would it sound too saccharine for words to say I recognised him from the first? The minute Nick pulled that incredible mask off, I knew I'd found the man I'd been looking for all my life.'

'Oh dear, oh dear. I just hope it won't end in tears, that's all,' said Emma, unappeased.

Clem laughed and gave her friend a hug, then ran downstairs, handing her bag to Nick as he met her in the hall. He slid his free arm round her waist and smiled at Emma and Jane.

'I enjoyed meeting you both. See you again soon.'

It was patently obvious to both girls that neither the tall, dark man nor their glowing, radiant friend could wait to be alone together again, and Jane exchanged a wry look with Emma, then opened the front door.

'Off you go, then, children. Be good.'

Nick looked very deliberately at each girl in turn and smiled in reassurance. 'I'll take great care of her, I promise.'

Emma eyed him steadily. 'Do that, Nicholas Wood. We're quite fond of her, you know.'

Clem flushed, but Nick nodded, unruffled. 'Don't worry. So am I.'

When they were in a taxi on their way back to Parson's Green, Clem smiled ruefully at him. 'I hope Emma didn't embarrass you.'

He grinned down at her, sliding an arm round her waist. 'It would take more than Miss Emma Reeves to do that, darling. Besides, after some of the things I've seen in various places round the globe, concern for other human beings is something I appreciate in anyone, believe me. Your friends' concern for you is highly laudable, but unnecessary, you know. I meant what I said.'

Clem stayed silent after that, mulling over his words. It seemed Nick was telling her he was fond of her. Which was all right in its way, of course. But not enough. Not nearly enough. She wanted him head over heels in love with her, as she was with him. To be consumed with this desperate longing to be as close as humanly possible, physically and mentally, to be together for the rest of their lives. In short, marriage; a state she had never yearned for before with any man until now. It was true she had contemplated it with Hugo, at the dictate of her brain, but had never longed for it with all her heart as she did now with Nick. After only a few days spent in his company she knew beyond any shadow of doubt that he was the only man capable of providing the happy ending to her own particular story.

'Penny for them,' said Nick, as the taxi drew up outside the house.

Clem shook her head, smiling. 'Not for sale.'

She put thoughts of marriage firmly from her head, determined to enjoy whatever life offered, refusing to allow doubts about the future to cloud the present, which passed in a dreamlike sequence of laughing and loving, and the sheer enjoyment of being together as she wandered with Nick along the Fulham Road, windowgazing at antiques and pictures, or patronising the various fashionable little eating places in the neighbourhood. They frequented the White Horse at lunchtime in Parson's Green, where Nick cracked jokes with a cheerful young Australian barman, then afterwards they wandered in Fulham Palace Gardens, enjoying the afternoon sun, pretending they were walking in the country in the cottage-garden atmosphere of its seclusion. They bought luscious pastries to eat with the tea they drank on the tiny patch of lawn behind Nick's house, and later when it was cooler they prepared a meal together, or went out to eat, and one evening went to the cinema near Putney Bridge, squabbling amicably over their choice of the three films on offer, and afterwards sitting hand in hand in the darkness, the choice of film irrelevant, since their enjoyment was heightened by the simple fact of watching it in each other's company.

CHAPTER FOUR

THE WEEKEND brought Clem back to earth before she was ready for it. The outer world intruded on her idyll in the shape of Nick's agent, who rang him on the Thursday evening with a reminder of lunch with his editor the following day.

'Blast!' Nick scowled as he rummaged for the diary on his desk. 'I'd forgotten.' He looked across at Clem, who lay full length on the leather chesterfield across the room, watching him. 'Do you realise you've made me forget anything existed other than you and me? While all the time there's a noisy, brash world out there ready to pounce on a poor be-glamoured mortal and haul him kicking and screaming back to reality.'

Clem sighed. 'Does this mean you can't make it this weekend?'

'No, of course not. But I can't get there as early as planned, obviously. Must you start off in the morning?'

'It's my father's birthday. I promised Mother I'd be there early to help with dinner.' Clem sat up, stretching. 'You'll just have to follow on later, after this lunch of yours.'

'Not much option, I suppose.' Nick eyed her morosely. 'If you refuse to wait for me at least make sure you provide me with detailed instructions, so I can roll up in good time to wish your father many happy returns.'

'Are you sure you're up to driving all that way?' She smiled at him coaxingly. 'Take the train, Nick—please. I could meet you with Dad's car in Newport.'

He shook his head and let himself down beside her. 'No, I'll be fine, I promise. On my own in the car I can wear dark glasses instead of the patch, which takes care of the vision—and there's nothing wrong with my leg now——'

'True,' she murmured, and ran a delicately questing finger along his thigh.

Nick breathed in sharply and captured her hand. 'So I'll drive down the M4, cross the Severn Bridge, and I'll be in Llanhowell if not afore ye, at least in time for dinner.'

Clem chuckled at his pronounciation. 'Not *Clan*howell, Englishman. *Ll*anhowell. Put a little breath in before the L.'

'I can't reproduce the exact lilt. Yours is unique.'

'Not a bit of it. We Vaughans all talk alike.'

'Impossible.' He moved nearer, drawing her against him. 'There couldn't be anyone like you in the whole wide world, Highness.' He laid a finger on lips that opened to protest. 'No, don't let's talk any more right now. Let's just do this, and this . . .' He laid his mouth on hers and pushed her back on the couch and began to caress her in a way that promptly drove thoughts of anything but his love-making from her head. They caught fire from each other's urgency. Clem pulled Nick's shirt free from

his jeans and ran her fingers up his spine, putting
her open mouth against his shoulder, breathing in
the warm, clean scent of his heated skin, delighted
as his muscles tensed beneath her wandering
fingers. Soon he could bear it no longer and sprang
to his feet, taking her by the hand, pulling her
along with him as he strode upstairs to the cool
bedroom. They were both breathing raggedly as he
undressed her in the half-dark and laid her urgently
on the bed, taking her with no preliminaries of any
kind, their mutual need so intense that nothing was
necessary to their pleasure beyond the meeting of
two bodies already so well-tuned to each other that
they reached crescendo swiftly in perfect harmony,
and lay locked together in wonder afterwards, as
always, at the perfection of their union.

'I'm sorry,' murmured Nick at last. 'I was
intemperate.'

'I liked it like that.'

'As though I'd die if I didn't have you?'

'Is that how you felt?'

'Yes.'

Clem stretched, luxuriating in the feel of his hard
body against hers. She stroked his hair, her fingers
halting as they encountered the cord of the eye-
patch he stubbornly refused to take off. 'Let me see
your eye, Nick.'

He rolled away on to his back and stared at the
ceiling. 'No.'

'Why not?'

'It's ugly.'

'What difference does that make?'

'A lot. To me, anyway.'

Clem lay in silence, achingly conscious of his tension. 'I've seen the scar on your leg,' she pointed out after a time.

'That's different.'

She was sure that whatever lay under the patch would be a lot less disturbing than the picture her imagination kept conjuring up, but she gave in at once. 'All right, Nick, I won't nag any more.'

He turned towards her and pulled her close, rubbing his good cheek against hers. 'Everyone needs to keep something back, Clemency.' He stared down at her. 'I'm sure there are plenty of things about you I don't know, even though we've talked non-stop about ourselves for days, but I honestly believe every individual must hang on to something of themselves—just to remain an individual.'

Clem wasn't sure she liked the sound of that. 'You mean I've been too forthcoming about the way I feel for you?'

'God almighty, no!' He shook her hard. 'That's not what I meant at all. I delight in your honesty and your lack of affectation. Your response to me has done more for my convalescence than anything the medical profession could ever have come up with, apart from actual surgery.'

Clem detached herself gently and wrapped herself in his cotton dressing-gown, then went over to one of the windows to look down at the moonlit garden. Nick lay very still, watching her, his face obscured by shadow.

'You mean that between us you would always expect areas of our lives to remain closed books to each other?' she asked.

'Not exactly.' He locked his hands behind his head. 'I meant that no human being should ever demand everything of another.'

Clem thought this over at length, sorry now she had asked to see his eye. Yet the black silk patch still represented a barrier between them in some strange way. While whatever lay beneath it remained hidden from her she had the illogical feeling Nick could never wholly be hers. She jumped as his arms slid round her waist from behind.

'You gave me a fright!' she said, breathless.

'Did I? One learns to move quietly when necessary in my line of business.'

'Very likely. But I don't appreciate being crept up on.'

He smoothed the hair away from the nape of her neck, opening his mouth against her skin, so that she felt his lips and tongue, warm and persuasive, as they roved, planting kisses in the hollows behind her ears, raising trickles of response along her spine. He turned her in his arms and kissed her. 'If it means so much,' he muttered against her mouth, 'I'll take off the patch, since it's only moonlight. I'm not up to the full light of day yet. But promise not to scream.'

She held her breath as his hands went to the cord that secured the patch, nervous now that, Pandora-like, she had her wish, as Nick turned away to toss the patch on the dressing-table, then back again so that moonlight shone fully on his face. Relief flooded her as she looked steadily at the scar which puckered his eyelid and held it half open, then furrowed deeply through his heavy eyebrow before continuing up into his hair on the path already familiar to her. Instinctively she moved to touch a hand to his cheek, then stretched up to kiss the corner of the maltreated eye.

'So that's all it is,' she said scornfully, as he replaced the patch.

'Isn't it enough?' he demanded.

'More than enough, when I think of the pain you must have suffered—how easily you could have been killed. But nothing at all in terms of revulsion, on my part or anyone else's! Has everything been done that can be done?'

'Not yet. The vision's impaired in the eye itself, of course, but plastic surgery will improve my appearance soon. And until I can close my eye fully I'm advised to wear the patch.' Nick held her lightly. 'Can you put up with it until I've been re-modelled?'

'Now I can.' Her chin lifted. 'Because I know. Not that there could have been anything under that patch that would have made a scrap of difference. And,' she added tartly, 'it's the only secret I'll ever ask about, I promise.'

His face was inscrutable. 'So you won't be angry if you happen to discover other things I didn't mention?'

'No.' Her eyes narrowed. 'Unless, of course, you're about to tell me you're a married man,

Nicholas Wood.'

'No. I've had relationships of varying importance in the past—I won't deny that. But I've never found anyone I wanted to marry. Until now.'

Clem stood very still, her lashes falling to hide her eyes. Until now. The blood throbbed in her veins, she could hear the traffic outside, music from someone's radio through the open window, but she felt like one of the posies favoured by the Victorians, enclosed in glass in a cloche of silence.

'Clemency,' Nick whispered, and drew her unresisting body against his. He smoothed the dressing-gown away, then bent and picked her up, carrying her to the bed. He laid her down in a shaft of moonlight which turned her golden skin to marble, and he hung over her in silence, as if the sight of her lying there inspired reverence rather than urgency and heat.

Clem held up her arms in mute invitation and he sank down into them, stretching himself beside her as he held her close with a tenderness that thickened her throat with tears that reached her eyes and overflowed until he tasted their salt on his lips.

'Darling, don't cry!'

'I rarely do,' she whispered, sniffing, and he took her face in his hands and kissed the thick, damp lashes and wet cheeks, licking the tears away with a tongue that quickly grew bolder, flicking over the contours of her lips, then thrusting boldly between them as her quivering mouth opened eagerly. Suddenly Clem was no longer still. As Nick's mouth grew more urgent her hips thrust upwards, and he laughed deep in his throat and slid his hands down to her breasts, which rose to his touch, taut under his stroking fingers, the nipples hard as he teased them with bold lips and delicately grazing teeth, before moving his mouth lower, to her waist, her navel, and on down to the silky curls below, to invade their privacy and discover the exact nature of her response to his caresses.

'Please!' she gasped, and he poised over her, dark and tense with a desire that matched her own in the final moment before he gave in to her pleas and began to make love to her with all the subtlety at his command, until at last his control snapped and they moved together convulsively, in a basic need that joined them in the few throbbing, fleeting moments of unity nature allows.

'Happy Birthday, Dad!'

Dr Harry Vaughan smiled warmly at the radiant apparition advancing towards him outside Newport station the following afternoon, and hugged his daughter fondly. 'You look well, sweetheart! A different girl from last weekend. Your mother was a bit worried.'

Clem settled herself in the car with a contented sigh as her father threaded through the busy Friday traffic and headed out of Newport on the Maindee road.

'Was Mother surprised I invited someone else this weekend, Dad?'

Dr Vaughan grinned. 'Curious, rather. So am I.

How come we got Hugo Barrington last week, and some chap we've never heard of this week?'

Clem explained at length, her happiness radiating from her as she talked non-stop about Nicholas Wood all the way to the Cauldra roundabout, and long after they'd turned off on the dual carriageway to Monmouth. Dr Vaughan was, fortunately for his patients, an attentive listener, and he let his daughter pour out her excitement over the new man in her life without interruption until she ran out of steam.

'Does this mean,' he said, when his daughter paused for breath, 'that at the ripe old age of twenty-eight you've finally fallen in love?'

Clem nodded, her eyes shining as she smiled up at her father. 'Yes. At long last I know what Kit and Chatty meant, about recognising the right man when I found him.' She shook her head. 'I genuinely thought I'd never find someone who—who makes me feel the way I do for Nick.'

'Neither did your mother. She'll be pleased.'

'Are you?'

He slanted a whimsical smile at his daughter's anxious face. 'Let's say I look forward to meeting this Nicholas Wood. Very much.'

Angharad Vaughan took one look at the glowing daughter who burst into the kitchen, and needed no further enlightenment. She had seen that particular radiance before, on the faces of her other two daughters, had personal experience herself of the feeling that generated it, when she first met a medical student by the name of Harry Vaughan.

Clem's excited spate of explanations merely served as confirmation that Mrs Vaughan's one remaining single daughter hoped to change her status as soon as this extraordinary wonderful man called Nicholas Wood officially popped the question.

All through the afternoon Clem worked with her mother on the birthday dinner, tireless in her joyous anticipation of Nick's imminent arrival, the mere prospect of which lent enchantment to even mundane tasks like scrubbing new potatoes and polishing knives and forks.

It would be just the four of them, explained Mrs Vaughan, after her husband had left for his afternoon surgery. Kit and Reid were still coping with the aftermath of their sons' German measles, and of course it was high season at the hotel Charity's husband Luiz owned near Gerona in Spain.

'How about Penry?' asked Clem.

'On duty this weekend, unfortunately. He dashed down yesterday instead and went off to the local with his father as a sort of substitute celebration—men only.' Mrs Vaughan smiled. 'An arrangement I deeply appreciated. After feeding my son, I was only too pleased to put my feet up on my own before tackling tonight's menu.'

Clem giggled. 'The walking appetite! How that boy eats!'

'That "boy", as you put it, is only a year or so younger than you, Grandma! How old is this Nicholas of yours, by the way?'

'No idea. Thirty something, I suppose. I haven't asked.'

Mrs Vaughan asked a few questions about Nick's family and background, and laughed when Clem proved vague on hard facts. 'What *have* you been talking about all week, child?'

'Ourselves.' Clem's brilliant blue eyes softened to dreaminess. 'Funny, isn't it. This time last week I had no idea Nick even existed. And now I can't imagine life without him.'

Mrs Vaughan's eyebrows rose. 'It hasn't taken you long to decide that.'

Clem met her mother's questioning look point blank. 'I knew it from almost the first moment I set eyes on him.'

'Just like Charity did with Luiz, I suppose.'

'Only I'm ten years behind!'

Mrs Vaughan laughed. 'Go and change. If my memory serves me correctly, being in love adds considerably to the time necessary for prettying up, if Kit and Charity were anything to go by. You've only got an hour before your Nicholas is due, so get moving.'

The doorbell rang slightly less than an hour later, just as Clem was putting the finishing touches to her face, and Dr Vaughan was relaxing over a much-needed gin and tonic with his wife in the sitting-room. Clem raced downstairs, shouting, "I'll answer it," and threw open the front door expectantly, her face blank with amazement as she found, instead of the lean brown person of Nicholas Wood, an even darker-skinned man, elegant in a lightweight fawn suit, grey eyes gleaming in greeting under light brown hair, and in the crook of his arm a tall, voluptuously curved beauty with a mass of curling ash-fair hair, her cornflower-blue eyes alight with mischievous laughter in a face identical to the one Clemency Vaughan saw in her own mirror every morning.

'Surprise, Clem!' cried Charity, and held out her arms to her twin, who fell into them, hugging her and crowing with laughter as Luiz Santana detached his sister-in-law from his wife's arms and demanded, and received, his own kiss in greeting.

'*Gran Dios*,' he breathed in wonder, as he held Clem at arm's length. 'All the time I forget how much you two are alike, until I see you together again.'

'Never mind that.' Chatty pulled her sister back. 'Don't let's go in yet.' She eyed Clem's face closely. 'So who is he, then?'

'Who's who?'

'The man who's switched your light on, baby sister.'

Clem needed no urging to embark on her tale yet again, or as much of it as she needed to tell. From the time they could first speak the twins had possessed their own particular form of verbal shorthand, and Chatty would need only the bare bones of the story to know the whole, as always.

Their parents came hurrying from the house, smiling in delight at the unexpected arrivals, hardly able to believe their eyes. Luiz explained that his darling daughters had been entrusted to the care of his cousin Milagrita and her husband Juan Carreras in Granada, for the short time required.

'They will spoil the *ninas*, of course,' he laughed, 'but it is only a short time, because I cannot afford to be away from the hotel for longer than a day or so at this time of the year.'

'Luiz's uncle nobly volunteered to keep an eye on the place until we get back, otherwise we'd never have managed it.' Charity kissed her father affectionately. 'Couldn't pass up the chance to wish my dear old Dad many happy returns, now, could I?'

In all the excitement Clem had forgotten the time. But when her mother retreated to the kitchen to check on the meal she realised it was late. She frowned, then shrugged, smiling, as Charity raised an eyebrow.

'Nick's a bit later than expected. Usual Friday traffic, I expect.'

But an hour after that, when dinner could wait no longer, and as many drinks had been consumed as was prudent, Clem was very worried indeed.

'I'll give Nick's house a ring, just in case——' She left the rest of her thought unspoken, and stood in the hall, tense with anxiety, as she listened to Nick's unanswered phone ringing.

'He must be somewhere en route,' she said cheerfully, as she joined the others, and avoiding Charity's all-seeing eye. Determined not to spoil her father's birthday celebration, Clem talked vivaciously, catching up on news of her nieces, Dolly and Luiza, offering congratulations on the forthcoming event as, at her own insistence, they all went in to dinner.

'A son this time, I suppose,' she said, grinning,

and Luiz Santana laid a hand caressingly on his wife's arm.

'It is of no importance, a son or a daughter, only that my wife is safe and the child healthy.' The look on his face as he gazed down at Charity gave Clem a sharp pang, underlining the fact that Nick was missing.

All evening, as the minutes ticked by, Clem gave the greatest performance of her life as she battled hard not to ruin the occasion for everyone else. But as she laughed and talked her mind was frantic with worry, as she imagined Nick in a car crash, injured or—no, she told herself firmly. He couldn't be dead. She would know. But what in heaven's name had happened to him? Why hadn't he rung? Eventually she excused herself from the others and went into her father's study to try Nick's number one last time before she went to bed. Her heart turned over as this time Nick's deep voice barked in answer.

'Nick, it's Clemency. For God's sake, what happened? Are you all right, darling?'

'Yes,' he interrupted stonily. 'Or perhaps I should say as well as can be expected.'

'Did something go wrong at the lunch? I've been out of my mind all night, Nick——'

'And I've been out of mine all week. But not any longer. In fact you could say I'm in my right mind at last. So let's just call it quits, my dear. It was great fun and all that, but obviously just one of those things, as the song says.'

Clem's knees gave, and she sat down abruptly on the edge of her father's desk. Every drop of blood in her veins seemed to turn into ice, as she stared blindly through the window, wondering if this were a nightmare; if she were likely to wake up any minute to find the last week had all been a dream.

'What exactly are you saying?' she asked carefully.

Nick laughed, a sound that chilled her to the bone. 'It's over. Finished. Kaput. You're a bright girl, Clemency, you know very well what I'm saying.'

Clem knew, but she just couldn't take it in. This was the man who'd kissed her goodbye this morning with such tenderness, such—such *love*. How could he be saying it was all over between them? Perhaps she hadn't heard him properly. 'Are you saying that you don't want me any more, Nick?'

'No,' he said savagely. 'I still *want* you, God help me. But I'll get over that in time, never fear. There are other women in the world. But as far as you and I are concerned, that's it. In short, from now on just stay out of my life.'

He hung up, and after a long, long time Clem replaced the receiver and walked slowly towards the door. It opened before she reached it, and Charity stood in her path, staring at her in horror.

'Oh, my God. Clem—love!' She threw her arms round Clem and held her tight, and a little of the numbness went, and Clem's teeth began to chatter, great tremors running through her body as Charity kept up a non-stop flow of soothing encouragement as she drew her gently towards the stairs. Clem realised vaguely that her knees were buckling. Her legs refused to hold her up.

'S-sorry,' she got out with difficulty. 'Feel—funny.'

'Luiz! Dad!' yelled Charity, and her husband came down the stairs three at a time, converging with the Vaughans as they ran into the hall from the sitting-room.

'*Dios!*' Following his father-in-law's swift instructions, Luiz carried the shivering girl upstairs, while Dr Vaughan ran for his bag before hurrying after the others to the room Clem and Charity had shared as children.

'She's in shock,' said Dr Vaughan tersely. 'What the hell's happened?'

'Never mind now,' said his wife, white-faced, and hurried off to fill a hot-water bottle while Charity held her sister in her arms on the bed.

Dr Vaughan gave his daughter a swift examination, checked the racing pulse, then produced a capsule from his bag. 'Water,' he commanded, and Luiz ran to fill a toothmug at the washbasin. Without ceremony Charity prized apart the chattering teeth and popped the capsule in Clem's mouth, then held the glass for her to drink, water spilling over them both before her object was achieved.

'All right, Dad, I'll see to her.' Charity turned to smile in reassurance as Angharad Vaughan appeared. 'She'll be fine in a while, Mother. Better to leave her with me.'

Mrs Vaughan looked as shattered as Clem, but she nodded briskly. 'Yes, darling, I know. But call the instant you need anything.'

After the reluctant departure of the Vaughans, Luiz Santana scowled blackly as he smoothed his wife's hair.

'I would give much to kill this—this Nicholas Wood.'

Charity nodded grimly. 'I'd help.'

'I'm—not—dead,' said Clem faintly. 'No need to—hold a wake.'

'What happened?' demanded Charity. 'Did you speak to him? What did the brute *say* to you?'

Clem's eyes focused with difficulty on the two anxious faces hanging over her. 'Not a lot. Just—to stay out of his life.'

Luiz swore sibilantly in his native tongue, his eyes bright with rage.

Charity gripped Clem's hand fiercely. 'Did he give a reason?'

'No.' Clem experimented with unruly lips and found she could manage a faint smile, now her teeth had quietened down. 'Today was our first time apart since—since we got together. I suppose he had time to think. Time to reconsider. I don't know.' Her eyelids drooped. 'What's Dad given me? My tongue feels numb.'

'A mild sedative.'

'Sorry I fell apart. Never felt quite like that before. I thought I was dying.' Her eyes opened on Charity's. 'I think a bit of me *did*, Chatty.'

Charity swallowed hard, then held up her face for her husband's kiss. 'Go to bed, *mi amor*. I'll join you as soon as Clem's settled.'

Luiz kissed the beautiful, upturned mouth, then bent to touch his lips to Clem's cold cheek. '*Buenas noches, chica*. Do not grieve. There are other men. Come to us in Cabo Feliz soon. Play with the children and lie in the sun—and forget.'

Clem smiled drowsily. 'Thank you, Luiz.'

Charity went to the door with her husband for another kiss, then undressed her sister and sponged her face. 'Did you sleep with this man?' she asked bluntly.

'Not a lot. We made love most of the time.'

Charity groaned. 'Oh, Clem! I'm so sorry, love. Have a good cry, for pity's sake!'

'No tears,' muttered Clem indistinctly. 'Can't cry without tears.'

'I just wish there was something I could do!'

Clem's eyes opened wide for a moment. 'No one can do a thing, Chatty. Except Nick. And he doesn't want me any more.' Her lids closed over the forlorn lost look, and she gave herself up to blessed oblivion as Charity tiptoed away, the tears her twin should have been shedding streaming down her own face as she fled to the comfort of her husband's arms.

CHAPTER FIVE

LADY ROBINA CRICHTON was the daughter of an earl, wife to the son of another, and indulged her considerable artistic and business flair by designing and making grand-occasion dresses for favoured friends in her own social circle. Clem and Charity had first come across her in art college, but it was only after Evan Rees died that Clem ran into her again. Robina, tall and commanding, with chestnut hair and fair, flawless skin, had spotted Clem quite by chance through the window of a coffee bar one day, and had sailed into the small, crowded café, superbly indifferent to curious looks as she hailed Clem with delight. She promptly ordered fresh coffee and settled herself to catch up on what had happened to them both since college, eager to tell Clem about her new venture. She described it as a 'sort of studio in Pimlico, because Oliver gets so frightfully fed up with pins and yards of satin and ribbon and things all over the house'.

When she heard Clem was still looking for the right niche in life, Robina's green eyes lit with sudden excitement, then she launched into a flood of persuasion. Clem had always been wonderful at design in college, she said firmly, and, by the look of the dress she was wearing, still marvellous at making her own clothes. And Robina needed another brain. Not just someone to do the donkey-work, but a friend who could share in the the designing and take over when Oliver wanted his wife at his side in the Royal Enclosure at Ascot, or for a bit of shooting in Scotland. And of course, she added, the arrangement could be just as elastic and convenient for Miss Clemency Vaughan in return if she were sensible enough to accept the offer.

At first Clem had been doubtful. Sewing had been something she did solely because it was cheaper to make her own clothes. But it was also something she enjoyed doing, she admitted, and in the end Robina's enthusiasm proved so infectious that Clem found herself agreeing to attend a certain London establishment where well-connected young ladies were taught the finer points of sewing, including the virtues of perfect finishing, the requisite hallmark of the expert dressmaker's craft.

'You can do the rest, anyway,' said Robina, and smiled jubilantly. 'And this place Oliver's bought for me in Pimlico is such fun—flowers everywhere and baby-blue telephones. You'll love it.'

And Clem did. After she'd completed her crash course in fine sewing, she joined Robina in her smart little studio and very soon found that this new way to earn her living was one she thoroughly enjoyed. The design side of the business appealed strongly, as expected, but Clem rapidly developed a particular talent of her own that became the hallmark of a Robina Crichton creation. Clem found she possessed not only a talent for the exquisite embroidery Robina required, but an absolute genius for the creation of lifelike silk flowers to embellish the dramatic Victorian and eighteenth-century designs popular with Robina's clients for the ballgowns and wedding dresses they commissioned.

'You look seedy,' observed Robina, when Clem returned to the fold the following Monday. 'What can I order for you, darling? Tea, coffee, aspirin?'

'Just work, Robina. Lots of it.' Clem smiled bleakly. 'My energies are in sore need of channelling. So wheel it all out.'

Robina looked troubled, but as usual asked no questions. 'All right, darling. How about ten bridesmaids, one bride and one bride's mother for starters?'

'Perfect.'

The work helped. Long hours in company with other people while she worked her fingers to the bone on the Sheringham wedding 'set' were an anodyne which blunted a little of Clem's anguish. Emma and Jane were usually there in the evening in Putney when she got home, which was another form of help. Clem's carefully erected barrier of brittle gaiety deflected the questions it was obvious they were burning to ask, but after the first terse statement that Nicholas Wood was history, nothing more was said; not even when a parcel arrived for Clem addressed in Nick's scrawl, and contained only some freshly laundered underwear, and a single gold hoop earring. Clem suffered a serious setback in her recovery programme that day, but somehow survived the night by sole courtesy of her temper, since she spent the dark, hot hours cursing a man who could make love to her one minute as though his very life depended on it, then tell her to get lost almost in the next breath.

At first Clem had been convinced her heart was broken. In those first moments after Nick had hung up on her she had genuinely experienced an odd cessation of her life force, as though his words had been arrows which had pierced a vital organ. But as time wore on she came to acknowledge and give credit to the resilience of the human animal. Recovery was slow, admittedly, but recover she did, by telling herself over and over again that one week out of her life was not to be allowed to ruin the rest of it. Sometimes she longed to move from Putney, it was true, to leave the place that was such a short distance from Nick's own particular home ground. But stubborn resentment always changed her mind. Why should she move? Even if they did meet—so what?

Clem's recovery was slow and hard-won, but fairly well-established by the time she got home one night to find Emma and Jane preparing a meal minus Hamish and Don, their respective loved ones, which was a relief. Clem had no yen for male company at the end of a hard working day, and was grateful for the plate of microwaved tagliatelli thrust in her hand by Emma while Jane switched on a video she'd found pushed to the back of the bookshelf.

'I recorded *Singing in the Rain* ages ago,' said Emma with satisfaction. 'We'd forgotten all about it.'

The film was exactly the entertainment Clem needed after a long day dealing with a bride who had proved very difficult at her first fitting, and demanded several alterations to the style of the dress originally chosen. Clem laughed with the others, and enjoyed the inimitable dancing of Gene Kelly as always, and felt restored enough afterwards to volunteer for washing-up duty as the credits rolled up the screen at the end of the film. Jane dried dishes with Clem in the kitchen, leaving Emma to rewind the video, when suddenly a scream from the parlour sent Clem and Jane dashing to find out what was wrong. They found Emma with the remote control in her hand, her finger on the rewind button.

'Clem,' she said urgently, 'take a look at this.'

Mystified, Clem stared at the screen as a lady newsreader informed them about a news item several months old.

'Why are we watching an ancient newscast, for heaven's sake?' she demanded.

'Sh!' said Emma, her eyes fixed on the screen. 'It came on after the film—look!'

The scene switched from the newsdesk to a hot, dusty location, with sporadic shooting going on in the background and people running in all directions as vehicles exploded and the voice of the reporter sounded breathless, as though he'd been running too. Breathless and familiar. In sheer disbelief Clem stared at the tall figure of the reporter in thin cotton shirt and khaki trousers as he described

the riot going on in the background. His face was
sweating and smeared with dust, but unscarred,
and both his eyes were perfectly normal, but the
mop of untidy black hair and bony face were
unmistakable. Clem hardly took in what he was
saying, her eyes incredulous as he finished with,
'This is Nick Wood for the nine o'clock news——'
Then the screen went blank and Emma rounded
on Clem in excitement.

'That's where the timer stopped the video,' she
said. 'But did you see Nick? Did you know
about——'

'Oh yes, I saw.' Clem's eyes sparked with anger.
'But I didn't know about the rest. Nick has this
thing about keeping certain areas of his life
private. He really meant it, didn't he? I naturally
thought he was a newspaper reporter.'

'No wonder we felt we knew him,' said Jane.
'We must have seen him dozens of times, only
without the black patch and the scar. He looks a
lot different without them, doesn't he?'

Clem snatched the remote control from Emma
and rewound the video to the newscast again,
freezing it at the point where Nick began to speak.
She stared at his unscarred face, while her two
friends looked on uneasily. 'So that's the sense of
recognition I felt,' she said slowly. 'What a let-
down!' She pressed the rewind button and sat
down abruptly on the couch. 'I really believed he
was the man I'd been waiting for all my life, you
know. And all the time it was just because he was a
face on a television screen. His name didn't mean

anything. Because it's short and ordinary, I suppose.'

'Let's have a drink,' said Emma briskly, her eyes meeting Jane's in dismay.

'I'd rather have tea,' Clem smiled wryly. 'Sorry to be such a wet blanket these days.'

'Nonsense,' said Jane, while Emma went off to make the tea. 'Men can be such swine.'

'And women such lunatics over them. Well, no more of that for me. I'll settle for being an aunt to my nieces and nephews from now on, and leave the domestic bit to you ladies lucky enough to find nice, straightforward mates.'

'Sounds dull and unexciting, put like that.' Emma handed her a mug of tea.

Clem laughed. 'Sound and reliable, not dull. I can't imagine either Hamish or Don hugging dark secrets to their respective bosoms.' Nor telling their ladies to get lost either, she added to herself, depressed.

'You could do with a holiday,' said Jane. 'When are you off to Spain?'

'I was going to leave it until Chatty and Luiz were less busy towards the end of the season, but I think I've changed my mind. They rarely let their private villa, even if the hotel's full, so there'll probably be some corner for me to squeeze into.' Clem drank her tea and got up. 'I'll ring Charity now, then book a flight to Gerona if she says yes. I'll have finished my part of the Sheringham wedding set soon.'

Clem's arrangements were soon made. Charity

was only too delighted, and Robina perfectly amenable to the change of plan.

'As long as you're back in time for my cruise with Oliver, darling, off you go. Enjoy yourself. Stop eating your heart out for whoever it is you're eating your heart out for.'

When everything was arranged Clem had just under three weeks to finish the embroidery on the Sheringham bridal gown, make herself a couple of dresses and go down to Llanhowell for a weekend somewhere in the middle. After two days of cosseting by her mother, and pointed advice on looking after herself properly from her father, Clem returned to Putney in the rain on the Sunday evening to find Emma prowling up and down, waiting for her as she let herself in.

'He's been here,' blurted Emma, pouncing on her.

Clem's eyebrows rose. 'Good evening, Emma, and thank you, I've had a very nice weekend, Emma, and just exactly *who's* been here?'

'Nick.'

Clem blinked, and turned away quickly to hide the sudden breathlessness that hit her. 'How extraordinary. What did he want?'

Emma sighed in exasperation. 'To see you, of course!'

Clem sat down on the bottom stair and thought this over. After weeks of misery, followed by a period of hard-won calm, she found that her major reaction to the news was resentment. 'Good thing I was out, then, wasn't it, because I certainly don't want to see *him*!' She jumped to her feet as the doorbell rang, staring at Emma accusingly.

'I told him you'd be home later,' confessed the other girl, biting her lip.

'Then *you* can open the door, my fine friend. Because I'm going to bed.' And Clem hoisted her weekend bag and marched upstairs, slamming her bedroom door behind her. She unpacked angrily, flinging clothes about and banging drawers to drown out the sound of the deep male voice downstairs in conversation with Emma.

A knock on the door made her heart miss a beat, but it was Emma who peeped round the door, looking utterly miserable.

'It's Nick. He won't go away.'

'Oh, won't he?' Clem brushed past her friend and marched downstairs like an avenging angel, her eyes glittering like blue diamonds as she glared at the man watching her. He looked tired, and even thinner than before, the eye-patch replaced now by dark glasses which successfully hid any expression in the eyes watching her from behind them.

'Hello, Clemency,' he said quietly.

'Why are you here?' Clem stood very erect, half-way down the stairs.

'Because I couldn't stay away any longer.' His voice grated, as though the admission hurt him to make it.

'Is that supposed to be of any interest to me?' Clem managed to keep her voice light—conversational almost, as though the sight of him wasn't breaking her in pieces. 'As I remember it, you told me to stay out of your life. And I have.'

'I was out of my skull with jealousy when I said that.' Nick threw out a hand in an awkward gesture, obviously very conscious of Emma in the background. 'Look—couldn't we talk somewhere?'

'No.'

The single negative dropped like a gauntlet flung down between them, and Nick stepped back, hunching his shoulders.

'Clemency——'

'Please go.' Clem stood rigid, her face cold as she stared down at him from her vantage point. 'If you had an apology in mind for—for ruining my father's birthday, it would have been more acceptable if you'd made it nearer the time. It's too late now.'

'I've been in hospital.' He took off the sunglasses and turned his face up towards her. 'They did some work on the eyelid and tidied up the scar.'

Clem viewed the result woodenly. 'So I see. Quite an improvement. No doubt it was necessary—because of your particular livelihood, I mean.'

His mouth twisted as he replaced the glasses. 'So you've remembered where you saw me before, I take it. Nick Wood, television reporter.'

'Why did you think it necessary to hide the fact?' she asked before she could stop herself.

He shrugged morosely. 'You may find it hard

to believe, but some women rather like the idea of being seen with someone like me. Because my face appears on television, I mean.'

'Really?'

His teeth showed fleetingly in a humourless smile. 'But none of them fancied me as a disfigured, *retired* television reporter.'

'You choose the wrong companions.'

He nodded. 'How right you are!'

Clem clenched her teeth, stung by his tone. 'From which I gather you count me as one of the number.'

Nick shook his head. 'No. As I must have said before, several times, you are unique. And if I never mentioned the precise nature of my occupation, I suppose I wanted you to l-like *me*, Nick Wood the man. Not Nick Wood the television reporter.'

'I don't really care who you are. I've had time to think since I saw you last, and I've decided first impressions are the most important, after all. If ever I *do* think of you—which isn't often—I'm inclined to remember the Beast.' Clem turned to go upstairs, but Nick sprang to the newel-post, looking up urgently into her cold face.

'Tell me who he was, Clemency!'

She stared at him blankly. 'Who are you talking about?'

'The man who was kissing you that night.' Nick reached up and seized her hands. 'I've got to know. It's killing me, wondering who the hell he is.'

Clem pulled away, eyeing him with distaste. 'You're mad. Or confusing me with someone else. I don't go round kissing every man I run into.'

'Perhaps your conduct in my own case misled me,' he said cruelly.

She went pale. 'Get out! Now!'

Nick reached up and caught her wrist, pulling her down forcibly until she was on a level with him. 'Not until you tell me who you were kissing in that bloody garage that night.'

Clem began to feel genuinely frightened. She tried to twist away, but Nick held her in a bruising grip. 'Emma!' she screamed. 'Call the police—tell them we've got an intruder, and he's assaulting me!'

Nick cursed and dropped her hand. 'So you'd set the law on me,' he said bitterly.

'Do you blame me?' She tossed back her hair, glaring at him. 'Besides, think how convenient it would be. You could report the incident yourself—get the cameras here. Nick Wood, for the nine o'clock news, Putney.'

'You're right about one thing,' he snapped. 'I *must* be mad—to love a woman like you.' And before she could stop him he pulled her into his arms and kissed her savagely, one hand wound in her hair to hold her still as his lips and tongue played havoc with hers. She was panting for breath when he finally flung her away from him and strode out of the house, banging the door behind him.

'Glory!' said Emma in awe as she crept down to Clem. 'Are you all right, love?'

Clem nodded dumbly, then screamed as the door flew open again.

Jane stood looking from one to the other, breathing hard. 'Nick Wood nearly knocked me over as he stormed down the path out there. What on earth's been going on?'

'You may well ask!' said Clem unsteadily, then began to laugh as Emma launched into an explanation. To her horror Clem found she couldn't stop laughing, and went on and on until Jane slapped her face and told her to cry for once like other people, and Emma held her tight for a while until she was calm.

'You know,' said Clem hoarsely at last, as the three of them downed large glasses of medicinal vodka spiked with orange juice, 'Hugo was a lot less trouble, one way and another.'

Emma agreed, sighing. 'But I just can't picture Hugo kissing you senseless like that. I came over quite peculiar just watching you.'

'Damn, damn!' said Jane bitterly. 'Why didn't I come home earlier? I missed all the best bits!'

At which Clem started to laugh again, but in genuine amusement this time, and the other two joined in, relieved to see her rational again.

'One thing though, you two,' said Clem soberly, as they went up to bed. 'I don't suppose for a moment that he will, but if by any strange chance Nick Wood comes here again, just shut the door in his face. Don't let him in. Don't tell him anything about me. Don't even say hello.'

'Are you sure?' Emma looked wistful.

Clem paused in her bedroom doorway. 'Yes, perfectly sure.'

But afterwards she lay awake for half the night, tossing and turning at the thought of those few moments when Nick's arms and mouth had taken her by surprise. Her brain told her to be sensible, to pretend the incident had never happened, but her body refused to go along with the idea, reminding her that her bruised mouth tingled, and her ribs hurt where he had crushed her in his arms, and quite shamelessly made it clear it longed to undergo the same sweet punishment all over again.

Clem had a lot to make up as far as her recovery programme was concerned after Nick's visit. Seeing Nick again had made it humiliatingly plain that she was only immune to him, it seemed, as long as she never laid eyes on him. The moment he'd appeared on her own doorstep, her carefully built carapace of indifference had disintegrated, leaving her as vulnerable to him as she'd ever been.

To make matters worse, from then on fate seemed to take infinite delight in conspiring against her. Only a day or two later Clem met Nick face to face as she hurried out of East Putney Underground on her way home. She flushed bright red, his face went a sickly colour under his faded tan, then she brushed past him in the crowd and made for home as if the hounds of hell were after her. She kept quiet about the incident to Emma and Jane, hoping that by pretending Nick didn't exist she might somehow get over him faster. She carefully avoided all the places they were likely to meet, which meant no more Sunday strolls in Fulham Palace Gardens, or an occasional drink in the White Horse in Parson's Green, though a trip to the cinema with Emma seemed safe enough one evening, since Clem knew Nick was by no means a regular cinemagoer. Her luck was out. As Clem and Emma went out into the hot summer night, discussing the film they'd just seen, they almost collided with Nick and a very pretty girl who never even noticed that her escort stiffened and tried to accost the fair, beautiful girl who swept past him, her stony blue eyes cutting him dead.

'Gosh, that was Nick,' said Emma, craning her neck to look behind her.

'Yes.'

'With a very attractive companion too.'

Clem glared at her friend. 'Do you think I didn't notice?'

'Well, you *did* tell him to push off, Clem.'

'Oh, shut up, Em!'

'Sorry.'

At the weekend Clem went shopping with Jane in the King's Road. She wanted a birthday present for her brother Penry, and spent a pleasant morning browsing through the fashionable shops with her friend before buying an ultra-large sweater in Hackett's.

'A bit pricey,' said Clem ruefully, as she left the shop clutching a stiff white paper carrier bag. 'There's a lot of Penry to cover, unfortunately.'

Jane laughed, then broke off to examine a shirt in the window, wondering aloud if it would suit her Don. Clem peered at it over her shoulder, then felt a touch on her arm and turned quickly.

'Oh!' She stared up in dismay at a familiar scarred face, lost for further words for a moment until Nick seized her by the elbows, the touch of his fingers hot on her bare skin.

'Clemency——' he began urgently, but she jerked free of his grip and literally dragged an unwilling Jane away and made off at a tremendous rate, leaving Nick staring after them in anger.

'He's livid,' panted Jane, looking back.

'I should be sorry?' Clem strode blindly through passersby on the pavement, the unfortunate Jane, who was much shorter, hurrying after her as fast as she could.

'Couldn't you just have a talk with him?' gasped Jane. 'There may be a simple explanation of what happened.'

'Nothing happened. So what's to explain?'

Jane gave up. 'Oh, all right. Make a mess of your life—it's your life!'

And a very hard life it was for the moment, Clem found, as the chance meetings with Nick fanned what she had fondly believed to be the ashes of her feelings for him into bright, unendurable flames again. She worked like someone possessed during the day, hoping to tire herself out so she could sleep at night instead of physically yearning for Nick during the long, hot hours of darkness. It would pass, she told herself firmly. It was nothing to worry about. All she had to do was treat the episode with Nick like an illness that required a long convalescence and careful nursing to effect full recovery. To which end she applied herself to the new dresses she was making for herself in the evenings, and lived out the time until her departure for Spain with grim endurance, almost afraid to look about her in shops and in the street in case she laid eyes on Nick again and found herself back to square one.

'There's a tall, dark hunk of man asking if he can take you home,' said Robina gaily, as Clem was getting ready to leave the Pimlico studio one evening.

Clem swallowed hard, clenched her teeth and said: 'Tell him to get lost.'

Robina's eyebrows shot into her hair. 'Little quarrel, darling? If so I think you'd better tell him yourself, he's bigger than me. Anyway, I told him to come in and get you.'

'What's up with you, Clem?' demanded Dr Penry Vaughan, aggrieved, and relieved his sister of the large bag she was holding in front of her like a shield.

Clem sagged. 'Oh, it's you, Pen!'

'Well, thanks—I'm pleased to see you too.' Penry exchanged glances with Robina Crichton, who shrugged very slightly and laid a long fingernail against her lips for an instant.

'How *are* you, Penry, you gorgeous creature?' she said, smiling. 'Still rocketing the nurses' blood pressure in your temple of healing?'

'Certainly not,' he retorted primly. 'Penry the Pure, they call me.'

Clem had recovered enough to give him a sisterly shove as they took leave of Robina. 'Penry the Pain, you mean. Does this unexpected honour mean I'm obliged to feed you tonight?'

'Yes, please. Then I'll buy you a drink afterwards to say thank you.'

Once the humiliating shock of disappointment receded, Clem brightened at the prospect of an evening with her brother, who was a great favourite with Emma and Jane. When Clem let herself into the house, the two girls were in the kitchen. They exclaimed in delight at the sight of Penry, and Jane promptly tossed another packet of spaghetti in the pot, while Emma threw more bacon and tomatoes, and anything else she could think of, into the sauce she was concocting.

'This is what I call a meal,' said Penry blissfully, as he polished off a second helping of pasta, accompanied by the last of the outsize salad. 'Great food, and three beautiful women to eat it with.'

'And everything free!' said Clem drily.

He rolled his smoke-blue eyes at Emma and Jane. '*Everything*?'

They both giggled and plied him with chocolate cake, followed by a hunk of cheese to eat with most of the loaf of bread intended for the following morning's breakfast toast.

'Food and sparkling conversation's all you get,' said Jane, not without a trace of regret on her pretty face as she smiled at Penry.

'Ah, well,' he said philosophically, 'one mustn't be greedy. Let me take you out to the White Horse for a drink, girls, as a token of my deep appreciation.'

'No,' said Clem involuntarily.

Penry eyed her searchingly. 'No drink?'

'No White Horse. Couldn't we go somewhere else?'

'Sorry, Sis. Said I'd meet a chap there.'

'Then I'll sit this one out.' Clem got up and took a tray of used plates into the kitchen. Emma and Jane followed her to help.

'You can't stay in for ever just because you're afraid to bump into Nick,' said Emma, forthright as usual.

'No. But I can until I get back from Spain. Until my armour's stronger.' Clem went on swishing china through the detergent bubbles.

'I thought I'd come out this evening too,' said Jane casually as she wielded a tea-towel. 'If you go, that is.'

'*I* can't,' said Emma, and fixed Clem with a straight look, 'because Hamish is coming round later.'

Clem sighed, resigned. 'I see. And if Jane and I leave you in peace for a change, you and Hamish can have a private little orgy on your own.'

'Hamish isn't into orgies,' said Emma regretfully. 'But we haven't had much time to ourselves lately, now you come to mention it.'

Clem knew when she was beaten, and went upstairs to change into a white-spotted blue shirt and white cotton trousers, gathering her hair up on top of her head in a loose knot tied with a blue ribbon. Jane, who was small and brown-haired, sighed as Clem sent Penry to tidy up.

'I wish I had your looks, Clem.'

'You're welcome to them, as far as I'm concerned!'

Jane looked unconvinced, but brightened, smoothing down her yellow dress as Penry reappeared.

'Where's Don tonight?' said Clem in her ear.

Jane turned blank eyes on her, as though she'd forgotten who Don was. 'Oh—he's off on a course for a couple of days.'

Clem was on pins as the three of them threaded their way through the crowded tables on the pavement outside the White Horse in Parson's Green. She sighed with relief once they were inside. No familiar dark head was among the crowd. Penry pointed out an empty table on the raised platform in the corner, and sent the girls to take possession of it while he went off to the bar.

'You Vaughans are a striking lot,' said Jane, as she watched Penry laughing with one of the barmen. 'Penry's a very attractive hunk of male, Clem.'

Clem shot an uneasy look at her friend, rather

alarmed by Jane's expression as she gazed after
Penry. It could hardly be described as suitable for
the face of a girl due to walk up the aisle with
another man in the not so distant future. Then
she remembered one of Jane's remarks and kept
quiet. If was Jane's life, after all. And an innocent
hour in a pub with her friend's brother could
hardly be described as infidelity, even if the
absent Don did happen to suffer a bit in contrast
to young Dr Vaughan, both in size and looks.
And who was she anyway, thought Clem in
derision, to put her oar in anyone else's love-life
when her own was in such a mess? She chatted
with Jane while they waited, trying to ignore the
pain she felt inside. Her last visit to the place had
been with Nick, and this fact dominated her mind
to such an extent she hardly knew what Jane was
talking about. It was a relief when Penry came
back, juggling with a pint of beer and two glasses
of lager.

'My chum isn't here yet,' he announced as he
folded his considerable length into a chair. He
smiled at Jane wickedly over his beer. 'Do you
come here often?'

She giggled. 'I think there's a rude answer to
that!'

Jane's eyes sparkled as Penry flirted with her,
and Clem looked on absently, comforting herself
with the thought that in a few days she would be
in Spain, where she could stop looking over her
shoulder all the time, in constant fear—and hope,
she realised unhappily, of meeting Nick every-

where.

'I say,' said Penry, who sat facing the bar, 'there's a chap over there who looks familiar.'

'One of your medical men?'

'No.' Penry frowned, thinking hard, then shook his head. 'Can't place him, yet I know him, I'm sure.'

'Maybe he's an actor,' said Jane.

'Whoever he is, he's certainly interested in me,' said Penry, grinning.

'Perhaps he fancies you!' Jane chuckled, and craned her neck to see over the crowd.

Clem went cold. She kept her back turned and swallowed some of her drink swiftly.

'He certainly doesn't fancy me,' said Penry. 'In fact, if looks could kill——'

'Oh dear,' said Jane. 'It's not you he's interested in, Penry.'

'You haven't been been doing naughties behind your Don's back, by any chance, Jane?' Penry smiled at her reprovingly, then his eyes narrowed at the anxious look on her face.

'It's Nick, Clem,' said Jane in a small voice.

Clem nodded, resigned, and stared into her drink. 'I thought it might be.'

Penry demanded enlightenment, but received only as much as Clem thought fit to provide. She gave a quick look in the direction Jane described, and decided she could make it through the nearest door, since Nick was standing by the bar at a point near the farther exit.

'I think I'll make a run for it,' she said. 'I can get

a taxi home.'

'Look,' said Penry, 'if you want me to sort this chap out, Clem——'

'God forbid! It's the last thing I want.' She turned to Jane. 'Go to the loo, Jane, and say hello to Nick on the way back. Keep him talking while I get away.'

Jane looked appalled at the prospect, but reluctantly went off to do as Clem wanted.

Penry subjected his sister to a very close scrutiny. 'Hurt badly, love?' he asked quietly, and Clem nodded, touched by his unaccustomed gentleness.

'Yes. But I'll get over it.' She kept an eye on Jane, who was making her way towards the spot where Nick was talking to the young Australian barman Clem remembered from another, happier time. 'Right, I'm off now, Pen. Will you see Jane home, please? In one piece, preferably,' she added with meaning.

Penry nodded, and stood up to kiss her, giving her a hug as she braced herself for escape. 'I'll sort this chap out for you gladly, you know.'

'No, thanks, I'll do my own sorting out.' Clem smiled up at her young brother affectionately, put a hand to his cheek, then slipped away as quickly as possible, only to run into Jane on her way to the door.

'You can come back to the table now,' her friend informed her. 'I barely had time to say hello to Nick before he saw you and Penry. He looked absolutely murderous, then muttered goodnight to me and dashed off. So there's not much point in your doing likewise, love. Come and have another drink.'

Clem nodded glumly, because she knew how much Jane wanted her to, but it took all her strength of will to stay chatting and laughing with the other two, and later to make an effort to be pleasant to Penry's colleague when he put in an appearance. It was late before the foursome broke up, the young men to get back to their flat near the hospital, the girls to Putney in a taxi. When they arrived Jane went on into the house, leaving Clem to settle with the taxi-driver, feeling decidedly worn.

'Don't go in yet,' said a deep voice, as she turned to go up the path.

The hair on her neck stood up, and she bit back a scream as a hand reached in front of her in the darkness and closed the front door very quietly. She whirled round to face Nick, who took her by the elbows and held her fast, looming over her forbiddingly.

'And who was *this* one?' he said very softly, his fingers biting into her skin. 'Tell me—to the nearest figure—just how many men you need, Clemency?'

Clem was frightened, and angry with herself because of it. She raised her chin and met his angry eyes squarely. 'It can hardly matter to you who I go out with, or drink with, or—or kiss. As I remember it, you told me to stay out of your life. And I have. So I'd be much obliged if you'd return the compliment, Nicholas Wood, and stay out of mine!'

'Who was he?' he snarled, ignoring her.

'My *brother*!' Clem tried to shake his hands off as he gave a savage bark of laughter.

'Oh, come on, Clemency, you can do better than that!'

'It may come as a surprise to you, but I don't *have* to do anything. I'm my own woman.'

'Unfortunately for my peace of mind—and body—I can't rid myself of the feeling that you're mine.' He bent and kissed her hard, but her mouth stayed closed and unyielding as she stiffened in outrage in his arms. He lifted his mouth a fraction. 'No response?' he muttered against her lips. 'Would it help if I abased myself completely, Clemency, told you I was willing to go against every principle I've ever lived by just to have you in my bed again?' He let out a long, unsteady breath, and tightened his arms, subduing the sudden lunge she made to break free. 'No, you don't. I want you to listen to me. What I'm trying to say is that I've come to a very soul-destroying conclusion. I can't live like this. I want you so much, I'm willing to turn a blind eye—appropriately enough—to any occasional lapses on your part, if only you'll come back to me.'

Clem felt sick. She fought the nausea down, drops of perspiration pearling her upper lip as she clenched her teeth.

'Well?' he demanded hoarsely, shaking her a little. 'God almighty, Clemency, what more do you want me to say? Isn't it enough for you to see me reduced to this?'

She shuddered. 'What you suggest is an insult, to us both. You must be drunk!'

'Not drunk—demented.' And he crushed her to him and kissed her until she clutched him to keep her balance, her mouth opening to gasp for air, and he gave an exultant laugh and kissed her parted lips in triumph, his tongue seducing her into shaming response. Clem shook with rage at herself and pushed at him, but Nick was lost in a desire so introspected that he seemed blind and deaf to anything but the feel of her body against his. Then his fingers slid to the buttons on her shirt and Clem seized the advantage. Her sudden, eel-like wriggle took him by surprise, and somehow she managed to twist out of his grasp and lunge for the door, which opened as she reached it and sent her sprawling on her hands and knees on the hall carpet, to the astonishment of Jane, who'd come to see where she was.

'My God, Clem, what happened?' she demanded, helping her up. 'Did you lock yourself out? I heard the door close and thought you'd gone straight up to your room, then Em just said you weren't there and I panicked . . .' She trailed into silence as she caught sight of the man outside.

'I got waylaid,' panted Clem, and turned on Nick, staring at him balefully. 'Why don't you just go?'

Nick stood looking down at her, his fists clenched. The hall light threw his scar into cruel relief, and for a moment Clem's heart contracted, then he put out a hand in appeal, and she stepped back deliberately.

'Clemency——'

'Just go,' she said, in a voice so deadly quiet his head went up as though she'd struck him. 'Tomorrow, when you're sober, you'll be sorry you sullied your precious principles by the offer you just made.'

Emma was peering over Jane's shoulder, and both girls' eyes opened wide at this.

'And glad,' went on Clem inexorably, 'that I rejected it. And you.' She gave the still man a look of cold disdain, then turned her back on him and went upstairs, leaving Nicholas to bid Emma and Jane a punctilious goodnight, and to apologise for his intrusion before he walked away into the warm summer night.

As they locked up, Jane and Emma had a whispered discussion about whether to ask Clem if she needed tea, or sympathy, but in the end decided privacy was their friend's major requirement, and left her alone to enjoy it. Not that 'enjoy' was an apt term, because Clem lay awake all night long, racked by misery over Nick's humiliating proposal.

It was, she decided, staring out at the stars, a very mortifying thing to be wanted by a man just because he had an urge to possess her body; an urge so strong, moreover, that he was actually prepared to share her with the mythical 'others' of his imagination. And the great joke of it all was that, in spite of all the things he'd said, she still loved the man. Clem sat bolt upright in bed, pushing her damp hair away from her neck as the truth struck home. It *was* true, she thought, panicking, and slid out of bed and went downstairs to get a drink. Almost immediately the other bedroom doors opened and Emma and Jane went running downstairs after her.

'Are you all right?' they asked in unison, and Clem laughed shakily and offered them some of the orange juice she was pouring.

'I just had a collision with the truth, that's all. And it hurt.'

'Is there anything we can do?' asked Jane anxiously.

Clem's eyes softened. 'No. My problem is simple. It took me all these years to fall in love, and then when I did I chose the wrong man. Mind you, I suppose I should be flattered. Not many men would be willing to take on a woman with all faults, so to speak, which was the gist of Nick's offer tonight.'

Emma frowned as she poured juice into two glasses. 'Would we be horribly inquisitive if we said we're dying to know just what these "faults" of yours are supposed to be?'

'Search me. God knows, I'm not perfect, but for some reason Nicholas Wood thinks I'm first cousin to the whore of Babylon.' Clem smiled wryly. 'Funny, isn't it, when I'm really just an old-fashioned one-man girl.'

'So Nick thinks you've got a couple of interests

on the side, then?'

'Certainly does. One of whom he saw kissing me in the White Horse tonight.'

Jane groaned. 'Oh Lord! Didn't you tell Nick it was your brother?'

Clem shrugged. 'He didn't believe a word of it. He's obsessed by some outsize bee in his bonnet about my liberal tendencies towards his sex.'

'So what now?' asked Emma.

'I go to Spain. Where I can relax, and where Nicholas Wood won't be popping up in front of me wherever I go.' Clem downed her orange juice. 'Only first I've got a wedding dress to finish, and if I don't rest my weary eyes for a while, Miss Annabel Sheringham is likely to find some very peculiar motifs embroidered across her aristocratic bosom!'

CHAPTER SIX

A FEW days later Clem lay supine in the early morning sun on the tiny beach exclusive to the Villa Isabel near the village of Cabo Feliz, on the coast not far from Gerona. Her nieces, *las senoritas* Dolores and Luiza Santana, were sitting at her feet, absorbed in the jigsaw puzzles their aunt had brought them from London. Clem watched them from under the brim of her white cotton hat, enchanted by the grave consideration the little girls accorded each large wooden piece as they tried to fit it into the pattern, her eyes soft as they rested on the two curly blonde heads.

'*Hola*, Clem,' called a husky voice, and Clem sat up, smiling, to wave at Milagrita Carreras, Luiz's cousin, who had arrived the night before. She was picking her way over the pebbles, looking elegant as always, in a filmy shirt knotted over a perfectly cut one-piece bathing-suit.

'*Tia, Tia!*' clamoured the little girls, who rushed to lift their faces for the kisses their Spanish aunt rained down on them.

'And how are you today?' asked Milagrita, settling herself on the sunbed beside Clem.

'I'm very well.'

'*Es verdad?*'

'Yes, truly.' Clem smiled, and began to rub oil

113

into her long brown legs. 'I haven't been ill, you know.'

'No. Only the lovesickness.' The grey eyes were shrewd. 'And when love comes late, it comes hard, *querida*. I have watched you. Sometimes you are sad. He must be *mucho hombre*, this man of yours.'

'He's not mine.' Clem kept her eyes on the blue, blue sea, and pulled her hat low on her forehead. 'Let's not talk about him. Tell me about Juan instead.'

'Juan is busy, as always, but he will drive down from Granada this weekend.' Milagrita smiled serenely. 'I do not leave him often, but I thought I would like to see for myself how you are.'

'I'm flattered!'

'Also, I thought you might need some company because Charity is so busy at this time of the year.'

'Thank you—I'm grateful. Not that I'm lonely, of course, with these two charmers for company, but I do tend to worry about Chatty a bit. Should she be doing so much now she's pregnant again?'

Milagrita shrugged. 'I think she does far more than Luiz wishes, but she is so proud of this hotel of theirs. It is their baby too, I think. They have worked so hard together for its success.'

Clem agreed, remembering how Luiz had seized the chance of owning his own hotel, after years of managing his uncle's in Marbella, as he had done when he had first met Charity.

'At least they've got the villa to come home to

at night,' said Clem. 'And Chatty's promised to spend the rest of the day with us today, once lunch is over at the hotel.'

'Now I am here she can spend the rest of the week with you, *chica*. *I* shall help in the hotel.' Milagrita smiled in triumph.

Clem's face lit up. *'Really?* I offered to lend a hand myself, but Chatty and Luiz wouldn't hear of it.'

'I shall enjoy it. Do not forget, I was brought up to the hotel business, Clemency. My name is not "Little Miracle" for nothing!' Milagrita laughed, then settled herself comfortably under the big striped umbrella. 'Now, tell me all the news about Kit and my old friend Reid, and their beautiful sons, also the so charming Penry, that heartbreaker of a brother of yours!'

The morning passed pleasantly and quickly until it was time to take the little girls up to join their mother at the villa for lunch on the vine-framed patio. Afterwards Clem was adamant her sister had a rest.

'Since Milagrita has volunteered so nobly for duty, I just might,' yawned Charity. 'I get so sleepy when I'm pregnant. Come on, my darlings, siesta time.' She rounded up her little daughters, then eyed Clem. 'And what about you? Any plans for this afternoon? I'll be up and around again by four or so.'

Clem's programme was to return to the beach, swim a little, lie in the shade and read or doze. 'I shall wallow in sheer laziness,' she said, stretching luxuriously. 'I've been working like a maniac these past few weeks.'

'Sounds as though Robina's running a sweatshop!'

'Not a bit of it. She's a dear, actually. We get on surprisingly well together. And believe me, she's no dummy when it comes to business. She can tell at a glance what suits a client best.' Clem giggled. 'She has her work cut out sometimes, when a well-upholstered chum fancies skin-tight satin bristling with beads, but in the end the lady always goes away convinced the flattering black chiffon, or whatever, was her own idea in the first place, and everyone's happy.'

'Robina always was a bossy soul.' Charity laughed and kissed her sister, then shepherded her daughters off to rest.

With Milagrita's help the days soon took on a pleasant routine. Clem insisted on taking charge of the children during the early part of the morning, then Charity joined them on the beach for an hour or two before lunch, after which she took her daughters off to bed for a rest, adamant that Clem had the afternoon to herself. The student son of the head waiter, Luiz discovered, was only too glad to earn some money by acting as Clem's chauffeur and guide on her expeditions into the neighbouring countryside, since Cabo Feliz itself offered little in the way of diversion apart from the hotel itself, which, though beautiful, possessed one main disadvantage from Clem's point of view.

The Hostal Isabella, situated in the centre of the village itself was over a century old, and had once been a *hidalgo's* country residence. It was built around a central cobbled patio with a fountain, with geraniums in splashes of red and green against walls decked with the frivolous black lace of iron balconies. Luiz was too much the experienced hotelier not to exploit the commercial possibilities of his hotel to the full, but at the same time he took great care to maintain its gracious, old-world atmosphere, using the original *sala* of the old house for his reception area, where the great curving staircase was only one among many features which brought visitors back to the hotel year after year, pleased by the efficient courtesy of the staff and the charm of the owner and his beautiful wife. But Clem had learned early on during her first visits that it was best to keep away from the hotel on her own, purely to avoid the inevitable confusion over her resemblance to Charity.

José, or Pepe, as he asked Clem to call him, was a dark-eyed, rather serious boy, who spoke enough English to make their daily excursions very pleasant, and because he was a history student he took great pride in showing his companion as many monuments, Romanic churches and monasteries as she could take in, until she begged for mercy at last and proposed an afternoon spent in Gerona itself. The trip was a great success. Pepe parked the car on the north side of the town near the park, only five minutes

away from the old quarter, and Clem followed
obediently as he conducted her to the places he
considered most important. She enjoyed the bustle
of a busy city again after days of sea and sand, but
was resigned to a visit to the cathedral first before
Pepe would allow anything more mundane. After
paying due respect to the grand approach of the
edifice and its enormously wide nave, Clem was
able to wander with a free heart through the
fascinating lanes of the city, to climb up steep steps
and peer through arches, to inspect the Arabic
baths and the medieval Jewish quarter, and take
photographs of the painted houses which rose
straight up from the banks of the River Oñar.

After the urban delights of Gerona, Pepe thought
they should return to the scenic delights of the
coast next day and drove Clem past curving
beaches and pine-encrusted bays to Cadaques, the
St Tropez of Spain, where as a matter of course, by
this time, she first inspected the baroque church
before wandering through the cobbled streets of the
town to gaze at the ancient roofs and whitewashed
walls of houses which Pepe informed her more
often than not contained architect-designed
interiors. And, since Pepe was adamant that the
senorita could not possibly leave the area without a
visit to Salvador Dali's house in Port Lligat before
returning to Cabo Feliz, it was a rather tired Clem
who finally arrived, yawning and apologetic, at the
villa later that evening.

Charity plied her with tea and questions about
the expedition, then handed Dolly and Luiza over

to Pilar for a while and took Clem upstairs to her bedroom.

'Just look at me,' said Charity disconsolately, waving a hand at her reflection in the full-length mirror. 'My waistline is quite definitely thickening already. It's happening sooner this time, Clem. Hardly any of my dresses fit me properly, but I really don't fancy getting into maternity gear just yet.'

Clem smiled soothingly. 'I may have just the answer.' She went off to her own room and returned with a dress. 'Try this. It's a sort of wrapover effect. Put it on like a coat, and tie it at one side, then presto, deep neckline—perfectly cut, I might ·add—flattering full skirt, and a waistline you can adjust as you go along.'

Charity's face lit with pleasure as she revolved in front of the mirror. 'It's perfect, Clem. Luiz will just love me in this!'

'No kidding!' Clem grinned. 'Keep it. And if you like, we'll get some dress lengths tomorrow, and I'll make you a couple more in return for my bed and board.'

Charity was indignant at the mere idea of any return, but accepted the offer when Clem insisted, hugging her twin before she took off the dress and pulled on a swimsuit.

'Come on, let's go down to the beach with Dolly and Luiza until their suppertime. Luiz is dragging Milagrita away from the reception desk later on and we'll have one of the chef's specials for dinner. I yearn for Franco's *huevos a la flamenca*—eggs baked with tomatoes, onions and diced ham to you, *cariad*, not to mention the asparagus and peppers and sausage he throws in—mm, yummy!'

'If having babies makes you eat all the time, I don't think I'll bother with the experience.' Clem stopped short, her eyes clouding, then she ran off ahead of Charity to collect her small nieces, making them shout with laughter at her sudden bear-hugs as she helped them into their bathing-suits. For the rest of the afternoon she was untiring in her efforts to entertain the children, playing ball with them on the shallow half-moon of sand beyond the pebbles, encouraging them with their tentative efforts at swimming, then reading to them in the shade from one of the pile of illustrated books she'd brought with her from England.

Charity joined in some of the games, just watched some of the others, and never said a word about the admiration she felt for this beloved other half of herself, who she knew only too well was still licking her wounds in private, behind the brave front put on for the world at large.

Not that Clem believed for a moment her act was deceiving Charity. The silver cord that bound them was too strong for successful subterfuge between them. But forbearance was given unquestioningly. Charity felt the hurt as if it were her own, Clem knew, but let it pass without comment, for which her twin was deeply grateful as they sat together on the beach watching the shadows cast by the umbrella pines as the sun headed for the sea, and the little girls squabbled a little over the books they were colouring, as bedtime grew nearer.

'They could almost be you and me at that age,' said Clem, after settling a dispute on whose crayons were whose. 'Only Dolly's older than Luiza, of course.'

'And we never squabbled over anything much.'

'True.'

They lounged in comfortable silence for a while, until Pilar, the young girl who helped with the children, could be seen making her way down from the house.

'It's high time *you* had a husband and children,' said Charity, gathering her children's belongings together. 'You can't go on making other people's wedding dresses all your life.'

'I don't see why not.' The identical pairs of blue eyes locked. 'I truly believe there's no alternative for me, Chatty. The only man I've ever wanted wants *me* for all the wrong reasons.'

'But surely you'll find someone else?'

'I don't want anyone else.'

'But you only spent six days with this man, Clem!'

Clem pulled on her shirt and stuffed her belongings in her bag. 'That's right. The Israelis had their six-day war, and I had my six days of love. More than some women ever have, perhaps.'

Charity looked almost ready to cry as the young maid reached them to carry off her daughters. '*Gracias*, Pilar.' She turned on Clem fiercely. 'This Nicholas Wood isn't the only man in the world!'

'I know that. But he's put me off the rest of his

sex, believe me. Luiz excepted, of course!'

Clem took longer to dress than usual that evening. The bedtime story her nieces chose was the longest they could find, so she was late having her shower and extra time was necessary to shampoo the salt from her hair. Not that it mattered much in Cabo Feliz. Everyone dined late anyway, and Luiz liked to make sure everything was in order at the hotel before he could relax with his wife over their own evening meal, which was by no means mere eating, but more in the nature of the main entertainment of the day, with plenty of wine and conversation to accompany the food. There was no set pattern to the menu. Sometimes Charity cooked dinner, sometimes it was sent down from the hotel, and occasionally it was provided by Luiz himself, when dinner was invariably a cold buffet, since where food was concerned Luiz was more by way of a chief than one of the Indians, Charity said, which somewhat mystified Milagrita.

As Clem dried her hair she could hear voices floating up from the patio below as Luiz and Charity relaxed together in the sea-scented dusk. She smiled a little wistfully and lingered deliberately in front of the mirror, taking her time before joining them. She felt rather pleased with her appearance, since in the time since her arrival her hair had become streaked by the sun like Charity's, and her eyes shone more deeply blue than ever in the deep gold of her face, even to her own clinical gaze. She put on one of the new dresses she'd made for herself, in thin black cotton, cut like the one given to Charity, but with a cluster of her own handmade white rosebuds at the waist instead of ties. The deep V-shaped neckline showed off her new tan rather well, she thought, pleased, as she fastened large white hoops in her ears. Then she frowned, startled, as she heard a sudden commotion from below. Angry voices were raised, then a scream came from Charity, followed by sounds of scuffling, and chairs being overturned.

Clem tore from the room, afraid someone had broken in, and flew downstairs to the patio, her eyes starting from her head at the scene confronting her in the dusk. Charity stood pressed against one of the vine-clad stone pillars, her hands to her mouth as she stared down at the body of an unconscious man, while Luiz stood over the intruder, fists clenched, still bristling with the rage that had obviously just driven him to knock the man down.

'What on earth is going on?' demanded Clem in alarm, hurrying over to her trembling sister. 'Hey! Steady—calm down now. Remember the baby.'

Luiz abandoned the body in the shadows and took his wife in his arms, smoothing her hair as he explained what had happened, since Charity seemed struck dumb for the moment with shock, and Clem bent to peer at the intruder, her heart flipping over in her chest as she realised who he was.

'I went upstairs to see the children,' Luiz said, his voice shaking with anger. 'I stay with them a little. When I come back a man is molesting my wife, so I hit him.' He released Charity reluctantly. '*Mi amor*, I must call the police.'

'No!' gasped Charity at last. 'He thought I was Clem, Luiz. That's why he tried to kiss me——'

By this time Clem was on her knees by the fallen man. 'I know him. It's Nick Wood. I-I think you've killed him, Luiz.'

There was a wail from Charity as Luiz thrust her aside to drop down beside Clem. He felt Nick's wrist and put an ear to his mouth, then let out an explosive sigh of relief. 'He breathes. I knocked him unconscious only. Help me move him.'

'Should he be moved? Maybe he's broken something.' Clem's voice was unsteady as Luiz ran his hands over the long body her own hands had once caressed with such pleasure.

'I think all is well. And if we get him to the sofa in the *sala* he will be more comfortable. Or shall I ring the hotel and get one of the waiters to come?' Luiz's worried grey eyes met Clem's questioningly, but she shook her head.

'No, let's not involve anyone else. I'll take his head and shoulders, you cope with the rest.'

Not without a struggle, they managed to manhandle Nick's slim, surprisingly heavy body inside to the *sala*, where Clem could see better. After a swift examination, her probing fingers found a contusion under the thick black hair at the back of his head.

'Must have knocked himself out when he fell on the tiles out there,' she said tersely, then gave Luiz a crooked smile. 'He'll have a fair bruise on his chin

first. I have sympathy with him. If Charity had not returned my love, life would have been meaningless for me.'

Clem stared at him in surprise, not a little embarrassed by such a dramatic statement. 'Why, Luiz——'

'In other words,' said Charity, with a luminous look at her husband, 'why keep Nick on tenterhooks when it's as plain as the nose on your face the man's bananas over you?'

'It may be to you. Personally, I'm not convinced.' Clem smiled at them both and went off to bed, rather shaken just the same. Luiz was an unexpected champion for Nick, in the circumstances.

To her surprise Clem slept well, and was up early with the children, insisting Charity stayed in bed until mid-morning. When breakfast was over Clem bundled a few necessary belongings into her beach bag, took Dolly and Luiza by the hand and went off down to the beach to play with them on the sand before the sun grew too hot. They ran about with a large ball for a while, then splashed about in the sea for a few minutes, while Clem encouraged her small nieces' efforts at swimming, then she took them back to the sunbeds for a rest. The three of them were enjoying mugs of cold orange juice from the insulated jug Clem produced from her bag, when footsteps crunched behind them on the pebbles, and Dolly and Luiza jumped up in excitement to greet the stranger they had taken to with such enthusiasm the day before.

In the face of such a vociferous welcome from her

nieces, Clem had no option but to smile politely at Nick, and ask him to join them.

'Are you feeling better this morning?' he asked.

'Much better. Sit down and have some orange juice.'

Nick did as she said with flattering alacrity, the wary look fading from his face as he sat on the other sunbed with a small girl close on either side of him.

'Actually I slept like a log last night,' she said. 'How about you?'

'I can't say the same, exactly.' He gave her an unsettling look. 'I seem to have lost the habit of sleep since I met you, Clemency. In the short time you were with me it seemed a waste of precious time, and since then I've been too bloody miserable to sleep much at all.'

Clem felt the colour rushing to her face, and turned away to pick up the shirt she'd worn to walk down from the villa. Suddenly she seemed in need of protective covering, and thanked Nick breathlessly as he bent forward to help her on with the shirt.

'Can you do puzzles?' demanded Dolly, and Nick blinked, then smiled at the small girl at his knee, assuring her he was an expert. The tense moment passed as Clem helped the children unpack the supply of books and puzzles they insisted on taking with them everywhere.

It was oddly enjoyable to sit under the big umbrella with Nick and the children, especially after they tired of their jigsaws and demanded a story. Clem lay back, listening to the deep, articulate voice telling an updated version of Goldilocks and the

Three Bears, her eyes dreamy as she watched the relaxed dark man holding her nieces in thrall, thinking what a good father he'd make. Her mind skidded to a stop. The thought of Nick as a father took her breath away. Because suddenly it was crystal clear to her that, if Nicholas Wood had any intention of fathering children, she very definitely wanted to be their mother.

When the tale was finished, the little girls looked up beseechingly at Nick.

'Do you know more stories?' asked Dolly eagerly, always the spokeswoman for the two children.

Nick admitted he did, then looked across at Clem very deliberately. 'I know a very beautiful story about Cinderella, but I can't tell it yet, sweetheart, because I'm not sure of the ending.'

Clem gazed back at him dumbly, unable to tear her eyes away from the sudden heated intensity in his.

The intrusion of Pilar was a welcome relief from the flood of emotion threatening to overwhelm her. Charity, it seemed, had coffee ready at the villa, and would be pleased if the *señor* would accompany the *señorita* and the *niñas* to the house to join her. Nick accepted without hesitation, and took Dolly and Luiza by the hand as he walked up the beach with Clem. She was very conscious of the picture they made as they went up to the house: tall, dark man and tanned, fair woman, the children resembling the latter enough to make them seem like a family. And Clem knew very well the same thought was in Charity's mind when her sister gave a warm welcome to the visitor. Her penetrating blue eyes had a habit of homing in on her twin's thoughts far too easily for Clem's peace of mind.

'You haven't changed your mind, Clemency?' said Nick, as he rose to go later. She looked at him blankly. 'About driving to S'Agaro tonight,' he added quickly.

'No, I'm looking forward to it,' she said candidly, and was rewarded by a smile of such warmth from Nick that her colour surged up under her tan in response.

'Thank you——' He made an involuntary move towards her, then checked himself quickly. He turned to Charity and the little girls to say goodbye, then looked back at Clem. 'Will eight o'clock suit you?'

She nodded, smiling, and returned his wave as he went away.

Clem had never been to S'Agaro, which Charity warned her was considered the cream of the coastal resorts, and merited something dressy if Nick was taking her out for an expensive dinner.

'I don't know that a pricey meal is what he has in mind.'

'He is taking you to the Hotel de la Gavina,' said Luiz, who had joined them for lunch. 'He asked me to advise him earlier,' he informed them smugly.

'Did he now?' said Charity, greatly impressed.

Clem's eyebrows rose. 'Is it a very smart place?'

Luiz nodded. 'The most luxurious hotel in these parts, *chica*.'

Charity kissed her husband and jumped to her feet. 'Then you'll need to borrow a dress, Clem. I don't suppose you've brought anything formal.'

'Formal?' protested Clem as she was dragged upstairs. 'I'm on holiday, Chatty. Surely my black dress will do?'

'No. You'd better wear the white one you made for me. I can't for the moment, it's too tight.'

'But it's not my style,' protested Clem, whose taste was different from her twin's when it came to clothes. Her own tendency was to minimise her curves, whereas Charity made no bones about emphasising the assets given her by nature.

Clem's protests were useless. Charity brushed them aside ruthlessly, and when Clem finally went downstairs that evening, shortly before Nick was due, she wore a clinging white silk sheath whose exquisite cut was its only ornament, apart from a cluster of green-stemmed silk lilies of the valley Clem had made to wear on one shoulder.

Luiz rolled his eyes and kissed her hand. 'The miracles God is able to perform! Almost I believe you are Charity.'

'Well, she's not,' said his wife, pulling him away. 'So hands off, *mi marido*.'

'Tell me where I may put my hands instead,' he said promptly, kissing her, and Clem protested loudly.

'Do me a favour, you two. Wait until I'm gone, at least!'

Nick arrived promptly, formally dressed in lightweight suit and white shirt with a dark tie. As he accepted a drink from Luiz, Charity caught Clem's eyes in triumph, with no need for the unspoken 'I told you so' as her glance flicked up and down the white silk dress. After a pleasant interval Nick smiled regretfully and said it was time to go if they were to be in time for dinner in S'Agaro, and ushered Clem outside to the small open area on the cliff-top where he'd parked the Mini hired for his stay.

'Is it far to S'Agaro?' she asked as they set off.

'Only a few kilometres. I booked dinner for nine.' Nick's voice sounded a little weary, and she stole a look at him, wondering if something were wrong.

'Is your head still aching?' she asked.

'No.' He smiled at her briefly as they left the village. 'Otherwise I wouldn't attempt this coast road, which is undeniably beautiful, but makes for tricky driving with all the doubling back around the inlets in the cliffs.'

Nick was right. The route was scenic, but demanded full concentration from the driver, and Clem made no attempt at conversation until they arrived in S'Agaro itself, where the palatial setting of the Hotel de la Gavina among its tree-shaded lawns was so impressive, Clem was gladder than ever of the dress and the silk sandals Charity had been adamant on lending her to go with it.

'You look absolutely dazzling tonight,' commented Nick when they were sitting over pre-dinner drinks. The look in his eyes was eloquent. 'That dress is superb.'

'It's Charity's,' said Clem, shrugging. 'She spurned all mine as unworthy of this.' She waved a hand at her surroundings.

Nick leaned back in his chair. 'By which I gather you think I've brought you here to impress.'

Her eyes opened in surprise. 'No, I don't. I can't have been *that* mistaken about you,' she said rashly, then bit her lip, annoyed with her unguarded tongue.

He smiled. 'Actually it's by way of a celebration. Maybe you've forgotten, but I've got a new job.'

Clem had not forgotten. She'd been wondering about it ever since he'd mentioned it.

'I'm leaving television to do a current affairs programme on radio.' He studied her closely as he spoke, as if gauging her reaction.

'Sounds safer, at least. Fewer bullets in a broadcasting studio, for a start.'

'True. It means I also stay in one place for a change.' He looked up impatiently as the waiter arrived with more drinks. Clem smiled her thanks as she accepted hers, which was her favourite Andaluza, a mixture of dry sherry and orange juice, served with soda and shaved ice.

'Good thing Dad isn't here to see my treatment of good Spanish sherry,' she commented.

Nick grinned. 'Not a drink for the purist, but if you like it, why not?'

Clem raised her glass. 'Exactly. Here's to your new job then, Nick. Every success.'

'It's a double celebration, actually.' He took a swallow of his gin and tonic. 'The first half of my book met with surprisingly warm approval from the publishers, so I'm finishing the rest of it at top speed before I start on the new job.'

'Congratulations!' Clem's eyes glowed. 'That's terrific news, Nick!'

His dark eyes lit with sudden heat, and he leaned closer to take her hand. 'Clemency——' He broke off with a stifled curse as menus were placed in front of them.

The moment passed as they began a discussion of what to eat, Clem frank about feeling hungry.

'I haven't eaten much since those famous prawns.'

'Choose anything you like,' he said, amused. 'If that dress will let you.'

'Do you think it's too tight?'

'Only as far as my blood pressure's concerned,' he said without expression, and applied himself to the complications of the menu.

Clem expressed a yen for something ethnic. 'Not too adventurous, though.'

With the waiter's help she chose *jamón serrano*, red mountain ham sliced so thinly it was translucent, served with ice-cooled melon. 'And at the risk of sounding like a tourist,' she said, smiling up at the waiter, 'I would really love a *paella*.'

'From the dazed look on the poor chap's face, I think he'd have probably tried to bring you the moon and stars as garnish, if you'd asked,' said Nick drily afterwards, his smile rather twisted as she turned innocent blue eyes on him.

'Sweet, wasn't he?' she said blithely. 'What was he saying about the *paella*?'

'Merely reminding me that it was prepared in the Catalan style, without chicken, as is considered proper in these parts. I also told him easy on the garlic, as Catalans tend to be rather liberal with it unless curbed.'

'How come you speak such good Spanish?' Clem asked curiously.

'I suppose I possess what's popularly known as an ear for languages. Useful in my line. But I confess I used to come to this part of Spain as a child every summer. My parents loved the area. There were only about a dozen hotels along this coast then. It was a magic sort of place to me. I used to hang out with local fishermen's kids—you could hardly tell me apart from them once I'd been here a day or two, and I just sort of mopped up the language osmosis-fashion.'

'While I, on the other hand, never managed to get to Spain at all until I was nineteen or so. Late developer!' Clem smiled. 'Actually it was a fairly momentous holiday. Practically the moment we arrived, my sisters met the men they're now married to.'

'Didn't anyone take *your* fancy?'

She shook her head. 'No, nary a one.'

'Don't try to tell me it was lack of male interest!' Nick took a look around him. 'Every man in this room envies me my companion, for a start.'

'*Muy guapa!*' said Clem, unimpressed. '*La rubia Inglesa.*'

'Ah! You've heard it all before.'

'Blondes go down well in Latin countries.'

'You sound as though the term "blonde" doesn't please you much.'

'Only because "dumb" tends to get bracketed

with it.' Clem looked up with a sudden dazzling smile as the waiter returned to escort them to their table in the Candlelight Room. The attractive young Spaniard almost fell over himself in his efforts to hold her chair for her, then flicked open the linen napkin for her with panache.

'You see?' murmured Clem, as she began on her delicious cured ham. 'Easy as pie, isn't it?'

'Do I get the feeling you're trying to make a point?' Nick raised his glass of champagne in silent toast.

'Merely that every man you imagine is—is fancying me is after this.' She flicked a finger at her face, then down at her silk-covered breasts. 'The body. Not one of them cares a damn about the fact that I think and hold an intelligent conversation, earn my own living. Mind you, the last would probably meet with approval because sewing is such a *feminine* occupation, isn't it? Highly suitable for a "damn fine woman" like me.'

'Some men have really trodden on your toes, haven't they?' said Nick, whistling. 'Do you lump me in with the rest, Clemency?'

'No. I honestly believed you were different.' She raised probing blue eyes to his. 'I thought you'd seen through the wrappings to the real me inside, otherwise I'd never have let you through my front door, Mr Wood, let alone into my bed.'

He returned the look steadily. 'Where it's just possible I'd still be welcome if you'd ever said the one key word to the whole mix-up. What's so bad about being a twin?'

'Very little.' Clem looked at him thoughtfully, then decided to tell him the story of a young solicitor she'd seen quite a lot of at one time. 'He was someone I liked, fun to be with, and we got on really well. I genuinely believed we had a lot in common. So after a while I told him I had a twin, who was an exact mirror image of myself. He said nothing very much at first, except for the usual surprise. Then eventually he confessed he was tormented by a fantasy which kept him awake at night, maddening him, about having two girls like me in his bed, making love to him at the same time.'

Nick's eyebrows shot into his hair as he glared at her. 'Are you telling me you imagined I was similarly inclined?'

'No, no, I'm just trying to explain why it was so difficult to say I had a twin. At first, anyway. Then afterwards, each time I tried to bring it up . . .'

'I shut you up by making love to you.'

The arrival of the *paella* provided a welcome interruption, after which further conversation was confined to comments on the food for a while, as Clem began on her portion with an appetite she was pleased to find quite unimpaired by her reluctant revelations.

Afterwards, when dessert had been refused in favour of *café solo* and a *coñac*, Nick asked if Clem felt like a walk.

'Or aren't those shoes up to it?' he asked, as they left the hotel.

'Certainly they are!' The night was so beautiful, Clem had no wish to return so early, and agreed readily when Nick proposed walking along the tamarisk-lined belvedere, which led past numbers of inlets on its way to the beach of Sa Conca. Clem was very much intrigued by the oddly dated atmosphere of the resort, with its smattering of elegant houses and beach huts, unsurprised when Nick told her the place dated from the twenties, the design of a Barcelona businessman.

'The Hostal de la Gavina,' he said, as they strolled away from it, 'is still in the hands of the family who built it in the early thirties.'

'It was quite an experience.' Clem looked up at him with a smile. 'Thank you for bringing me, Nick.'

'The pleasure, believe me, was all mine!'

At the note in his voice she turned away hurriedly, and began to talk about the various expeditions she'd made with the obliging Pepe.

'And just who might Pepe be?' asked Nick.

'The son of the maître d' at the Isabella.' Clem gave him a sardonic look. 'All of nineteen years old, and very keen to earn some pocket money while he subjects me to as much religious architecture as he can possibly pack into the space of a couple of hours each afternoon.'

Nick laughed rather sheepishly, and entered into a discussion on the things she'd seen, until without realising it they found they were at the end of the belvedere.

'Sorry, Clem.' Nick smiled down at her ruefully, as they lingered to look at the moonlight silvering the sea of the beautiful Sa Conca beach. 'Are your feet hurting?'

'Really,' she said mockingly. 'All this ravishing scenery spread out in front of you, Nick Wood, and all you can think of is aching feet?'

'By no means.' He pushed his hair back from his face and stared out to sea. 'But it seemed the least inflammatory of the various subjects I *could* put up for discussion.'

There was silence for a while.

'That moon's up there again,' said Clem at last, finding the quiet oppressive.

Nick glanced down at her. 'Are you a moon child, Clemency? Born under the sign of Cancer?'

She shook her head, grinning. 'No fear. My sign is Gemini, of course—the heavenly twins!'

He joined in her laughter, sobering at last as he gazed down into her eyes, oblivious of passers-by. 'You look like a moon child to me. In that dress, in this light, you're almost unreal,' he said huskily.

'Believe me, I'm not, Nick. I'm exactly the same girl you knew in Putney in the rain.'

Their eyes locked for several tense moments, then very carefully Nick took her hand in his as they began the walk back past the tamarisks to the car. Neither seemed willing or able to break the silence between them as they strolled slowly along the belvedere, the way back seeming far longer than the couple of miles Clem knew it must actually be. As they walked in apparent outer harmony, she knew only too well that Nick was as burningly conscious as herself of the simple contact of their hands, of the fingers which formed a junction for the currents of heat and longing that coursed through their veins, as powerful as though they were joined in the ultimate intimacy of love.

Clem felt utterly drained by the time they reached the Mini, and a swift glance at him showed plainly that Nick felt the same. He thrust a hand wearily through his hair as he opened the door for her, and she eyed him closely.

'It may be the moonlight, but you look pretty ghastly to me all of a sudden. What's the matter, Nick?'

'Headache. I get them now and then since this.' He touched a hand to his eye and smiled crookedly. 'Contact with Luiz's fist and the patio floor haven't exactly helped lately, either. I'm determined to lead a quieter life from now on.'

Clem studied his face anxiously in silence, thinking hard. Finally she came to a decision and held out her hand. 'Give me the keys. I'll drive back.'

'I didn't know you could.'

'There's a lot about me you don't know!'

'I'd give my soul for the chance to learn, Clemency!' he muttered thickly.

She pushed him into the passenger seat, very worried by the fact that he offered no argument. Since it was obvious he was feeling far worse than he let on, she slid into the driving seat, took a few minutes to study the details of the unfamiliar right-hand drive, then switched on the ignition and cautiously nosed the car out into the traffic.

'This will probably be a very slow journey,' she warned. 'And don't doze off, please. I'll need instructions. I've never driven on the right-hand side of the road before.'

'Now she tells me!'

'You said you wanted to learn everything about me,' she reminded him.

'Careful! You're a bit near the edge!' Nick sat rigid, staring ahead at the moonlit road.

'Look—do you want to drive?' she demanded irritably.

'Can't. Eye's gone.'

'Gone where?'

'Vision goes in the bad one with migraine—God! You're too close to that car!'

After a while Clem got more into the rhythm of things, growing used to the car as the journey progressed. She blessed the illuminating moonlight, but had no attention to spare for the beauty of the night, all her energies concentrated on the unfolding ribbon of road, which looped in and out of the pine-topped cliffs in relentless hairpin bends that raised beads of perspiration on her forehead, and made her palms so slippery with sweat that she was obliged to wipe a hand down the silk dress every now and then when she could bring herself to spare one from the wheel. It seemed like hours before Cabo Feliz finally came in sight, by which time it was difficult to judge which of the car's occupants was the more exhausted.

'Just park it here. I'll walk you down to the villa,' mumbled Nick, when they reached the hotel.

'No fear,' said Clem after one look at his ravaged face. 'You get out and go straight up to bed. It's only half a mile to the house. I'll drive down and leave the car parked there. You can pick it up in the morning.'

Nick protested feebly, but gave in without much struggle, quite obviously too ill to argue any more. Clem kept the engine running until he was safely inside the hotel, then drove the Mini down to the villa at a crawl and reversed the car inch by inch into the open space on the cliff-top next to Luiz's Mercedes.

Her knees were knocking like castanets as she got out, and she breathed in great thankful gulps of night air as she tried to discover which key locked the doors of the Mini. She found she could laugh a little now the journey was over, thinking it was a blessing she hadn't explained to Nick that, although she owned a current licence, driving was something she actively detested, and only the fact that he was in such dire straits had driven her to volunteer her services. By a process of elimination she found the right key at last, but before she could insert it in the lock found to her horror that the car was slowly moving backwards.

'Oh, my God!' she gasped, and yanked at the door handle, some instinct prompting her to try to get at the handbrake, but the momentum of the car defeated her, knocking her over despite its size, and by the time she scrambled to her feet all she could do was watch in utter horror as in graceful slow-motion the car slid backwards over the cliff and disappeared from view. She screamed and rushed to the edge, in time to see the Mini somersault in its fall to the pebbles below, landing upside-down with a final, sickening crash. She moaned, clutching her arms across her chest, waiting with staring eyes for the inevitable explosion. Nothing happened. She waited, teeth chattering, then raced up to the house, to collide with Luiz, who was running towards her.

'*Qué pasa?*' he demanded, putting his arms round her. '*Dios*, Clem, what happened?'

'Nick was too ill to drive back,' she panted, 'so I did. I let him off at the hotel and drove down here to park, but I couldn't have ratcheted the handbrake up properly. Oh God, Luiz, it was a hire car, and I just let it fall off the cliff!'

Charity had arrived by this time, and snatched her sister into her arms as Clem gasped out her story again while Luiz ran down to the beach.

When he returned, Luiz spread his hands, shrugging. 'I think it is a write-off, *no?*'

Clem let out a wail of despair.

'All right, all right, love. It's only a car.' Over her twin's dishevelled head Charity exchanged a look with her husband, and Luiz put an arm around both girls, and led them into the house.

It was a long time before Clem was restored to anything like normal, requiring tea and a great deal of straight talking from both Luiz and Charity before she was able to put the accident into perspective.

'*Querida,*' said Luiz earnestly, as he held her hand, 'there was no life lost, no one else involved, no one was even hurt——'

'Except Clem's hands and knees,' muttered

Charity, sponging the grazes.

'But just look at your dress, Chatty!' moaned Clem.

'Who cares about a dress?'

'And if the matter of money worries you, I am sure the insurance will cover it,' Luiz added.

'But what on earth am I going to say to Nick?' Clem put her head in her hands and groaned.

'Shall I talk to him for you?'

'No, Luiz. Please. I'll tell him myself. I'll come up to the hotel first thing, before he finds out.'

'How did you come to be driving, anyway?' demanded Charity.

Clem explained about Nick's migraine and the nightmare journey home.

'You mean you drove all the way from S'Agaro?' said Charity in awe. 'Good heavens, I think you'd better have a brandy. Llanhowell to Monmouth is usually your limit—and unless the law's changed lately, they still drive on the left over there.'

'I'll admit I was a bit nervous—no, I wasn't, I was petrified! So was Nick, I think, but he was too polite to say so. In fact he was very restrained—unless he was too ill to care.' Clem shrugged and accepted the brandy Luiz gave her. 'But since he couldn't see properly, I didn't see what else I could do.'

'You must have been shaking so much by the time you got out of the car, you weren't even capable of pulling up the handbrake properly.' Charity let out a sigh. 'Anyway, the important thing is that you're in one piece. To hell with the car!'

Clem put out a hand to cover her sister's. 'I really

am sorry, Chatty. Did the crash give you a shock?'

'No. I was just getting out of the bath when I heard a dull thud in the distance, then I went out on the balcony and saw Luiz running one way, and you the other, and I got myself down here pretty fast.'

Clem stood up. 'I'll let you get to bed. My apologies again. Frankly, I think I'd better get myself back to Putney.'

Charity protested at once, but Clem shook her head decisively.

'If anything else upsetting happens, you'll be lucky to stay pregnant, Chatty. I've caused too much commotion one way and another as it is. I'll come back to you again after the baby's born, when—when I'm a bit more sorted out.'

Whenever that was likely to be, Clem thought morosely, as she tried to get to sleep. A shower had dispelled the effects of the brandy, and the prospect of having to own up to Nick about the car next day was not a thought that wooed sleep. She dozed a little intermittently at last, but as the first rays of light lit the sky she woke up again and decided to get dressed. She pulled on shorts and a sweatshirt and crept downstairs very quietly to shut herself in the kitchen and drink cup after cup of strong tea until the day was advanced enough for her to go down to the beach.

She let herself out of the house and went down to the small cove to inspect the car in despair. It lay like a dead red beetle, wheels turned up to the sky. Luiz was right, thought Clem. It was a total write-off, even to her own inexpert eye, and she turned away disconsolately to head for the sunbeds which Pilar always pushed well up the pebbles at night. Clem slumped down on one, noticing a forgotten beach towel lying half hidden under the other bed. She picked it up and sniffed at the salt and sand dampness of it, then curled up wearily on one of the beds, huddling the towel around her like a blanket.

She dozed a little for a time, worn out by her restless night, then she jerked upright at the sound of pebbles flying as Nick's unmistakable figure hurtled down the private path to the beach. He ran like the wind towards the wrecked Mini, and Clem tore after him, calling to him hoarsely as she ran across the beach, but even before she reached him it was plain he was too frantic to hear anything. She put on a burst of speed as she saw him push frenziedly at the car, reaching him as he fell on his knees beside it, maniacal in his attempt to see inside.

Sobbing for breath, Clem touched his shoulder and he leapt to his feet, staring at her as though she were an apparition, tears pouring down his haggard face.

'I'm sorry,' she choked, and began to cry in sympathy. 'I didn't put the handbrake on properly last night, Nick.'

Nick spat something excessively vulgar about the handbrake and dragged her into his arms, kissing her feverishly, his hands running all over her body to convince himself she was all in one piece. Clem locked her arms round his neck and kissed him back, her tears mingled with his as she sobbed out an explanation which he interrupted every other word or so to kiss her again and again.

At last he thrust her away from him and held her by the elbows, shaking her hard until her teeth rattled.

'I saw the car from up there.' He jerked his head towards the cliff-top. 'I thought you were *in* it, woman! When I came running down here, it felt like the descent into hell. Stop *crying!*'

'I will if you will,' she retorted, brushing the tears from her eyes, and he stopped dead, touching one of his hands in amazement to the wetness on his face.

'See what you reduce me to!' he said wrathfully, and fell to kissing her again; hot, salt kisses fired by the violence of relief.

Clem returned them with equal ardour, clutching him to her until after a while her knees began to buckle, and she tore her mouth away long enough to gasp, 'Let's sit down!'

She led him to the sunbeds, where, careless of who might be watching from the villa, Nick drew her down to lie full length against him, holding her tightly in his arms as he kissed her mouth and nose and red, swollen eyes.

'Don't cry any more, darling,' he whispered, but the very tenderness in his voice made her tears well up again. Clem sniffed inelegantly and tried to smile.

'No one would believe it if they saw me crying, you know. Charity was always the one who cried. Once I was grown up I shed very few tears until I met you. And even then they weren't for the usual reasons.'

Nick stroked her hair back from her damp forehead, the light in his eyes making her breath catch in her throat. 'What were the reasons?'

'That night, in the moonlight in your house, when everything was still so beautiful between us, I cried because I was so happy.'

'How about afterwards?' he asked soberly. 'When everything blew up in our faces?'

'I just went sort of numb with shock when you told me you didn't want me any more——'

'Oh no, I didn't,' he corrected swiftly. 'I've never stopped wanting you.' And to prove it he began to kiss her again, caressing her with growing urgency, driven by an instinctive urge to mate after the near-brush with tragedy.

'Come up with me to my room!' he said hoarsely.

'I can't!'

'Why not?'

'I look far too much like the owner's wife!'

Nick groaned and crushed her to him so hard she feared for her ribs. 'I begin to realise the drawbacks of this twin arrangement,' he said bitterly.

'And you can't make love to me here!' Clem protested after a few ecstatic moments.

'Where can I, then? Because if I don't soon, I think I'll go insane!'

She pushed him away, staring up at him searchingly. 'Nick, is that what you want most?'

The hot urgency faded in Nick's eyes as they held hers. 'You mean you think I'm too obsessed with thoughts of possessing your body?'

'Not exactly. After—after what I witnessed just

now . . .' She trailed into silence, flushing.

'You mean when you saw me go mad because I thought you were dead?' He smiled ruefully. 'Did that convince you that maybe my feelings for you were more cerebral than you suspected?'

'Yes, it did.' She touched a hand to his face, and gave him a wicked smile. 'But the thing I find even more convincing is that you haven't said a word about the car.'

Nick grinned. 'Which demonstrates very clearly where my priorities lie, apart from all the hundreds of other reasons I shall list for you when I'm in a calmer frame of mind.' He took her face in his hands. 'Just now I experienced the worst moment of my life when I thought you might be dead—or injured. I never want to go through that again. I just can't face the thought of life without you, Clemency Vaughan. These past few weeks have been a nightmare.'

'I haven't enjoyed them overmuch myself.' She looked away, feeling oddly shy. 'So what now?'

Nick laughed in delight at her embarrassment, and put his arms round her, drawing her close. 'Before anything else happens to prevent it, I vote we get married, my darling, as soon as humanly possible.'

Clem smiled at him blissfully. 'Yes, please!'

'I'd appreciate a very early date for the wedding, Miss Vaughan, because I've just come to a very difficult decision,' he went on, sighing. 'Until we're legally and permanently bound in holy wedlock, my beautiful girl, I'm determined I'm not going to allow myself more than a few kisses and maybe a cuddle or two.'

Clem's eyes narrowed to a laughing blue gleam. 'Oh? Why?'

'As an act of faith. To prove that I want not only your unquestionably tempting body, but your company and your conversation, and, even more important, your helping hand when it comes to scraping paper off walls——'

'My what?'

'We'd better redecorate the house, don't you think?' Nick's eyes danced. 'Unless you don't like my house, of course, but I very much hope you do. For a start it really *is* mine, lock, stock and barrel, and anywhere else in the same area is bound to cost an arm and a leg. Besides which I have some very sentimental associations with that bedroom of mine. Not that you're going to share it again until we tie the knot, of course,' he added virtuously.

Clem was so inordinately pleased by this declaration of intent, she hugged him close, raining kisses on his smug face. 'That's the nicest thing any man's ever said to me!'

'The reverse, I gather, from some of the propositions you get!'

'I seem to remember a singularly unique proposition from you, Nicholas Wood, the night you saw me in innocent company with my brother.'

Nick closed his eyes, shuddering. 'The worst part of it was that I meant it. I was driven to the prospect of sharing you with other men, just so long as you included me among the number.' He shook his head violently. 'I'd never have kept to it.'

'So the offer no longer stands?' she asked, straight-faced.

He growled, his eyes glittering. 'No. Or I strangle you.'

'Persuasive argument. OK—just you, then. Which it has been from the moment we met,' she added matter-of-factly. 'I've never loved any other man, Nick, nor ever will. Only you.'

They melted together in a trembling embrace which grew prolonged and almost unbearable, until it was interrupted at last by a small, resigned voice.

'Mama says breakfast's *ready*.'

Nick released his flushed bride-to-be and grinned at the two little girls regarding them with stern disapproval. '*Hola, señoritas. Buenos días.* Am I invited too?'

Dolly and Luiza nodded enthusiastically as Nick held out his arms to them, their brown faces glowing up as he swung one up in either arm to walk up the beach.

'Mama says you're Tío Nick now,' announced Luiza with satisfaction.

'Your uncle, eh?' Nick's eye met Clem's over the curly fair heads. 'How did Charity know that already?'

Clem shrugged. 'We're twins, remember.'

He rolled his eyes at her. 'I hope this private hotline you share is—er—selective in certain delicate areas.'

'Don't be rude!'

* * *

In the garden the moon silvered the grass and smudged in dark shadows under the bushes, but this time frost added sparkle to a lawn which was not only small and a long way from any lake, but bounded by fences and houses in one of the streets of Parson's Green. It was a cold February night, and Mr and Mrs Nicholas Wood were At Home to a large number of friends and relatives invited to celebrate the success of the best-selling novel *Flight from a Far Horizon*.

The house, newly decorated, was alive with music and laughter as Clem and Nick circulated among their guests, receiving congratulations on all sides.

'Fantastic book, Nick,' said Robina, who was a superb advertisement for her own business in a watered silk suit with an exquisite camellia on her lapel, made by her partner's unmistakable hand. 'I mean, even Oliver was enthralled by it—I couldn't get him to put it down every night in bed.'

'Then you're slipping, Robina,' said Charity, standing, as always, in the circle of her husband's arm. 'Luiz never reads in bed.'

'No,' he agreed solemnly, his grey eyes gleaming wickedly. 'I work so hard all day, my eyes refuse to stay open!' But he kissed his wife's cheek, in loving contradiction to his words.

The book had been gratifyingly well-received, but the party was by way of a housewarming, as well as a celebration, since the months since the Wood/Vaughan wedding day had been spent in redecorating the house to a standard Clem had finally pronounced satisfactory only a week or so previously.

'It's lovely, darling,' said Angharad Vaughan, who, with Kit her eldest daughter, was helping with the buffet Clem had insisted on catering for herself.

'You've got quite a flair,' agreed Kit, who was looking particularly beautiful in a black velvet dress of Clem's own design. 'You've worked wonders here in a very short time. I don't know where you get the energy to do everything you do.'

'Secret source,' said Clem, smiling as Nick appeared at her elbow, exchanged a silent look with her, smiled back in apparent satisfaction, then went off again to ply his guests with drinks after a brief word with his father-in-law.

Dr Vaughan shook his head in wonder. 'Amazing how you and Nick communicate, *cariad*. Just like you and Charity.'

Clem smiled at her twin. 'It was the acid test, I suppose.'

'Finding a man on the same wavelength,' Charity nodded, serious for a moment. 'I was lucky enough to find my man very early on in life.'

'Whereas I've been very backward at finding mine!'

A pretty girl with long, dark hair came running into the dining-room. 'Shall I start handing round some of the goodies, Clem?'

'Thanks, Melanie. Get Penry to lend a hand.' Clem smiled affectionately at Nick's young sister, and handed her a tray of canapés. 'Tear him away from whichever female he happens to be seducing.'

'Females, plural,' said Melanie, grinning. 'There's a ring of them in the conservatory, drooling over his bedside manner, but don't worry. Just leave 'em to me.'

It was a happy occasion, with a mixture of guests who hailed from many and various backgrounds, but blended happily to enjoy each other's company, only a few of the newest of the Woods' acquaintances open-mouthed when they saw Mrs Nicholas Wood and Senora Luiz Santana together for the first time. Most of the company were used to the phenomenon, but even to those who weren't there was less difficulty than usual for the time being in telling the former Vaughan twins apart.

Charity, dazzling in cobalt silk, had recovered her usual curvaceous slimness again following the birth of her son, but was easy to tell her apart from her sister for once because, although Clem's dress was exquisite, of midnight-blue pleated chiffon, with crystal beads and embroidery at the low-cut neckline, it was nevertheless a maternity dress. For the time being its clever cut concealed the fact, but nothing could conceal an extra dimension to Clemency Wood's looks on this particular evening. Her eyes shone like sapphires in her radiant face, and her hair seemed to curl about her face with a life of its own as she laughed and chatted with Nick's editor, and Nick's parents and friends, Emma and Jane and their respective escorts, flitting from one group to another like a glittering blue butterfly.

'It was a great party,' she said, yawning, after the last of the guests had finally gone. 'But I'm glad the rest of my family are staying with Kit, much as I love them all. It's good to have the place to ourselves.'

Nick sat on the edge of the bed and drew her down beside him, eyeing her in a possessive way she responded to at once, sliding her arms round his neck and bringing his dark head down to hers as she kissed him slowly and pleasurably on the mouth.

'You are so incredible,' he said huskily after a while, as he held her close. 'I could hardly take my eyes off you tonight. You seemed to be lit up like a torch, eclipsing every other woman in the room —which was no mean feat among the beauties assembled under our humble roof.'

'You mean with Chatty and Kit and Melanie and Robina——'

'To name but a few. And not one of them could hold a candle to you tonight, darling.'

'You're prejudiced!'

'Not a bit of it. Even Penry commented on it, so it must have been blindingly obvious. And your father positively bristled with pride.' Nick grinned. 'By the way, did you notice Jenny's husband? He couldn't take his eyes off you.'

Clem pulled a face and stood up, turning her back so Nick could unfasten her dress. 'Mustn't alienate your editor, darling.'

His lips touched the satin-smooth place where her neck curved into her shoulder. 'Never mind anyone else. My turn now, since we are finally, as they say, alone at last.'

'Ah yes, Nick Wood, but there's a difference. It's not just your *eyes* you can't take off me, is it?'

'Very true. I intend to take off this dress too, and this, and these—' And Nick slowly undressed her, with delicate care, until they were together in the big new bed and everyone else was forgotten in the rapture they shared together, gentler and less fierce now, in deference to the future arrival, but their loving as intense and joyous as it had been from the beginning.

'There's a moon out there,' said Clem later, smoothing the tumbled dark hair away from Nick's forehead. 'Just like there was that first night. Only it was summer, and warm then.'

'I'm not exactly cold now, sweetheart,' Nick raised his head and looked into her eyes. It's doesn't make any difference, you know. I love you in the rain and mud as well as the moonlight. All the ways there are. And other ways I'll make up as I go along.'

Clem eyed him thoughtfully. 'I'm pleased to hear it. I hope you'll love me when I'm tired and crotchety from getting up in the night, and even before that stage, when I'm what's popularly known as "great with child".'

'All the time. Always,' Nick assured her.

'Good. Because I'm going to be both with a vengeance, believe me,' she smiled at him smugly. 'I had another reason for celebrating tonight, Nick, but I wanted to keep the news until we were alone together without any interruptions.' She paused dramatically, her eyes dancing. 'Would you believe that at my check-up today they said we're going to have twins?'

He stared at her incredulously, then his eyes filled with unholy glee, and he began to laugh, hugging her to him convulsively. 'I told my mother tonight I was twice as fortunate as most men. I didn't know then just how right I was!' He raised his head to look into her radiant face in question. 'Hey, wait a minute! I thought identical twins were a freak of nature, not hereditary.'

'True.' Clem looked inordinately pleased with herself. 'I really put one over on Chatty for once, didn't I? The Vaughan brand of twin might not be hereditary, but the Wood family are about to be blessed with two little simultaneous darlings just the same.'

Nick smoothed her hair away from her face and shrugged. 'I'm not surprised, really.'

'Oh? Why?'

'It seems quite logical to have produced two babies at once, now I come to think of it.'

Clem looked up into her husband's face, intrigued. 'Go on—I'm all ears.'

'And not just ears by a long way,' he said with feeling, looking down at the picture she made in the lamplight.

'Don't wander from the point! Tell me exactly why you consider our imminent production of twins so logical?'

'Twins are a perfectly fair result, in my opinion, if one takes into account the fact that I love you twice as much as any man ever loved his woman, all the way back to——' Nick paused tantalisingly.

'When?' Clem demanded, touching a loving hand to his cheek.

He smiled down at her. 'Oh, I don't know, at a rough estimate, I suppose you could say the Garden of Eden!'

Jessica Steele lives in a friendly Worcestershire village with her super husband, Peter. They are owned by a gorgeous Staffordshire bull terrier called Florence, who is boisterous and manic, but also adorable. It was Peter who first prompted Jessica to try writing, and after the first rejection, encouraged her to keep on trying. Her first book was published by Mills & Boon® in 1979 and since then Jessica has written 65 novels, published in more than 20 languages. Luckily, with the exception of Uruguay, she has so far managed to research inside all the countries in which she has set her books, travelling to places as far apart as Siberia and Egypt. Her thanks go to Peter for his help and encouragement.

HEARTLESS PURSUIT
by
JESSICA STEELE

CHAPTER ONE

BELVIA parked her car on the drive and let herself into her house and, dressed in old jodhpurs, she went straight to the kitchen where she was fairly certain she would find her sister busy preparing the evening meal.

'How was she?' Josy asked as soon as she saw her.

'You could come with me tomorrow and see for yourself,' Belvia suggested gently. Hetty was Josy's horse, but Josy just couldn't bring herself to go to the stables. It had not always been like that. At one time Josy had been up at the stables every minute she could spare—but that had been before Marc...

'I'm not——'

'I know, love, you're not ready yet,' Belvia interrupted quickly, her heart going out to her twin who, although like her in some ways, was so unlike her in others. 'What are we having for dinner?' Aware that Josy was hurting, she swiftly changed the conversation.

'Father's favourite.'

'Ham, peas, potatoes and parsley sauce!' Belvia recited. 'I'd better go and get showered and changed.' She was on her way out of the kitchen when she hesitated. She might have continued on her way, but saw that Josy was watching her. 'Er—do you get the feeling that Father's up to something, or is it just me and my imagination?' she asked.

'He's been a bit—um—pleasanter than usual this last couple of days, if that's anything to go by.'

'Then he *is* up to something!' Belvia needed no more confirmation than that. She knew her father of old. He could be charming—but seldom without a reason.

'He was saying last week how money was tight and how we might have to make more economies in the home.'

'According to him money's always tight,' Belvia laughed, and, unconcerned with their father's wheeling and dealing, commented, 'Thank goodness Mother left us both a little nest-egg, so we don't have to ask him for anything!'

Belvia left the kitchen and went up to her room, thinking that it was only eighteen months ago, when she and Josy had had their twenty-first birthday, that they had inherited the money left to them by their mother. It was a tidy sum, but not vast by any means. But, even so, their father had wanted them to invest the whole of it in his engineering business. Josy would have let him have the lot, but Belvia would not let her.

'He's more likely to spend it on his women than his business,' she'd persuaded her. 'And I'm sure Mummy would never have tied it up so that he couldn't get his avaricious fingers on it if she'd wanted him to have it.'

'That's a point,' Josy had agreed, remembering as Belvia did their sensitive and long-suffering mother. She'd had no money herself to start with, but the twins had been fifteen when she had inherited from a relative— and had been married for long enough to have the scales drop from her eyes. She had seen him for what he was, a philanderer and spendthrift. She had taken immediate action to ensure that, while keeping a little for herself, her two girls should have a secure future. A year later she was dead.

Belvia stripped and stepped into the shower, the water darkening her long hair. She and Josy were not identical twins: Belvia was the taller of the two and, while they both possessed dainty features, creamy complexions and the same large, deep brown eyes, Josy had hair with a reddish tint to it, while Belvia was blonde.

Belvia was the younger twin by ten minutes but, with Josy at a very early age showing signs of being painfully shy, it had seemed inborn that Belvia should protect her wherever they went.

Josy never had outgrown her shyness and, when they had left the all-girls school they attended, while Belvia had got herself a job in an office, Josy had urged her to talk to their father about letting her stay at home and keep house for them.

'Are you sure? It might be better if you got out and met a few new——'

'Oh, please, Bel!' Josy had begged in agony—and Belvia had been immediately contrite.

'All right, don't worry, I'll see to it,' she had quickly soothed.

Belvia had talked long and hard to their father, but she was sure that in the end it was purely in the interest of his own comfort that he had agreed. And matters had gone on fairly smoothly from there.

There had been a flurry of excitement when last year she and Josy had come into their inheritance. Belvia had learned to drive, purchased a good second-hand car, and had subsequently taught Josy to drive. Josy had purchased a good second-hand car too, and had then started to realise that she could also afford to buy and keep the horse she had always so passionately wanted. Belvia, her

staunchest ally, had phoned around for her and found
a stables which would allow her to keep a horse there.

Stepping from the shower, Belvia began towelling
herself dry, a smile coming to her face as she remembered her twin's joy, how Josy had forgotten to be timid
or shy the moment she had cast her eyes on Hetty.

Josy had bought Hetty without quibbling over the
price, and over the next few months had spent every
spare moment she could find up at the stables. Belvia
had thrown up her dead-end job and, her school grades
being excellent, had persuaded a firm of accountants to
allow her to train with them. She had been so keen, in
fact, that she would have trained without salary, but it
had not come to that, and she had begun to enjoy every
minute of it.

Then in the months that followed she had become
aware that, while everything in her life was metaphorically coming up roses, Josy too was beginning to
blossom.

She had found out why one lunch-hour when, her sister's car being in the garage for a service, she had driven
up to the stables to give her a lift home, and had seen
her in easy conversation with a jodhpur-clad male.

She had been more than a little amazed to see that
Josy, whom she'd never heard utter more than a few
words to any man near her own age, was smiling and
actually *chatting*! Belvia at once felt sensitive to her sister
and, while joy warmed her that Josy might be losing
some of her paralysing shyness, she was on the point of
going quietly away so that Josy might chat with her
fellow-rider the more, when her sister turned
and saw her.

'Oh, Belvia!' She welcomed her with a loving smile, and with not a stammer or a stumble in sight she introduced Marc to her.

Marc was French and, it emerged, was a groom at the stables. He was twenty-five and was, Belvia discovered, almost as shy as Josy. But he was unfailingly gentle to her sister, and Belvia could not help warming to him for that alone.

It seemed to Belvia after that that there was seldom any conversation she had with Josy in which Marc's name did not come up.

'Who's Marc?' their father, on overhearing them, enquired one day.

'He's a groom up at the stables,' Josy answered, and, to Belvia's surprise—and their father's astonishment— 'May I bring him home? I'd like to intro——'

'A *groom*!' It was all Edwin Fereday said, but it was enough.

One day four months ago Josy had come and sought her out in her room and told her that she and Marc were getting married. 'Oh, darling!' Belvia had squealed on the instant, leaping up and going over to give her sister a hug.

One look at Josy's excited face, as she spoke of there being a flat available at the stables where she and Marc would live after their marriage, was all she needed to know that her sister was very happy.

'Have you decided when?' Belvia asked, her heart bursting with joy for Josy.

'Soon—next month.'

'That doesn't give us long to get ready, but we'll manage. I shall have to——' Something in Josy's sud-

denly haunted manner caused her to break off. 'What
is it?' she asked quickly.

'I don't want a big wedding!' Josy cried in alarm.

'Nobody can make you do anything you don't want
to,' Belvia soothed calmly, having had years of practice
in dealing with her dear sister's sudden panics. 'I'll talk
to Father if you like——' She broke off as a sudden
thought struck. 'Sorry,' she smiled. 'I expect Marc will
want to speak to him himself.'

'Marc would just about die at the very thought,' Josy
replied, and went on to reveal that she and Marc had
decided to get married in secret and go to Marc's home
in France for their honeymoon, and then return to the
flat.

'You're getting married without Father or me there?'
Belvia queried gently. While it was unthinkable to her
that her twin should marry without her there, she at the
same time strove hard to remember what she had just
told her—that Josy did not have to do anything she did
not want to.

'Of course I want *you* there!' Josy answered at once.
'But not him. Marc's as nervous as me about it, and
I'm not having Father looking down his snobby nose
because Marc happens to be a groom and not a brain
surgeon.'

Belvia felt more joy that the sister she had tried all
her life to protect should now, in her love for the man
she was to marry, be in turn protective of him.

'Are you going to tell Father before or after your
wedding?' she teased, and, straightening her face, asked,
'Would you like me to tell him?'

'I'll do it—after. I'll tell him I'm going on holiday—and I'll come and move out and tell him when I come back.'

'Oh, love!' Belvia cried on a sudden note of anguish—she had never thought of Josy leaving home—'I'm going to miss you dreadfully!'

Belvia came out of her reverie on hearing the sound of her father's car on the drive. He was home early—perhaps he was dining out. Typically he would not have thought to phone to let Josy know he would not be in for dinner.

Belvia forgot about her father as she turned to go and seek her sister out. She recalled how at Josy's wedding she had been unable to stop crying in her joy for her—but recalled too how, only a day later, Josy had telephoned her from France, stunned and in shock that Marc, her husband of such a short while, had been killed in a fall while they were out riding.

Barely able to take in the tragedy that had taken place, Belvia had sensed that her twin would not want her to tell their father anything of what had happened, so she had phoned his secretary and left a message that she was going off on a week's holiday. She had gone at once to France. She and Josy had stayed in France until after Marc's funeral and then returned to Surrey.

There was then no question of Josy going to live in the flat which she and Marc had got ready. And, save for Josy saying that she did not want her father to know she had married, that she could not bear any insensitive remarks he might make if he knew that in the space of just over twenty-four hours she had been married and widowed, she had seemed to retreat into a world of her own. So much so that Belvia, who knew her better than anyone, began to be greatly worried when, although her sister appeared to be outwardly functioning normally, it seemed to her that she was going around in a daze. Josy still seemed to be deeply shocked when the whole of Belvia's holiday allowance from her office was used up, but she felt she could not leave Josy for hours on end by herself while she was at work.

'Aren't you going to your office today?' Josy surfaced to ask one day, seeming not to have noticed that Belvia had not been to her office for the past six weeks.

'I've given it up,' she smiled.

'But I thought...'

'I didn't think about it deeply enough before I took up the training.' Belvia made light of it. 'I've decided to take some time off while I have an in-depth think about what I want to train for.'

'Meantime you'll continue exercising Hetty for me?'

'Of course,' Belvia smiled. It was no hardship for her to go up to the stables each day, but each day she hoped that Josy would want to go and exercise her horse herself. She could not bring herself to sell Hetty on, and spoke of how much she loved her horse, but Belvia felt that only when she could go to the stables herself would she start to accept Marc's death.

Belvia left her room and went downstairs to check that Josy was all right. Marc had been dead three months now, but it still seemed like only yesterday.

'I'll make the parsley sauce if you want to go and tidy up a bit before dinner,' she offered, and Josy, with a smile of thanks, left her to it.

Contrary to Belvia's expectation, her father did not go out to dinner that night, but was seated in his usual place at the dining-room table when she helped Josy wheel the heated trolley in.

'Good day at the office?' Belvia asked, to cover for her silent sister. Only last week her father had said Josy seemed to be getting worse in that she barely spoke a word to him these days.

'As well as can be expected,' he answered pleasantly as Josy placed his soup in front of him. He's up to something, Belvia thought yet again, and wished he could give a hint so that she could prepare both of them for it.

'Business booming?' According to him, within their home four walls, it never was, so she reckoned it would keep his attention off Josy while he related how dire matters were.

'To be honest, no,' he answered right on cue. 'Though there's nothing wrong that can't be cured by a bit of financial investment.' Here it comes, Belvia thought, as she prepared to be strong for both herself and Josy. Had their mother wanted him to have their money, she would have left it to him.

'These are hard times,' she commented pleasantly as she searched for words that might be kinder than a blunt no. She was not blind to his faults and she knew he would try to bully her if she was not firm at the outset but, despite not wearing blinkers where he was concerned, he was her father and, while she might not like him very much, she loved him.

'They certainly are. Though I've every confidence that I'll weather my present little crisis.'

Not with our money you won't, Belvia thought, hoping with all she had that she could be as strong as she had to be. 'If you'd like me to go over the firm's books...'

She threw in a neat red herring, guessing, since he had not wanted her to work in the firm his grandfather had started, that he'd burn the books before he would allow her loose among the figures.

'There's no need for that,' he replied shortly, but was back to being pleasant again when, to her amazement, he leaned back in his chair and revealed, 'I've one of the keenest financiers in the country coming to dinner tomorrow evening.'

'You...' Belvia could not believe it. He never invited anyone home to dinner, and certainly never any keen financier! As far as she was aware, he did not know any who were *that* good. 'You've invited...' Her voice trailed off again. 'Who?' she asked.

Edwin Fereday smiled, waited a moment for effect, and then announced, 'Latham Tavenner, that's all.'

Belvia's eyes shot wide open. The name Latham Tavenner was known to her as that of one of the sharpest, if most honourable, financiers in the business. But what in creation, if her father was to be believed, was he doing having anything to do with Fereday Products? While the firm which her great-grandfather had started was quite a sizeable outfit, it would be small fry compared with the companies he had dealings with and, she would have thought, was way beneath his notice.

'What's he coming here for?' she asked suspiciously.

'Because I asked him to!' her father retorted, doing away with any pretence of pleasantness at the note of challenge in her tone.

Belvia might have inherited all her mother's sensitivity and none of her father's insensitive ways, but she had also inherited from somewhere a fair degree of intelligence. She used it then, and, knowing her father too well, she asked sharply, 'Does he know he's going to invest in Fereday Products?' and drew forth a swift and bullying reply from her parent.

'No, he doesn't!' he retorted. 'Not yet! And don't you tell him either. You just keep him——'

'*I*,' Belvia jumped in, not for a moment prepared to be bullied by him or anyone else, 'won't be here.'

'Yes, you damn well will!'

'No, I won't! Kate Mitchell, who I used to work with, is having a retirement party. I promised I'd be there.'

'Then you can just ring her up and unpromise!'

'No, I can't!'

Her father favoured her with a spleenish look, glancing from her to her sister irritatedly. And then suddenly he was smiling a smile which Belvia did not like at all, with his look coming back to her. 'Very well,' he agreed. 'If that's your last word, so be it. We'll just have to leave it to Josy to entertain our guest.'

That was when Belvia knew why she so often disliked her father. She looked from him to where Josy was just about dying a thousand deaths. She had never met Latham Tavenner either, but she did not have to: any man who was as successful and therefore as worldly as he must be would terrify her. Belvia knew in that one glance at her sister that she was crumbling just thinking about entertaining the man at their dining-table.

'So I'll stay at home!' she agreed shortly, unable to take her support from Josy now. She caught Josy's grateful look and smiled at her before she turned back to ask her father frostily, 'And what, in particular, would you like us to cook for your guest?'

'I don't give a hoot what it is, so long as you keep him sweet,' he answered.

So that was it! The something she had thought her father was up to was now very clear. He needed quite substantial investment in the firm and, the banks being unmistakably disinclined to lend him any more, he was hoping that Latham Tavenner would. Why he had invited him to dinner was a bit mystifying, but perhaps that was how these things were done—probably over a glass of port. She did not at all like her father's instruction that she 'keep him sweet', and indeed cringed at the very idea of being nice to the man purely so that her father should have him good-humoured when he asked for his money.

Belvia was up early the next morning, and was starting to feel indignant at her father's 'keep him sweet' edict. She hoped her manners were such that she would be polite and pleasant to any guest in their home.

On going downstairs, she discovered that, early as she had arisen, Josy was down before her and was already worrying about what to give their guest for dinner that night.

'What were you going to give us?' Belvia asked.

'Chicken curry, rice and a side-salad, and bread-and-butter pudding.'

'Then that's what we'll have. I'll make some celery soup, if you like.'

'Oh, would you?' Josy accepted as she attended to their father's breakfast.

He had gone to his office by eight, and at a minute past nine Josy, as if afraid Belvia might yet change her mind, was reminding her to ring Kate Mitchell to let her know that she could not come to her party.

'Hello, Kate,' Belvia greeted the kind lady who had taken her under her wing when she had first gone to train at Newman and Company. 'Enjoying your last day?'

'Mixed feelings now it's come to it,' Kate replied. 'I'll see you tonight at the party w——'

'Er—the thing is, something's cropped up...'

Five minutes later Belvia put down the phone and went in search of her sister. 'Did she mind very much?' Josy asked at once.

'A bit. I've promised I'll look in later. Much, much later,' Belvia added in a rush when she saw her twin blench. 'Father won't want either of us there when he taps Mr Tavenner for his money, so once dinner's out of the way and we've been "sweet", we'll be free to disappear.' Belvia had been about to tack on what Kate had said when she had casually asked if Newman and Company had ever had anything to do with Latham Tavenner and his outfit, but Josy was already looking uptight, and she felt it best to get away from the subject altogether.

They spent the whole of the morning giving the already spruce sitting-room and dining-room another sprucing. And what with one thing and another—all preparations made for the evening meal, right down to the best china being brought out and rinsed—it was early afternoon before Belvia felt she could leave her sister and go up to the stables to exercise Hetty.

If their father wasn't happy with their efforts that day, then hard luck, Belvia thought as she sat astride Hetty and they cantered around the countryside, though she admitted to feeling uncomfortable inside that her father was entertaining the financier purely for his own ends.

But, while not wanting to be a party to any of it, she had to own to a sneaking curiosity to see for herself the hard-headed businessman Kate had told her about. Kate had never met him, but had said he had a reputation for being a shrewd, if fair, operator. Kate had not been able to tell her much more about him other than that he was still a bachelor, though not for want of half the female population around trying to do something to alter that. Kate also thought that he and his sister, to whom he was said to be very close, had been orphaned quite young and had been brought up by relatives.

Not much to go on, Belvia mused as she returned home. If he was still a bachelor, with women running after him, then how old was he, for goodness' sake? Or was it perhaps that he was getting on in years, bald and fat, and, since it was plain that he was not short of a penny or two, was it his fortune that half the women in town were after?

She stepped lightly into the kitchen, where she found that Josy was getting into a state as the time when she was going to have to act as co-hostess came nearer.

'It'll be a breeze.' Belvia tried to bolster her up. 'Come on, leave this and go and take a shower and put something pretty on.'

Belvia went up the stairs with her and they parted to go to their separate rooms. Now what, Belvia wondered, bearing in mind that—with no time to change—she would be going on to a party later, should she wear?

'Oh, Belvia, you look stunning!' Josy exclaimed when she joined her in the kitchen. Belvia was dressed in a simple—although expensive—black dress.

'Have you taken a look at yourself?' She smiled encouragingly at Josy, who had made a tremendous effort

to build her confidence and was wearing an equally
simple dress of pale green that brought out the red in
her hair. 'You're beautiful.'

'Tosh,' Josy responded, and Belvia went and gave her
a hug.

'We're going to have to do something about your low
self-esteem,' she told her seriously, then the doorbell
sounded and a look of panic immediately came over her
shy sister's face.

Ten minutes later Belvia judged it was time to leave
the kitchen. By the time they reached the sitting-room,
Josy had her panic under control. Belvia gave her a quick
reassuring glance, then opened the door and led the way
in—and stopped dead!

Latham Tavenner was neither bald nor fat, nor in his
dotage. He had turned as they went in and, as she looked
at the tall, dark-haired man in his mid-thirties, who with
all-assessing, cool grey eyes looked back and appeared
neither interested nor uninterested, for no known reason,
her heart gave a crazy flutter.

Ridiculous. She dismissed such nonsense as not worth
consideration and, knowing that Josy would stick close
like glue, she went forward so that her father could make
the introductions.

'This is the youngest twin, Belvia,' her father announced jovially. 'Belvia, our guest Latham Tavenner.'

'How do you do?' Belvia trotted out, extending her
right hand, and felt her whole body tingle as Latham
Tavenner took her hand in a firm but cursory grip then,
unsmiling and without a word, dropped it and turned
his attention to Josy, who was close by her side.

'And this is my other daughter, Josy.'

Protectively Belvia stood watch as Josy stretched out a nervous hand and gulped, 'Hello.'

Belvia moved a fraction closer to her and saw Latham Tavenner look from Josy to her and, after a barely perceptible pause, back to her sister again. 'Hello, Josy,' he responded, and—although Belvia had formed the view that the man did not have a smile in him—he smiled.

Although Josy's smile was a degree on the shaky side, she made it. But as Latham Tavenner let go of her hand and seemed as if he would engage her in conversation Belvia discerned in the quick look that Josy shot to her that she was signalling, 'Help me'.

'If you'll excuse us,' she butted in before he could address another word to her sister, 'Josy and I need to go and do things culinary.'

Oh, heavens, Belvia thought as she offered up a phoney smile to go with her words, and in return received the full blast of not just cool but arctic grey eyes.

Who the hell did he think he was? she fumed as she grabbed hold of Josy's arm and took her kitchenwards.

'He's terrifying!' Josy cried, the moment they were out of earshot.

'How?' Belvia queried calmly.

'Didn't you see him! Smooth, sophisticated...'

'And eats little girls for supper,' Belvia teased, on the brink of being panicky herself, she realised, for sophisticated he certainly was. And smooth. Though for herself she had no need to worry for, from what she could make of it—and it couldn't be just his suave manner or he would have smiled at her too—Latham Tavenner had taken a shine to her sister!

That notion was further endorsed when, everything ready, they moved to the dining-room and, as the meal got under way, Latham Tavenner seemed to make a point of trying to draw out her shy sister.

'Do you have a career, Josy?' he enquired pleasantly as he took a spoonful of soup.

Belvia saw her slop her own soup. 'Josy prefers to stay at home and look after Father and me,' she hurried in. Not liking him any better when he tossed her a 'who-asked-you?' look she added swiftly, 'And very well she does it, too.'

Having brought the financier's attention on herself, Belvia then had to weather his cool appraisal. Clearly he was not liking her any more than she liked him, but he brought out his 'polite guest' manners to enquire distantly, 'And do you follow a career?'

'Belvia was in training to be an accountant,' her father answered for her.

'Was?' their guest picked up.

'She got bored, and threw it up.'

Thanks, Father, Belvia fumed, and, what with one thing and another, decided she'd had enough of the pair of them.

'You manage to keep busy, no doubt?' Latham Tavenner addressed her directly.

'Some,' she managed through gritted teeth.

'What did you do today, for instance?' he wanted to know, and Belvia knew at that point that he was not one iota interested in any cooking or cleaning she might have done. All too obviously he had formed an opinion, aided by her father, that she was an idle layabout, intent on nothing but pleasure.

Far be it from her to spoil his opinion. And at least while he was talking to her he was leaving Josy alone. 'Ooh, nothing much,' she replied, sending him another

phoney smile. 'I messed about for most of the morning—
ringing up friends, that sort of thing—and then this
afternoon I went out for a ride on Hetty...'

'Hetty?'

'Josy's horse. And——'

'Doesn't Josy mind you riding her horse?'

Had they been better acquainted, she might have
kicked his shins—she'd had just about enough of him
and the way he looked down his nose at her.

'Not today,' she returned, her attempt to keep smiling
wearing thin. 'Today Josy was too busy in the house to
exercise her herself, so I thought I'd do her a favour.'

'How very generous of you!' he clipped curtly.

Good. Now perhaps he'd leave her in peace and chat
to her father! To goad her further, however, it was to
her sister that he turned, and Belvia did not know just
then whether she felt piqued or protective about that.

'Have you been riding long, Josy?' he enquired.

'Yes,' Josy whispered and, as Belvia saw the mist of
sadness that came to her sister's eyes, it was protectiveness pure and simple that rushed to the fore.

'Will you have some chutney with your curry?' she
said in a rush, picking up the mango chutney and placing
it in front of him.

'Thank you,' he accepted politely enough, but there
was a tough look in the hard grey glance he served her
with that left her with an unmistakable impression that
one Latham Tavenner had no time whatsoever for her.

Which was just fine by her—she had no time for him
either. And if he had some notion—picked up, no doubt,
from the fact that she was jobless—that she was work-
shy and that the house could be six feet deep in dust
before she would pick up a duster, it was nought to her.

Thankfully her father was taking a hand in the conversation, which was just as well. By the look of it, Latham Tavenner had given up trying to address Josy, only to be answered by Belvia. Which suited her fine, since that meant that she did not have to talk to him either.

When the meal came to an end Belvia had long since got over any feeling of awkwardness that her father was entertaining Latham Tavenner for his own ends. She was liking neither her father nor his guest just then, and in her view they deserved each other.

'That was a very nice meal,' Latham complimented her sister as he placed his napkin on the table.

'Thank you,' Josy answered quietly, but added—and Belvia wished she had not—'Belvia made the soup.'

You needn't look so surprised, she fumed crossly to herself. 'Anyone can open a tin,' she offered uncaringly, and saw a glint in his eyes that spoke of his knowing the difference between home-made and tinned—and not taking kindly to being lied to on any subject, no matter how trivial.

'If you'll excuse me.' Josy's voice penetrated, and Belvia switched her glance to where her sister was taking a tray from the room. Her duty done, she would not show her face again that night, as Belvia well knew.

And, since it was only for Josy's sake that she had delayed going to the party, Belvia could find no good reason why she should not disappear too.

'If you'll excuse me, also,' she murmured, and was on her feet when she was staggered to hear her father—in front of company—take her to task!

'Where are you off to?' he demanded.

'I'm going out,' she replied.

'At this time of night?'

Belvia stared at him, barely able to credit that, in the belief that it made him look important, he should speak to her so in front of his guest. 'I've got a date,' she replied flippantly. Casting a quick glance to Latham Tavenner, she could hardly credit either that, without bothering to hide his look of total dislike, he was staring contemptuously at her! Who *did* he think he...? He might have been orphaned at a tender age, and might well be of the opinion that she should show more respect for her father, but...

Belvia made for the door but, feeling suddenly goaded beyond what was reasonable—by the pair of them—she turned. 'After dinner is the only time he can get away from his wife,' she tossed at anyone who might be interested.

She saw her father dart a hasty glance to his guest, but cared not if she had embarrassed him. He'd asked for it—speaking to her like that in front of a guest. She slid her glance to that guest, and was shaken by the harsh anger in his face—almost malevolent! He was not embarrassed—he was furious.

Finding his look threatening, she dragged her gaze from him and, feeling oddly all of a tremble inside, she left the dining-room.

Out in the hall, away from him, she told herself not to be so ridiculous and went upstairs to collect her bag and car keys. Grief! To look like that—just because she had been saucy to her bullying father, whom she knew far better than he did!

Belvia went out to her car, but was still feeling a trifle disturbed when she arrived at Kate's party. She made herself think positively and decided that, on the up side, she had done her father a favour. Because if Latham Tavenner was so incensed about her manner to her parent, then he might feel more inclined to let him have the investment he wanted. And, on the double up side, she doubted that Latham Tavenner would accept an invitation to dine at her home a second time. Which meant, happily, that she would never have to see him again.

CHAPTER TWO

FOR all that the party was good, Belvia came home dogged, as she had been at the party, by thoughts of Latham Tavenner. Damn the man, she fumed, then showered and climbed into bed, to sleep badly and dream of the wretched man.

She slept late and found that her father, off on his weekend pursuits, had already left the house to pick up his present lady-love.

'Good party?' Josy asked, looking up from stacking the dishwasher as Belvia walked into the kitchen.

'It was, actually,' she replied, and sank down on a kitchen chair and related some of the highlights.

'Coffee?' Josy enquired.

'Gasping!'

Josy busied herself making them both a cup of coffee, and then, placing a beaker down in front of Belvia, commented, 'You were shouting in your sleep last night.'

'Was I?' Belvia enquired, startled. In childhood she had shouted out in her sleep whenever she was disturbed about something, and she had gone through another bout of it shortly after her mother had died. 'I haven't done that in years. Was I yelling anything interesting?'

Josy smiled. 'Just gibberish.' And, her smile fading, 'Anything worrying you, Bel?'

'Not a sausage,' Belvia laughed, 'save for the mountain of clearing-up we left in the dining-room.'

'I'd have done it last night, only——'

26

'I know,' Belvia cut in gently, fully aware that, but for the fact that Josy had risked bumping into Latham Tavenner around the sitting-room area, she would have set to in the dining-room after the man had left it. Apparently there was something about the cool, detached man that disturbed both of them. She had been thinking of him when she had gone to bed last night, and could think of no other reason why she should have been visited by a return of shouting out in her sleep.

What she needed was exercise, and plenty of it, she decided, and quickly downed her coffee. 'I'll go and investigate the dining-room,' she remarked, getting to her feet.

'Don't you want any breakfast?'

'Not hungry,' Belvia replied, and, at the ridiculous thought that she had never been off her food until she had met Latham Tavenner, she realised that she was giving a man in whose company she had spent not much more than an hour far too much time.

She was in the sitting-room later that morning, plumping up cushions, when Josy went by to answer a ring at the door. She heard the door open and then close, and stopped what she was doing altogether when, her face pale, her eyes worried, Josy came into the sitting-room with a basket arrangement of flowers.

'Why, how lovely!' Belvia said spontaneously of the splendid arrangement.

'They're from—him!' Josy whispered in scared tones.

'Him' *had* to be Latham Tavenner! 'Well, it's only a thank-you for his dinner last night,' Belvia replied bracingly.

'But *your* name isn't on the card!'

Belvia would have been astonished if it had been. 'So?' she enquired.

'You helped cook dinner too. I—think he likes me,' Josy said worriedly.

It's for certain he doesn't like me, Belvia thought, and could not make up her mind whether she appreciated his honesty in leaving her off the card, or if she thought him oafish and sadly lacking in the manners department for the omission.

'Who could help liking you?' she teased—to no avail.

'Will you put them in your room?' Josy begged, clearly not wanting to catch a glimpse of them anywhere and so be reminded of the man whose sophistication all too obviously awed her.

'Of course,' Belvia replied easily before she could think—and then realised that she did not want to be reminded of the beastly man either. 'Or, better still, I'll take them to Tracey when I go to the stables this afternoon. She'll enjoy them, I'm sure.'

'Oh, she will,' Josy replied, starting to look easier. Tracey was one of the grooms up at the stables and had a positive passion for flowers. 'Only don't tell her that they came for me, will you?'

'I'll say they came from one of my many admirers,' Belvia laughed, liking the humour of that thought—an admirer of hers was something which Latham Tavenner most definitely was not.

The rest of the weekend passed without incident and Belvia was pleased to see that by Sunday evening, given that Josy was still suffering over the loss of her husband, as she would be for some time to come, she was otherwise back on a more even keel and calmer over Latham Tavenner's attentions to her.

Belvia got out of bed on Monday morning and felt more on an even keel herself. She went downstairs, saw her father in conversation with her sister through the open breakfast-room door, popped her head in and offered a 'Good morning,' then took herself off to the kitchen. She had just put a couple of slices of bread in the toaster when Josy joined her. 'I've put the toast in for us,' she began, but stopped when she saw that Josy was looking agitated. 'What's up, Jo?' she asked.

'I've just had a lecture from Father on the subject of shaping up and being more amenable to guests he brings into this house!'

By 'guests', since he seldom invited anyone home, Belvia knew her father could only mean Latham Tavenner. And that angered her. But while on the one hand she wanted to go straight away to see their father and let him know that she and her sister had not the smallest desire to be included in his devious games to finance Fereday Products, she felt it was more important just then to try to calm Josy down.

'Well, don't let it throw you, love. Since Father only invites a guest home once in a flood, you haven't a thing to worry about.'

'But what if he does?'

'He won't,' Belvia replied firmly, though she could see that Josy was far from convinced. 'And if he does, then you can make yourself scarce, and I'll look after Mr Latham Tavenner personally,' she promised lightly.

Josy still did not look reassured, and the day got under way badly, with their father going off to his office and with Belvia giving serious thought to her and her sister finding somewhere to live on their own and moving out. The only trouble with that, she mused as she took advantage of a lovely summer day and went into the garden to do some weeding, was that Josy was so shy with strangers, and any move they made would have to involve meeting new people.

She still had Josy on her mind when half an hour later she went indoors for a cold drink. Would it be better for her sister to be made to meet new people? she wondered, but at once cancelled that idea. Seldom a day went by now that she did not find her twin staring into space, hurting and still distraught over losing Marc. How could she think of...?

Belvia's thoughts came to an abrupt end when Josy came into the kitchen, looking more upset than ever.

'What's the matter?' she asked urgently.

'He's just rung!'

'Who?' Belvia asked, leading her over to a chair.

'Latham T-Tavenner!' Josy answered distractedly.

Belvia's breath caught; she had not anticipated this. Without haste she pulled up a kitchen chair close to her sister. 'What did he want?' she enquired as calmly as she could.

'There's a charity concert thing on in London tonight—some big affair. He's got tickets and wondered if I'd like to go.'

'You said no?'

'How *could* I?' Josy cried. 'Not after Father lecturing me this morning. He'd go wild if I had to tell him I turned down a date with the man he's breaking his neck to get in with.'

'All right, all right, keep calm,' Belvia instructed, seeing she was close to going to pieces. 'So what did you tell him?'

Josy took a shaky breath as she strove hard to recapture her self-control. 'At first, when I knew who it was, I just couldn't say a word. Then, quite pleasantly, he said, "You haven't forgotten me already, I hope," and I panicked a bit and—probably after what you said about you personally looking after him—I asked him if he wanted to speak to you.'

I'll bet that thrilled him, Belvia thought, but could see that Josy was in no mind to appreciate the humour of her thoughts. 'So he politely told you no, and then asked you out. And, since you didn't say no, you must have said yes,' she prompted.

'I must have done—he's sending a car for me this evening,' Josy gulped. 'Oh, Bel, I can't go! He's so sure of himself, while I'm so unsure of just about absolutely everything—he positively terrifies me!'

Belvia spent the next five minutes promising that her uncertainty about everything would pass, and that—while admittedly Josy had always been desperately shy—it must all be part and parcel of the dreadful loss she had suffered. 'And,' she ended, 'if you're so terrified of the man, then I wouldn't dream of letting you go anywhere with him.'

'You wouldn't?'

Belvia shook her head.

'But—what about Father? I can't let him down!'

'Leave Father to me—I'll ring him at his office.'

Belvia got on the phone straight away. Her father was not in his office and her call was diverted to Vanessa Stanley, his secretary of the last five years; according to him, the fluffily pretty woman was as hard inside as she appeared soft outside. Though whether this was because he had chanced his arm with her, only to be told she preferred men nearer her own age—the late twenties, Belvia could only conjecture.

'If you'd like to hold, I can go and find him,' Vanessa offered. 'Or shall I ask him to ring you?'

'I'll wait, shall I?' The sooner she got something sorted out for Josy the better.

The line went dead, and then, what seemed like an age later, her father, not taking kindly to being phoned at the office, was grumpily enquiring, 'I hope the house isn't on fire?'

'Latham Tavenner has phoned asking Josy out tonight, and she can't go!' Belvia told him bluntly, her spirits dropping—from the sound of it, she had caught him at a bad time.

'Why can't she go?' he wanted to know, equally bluntly.

'Because he terrifies her, that's why!' she answered aggressively.

'Rubbish!'

'Well, she's not going.'

'Put her on the line.'

Over her dead body. 'She's upstairs,' Belvia lied.

'Then you just tell her from me that we need his money. For God's sake, all she's got to do is go out with him—he won't eat her.'

'But she's shy! You know she is. She'll——'

'Then it's about time she grew out of it! Tell her from me that she's to go and that's an end to it!' With that, in a fine rage, her father slammed down the phone.

Stars above, how her mother had put up with him all those years...!

'What did he say?' Belvia was so angry that she had forgotten for a moment that Josy was in the same room.

'I—er—caught him at the wrong moment,' she had to confess, and thought fleetingly of suggesting again that she and Josy moved out. Then she saw that Josy looked near to tears, and it just wasn't fair—the little love hadn't been widowed four months! It just wasn't right that she should be put through this! 'You're not going,' she stated unequivocally. 'I'd sooner go myself.' It would not come to that, of course. 'Would you pass me the phone book?'

'What are you going to do?'

'You're going to have a migraine.'

Josy looked hopeful. Ten minutes later and she was looking downcast again. Belvia had got through to the Latham Tavenner building, and had even got through to his PA, but when she asked to speak to him, she had been politely, pleasantly, but firmly blocked.

'May I take a message for you?'

'I particularly wanted to speak to him personally.'

'Who did you say was calling?'

She hadn't said. 'My name is Fereday, Belvia Fereday,' she replied, and that was when the PA had said Mr Tavenner was out of town all day—and Belvia did not believe it for a minute. Though since it was highly unlikely that he had told his PA he had dined in her company on Friday and had taken an instant dislike to her, she did not know quite why she did not believe that Latham Tavenner was out of town—she just didn't. 'Should I leave a message, will he get it today?' she asked—her last hope.

'I'm afraid I can't promise that. Mr Tavenner sometimes rings through at the end of the day, but it's by no means certain.'

Belvia toyed with the idea of leaving a message that his date for that evening was off. But Josy would want her to give an excuse—and what excuse was there? On thinking about it, any migraine she invented could be better by this evening and, by speaking to Josy personally only a short while ago, he knew that she was not in bed with flu.

'I'll leave it, thank you,' she said politely, added, 'Goodbye' and hung up. 'Look.' She addressed her twin seriously as she turned round to see that Josy had already realised the negative result of that phone call. 'You don't *have* to go!'

A shuddering kind of sigh escaped Josy. 'I do,' she answered. 'For Father's sake, I have to.'

'Oh, damn,' Belvia groaned, and knew that, love him or hate him, when it came to the crunch, neither of them could let their father down. She let go a shaky breath too, loathing the whole of this as much as her sister did. Though when a glance at her showed that Josy seemed to be wilting where she sat, Belvia started to grow angry. This just was not on! 'You're not going!' she stated. No argument.

'I have to.'

'No, you don't. You——'

'Let's face it Bel,' Josy interrupted, 'we can't get in touch with him, and he's sending a car for me. By the time the chauffeur turns up without me, it will be too late for him to rustle up another female—date. That,' she ended in a choked voice, 'is certain to make it a foregone conclusion that he'll want nothing to do with any of the Fereday family again. I have to k-keep my word—the Fereday word.'

In the world of high finance a person's word meant everything; Belvia knew that. Oh, stuff it, she fumed, and knew then that if the Fereday word was to be kept one of them had to go. It was with a great deal of reluctance that she realised it was time to put her money where her mouth was. Though Latham Tavenner was not going to like it any more than she was.

'So,' she smiled, 'what am I going to wear?'

The only thing Belvia was grateful for when, right on time that evening, a sleek limousine pulled up outside was that, as sometimes happened, her father was not yet home. It was taking all she had to go through with this— she could do without his objections and arguments.

'Oh, Belvia, you look lovely!' Josy exclaimed as she went with her to the door, admiring the look of her in her strapless sheath of white satin, her only jewellery a pair of pendant crystal ear-rings.

Belvia needed to hear that. She was not shy nor timid where men were concerned, unlike her sister, but her insides were quaking. Lord above only knew how Josy would have been feeling had she been the one dressed in all her finery on her way out.

That thought alone was sufficient for her to know she was doing the only thing possible. Josy could just not have coped. 'Now, remember.' She went through what they had decided to tell their father again. 'If Father cuts up rough when he gets in, tell him you've got a tummy upset and that rather than have you throw up in the car, and in particular rather than break the Fereday word, I've gone in your stead.'

Josy nodded solemnly, and Belvia, her long blonde hair swept upwards in an elegant style on top of her head, went out to where the chauffeur immediately sprang to open the rear door of the most splendid limousine. Belvia got in and, with a cheery wave to Josy hovering on the doorstep, they were away.

What Latham Tavenner was going to say when he saw her she did not dare think, and by the time they were approaching the theatre, Belvia's insides were churning so much that she felt the tummy upset Josy was to tell their father she was suffering with was about to be visited on her.

There was no sign of Latham Tavenner when the limousine drew to a stop. The chauffeur got out and, with her insides in more of a knot than ever, Belvia prepared to get out too. Then the passenger door was opened—and suddenly it was not the chauffeur who stood there but, having appeared from nowhere, Latham Tavenner!

Oh, heavens! He looked magnificent in evening clothes! But as he stood there and just stared at her, he was clearly quite unable to believe his eyes. Belvia opened her mouth, her rehearsed excuses at the ready, but, with her stomach churning and her heart banging away against her ribs, all at once she could not remember a word of them.

Which left her to do the only thing possible. She dipped her head to avoid looking at him, and stepped elegantly out of the streamlined vehicle.

The next second she was standing close up to the athletically built financier—and would not have been at all surprised had he pushed her back into the limousine and instructed the chauffeur to deliver her back whence she came. For it was all there as he recovered from seeing that the wrong Fereday twin had turned up and snarled, 'I invited your sister, not you!'

His tone was what she needed—it nettled her. 'We——' she began snappily—and that was as far as she got. For abruptly, not giving her chance to say another word, Latham Tavenner caught hold of her by her upper arm. Though not, she swiftly realised, to push her back in the vehicle, but to turn her in the direction which they were to go.

'We're holding everything up!' he grunted, and, plainly irritated to find himself lumbered with her for the evening, he bent and closed the passenger door, and as the vehicle slid away and another pulled up in its place Belvia saw that cars were queuing up to drop off their passengers. The next she knew was that the firm hand was on her upper arm again and, while flash cameras seemed to be going off everywhere, Latham Tavenner was instructing her tersely—through a seemingly smiling mouth—to 'Try and look as though you're enjoying yourself—you'll probably see the result in the paper tomorrow.'

Belvia smiled and hated him, and walked with him into the theatre and into the crowded foyer, and was glad with all her heart that it was she who was there and not her twin. Aside from having this brute of a man steering her around, Josy would never have been able to cope with the attention of the Press and television cameras, even if well aware that it was more her escort they would be interested in than her. Nor, as Latham was halted here and there by people he knew and exchanged a few words, and occasionally introduced her to someone, could Josy have coped with that either.

To Belvia's surprise, however, while she knew without doubt that her escort must be furious to find himself having to put up with her, he was unfailingly polite to her in front of other people. Though she guessed it was only a matter of time before she felt the whiplash edge of his tongue.

They had made it to their seats, with about five minutes to go before the performance was about to start, when Belvia gave up all pretence of appearing intent on the programme he had purchased for her—and decided to get in first. Impulsively she turned to look at him. Though when he, sensing her movement, turned to look at her too and stared arrogantly down at her the words died in her throat.

But it was important for her father that she get through to him, so, 'I apologise that I'm here and not Josy...' she managed—ye gods, arrogant did not begin to cover it as one superior eyebrow went aloft! 'But when Josy was taken suddenly ill...' She ploughed doggedly on.

'Your sister is ill?'

'A twenty-four hour bug,' she lied brazenly. 'It was important, we both felt, that the word of a Fereday should be kept. So...' She let the fact that she was there finish the sentence for her, and was just congratulating herself that she had assured him that he could rely on a Fereday when she saw his arrogant look change to one of amazement.

'You thought I'd be inconsolable if the car arrived empty?' he queried incredulously.

'No, of course not. But——'

'Oh, shut up,' he grated, and for the first time in her life she came within an ace of punching a man on the nose.

'Bastard!' she muttered, and the lights in the theatre went down—and she would have sworn she heard his smothered laugh! Actually heard him laugh! As if he had heard her muttered expletive—as if she had amused him!

Belvia, while looking at the stage, saw and heard nothing of the first half-hour of the concert. Good grief, what was happening to her? She had never called anyone a bastard in her life! And what was more, if asked, she would have said she never would. The word was just not part of her vocabulary—or so she would have said.

It was him, his fault! He had goaded her to it. Well, she would be hanged if she would apologise. Come to think of it, she had never thought she would want to set about anyone physically either. But that too was his fault! Who the devil did he think he was, telling her to shut up? Infuriating swine!

By the time the interval arrived, Belvia had cooled down sufficiently to realise that, although it would irk her beyond measure, for her father's sake she was going to have to make amends for that 'bastard'.

She hoped, in a way, that she *had* amused Latham Tavenner, come to think of it. Because, if he was in a good humour, she might be able to get in a tactful word with which to ask him to leave Josy alone.

That chance, however, did not come. 'Would you care for a drink?' her escort enquired when the lights went up.

She much preferred to sit where they were so that she could talk to him—tactfully. 'No, thanks,' she smiled, realising as she stared into his strong, good-looking face that she must have been mistaken about having amused him, because his expression was now as arrogant—not to mention hostile—as she remembered it.

'You won't mind if I do, I'm sure,' he commented suavely, and so much for her decision to stay and talk

because—and she was having a hard time taking it in—
he did no more than get up and leave her!

The pig, the utter pig! She hoped the bar was dry by
the time he got there. She was still fuming many minutes
later when, startling her out of her thoughts, a man
somewhere around her own age came and sat down in
the empty seat next to her.

'Didn't I see you with Latham Tavenner?' he asked,
turning sideways in the seat Latham had vacated.

'Er—yes,' she agreed.

'Rodney Phillips,' the man introduced himself. 'At a
rough guess I'd say I've not much time before he comes
back—I don't suppose you'd like to let me have your
phone number, would you?'

After so much tension, it was a great relief to find she
felt like laughing. Rodney Phillips was transparent, and
harmless. 'Not a chance,' she laughed.

'Oh, you're so beautiful!' he exclaimed, and then, as
if fearing he was being too familiar, 'Can I get you an
ice-cream or something?' he asked earnestly.

'What you can do, Phillips, is get out of my seat,'
Latham Tavenner addressed to his earnest back.

Like someone shot, Rodney Phillips sprang to his feet.
'Sorry, sir,' he apologised, and as unexpectedly as he
had arrived so he went.

'Does he work for you?' Belvia enquired.

He nodded, and took his seat. 'Was he annoying you?'
he enquired crisply.

'I enjoyed talking to him,' she replied—and take that
whichever way you care to, she added inwardly.

Aggravatingly, Latham Tavenner did not take it that
she was hinting that it was nice to have somebody around
to be able to talk to, but made it sound as though she

liked to make a conquest of every male she came into contact with by commenting grimly, 'He's too young for you!' Again Belvia wanted to thump him. Was he warning her to keep away from his staff?

Belvia sat and fumed for the rest of the performance and, for herself, would have walked back to Surrey rather than spend another moment more in his company than she had to when the concert was over. But there was her father, who was relying on Latham Tavenner investing his money in his company, and, more importantly to her, there was Josy.

'Thank you. It was very good, wasn't it?' She forced the words out between her teeth as they made their way out from the theatre.

'I expect you're hungry,' he offered, which in her view was no sort of a reply, but it did hold a hint that he might feed her. Surely then she could get a word in to ask him to leave her sister alone, although, for her father's sake, it would have to be done with the utmost tact.

'Starving,' she lied; she had been too stewed up to eat a crumb before she had left home, and felt pretty much the same now.

As if by magic, the chaffeur-driven car she had arrived in pulled up alongside as they walked to the edge of the pavement. Latham said not a word to her as they drove, but she was unworried by that. She had better things to do—such as sorting her words into some kind of order.

They arrived at an old, stately-looking building and, getting out, Belvia realised he had brought her to his club to eat. Good, she thought as they went in and she looked about. She would have a far better chance to talk to him in these discreet confines than in any nightclub.

'I tried to phone you,' she opened, with the latest of her rehearsed lines, 'but——'

'Why the hell would you want to do that?' he demanded, and Belvia did not need any more than that to have it confirmed he did not like her and would take the gravest exception to her taking advantage of the fact that he had dined in her home last Friday.

'Surprising as it may seem—I don't fancy you!' she hissed, and was saved from ruining everything and upending the water-jug over his head when the waiter arrived with their first course. It gave her the chance to get herself under control. So she bit down the words to tell Latham Tavenner to go and take a running jump, and dipped her spoon into her soup.

'Mmm, this is good,' she remarked civilly, much too preoccupied to have any idea what it tasted like. 'Er— I'm sorry Josy couldn't make it this——'

'Your date for this evening obviously couldn't make it either!' he cut in sharply.

'My d——?' What *was* it about this man? 'Men aren't in the habit of breaking dates with me!' she erupted, her chin tilting at a lofty angle. She did not like the hard glint that came to his eyes, and knew that she would have been better staying quiet.

'My God, you need taking down a peg or two!' he rapped.

She hoped he did not think he was the man to do it! Not that she agreed with him, anyway. Though as it belatedly dawned on her that she was a mile away from being as tactful as she had decided she must be, she fought hard to hide the antagonism which this man aroused in her.

'Look, I'm sorry if I've offended you,' she began placatingly, and saw from his distrustful look that he was not placing any faith in her apology. 'But the reason I tried to phone you was because Josy had a sudden tummy upset...' She took a glance at him from beneath her lashes—and saw he was not believing that either. 'And I thought—if I *could* get in touch with you—that I could explain about Josy not—um—being well.'

'And when you couldn't get in touch with me—you decided to come in her place?'

The way he put it made it sound as if he thought she was some egotist to believe for a moment that he would consider herself a good substitute for Josy.

Oh, to blazes with him, Belvia fumed as her anger against him once more spiralled. Suddenly she checked. Anger was just something she could not afford right now. She had to think only of her sister, and forget all about her own emotions.

She looked across at him and knew that, even without his abrasive manner, her gentle, saintly sister would go under if she had to go out with him. He was so virile, so, so—absolutely everything. Poor, sad Josy just *had* to be protected.

'Um—if——'

'You seem to be struggling?' he interrupted urbanely. 'Surely not?'

Viper! She smiled. 'I'm searching for tact,' she confessed.

'Which means, no matter how you dress it up, that I'm not going to like it.'

Shrewd was not in it. 'Well, the thing is, Josy, my twin...'

'I know who she is.'

Somehow Belvia managed to keep the smile on her face, even while endearing thoughts of burying an axe in his head intruded. 'The thing is,' she forced herself to go on, 'Josy is very shy. Extremely shy,' she added for good measure.

'She sounded all right on the phone this morning.'

'She's also extremely well-mannered,' Belvia stated crisply, and had to weather his look that asked if they had both been brought up by the same parents.

'You're trying to tell me something?' he enquired mockingly.

Her temper flared; she forced it down, though her tone was sharper than she had meant when she told him, 'My sister is not used to men!'

'But you undoubtedly are!' he rapped.

Damn him, one of these days...

Her temper cooled. She doubted that she would ever get the chance to land him one—as he so richly deserved.

'Actually, I'm not,' she replied, and felt her palms itch to come into sharp contact with his face at the look of total derision which he did nothing to hide. 'But...' She dug her heels in—she'd finish this if it killed her. 'This isn't about me, it's about Josy and the fact that... Well, just this evening for a start—all those people, the cameras, the TV people—she's not used to that sort of thing, she'd...'

'She'd never cope?' he suggested.

'She wouldn't.'

'But you're not used to it either—and you coped.' Her beautiful brown eyes shot wide—she had not thought he had noticed. Not that he was offering a compliment of any kind.

'I'm not Josy,' she said quietly. 'I'm different.'

'I'll agree there—I've never seen such a pair of mismatched twins.'

'Don't dress it up—insult me!' she snapped—and actually saw his mouth twitch. A moment later and she knew from his stern expression that he was not in the slightest amused by her sharp tongue. And, oh, Lord, she realised, she was going to have to stop firing up like this! But his intimation that Josy was so likeable while she was quite the opposite had been hurtful—though why it should be hurtful when she couldn't stand him either was a mystery. She took a deep and steadying breath. Tact, she realised, was wasted here, so as calmly as she could, her voice taut from the control she was exercising, she stated distinctly, 'What I'm asking, Mr Tavenner, is that, if you feel you have to get in touch with my sister again, you bear in mind her painful shyness, and treat her with every kindness.'

Latham Tavenner surveyed her coolly, his grey eyes unhurriedly taking in her clear, creamy skin, her delicate features. His glance strayed to her mouth and lingered there, before going up to her eyes again. He drawled, insolently almost, 'I treat all women as they deserve.'

Belvia could hardly believe her ears. In the next split second, however, as what he was really saying hit home— that she deserved to be treated no better than he was treating her—she was instantly outraged! In that moment

she knew that she hated him more than she had hated
anybody in the whole of her life!

'Thanks!' she spat—and stood up. He was on his feet
too. She ignored him—and other interested diners—and,
with her head in the air, she sailed furiously out of the
dining-room.

CHAPTER THREE

BELVIA awoke on Tuesday morning, opened her eyes, and groaned. Oh, grief—too late now to regret her hasty temper. It was done.

She was in the middle of contemplating how, so far as she could remember, she had never had much of a temper, still less such a hasty one—so it had to be all *his* fault that he could provoke her to such anger—when her bedroom door opened and Josy came in with a cup of tea for her.

'It's late?' Belvia guessed.

'You were late in. Father's just gone to his office, but I couldn't wait any longer to hear if everything was all right last night. Did...?'

'You told Father I'd gone to keep the appointment?' Belvia asked, sitting up and playing for time as she tried to sort out in her head just how much she should tell her twin.

'I told him,' Josy confirmed. 'And save for grunting something cutting to the effect that at least one of his daughters was blessed with a sense of duty, he just had his dinner and went out.'

'Not to worry,' Belvia smiled. 'I don't think Latham Tavenner was too delighted that it was me in place of you last night, but his manners, in front of other people, were impeccable,' she stated honestly, deciding at that moment to keep quiet about her own abominable manners in walking out on Latham mid-way through

47

their soup course—she was feeling a tiny bit guilty that morning.

'He—didn't cut up too rough?'

'I explained you had a tummy upset, and he must have swallowed it,' she went on, wondering when she had become such an accomplished liar, 'because after the show he took me to his club for dinner.'

'Oh!' Josy exclaimed, and her feeling of relief was obvious in her face. 'Do you think he might transfer his attention on to you now?' she asked hopefully.

Belvia knew full well that there was not the smallest chance of that. 'You never know,' she smiled and, hoping to avoid further questioning, added, 'Thanks for the tea—I'd better get up.'

Belvia was barely out of bed when thoughts of Latham Tavenner pushed through her firm efforts to keep him out of her head. She had only been in his company twice but she found his good looks, his manliness unforgettable. She had been ill-mannered to get up and leave him the way she had—she could admit that this morning. But he had been very much out of order in her opinion, not even to pretend to believe her lies about Josy being ill, to tell her to shut up the way he had, to leave her sitting there in the theatre while he went and had a drink, and then insolently to tell her that he was treating her as he believed she deserved—and then expect her to sit there and eat with him!

She had a quick shower, realising she was angry again, and got dressed not caring a damn that she had walked out on him—she would do it again any time. She doubted, though, that she'd be so lucky a second time as to espy the chauffeur of the limousine in conversation with one of the club staff.

'You're ready to go home, Miss Fereday?' he had enquired courteously on seeing her alone and heading for the outside doors—by the sound of it he had been instructed to wait around to deliver her back to Surrey.

'Mr Tavenner will not need you again this evening,' she had been still angry enough to tell him, albeit with a smile. 'Shall we go?'

She was still not regretting any of her actions when she went down the stairs to join her sister. But as the day wore on she began to be visited, with a growing frequency, by thoughts about what her actions might have done to her father's chances of doing business with Latham Tavenner's company.

She took herself off to exercise Hetty and returned to her home just after three, to be passing the phone in the hall when it rang. She picked it up, and heard the cool, detached tones of the man who had been in her head for most of that day.

'You made it back to darkest Surrey, then?' he enquired arrogantly.

Since it had taken until now for him to pick up a phone to enquire, she doubted that her safe arrival home was on his list of priorities. But she swallowed the ire which just hearing him, arrogant and cool, produced.

He had not said who he was, and neither had he asked which twin she was. 'Thank you, yes.' She hauled her manners back into shape. 'How are things in darkest London?' she returned, well aware that he had not dialled her number merely to dally with her over the phone but realising that, for her father's sake, she had better make some effort.

Latham Tavenner, she was swiftly to realise, had no thought of doing the same, for, ignoring her question, he asked, 'Is Josy there?'

'What do you want her for?' she asked snappily, her protective claws unsheathed on the instant.

The taut silence at the other end spoke volumes, and that was before, his tone stiff with annoyance at her impudence, he spelt it out. 'I don't think that has anything to do with you.'

'It has *everything* to do with me!' Belvia countered. 'I told you last night how very shy she is!'

'Do you vet all her personal phone calls like this?' he barked.

'Why wouldn't I?' she erupted, that word 'personal' somehow catching her on the raw. Crazily, she did not like the thought of him getting 'personal' with her sister—and for one horrifying moment had the oddest sensation that that did not stem from any sense of protectiveness over Josy. Abruptly Belvia sent that peculiar notion on its way but, because of it, felt sufficiently weakened to be placatory once more as she lied, 'Josy's— er—still not well.'

'Oh, what a pity. She's so sweet and charming.' Belvia could almost hear him thinking 'unlike you'. 'I was hoping she might be up to coming out somewhere with me this evening.'

At that very moment Josy came quietly down the stairs and into the hall. 'I don't think she is but, if you'll hold on, I'll go and ask her.' With that she put her hand over the mouthpiece. 'Latham Tavenner,' she said in an undertone to her twin. 'He wants to know how you are today and if you'd like to go out somewhere.'

Josy was starting to look alarmed before she had half finished. 'No!' she exclaimed, vigorously shaking her head, distinctly starting to panic that he had not, as she had hoped, transferred his attentions to her sister.

'It's all right, don't worry,' Belvia assured her quickly, and, taking her hand from the mouthpiece, 'I'm sorry, Latham,' she told him, ploughing on even while she felt aghast at the natural way his name had just seemed to fall from her lips, 'but Josy feels she wouldn't be very good company just now.'

'Another time perhaps. I'll phone again,' he threatened as he ended his call.

Belvia put the phone down, knowing that she just could not tell Josy that last bit—she would be on thorns waiting for the phone to ring.

'What did he say?' she asked agitatedly.

Belvia smiled reassuringly. 'That he hopes you'll soon be better.'

Some lies, Belvia mused, as later that day she helped Josy with the evening meal, are essential. Already her sister seemed to have put the memory of that phone call behind her, and was even starting to look a shade less hunted. Was this the beginning of Josy starting to come to terms with Marc's death? She did hope so—the poor love had suffered enough.

Josy's sufferings were far from over, Belvia discovered when, with their father home early, the three of them sat down to dinner. For he was at pains to tell them how desperate matters were at Fereday Products and how, with his renewed entreaty to the banks for more capital falling on stony ground, it was now more essential than ever that Latham Tavenner looked on him favourably.

A squeak of an 'Oh!' escaped Josy's lips, and drew Edwin Fereday's attention.

'What was that "Oh" about?' he wanted to know.

'He—Latham Tavenner—he rang today,' Josy revealed shakily.

'Mmm—interesting,' her father replied, a speculative light appearing in his eyes which Belvia did not miss. 'What did he ring about?'

'I didn't speak...'

'I took the call,' Belvia took over.

'So what did he want?'

Her father was sounding tough, but that was when Belvia found that she had the ability to lie her head off without blushing, if it was to shield her sister. To lie to her father to shield herself, she could not. 'He wanted to speak to Josy—only I wouldn't let him,' she owned up—and brought his wrath down upon her head.

'You wouldn't *let* him?' he raged. 'Have you any idea what you're messing with here—the jobs that will go to the wall if I have to close down? How dare you offend the one person who can get us out of the hole we're in?'

'He wasn't offended!' she defended. 'Well, a little bit annoyed, perhaps,' she had to concede. 'But——'

'But nothing. It doesn't matter a damn to you, does it, that I might go out of business? That——'

'Of course it matters.'

'It sounds like it. Just because you have money of your own, everyone else can——'

'You can have my money if you want it,' Belvia cut in rashly before she could think.

'And mine,' Josy rushed in.

Their offer stopped him dead in his tracks. But, inside a very few seconds, he was off again. 'It's too late for that now. I need more than the pair of you have put together. I could have had it too, if only you'd been more pleasant to Latham Tavenner. It's just too bad of you, Belvia.'

Belvia did not like his laying all the blame at her door, though she started to realise that there was no one else whom he could, or perhaps should, blame, 'I'm sorry,' she apologised—and brought more of his spleenishness down about her.

'Sorry's an empty word unless you intend to right the wrong,' he told her heavily.

'Right the wrong?' she queried. 'How can I do that? Latham Tavenner wants to date Josy, not me!' She glanced at her twin, saw she was starting to look anxious again, and turned back to her father. 'I don't think Josy should have anything to do with him if she doesn't w——'

'You're the one who messed things up! It wouldn't hurt you to keep him sweet by ringing him and inviting him to dinner tomorrow.'

Like blazes she would! Belvia had already mentally rejected his suggestion out of hand—and then she saw her father watching her as if to say, See how empty your 'sorry' is when put to the test. She remembered too how he had spoken of jobs going to the wall, his staff losing their jobs, their livelihoods, and if all she had to do to get him the investment he needed—for himself and his workers—was to invite Latham Tavenner to dinner tomorrow evening, then was it such a high price to pay?

'He won't come for me.' Some stray strand of fear still held her back—though she was uncertain just then whether that fear was for Josy or for herself.

'Then tell him it's your sister's wish that he join us for dinner.' Her father at once knocked that argument away.

'I've already told him Josy isn't well. She won't be well enough by tomorrow to cook him dinner,' Belvia still prevaricated, and received one of her father's bad-tempered looks for her trouble.

'Well, for goodness' sake invite him for some time this week!' he bawled.

Belvia refused to be cowed. 'I don't know his home phone number.'

'I'll give it to you,' he replied, and took out his pen and a piece of paper from his diary, wrote the number down—then in angry silence finished his meal, and went out for the evening.

It was time, Belvia well knew, for her again to put her money where her mouth was. 'Is it all right with you if I ring Latham Tavenner?' she asked Josy.

'I don't see that you've got very much choice,' Josy replied bravely, and Belvia wondered if she would be putting too much pressure on her just now if she suggested that she would like her to think very seriously about the two of them leaving home in the near future.

On the grounds that their father seemed to need their full support at present, she decided to say nothing for the moment. But she got up and helped Josy clear the table, growing more and more aware that, while support him she would, once this crisis at Fereday Products was resolved, she was going to take Josy from under his roof and find somewhere else to live.

'Do you think you should ring him now?' Josy asked anxiously, once everything had been tidied up.

Had it been up to her she would never ring him, so why, when it was not for herself, did her insides feel like so much jelly as she dialled his number and waited, and waited? 'He's not in,' she reported to her sister, while trying to hide the mixed emotions she felt about that.

Suddenly though, just as she was about to put down the phone, an unmistakably all-male voice said, 'Hello,' in her ear—and her insides went all of a tremble.

'Oh, hello,' she answered, relieved to find that her voice sounded remarkably light. 'I was beginning to think you weren't in.'

'What can I do for you?' he asked, apparently recognising her voice at once, for he did not ask her who it was.

'I—um . . .' God, she felt all of a lather. 'I wondered if you'd like to come to dinner on Saturday.' She pulled herself sharply together and got the invitation out—and had to wait an agonising number of embarrassed seconds while he chewed her invitation over.

'Let me get this straight,' he queried, as if he was not quite comprehending what she had said, when she knew full well he had been at the forefront of the queue when intelligence had been given out, 'you're asking me to dine with you this coming Saturday?'

Say no, she silently begged, say you've got a previous engagement. 'My family would like you to dine with us— I'm their spokeswoman,' she replied, hoping he'd use some of that vast supply of intelligence she had credited him with to realise that for herself she'd starve rather than sit at the same table with him ever again.

'Josy—if she's better—she'll be there?'

Most peculiarly, Belvia found his question had reached her sense of humour. 'Er—if she's better,' she agreed.

'And—what about you?'

'Me?'

'I understood you were having an affair with a married man?'

There was suddenly such a toughness in his tone that Belvia at that moment knew that anyone who ever crossed this man would live to regret it. But she banished such thoughts. She had not crossed him—well, not to any great degree, anyhow—and, to get back to his statement, she guessed she only had herself to blame that he thought she was having an affair. Had she not said in front of him last Friday—flippantly into the bargain— that after dinner was the only time her date could get away from his wife?

She could, Belvia supposed, have owned up that she was not involved with any married man. But Latham Tavenner seemed to bring out the worst in her—and instead she found herself stating, 'I cancelled my date for Saturday when my father said it would be more agreeable for you if we were four at dinner.'

'You shouldn't have cancelled your date on my account,' he retorted sharply. 'You must have enough restrictions on the time available to meet your lover behind his wife's back.'

'That's true!' she retaliated, then caught sight of Josy, looking at her as if to say she was not going about getting him to accept her invitation in a very polite tone. But by then Belvia was well and truly upset by one Latham Tavenner, and demanded, 'Are you coming or not?'

'Get your sister to give me a ring!' he snarled—Belvia had an idea that they both slammed down the phone at the same time.

For two seconds more she fumed about the ghastly rattlesnake of a man—and then became aware of Josy watching her, all large-eyed and fearing the worst. Belvia forgot her anger with the financier to tell her, 'I—blew it!'

'Oh, heavens—Father will be livid! What did Mr Tavenner say?'

How to tell her? There was no way, Belvia realised, in which she could dress it up. 'He—wants you to phone him,' she said in a rush. And, as Josy lost some of the little colour she had, 'But you don't have to,' she told her firmly.

Josy stared at her and, Belvia realised, was patently remembering their father's attitude, his anger over dinner, and, 'Yes, I do,' she answered quietly.

'Well, not tonight you don't,' Belvia stated quickly, even as she said it wondering if she was right to get her sister to put off making a phone call that to anyone else might be a simple phone call, but which just thinking about would give her sister nightmares. 'Although it might be better out of the way.'

'I'll sleep on it,' Josy replied, clearly shrinking from having anything to do with the self-assured man.

Belvia was hating Latham Tavenner with a vengeance as she lay sleepless in her bed that night. When, however, fairness tried to nudge its honest way in—it was hardly his fault because, but for the Feredays needing to keep him sweet because they were after his money, they need have nothing to do with him—Belvia ousted such unwanted honesty. He *was* at fault. Of course, he had no idea of the dreadful tragedy that had befallen Josy when her husband had been killed, but that did not make it any better. He must have seen for himself how withdrawn Josy was before Belvia had told him of her sister's extreme shyness. Yet now he was waiting for Josy to telephone him—he wanted hanging up by his ears!

At that moment visions of Latham Tavenner's quite nice ears sprang into Belvia's mind out of nowhere—as, too, did a remembered image of his good-looking, if arrogant, face. Good grief, she fumed, and buried her head under the bedclothes—as if to escape him.

But there was no escape from him the next day. It started at breakfast. 'Did you ring Latham Tavenner last night?' her father asked, when she had barely sat down at the breakfast-table.

'I did.'

'And?'

Belvia avoided looking at her sister. 'Nothing's been settled yet.' Her father was waiting for more. 'But it will be before dinner-time on Saturday.'

'See that it is,' he grunted, then finished his breakfast in stony silence, and left for his office.

'You might like to give thought to you and me moving out from this house—once Father's got his loan,' Belvia blurted out to Josy, this time too upset by her father's manner to hold her thoughts back.

'I couldn't do that!' Josy gasped.

'You know, you could, love,' Belvia argued gently. 'We could find a small flat somewhere, and——'

'But what about Father—who'd look after him?'

'He's big enough to look after himself, and, if he isn't, he can jolly well pay a housekeeper.'

'I—couldn't, Bel—not now...'

'Well, don't fret about it. It was just an idea.' Belvia smiled—and hoped that, now the idea had been planted, perhaps as the days and weeks went on her sister might grow to the idea.

It was early afternoon when Belvia went up to the stables to exercise Hetty. She had said not a word to Josy about the fact that there was a phone call to one Latham Tavenner outstanding, but toyed seriously with the notion of dialling his number and saying that her sister had been called away for a few days and had asked her to ring. She would say that Josy would be back by Saturday, she decided, warming to the idea, and then again ask him to dinner.

She had it all worked out by the time she had returned home, and went looking for Josy. She found her in the sitting-room—and one look at her face was enough to tell her that something was wrong.

'What's happened?' she asked, going quickly over to her.

'I rang him.'

Belvia did not need two guesses. 'At his work?' she enquired, realising that it must have taken a great deal of courage for Josy to do that.

'I thought I was leaving much too much to you, so I...'

'Oh, love,' Belvia murmured.

'Anyhow, to be honest, it was with the bright idea in my head that if I rang Latham Tavenner at his office, he wouldn't have time to take my call and I could leave a message to say I'd rung, and...'

'And you'd be absolved from ringing him again?' Belvia took up.

'Only it wasn't such a bright idea as I thought it was, because after his PA had taken my name he came on the line—and I nearly died.'

'Never mind—you did it, and it's all over now,' Belvia comforted. Somehow, though, she saw no relief in Josy's expression that, her call made, she could forget about him until Saturday. 'Was he very much of a brute to you?' she asked, sorely wanting to set about him.

'No, not really. In fact, I suppose you could say that, given he was firm, his tone was quite kind.'

Kind! She would never associate him with 'kind'! 'Er—what was he firm about?' Belvia asked, a little puzzled. 'You mean he gave you a firm yes about coming to dinner on Saturday?'

Josy shook her lovely head. 'He was firm about not coming here to dinner,' she replied, her voice starting to break, 'but he suggested, since I'd cooked dinner for him the last time, that I must go to his place for dinner this time.'

'You're not going!' In a flash Belvia was up in arms, whether her sister thought she was going or not, making that decision for her. 'No way are you going!' she added forcefully.

'But, Bel, I've got to. You heard Father...'

'You've got to do nothing of the sort!' Belvia would not hear of it, and as she began to cope with the initial shock of Latham Tavenner's invitation to her sister continued, 'Was the invitation for you alone? Not you and Father?' she queried, not needing to enquire if she was excluded—that was a foreknown fact.

'Just me. He made that plain. I shall have to go!' Josy cried in panic. 'If I don't, Father will have to close down, and all those people will be put out of work, and——'

'And leave it with me. I'll think of something,' Belvia promised—and had until Saturday to come up with something brilliant.

*　*　*

By Saturday their father had been acquainted with the fact that Josy had been invited to dine with Latham Tavenner in his London flat. Edwin Fereday seemed much pleased by this news—so much so that, for the moment, and in the interests of a pleasant home-life, Belvia thought it better not to disillusion him. Latham Tavenner had suggested he would send a car for Josy, but she had said she would drive herself. But, Belvia fumed, over her dead body would Josy be dining with him alone in his flat or with him anywhere else.

Though how to get her out of it? Belvia thought up plenty of ideas, but none which could not be overcome. Josy's car could break down—Latham would send a car for her. Belvia thought perhaps she could ring him and say that it really was not on for him to expect Josy when she had told him herself of her extreme shyness—to which of course he might answer, 'Fine,' which would mean that not only would they never see or hear from him again but—immediately losing his 'in' with him—neither would their father.

'I shall have to go,' Josy said worriedly after lunch on Saturday.

Belvia did not need to ask, Go where? 'Where' was to the forefront of both their minds. 'I've told you you're not going,' she reiterated, and remembering that, although Josy was terrified of him, she had thought him kind, Belvia realised her only hope lay in hoping Josy had got that bit right—she would appeal to his kindness. 'I've decided to give him a ring and to ask if he'll see me. Then I'll explain that because—because you've recently suffered a great sadness in your——'

'You won't tell him about Marc!' Josy exclaimed, tears rushing to her eyes.

'Oh, love, would you mind so much?' In an instant Belvia was by her side, an arm about her shoulders.

'He'd tell Father—I couldn't take him ridiculing...'

'Shh, it's all right, don't worry.' Belvia calmed her. To her mind it had seemed a good, if not the only, option. If Latham had half the honour he was said to possess, then surely he would be appalled to know that he was not just trying to get on better terms with a very attractive woman, but was in fact causing more distress to an already distressed and grieving widow. 'I'll ring him anyway and ask if he'd mind seeing me,' Belvia determined.

'With what in mind?'

Belvia tried to bring all the confidence which she was far from feeling into her smile. And, having already told Latham Tavenner of her sister's shyness, she stated, 'I'll impress on him how shy you are, how—um—difficult you find it to make new friends.'

'D you think that will be enough?'

'We can give it a try,' Belvia replied brightly. 'Somehow I'll get him to leave you alone.' She went at once to the phone and dialled—and found he was not in.

From then she rang his number every half-hour, but there was still no reply. Damn him, she started to fume. As someone expecting a dinner guest that evening, he should at this very moment be slaving away over a hot stove!

Suddenly the minute hand on the clock seemed fairly to race round. Belvia tried Latham Tavenner's number once more and knew, when there was again no reply, that she had only one option left. She, as she had done before, was going to have to turn up, unwanted and unasked, in her sister's place. She went upstairs to bath and change.

'I feel dreadful letting you do this for me,' Josy fretted when, with Belvia already running late, she went out to the car with her.

'Just keep out of Father's way if he comes home early—which I doubt. He'll never know which one of us went.' Belvia smiled, and started up her car—her insides filled with dread. She did not need a barrow-load of premonition to know that there would be no welcome awaiting her.

With her thoughts varied—frequently panicky, less frequently calm—she somehow made it without mishap to the impressive building where Latham Tavenner had his apartment. And, having parked her car, she entered the well-lighted building to find her way blocked by a uniformed commissionaire.

'I've an engagement with Mr Tavenner,' she smiled prettily to tell him.

He had seen it all before, and smiled back. 'May I have your name, madam?'

'Fereday. B... Miss Fereday.'

Her insides were behaving no better than they had been before when she sailed up in the lift and got out where she had been directed. Oh, how she wished that this were all over and that she was on her way back home!

She found his door, rang the bell, and waited to be annihilated.

She was not far wrong. The door opened and he stood there, tall, sophisticated, casually clad—and disbelieving. Indeed, so disbelieving was he that while her voice died in her throat he took a step past her into the hall, as if to check for himself that, incredibly, it looked as if she had again come in her sister's stead.

'Where's Josy?' he demanded, clearly unimpressed as his eyes took in her shoulder-length shining blonde hair and her slender shape in a simple, classic, light wool dress of deepest lavender.

'She—er...' Her voice faded.

'I don't believe this!' he snarled, and to her consternation seemed about to close the door on her.

'I can explain!' Belvia burst out quickly.

He halted. 'I was expecting your sister an hour ago!' he rapped pointedly.

'She did try to ring!' Belvia lied desperately. 'Only you weren't in.' Not a smile, not a glimmer of any softening. 'I lost my way,' she added to her lie total. 'I'm sorry I'm late,' she offered appeasingly.

'I wasn't expecting *you*!' he emphasised.

And Josy had imagined he was kind! Belvia started to get cross, even while she knew that she could not afford the luxury. Then she remembered how this brute of a man had said that he treated a woman as she deserved to be treated. 'Can I come in?' she asked bluntly. Unmistakably, this swine had seen that Josy deserved a kind tone. Belvia knew for sure that she would never get that luxury.

'I'm going to eat!' he informed her curtly.

'I haven't had my dinner either,' she dared, and guessed she was about to be flattened for her sauce. But, miraculously, she saw his lips twitch in the way that they had that time she had mistakenly thought she had amused him. He was not amused this time either, though, she saw, when his mouth suddenly looked not at all like smiling. 'I wanted to explain—about Josy,' she added in a rush, when it still looked as if he might close the door on her—this thing had to be settled *now*.

'Is it going to take long?'

It could do; she had not a clue what she could tell him without bringing Marc into it. 'I'll be as brief as I can,' she promised—and did not know if she was relieved or otherwise when he relented and stood back from the door to allow her into his apartment.

'You'd better share my meal,' he grunted unenthusiastically.

As long as you don't put arsenic on my share, she thought sweetly, and entered a thickly carpeted sitting-room that was roomy enough to house half a dozen settees, but in actual fact housed only two, plus a few well-padded chairs and low antique tables.

'We'll go straight through to the dining-room,' her hungry, unwilling host stated, leading the way.

'Er, could I wash my hands first?' she enquired, as she desperately sought for time to find a way to tell him, tactfully, to leave her sister alone.

Latham threw her a look which she read as one of regret that he had agreed to let her in. 'Second on the right, through there,' he grunted, and left her to it.

Her mind was much the same blank as it had been when, ten minutes later, she joined him in the dining-room. There were two places laid at the highly polished table, and he was standing by one of them.

She gave him full marks that, despite his annoyance to find he was again feeding her, he waited until she was seated before taking his own seat. She picked up her knife and cut into a portion of pâté which obviously came from a high-class delicatessen.

'Mmm, this is good,' she murmured, all wide brown eyes. 'Did you make it yourself?'

Again she saw that minuscule movement of his fabulous mouth. But, as before, any suggestion of a smile didn't make it. 'You know bloody well I didn't,' he growled.

'Oh,' she mumbled, and knew that she had better watch her step. Another comment like that and he would be slinging her out before she'd had a chance to get through to him about Josy. Josy—think about Josy. Josy was why she was here. Belvia drew herself up short—how on earth had it come about that she could so far forget about Josy as to think that this man who terrified the poor love had a fabulous mouth! 'Mr Tavenner,' she said in a rush—and became aware on that instant that, surprisingly for such a hungry man, he had not been eating, but had been studying her for quite a few seconds. That realisation made her forget whatever it was she had been about to say.

Nor did she have any chance of remembering either when, quite out of the blue, he remarked, 'You're so beautiful.' She stared at him, barely believing her ears. Nor could she believe—his statement on her beauty had been so matter-of-fact—that he should follow it up with a churlish, 'Why the hell, with all you've got going for you, do you have to snare yourself up with a married man?'

Belvia supposed it must have been because she was still stunned that he had paid her a compliment, no matter how matter-of-factly put, that she did not at once deny that she had any liaison with a married man. In fact, she was sure she must have stared at him in shock for a full five seconds before the last of what he said made sense in her brain. 'Mr Tavenner,' she began.

But his churlishness had given way to mockery. 'Mr Tavenner—twice?' he drawled, as if to remind her that she had called him Latham when he had phoned on Tuesday afternoon.

'Are you suggesting I use your first name?'

'I'm suggesting you eat your pâté. There's a casserole in the oven drying up.'

Belvia was glad of the respite from having to launch into her 'hands off my sister' campaign. For good manners decreed she could not speak with her mouth full.

The casserole was not dried up, and tasted delicious. 'This never came out of any delicatessen,' she murmured appreciatively. 'Nor,' she added, knowing it for certain, 'did you make it.'

'There are other things I'm better at,' he admitted, which left her wondering if one of his lady-friends had served time in his kitchen. That thought disturbed her. She most definitely did not like that thought—though she could not think of one possible reason why she did not. Nor why she should feel immediately better when Latham added, 'My daily is also a genius in the kitchen.' So his cleaning-lady had made it for him. 'Wine?' he enquired.

'I'm driving,' she refused, wanting to keep a clear head, and smiled, then saw his glance on her smiling, upturned mouth.

His mouth, however, when she was somehow irresistibly drawn to stare at it, had never been more unsmiling. In fact, when she raised her eyes and met the granite grey of his arctic look, she knew that his mood

had changed yet again. She was not, therefore, totally
unprepared for his hostility when he snarled, 'So keen
to stay within the drink-drive laws that you abstain totally
when driving! What a pity you don't hold the laws of
marriage in such high regard.'

'What on earth are you talking about?' she gasped.

'Spare me!' he thundered, his expression taut and
menacing as he leaned towards her, his jaw jutting at an
aggressive angle. 'You've already admitted to having an
adulterous relationship.'

'No, I...' she began. 'Well, I...'

'Strange, I thought you could lie all the time!' he
grated, manifestly not taken by her amending her 'no'
to a prevarication.

'So I've lied—a little,' she had to admit.

'At every chance you've had, I'd say...'

'Listen, you!' she snapped, suddenly enraged. She did
not have to sit here and take this. Her meal was forgotten in her fury, everything forgotten as, eyes flashing,
she shot to her feet, slamming her napkin down. 'If I've
lied to you, it's been for good——'

'If? Ye gods!' he scorned.

'For good reason! And about having an affair
with——'

He was on his feet too, and, just as she was wishing
he was nearer so that she could ease her itching palm by
belting him one, he had moved, and in a couple of strides
he was standing directly in front of her.

But her urge to set about him physically was denied
her when, his fury suddenly matching hers, he caught
hold of her by her upper arms—making her powerless
to get a swing in at him—and roared, 'Don't lie to me
about that!'

'What?'

'About sleeping around—careless of whether he's got a married label att——'

'How dare you?' she erupted. 'I don't sleep around. I——'

'You'll be telling me next you're a virgin!'

'And you wouldn't believe that either!'

'You're damned right I wouldn't believe it.'

'Then to hell with you!' she exploded, and turned to leave—and found that he still had hold of her, refusing to let her go. The result of her fast, halted action caused her to stumble against him. 'Get away from me!' she shrieked, outraged, and gave him a push which, violent as it was, moved him not an inch.

She glared up into the blaze of fury in his fierce grey eyes, and her heart almost stopped at the intent she saw there. 'My God, when did you get to be so fussy?' he sneered cuttingly, and in the next split second the hands that had been on her arms were like iron bands about her, pinning her arms to her sides, and the split second after that, for all she tried to jerk her head out of the way, his mouth had found hers in a savage, angry kiss.

'*No!*' she screamed, the moment he took his mouth from hers. It was as much time as she had before he claimed her mouth again.

With what freedom of movement she did have she pushed frantically to try and break free, but he would not let her go. In fact, all she succeeded in doing was to make him hold her more firmly to him. She could feel his body, his warmth, and his strength. It scared her, made her own strength seem puny.

That fear made her fight the harder. She tried desperately to kick at his shins, but did not connect. She

twisted and turned her body in an attempt to be free—
and found that by wriggling up against him she had
earned herself more savage kisses.

'Keep that up, sweetheart, and we might have a lot of
fun.'

'Stuff your promises!' she returned spiritedly, and
gasped as, this time, instead of his mouth coming over
hers again, he opted to trail kisses down the side of her
throat.

She swallowed convulsively, realising that, while she
was still in a dangerous situation, she somehow no longer
felt so threatened as she had! Although still panicking,
she was in charge of that panic. Sufficiently at any rate
for her to realise that if her violent movements against
him to be free seemed to be inciting him to passion then
she must have the nerve to stay passive.

She had nothing to lose, she felt—when another unsuccessful attempt to be free only gave him the chance
to pull her to him—and everything to gain. She might,
by staying passive in his arms, get him to let go his steely
hold on her a little. Enough, anyhow, for her to find a
chance to scrape her foot down his shin—that should
make him hop a bit, and so would she—right out of
there.

On that instant, before she could think of it further,
Belvia stopped struggling. To her surprise, it worked!
For instantly Latham leaned back from her and, while
still holding her in the circle of his arms, stared down
into her face. And then he smiled, a smile which she
afterwards realised she should not have believed in. But
it was the first smile he had shown her personally, and
she was so shaken by it that, while still in the grip of
surprise that he was no longer forcing himself on her,

she forgot entirely her intention to scrape a few layers of skin off his shin.

And then it was too late. Because, as his hold on her all at once gentled, suddenly his head was coming down and, tenderly this time, Latham laid his mouth over hers in an all-giving kiss, and Belvia was lost. Never had she known such a beautiful kiss. Never had she known a kiss could be so beautiful.

'Latham!' she whispered when he broke that kiss, her world upside-down. She stared up at him and he stared back down into her receptive wide brown eyes.

She had no idea what signals she was giving off, but with her heart beating as it had never beaten before, she had not the smallest objection to make when his head came down and, gently, he claimed her mouth again. She moved her arms and found them free, and was glad, because she was then able to put them around him.

And it was bliss, pure bliss. He held her firmly, but without force. With expert fingers he slid the zip at the back of her neck down a little way, and she was entirely unaware that he had done so until she felt his warm, mobile, fabulous mouth kissing the nakedness of her shoulders.

She clutched on to him. She was not very sure about this. His mouth returned to claim hers, and she felt she had nothing to worry about. While his wonderful mouth still held hers, though, she felt his fingers caressing inside her unzipped dress at the back. And again she gripped on to him when warm, sensitive fingers caressed her shoulder, sliding her bra-strap to one side.

Then all at once emotions she had never dreamed of were licking into life inside her. She was conscious, vaguely, that as they kissed they moved. She had thought—while acknowledging that she was not thinking very clearly—that they had moved only a yard or so. But, when she opened her eyes from yet another gentle onslaught to her senses, she found that they were standing at an open bedroom door.

Her heart was thundering against her ribs. This was not right; she knew it was not right. Yet Latham had so awakened her senses that what was right and what was wrong were hazy. All she knew was that she did not want it to stop.

Yet somewhere, something was holding her back, 'Th-this is as far as I go,' she managed chokily, and felt she did not hate him after all, but really liked him when he smiled a wonderful smile.

'That decision is all yours, beautiful Belvia,' he murmured. 'Though—perhaps—one last kiss?'

What a wonderful suggestion—she would have felt bereft without another, just one last kiss. She smiled willingly, and he read her answer in that willing smile. And what a kiss it was! Belvia had thought she had learned a lot that night about the different quality there could be in a kiss. But as Latham's head came down once more and he pulled her slender body close up to him again yet another dimension was added, and as passion between them soared higher she went with him without protest through that open bedroom door.

'Do you want me?' he asked, teasing her lips apart with his.

'Oh, yes,' she breathed, aching for him—and abruptly hit terra firma with the cruellest of jolts.

For one minute she was in his arms—willing, eager to be taught everything he could teach her—and the next she was standing alone. Totally alone and isolated, for all that Latham was not a yard away from her. Feeling utterly bewildered, she stared at him, doing her best to comprehend that there was a look about him that seemed to say that he had not the smallest interest whatsoever in making her his.

'What...?' she gasped. 'I...' But, taking in his look of sheer mockery, she seemed totally unable to string two words together.

'What an actress!' he drawled, not a glimmer about him of a man wanting desperately to make love. Indeed, his look toughened, his tone became grating as he went on to gibe, 'And you say you don't sleep around?'

Her mouth fell open in utter shock. But she was not thinking or feeling as shock gave way to rage. A rage of rejection consumed her. A rage that came from being made to look a fool, being gibed at, stormed in and took total charge of her. He had been leading her on! He had been leading her on so that he could gibe, sneer, and throw back at her, 'And you say you don't sleep around!'

Never had Belvia been so almighty furious as when, taking a fierce step closer so as to be certain not to miss, she yelled, 'Not around here, sweetheart!' and hurled a blow across his face which almost sprained her wrist.

There was still a red mist in front of her eyes when she turned and went smartly out of there, with only the satisfactory, painful stinging in her right hand to tell her that indeed she had not missed, but had found her target—dead on.

CHAPTER FOUR

BELVIA woke early on Sunday morning after a fractured night's sleep. Oh, Lord, it seemed worse with the coming of daylight rather than better, as she had hoped.

Had that really been her last night? The wanton, the pugilist? She winced in her bed, still stunned by her behaviour, and never wanted to get up. Oh, grief, what was happening to her? Before she had met Latham Tavenner she had been an even-tempered and, for the most part, logical-thinking female. Yet, since knowing him, everything she knew about herself, or thought she knew about herself, had been turned upside-down!

She would have liked to think that it was all his fault. That had he not kissed her so expertly, touched her skin so tenderly, she would not have responded as she had. But she had been kissed pretty near expertly before— and had never come close to losing her head.

She heard Josy moving about in the room next door and, feeling impatient with herself, she jumped out of bed and headed for the shower. Josy, she knew, would be anxious to know how she had got on. Indeed, she had been waiting up for her last night, but her father had followed her in, and Josy had made herself scarce before he had a chance to see her.

Belvia owned that she had been glad of the respite, though she had no more idea now than she had had then of what she was going to tell her. The whole point of her going to see Latham had been to find some way of

making him see he should leave his pursuit of her sister—
yet not a word to him had she said in that direction.

Belvia came from the bathroom knowing that there
was no way she was going to tell her sister any of what
had taken place last night. How, when her intention at
the outset had been to keep him sweet, she had landed
him one and stormed out of his flat—doing up her dress
as she descended in the lift.

Her cheeks grew hot as thoughts that had racked her
through the night assaulted her again now. Would she,
after years of instinctively knowing that she would give
herself only when love was there, have given herself to
Latham Tavenner—this man she hated? That he had
called a halt before it had got that far was academic; it
was herself, her own reactions, which were crucifying
her.

Though what about him? Josy was the one he was
after, not her. Belvia admitted that her physical and
sexual knowledge of the opposite sex was limited but,
even so, she was not so green that she could not tell
when a man wanted her, even if he did have such control
over his sexual urges that he could suppress his wanting—
and reject her.

Was she greener than she had thought, anyhow? Had
he not wanted her after all, but been more intent on
proving that her 'I don't sleep around' claim was the rot
he believed it was? Swine. She started to grow angry
again. She was glad she had belted him. Then she remembered her father, and how he was desperate to do
business with Latham, and she gave a groan of despair.
Then she heard a light tap on her door, and Josy
came in.

'Hello, Jo,' Belvia greeted her brightly. 'You're up early.'

'So are you,' Josy commented, and, as Belvia knew she would, 'How did it go?' she asked worriedly.

And that was where Belvia knew that, even if she had to lie her head off, she was going to make sure that Josy had one day in which she was not going to be plagued with anxiety. 'Fine,' she smiled.

'You were able to convince him that he's wasting his time with me?' Josy pressed, and Belvia knew that her twin would not just be unable to cope but would be terrified if ever Latham took her in his arms as he had her last night.

'As you noticed, he has a very kind streak in him.' Like hell he did! 'He gave me dinner, and was very understanding—about you being shy, I mean. He asked me to give you his best wishes.' Belvia thought that should do it—any more and it might be over the top.

'And—he won't be phoning here any more?'

If she prevaricated, Josy would worry. 'No,' she replied positively, and determined to stand guard by the phone all week.

Fortunately their father seemed to have other matters on his mind and forgot to ask how Josy had got on with the financier at dinner the previous evening. Belvia later heard him on the phone arranging to spend the day with a lady-friend, and Sunday passed without anything happening to ruffle the calmer waters Belvia thought her sister was sailing in.

For the rest of the week that followed Belvia managed to make all the right responses whenever her father mentioned Latham Tavenner, which, as chance had it, seemed to be only when Josy was not around. For that week too, Belvia stayed close to the phone whenever she could. Because Josy might wonder why she was not exercising Hetty, if she followed through her fleeting idea to pay the stables to exercise her, Belvia went each afternoon to attend the horse. Each time she dashed home, though, it was to see that, given that everything was wrong with Josy's world, she was starting to look more and more relaxed as the week went by.

When Sunday rolled around again and not a word had Josy heard from Latham Tavenner, Belvia began to wonder if he had given up his pursuit of her sister.

Evidence, however, that he had by no means given up that pursuit came only a few hours later. Their father had not come home the previous night, and she and Josy were having a cup of coffee in the sitting-room when the phone rang. How she could have allowed herself to become so complacent Belvia could not explain. Though perhaps it was because she had been so keyed up all week, expecting Latham to ring, that, when he had not, she had started to believe that he would not—not now. Which was why, Josy being the nearer to the phone, she let her answer it.

'Hello?' said Josy, and went ashen.

In a flash, instinct screaming at her who was on the phone, Belvia was out of her chair and grabbing the phone out of her sister's hand. 'Hello!' she gasped.

Silence. Then, 'I was talking to Josy!' Latham Tavenner stated harshly. Oh, grief, he hadn't forgiven her for attempting to break his jaw, then—not that she had expected him to.

'I'm sorry,' she murmured politely, unsure if she was being polite for his sake, for Josy's sake—whom she would have believe she had nothing to worry about—or

for her father's sake, not to mention his employees'.
'Josy had to dash off. She's got something burning in
the oven.' She saw a look of relief wash over Josy's face,
and smiled encouragingly and nodded when she saw her
sister stack the coffee-tray and indicate that she was going
to take their used coffee-cups to the kitchen.

'We can't have your Sunday roast cindered,' Latham
offered sarcastically, and Belvia knew that he hadn't believed her excuse for a minute.

She waited to answer until Josy had closed the sitting-
room door behind her. This was dreadful! She had
thought... 'What did you want Josy for?' she asked
abruptly.

'Please,' he suggested, reminding her of her manners.

My God, he was doing it again, making her want to
thump him! Never had she met a man who could so
effortlessly upset her equilibrium. She swallowed hard,
and rephrased her question. 'What can we do for you?'
she enquired, trying to make her voice as pleasant as
possible.

'We?'

Her right hand itched. 'Me, then,' she pushed out from
between clenched teeth.

'You don't consider you've done—enough?'

Oh, my... She struggled to stay calm. 'I consider that,
when I b—— hit you on Saturday, you had it coming.
Which,' she tacked on swiftly, 'if you're half as
honourable as they say you are, you'll admit is——'

'Don't you dare talk to me about honour!' he clipped.

Oh, hell, he was off again about that affair she had
made out she was having with a married man. Now did
not seem to be the time to renew her denial. 'So we're
both in the wrong.' She swallowed down impetuous

words to get him to think better of her—grief, as if she cared! 'Um, Latham.' Damn, now why had his name just slipped out? Crazy. 'The thing is, it looks as if Josy's having a few problems in the kitchen—she really did go to the kitchen—er—can I take a message for you?'

Silence. Frantically, if belatedly, Belvia tried desperately for something to say that would retrieve a situation that looked to be rushing headlong into 'Who needs the Feredays anyway?' That might be marvellous for Josy, but would be ruinous for her father.

'It was your sister I wanted to speak to,' he stated at last. 'I hear she's pretty good about horse-flesh—I'd value her opinion on a horse I'm thinking of buying.'

And if I believe that I'll believe anything, Belvia fumed, knowing full well that if he wanted an opinion on horse-flesh he would go directly to the top expert. But she was feeling sick inside that all too clearly Latham's pursuit of Josy had never let up. Most probably he had been out of town on business this week—and this was his first chance... She took a shaky breath as she suddenly realised that she was going to have to do what she should have done a week ago, what she had gone to his flat to do, in fact—appeal to his better nature, if he had one.

'Look, Latham,' she began, her tone conciliatory.

'Oh, you're still there!'

Sarcastic swine. Did he think she had rushed off to drag Josy back to the phone? 'The thing is...' She hesitated, no more ready now with what she wanted to say than she had been before.

'Yes?' he prompted.

'Well...' She took a deep breath. 'Can I see you?' she plunged.

A dreadful silence followed her blunt request, during which she felt quite mortified. For herself, she would never ask. For Josy, she had to ask—even if it meant she had put herself on the receiving end of a ton of sarcasm for her trouble.

'You—want a return match?' he asked finally, and Belvia knew he was referring to the way she had put all her slender weight behind the blow she had struck him.

'No,' she replied quietly, so that he would know that it was not her usual habit to resort to physical violence— though, come to think of it, no one of her acquaintance earned it the way he did.

'You're saying—that you want a date?' he asked incredulously, deliberately misunderstanding her, she was sure. 'You're asking me to go out with you?'

'No, I'm *not*!' She blew it in no uncertain fashion, her aggressiveness out in the open. Who in creation did he think he was? she seethed, not mistaking that tone in his voice which clearly showed he was not one bit enamoured of the idea of a date with her. But she bit down her ire. 'I need to talk to you—to explain about...'

'Josy,' he finished for her. 'You didn't make a very good job of it last time,' he did not hesitate to remind her.

Rodent! she smouldered, wanting only to forget the whole of that 'last time'. Only, clearly, he was not going to let her. 'Please,' she swallowed her pride to utter— and again had to wait while he thought the matter over.

'I could give you lunch, I suppose,' he thought out loud. Today? What the dickens would she wear? 'But I don't see why I should.' Pig, she fumed, hating him afresh and starting to believe he was playing some cat-and-mouse game with her for his own amusement. There was nothing in any way remotely amused in his tone, however, when after a moment more of consideration he told her decisively, 'You know where I live—come here tonight.'

Belvia stared in disbelief at the dead phone in her hand. The misbegotten brute—he'd put the phone down on her!

A minute later and she was still finding fresh names for him. It had always been her prerogative to say yea or nay, but he, the monster, had just taken that prerogative away from her and, because of Josy, she could do nothing about it.

Thinking of her sister reminded her that Josy would be nervously waiting to hear what that phone call had been all about. And that was when Belvia accepted that, for quite some while now, because of Josy, because of their father, her yea or nay where Latham Tavenner was concerned had been immaterial. He stated, made his wishes known, and she had to comply.

Belvia tilted her chin at a defiant angle. So be it. She went in search of Josy facing that, because she had no choice; she would have to put up with being bossed around by Mr Come-here-tonight, End-of-conversation. She would go because she had to, because she would do anything she had to to end this particular torment for Josy—but, oh, how she wished she need never have anything more to do with him.

'What did he want?' Josy wanted to know the moment she saw her.

'Nothing to get stewed up about,' Belvia smiled. 'He'd merely heard, from Father probably, that you knew horse-flesh, and he wanted your opinion on a horse he's thinking of buying.'

'You told him I no longer have anything to do with horses?' Josy asked urgently.

'Of course. Don't be upset. I told you you had nothing to worry about with Latham, didn't I?' Belvia went on cheerily. 'Which you'd have discovered for yourself if I hadn't been such an idiot and grabbed the phone from you,' she laughed.

Belvia was not laughing later when, in the early evening, she began to feel extremely agitated about seeing Latham again. Oh, for goodness' sake. She tried impatiently to snap herself out of it. What could happen to her that had not happened to her already?

Because of her inner agitation, though, she dressed with special care, as if hoping her red short-sleeved crêpe dress would give her some confidence.

'You didn't say you were going out,' Josy remarked when she popped her head round the sitting-room door.

'I just thought I'd drive over and see Kate, in case she's feeling a bit lost since her retirement.' And, playing her ace, 'Would you like to come?' Josy had never met Kate; her answer was a foregone conclusion.

'No, thanks,' Josy smiled.

'See you, then. Shouldn't be too late—well, not unless Kate's starved for company and wants to talk late.'

Belvia did not hurry. While she was anxious for this meeting to be over, she was not so anxious to meet Latham again. She was not hungry and had no mind to share his dinner this time, so deliberately made sure that she did not enter the foyer of his apartments before nine.

The same commissionaire was on duty as before. 'Good evening, Miss Fereday,' he greeted her, and as he went over to the lifts with her and pressed the appropriate button Belvia understood how he had got his job.

Commissionaires did not come any more alert, tactful and smart than this man.

Her thoughts were all on another man, the man she was there to see, well before the lift stopped at his floor. With her insides churning, she walked along to his door and pressed the bell.

He kept her waiting, and that niggled her, and she was glad to feel niggled. Given that she was there to appeal to his better nature, she felt better able to cope with how she was feeling as she experienced a spurt of annoyance.

Then she heard him coming to the door, and her insides were aflutter again. The door opened, and he stood there, as she remembered him, dark-haired, grey-eyed, and cool with it. He was casually dressed in shirt and trousers, 'Come in,' he invited, his eyes taking in her blonde hair framing her face, her neatly fitting dress. 'I'm just finishing my meal.' She pinned a pleasant look on her face and went in. 'You can make some coffee,' he stated—it sounded like an order. Her pleasant look started to slip. Oh, for some rat-poison!

'I think I know where the kitchen is,' she murmured as evenly as she could and, to cover that she would prefer to punch his head, she went kitchenwards.

In the kitchen she found the makings for his coffee and, to the devil with it, found two cups and set to work making coffee and trying to restore her equilibrium. With him so close, it somehow was not easy, and she loaded a tray, working hard on an entry line. How's business? No, she couldn't say that! Latham Tavenner was a shrewd operator. She did not want to give him the smallest cause to associate her visit in any way with business—her father would be furious if she slipped up and gave away the smallest clue that he would not mind doing business with Latham. Her father always had played his cards close to his chest.

She carried the tray into the dining-room—only to find that Latham had transferred to the sitting-room. He took the tray from her when she went in, and set it down on a small table in front of a well-padded, luxurious couch.

'Have you lived here long?' She looked about as she offered an everyday question.

'Some while,' he replied, indicating she should take a seat on the couch. 'It's a useful base,' he commented.

Belvia did as he indicated and sat herself behind the coffee-pot—and at once felt her equilibrium slip when Latham opted to sit on the couch beside her. 'You're not here all the time, then?' she enquired, her brain picking that up from what he had just said while she tried to get the rest of her act together.

'I'm frequently away,' he agreed.

'You've been away this week?' She followed through her thought of earlier that day, that he had been out of town on business that week.

'I flew in this morning,' he confirmed.

Not merely out of town, but out of the country by the sound of it! It did not bode well for her sister, Belvia considered, that one of the first things he did on his return was to pick up the phone and ring Josy on the pretext of asking her about some horse he was interested in.

She poured him a cup of coffee, aware that she was skirting around the real issue of why she was there. 'Cream?' she enquired.

'Black, thanks,' he answered, and then, when she was mentally getting her words in order to talk of Josy, he upset her concentration by asking abruptly, 'Where's the boyfriend tonight?'

'There isn't one,' she replied, and saw his brow darken.

'You never felt it necessary to lie about his existence before!' he reminded her sharply, and Belvia realised the situation was going rapidly downhill—not at all the way it was supposed to go.

'Oh, that...' she began but, looking at him, she saw from the cold look in his grey eyes that things had gone too far for her to try now to convince him that there was not any married lover in her life. To try to convince him, she realised, would only make it seem she was protesting too much, and convince him of the opposite. Anyway, she thought, starting to feel niggled again, why should she try to convince him of anything to do with her? It was not why she was here. She placed her coffee-cup back on the table. 'Do you mind if we talk about something else?' she asked evenly—and found he would be the one to decide when to change the subject.

'It embarrasses you talking of your lover?' he grated toughly. 'The man you're enjoying behind his wife's back?'

'There isn't...' she flared, but saw, as Latham glowered, ready to disbelieve any denial she made, that she was wasting her breath. 'I'm not here about me!' she stated stiffly.

'No?'

'No!' she replied shortly, and, as he placed his cup down on the table beside hers, felt her right hand itch with wayward tendencies again.

'Then—let me guess—it must have something to do with your sister.'

'You know damn well it is!' she snapped—he really was asking for it.

'Do I?' he drawled. 'The last time you were here, supposedly on the same errand, you—er—forgive me for being indelicate,' he inserted, not looking in the slightest apologetic, 'you showed every sign of—wanting my body.'

That was it! In a flash she was on her feet—only to feel the firm grip of his hand on her arm pulling her down again. Clearly he was of the view that he was the one who would decide when this discussion was over. Fuming, furious, she resisted as long as she was able, but his superior strength won, and she was pulled back to the place she had just jumped up from.

Only in doing so, in Latham taking his hand from her arm, she fell awkwardly against him—and his hand accidentally brushed across her breast. 'Oh!' she gasped, frissons of electricity rocketing through her as her eyes shot to his.

Latham stared back, his aggression, like hers, dented. She felt powerless to move. His hand was still near to her breast, and she felt that she was not even breathing when, unhurriedly, as if he had liked that brief flirtation with her breast, Latham moved his hand—and cupped it over her breast.

She stared at him, the gamut of emotions rioting in her. She wanted to tell him no, but was too transfixed to move, too transfixed to speak. Gently then he began to mould her breast beneath his hand, and as she gasped, so she strove for calm.

Once more he gently moulded the full, rounded contour he held captive, and Belvia bore it as best she could. But when he teased, to find the hardened peak

he had created, Belvia could take no more. Desire for
him was making a nonsense of her. His warmth, the sen-
suousness of his touch through the thin material of her
dress, were blowing her mind.

'D-Don't—do that!' she whispered croakily, and on
the instant his hand stilled. 'I—I . . .' she mumbled, and
knew that, if she was to regain her scattered senses, she
had to get away from him.

Dragging her eyes from him, she stood up—and this
time he did not stop her. She knew vaguely that she could
not leave his apartment until she had settled things with
him about Josy, but, as she moved from the room, Belvia
was more concerned just then with finding some self-
control than with talking to him about her sister.

Why instinct should lead her not out of his apartment
but into his kitchen she had no idea, but it seemed as
good as any place to try and get herself back together.

The only trouble was that Latham followed her. Oh,
heavens, he had the lot, and she knew she did not stand
the remotest chance of gaining a scrap of control while
he was in the same room. Determinedly she turned her
back on him, as though hoping that not to see his intelligent and good-looking face might help her.

It did not, for the simple reason that Latham came
and stood close behind her, his breath against her hair
as he murmured, 'You want me, Belvia, don't you?'

She swallowed hard. Other men had kissed her and
she had remained cool. This man only had to be in the
same room and she wanted him. 'I'm—I'm...confused,'
she admitted shakily—and knew at that moment that
the advantage was all his.

Which made it more bewildering than ever that, when
her resistance to him was at its lowest, when she was his

for the taking, he did not take up that advantage, but, placing his hands gently on her shoulders, he just held her in a comforting clasp.

And she no longer seemed in charge of herself, nor in charge of her voice, for she could do no other than lean back and place her head against him. She felt the solid wall of his chest at the back of her. 'Oh, Latham,' she murmured.

His answer was to turn her without haste until she was face to face with him. She looked up at him and could see none of the coldness in his expression that had been there before. 'Latham.' She whispered his name again, and leant her head against him.

His arms came round her in a gentle hold, and it was bliss. He said not a word, but just held her tenderly in his arms, and she was enraptured—and knew that there was kindness in him.

She raised her head to look at him, and gently, as his head came down, they kissed. With an arm about her, he walked with her from the kitchen and back to the sitting-room, and there for long, long moments he looked into her all-giving wide brown eyes, and gently, without haste, he kissed her again.

Feeling shy suddenly, she smiled, and he smiled back, and her heart raced faster than ever. She raised her arms and put them round him and, purely because she wanted to, because she had to, she stretched up and kissed him. It was a lovely, wonderful kiss, and, when she pulled back to smile at him again, Latham responded by kissing her, by holding her that bit more firmly—and everything in her went haywire.

She pressed close to him; he pressed back. He kissed her throat; she clung on to him, the warmth of his body through his thin shirt making her want to feel more of him—and in no time fires of wanting were burning uncontrollably in her. As his hands caressed her back, so her hands caressed him.

She wanted him to undo the zip of her dress as he had the last time, but he did not, but just held her, and kissed her, and drove her mad with her need for him when long, sensitive fingers caressed the front of her ribcage, and upwards.

There was no thought in her head to tell him, Don't do that, when once more he gently cupped one of her breasts in his hand. 'Oh, Latham,' she murmured in joy. Nor was there any thought in her head that the last time she had been in his arms he had rejected her—this time it was different, not only because he had started to make love to her gently. It was just that she knew it was different.

'Are you all right?' he breathed.

'Oh, yes,' she replied gloriously, and knew more delight when his expert fingers did go to the zip of her dress.

A moment later and the zip was undone to her waist. With sensitive fingers Latham eased her dress from her shoulders, from her arms—and that, ridiculously she felt, was when she experienced such a shyness that, as her dress started to fall from her and a vision of herself standing there in little but her lacy underwear shot through her head, she caught a fast hold of it before it could fall from her waist.

'Something wrong?' he queried softly, teasingly.

'I'm—um—a bit shy,' she mumbled.

'Shy?' he echoed, but, as he bent his head to kiss her lace-covered breast, he seemed to accept that some family trait of shyness was getting to her.

But Belvia, even as her senses were assaulted by fresh, mind-boggling sensations at the feel of his mouth on the swell of her breast, suddenly knew why she wanted him to be her first lover—and, contradictorily, why it was just not right.

'I—don't want to!' she choked, and was not surprised, after the signals she had been giving off, that Latham should straighten and stare at her in disbelief.

'You—don't want to?' he echoed, his gaze going from the agitated rise and fall of her lace-covered breast and up to her face.

'It's—not right,' she choked. She wanted him to love her, for this first time to be with a man—who loved her.

'Not right?' He stared at her incredulously.

She took a step back, making a hash of it when with nervous fingers she struggled to get her arms back into her dress. 'I—just—can't,' she said helplessly—and started to get all het up again. He had undone the wretched zip—why the devil didn't he come and help her do it up again?

Her dress was at last done up, and she dared a glance at him. Any warmth she had imagined in his eyes was gone. Nor was his tone the sweetest she had ever heard, when he grunted, 'Are you like this with him?'

'With him?'

'Your lover!' he snarled.

'Oh, go to...' she began to erupt, then remembered very belatedly that she was there on behalf of her sister, but knew on her own behalf that she was too stewed up to start a discussion about Josy now. 'Can I ring you?' she asked.

He surveyed her sardonically. 'Am I to gather from that that you aren't staying the night?'

Again she wanted to hit him, even while she still wanted him. She hated the brutal, sarcastic swine. 'Not another minute!' she snapped, and got out of there. Damn him, damn him, damn him! She had wondered what could happen to her that had not happened to her already. And now she knew!

She, stupidly, idiotically, had fallen in love with him, and he—he did not care a button for her! He had desired her, but cared so little he had not pressed her to stay. And she, idiot that she was, felt that, had he asked her with any kindness not to go—regardless of her beliefs on a mutual love when she gave herself—she might have stayed.

CHAPTER FIVE

THERE had been a hopeful notion in her head when she went to sleep that she might wake up and find that she had made a mistake, would wake to find that she was not, after all, in love with Latham Tavenner. But, from the moment Belvia opened her eyes on Monday morning, she knew just how ridiculous that hope had been. She knew, and it was a part of her, that she was heart and soul in love with him.

It was not just physical, she knew that undeniably too. It seemed to her to be a love that transcended everything, even the fact that—given that she and Latham struck physical sparks off each other—he had shown distinctly that he preferred Josy to her. In fact, he had shown that he did not care for her at all.

'How was Kate?' Josy asked when Belvia went downstairs to assist with breakfast—and caused her to do a rapid rethink, to recall that she had used Kate as an excuse for going out last night.

'Fine. Enjoying life,' Belvia answered—and was glad to have her head in the cutlery-drawer so that she need not look her sister in the eye.

'It's about time you found yourself another job,' her father complained when Belvia placed a plate of bacon and eggs in front of him.

'What brought that on?' she enquired, and received a grunt for her trouble—no doubt his weekend had not come up to expectations. Or was it that his money worries were getting to him?

Oh, grief, she fretted, for it seemed to her that while keeping Josy out of Latham's clutches, she had been a bit tardy in remembering that—for her father's sake and for the continuance of Fereday Products—she also had most particularly to keep Latham sweet.

Great! How sweet was one furious blow to the side of his face? And how about—having shown herself more than willing to make love with him—suddenly halting proceedings by telling him 'I don't want to'? Sweet? If that was keeping him sweet, she would be lucky if he gave her father so much as the time of day next time he saw him—let alone the enormous finance he was after.

'More coffee?' She was brought out of her reverie by Josy waving the coffee-pot.

'No, thanks,' she replied, and with a sinking heart remembered that, for Josy's sake, she had asked Latham if she could phone him. But while her love for him made her want some contact with him again—quite desperately did she need some contact—at the same time she was most reluctant to make that call.

Would he expect her to ring? After last night, perhaps not. Though, since she had gone to see him with the specific purpose of talking to him about Josy, perhaps yes.

The whole of Monday went by and, although Belvia was close to the phone many times, she did not pick it up to make that call.

It was the same on Tuesday too, but on Wednesday Belvia got up and told herself she was made of sterner stuff than to go to pieces on hearing the voice of the man she loved on the other end of the phone.

Even so, nine o'clock came and went and she decided she would leave it a while and give him a chance to read his morning's mail. At half-past nine, Josy was in the vicinity of the telephone and, having let her sister think that she had nothing to worry about where Latham was concerned, Belvia did not wish her to overhear her conversation.

At half-past ten Belvia decided she was utterly and totally fed up with the dithery person she had become. She had just decided that she would go out and make her call from a telephone kiosk, however, when there was a ring at the doorbell.

'I'll get it,' she volunteered, and left Josy tidying up the sitting-room.

She had no idea who might be calling, and went to answer thinking more about the phone call she had to make than about who would be standing on the other side of the door.

Which left her totally unprepared. For, when she pulled back the door, her heart very nearly leapt out of her body to see the tall, dark-haired immaculately suited, sophisticated man she loved.

'Er...' Her voice dried and colour flared in her face—she loved him more than she had thought.

Latham's grey eyes rested on her flare of colour. 'Good lord, I didn't know women still did that!'

'And I didn't know men were so ungallant as to mention it!' she found a touch of spirit to retort, and hoped with all she had that he would think her colour came from the fact that she had been half-undressed the last time they had seen each other, and not from the fact that she loved him and that to see him was such a joy. Which was why, to counteract any stray 'I love you' vibe he might have picked up, she told him aggressively, 'Josy isn't in!'

Latham coolly studied her for some seconds, her aggressiveness not lost on him either. Nor was there any smile on his face when, grittily, he replied, 'I haven't come to see your sister.'

'Oh!' Belvia exclaimed faintly, and her heart fluttered idiotically and her throat dried. 'You've—come to see me?' she asked.

'There, you see—I knew you were intelligent.'

Sarcastic swine! she fumed on a loving instant. Though she had to concede, since it was a foregone conclusion that her father would be at his office, that if it was not Josy, then it had to be her Latham had called to see.

'Er—come in,' she invited, and knew her brain was addled when, as he stepped over the threshold, Josy, whom she had just told him was out, came round the corner of the hall. Oh, grief! Even while Josy's startled not to say alarmed look registered, Belvia was glancing swiftly to Latham. Oh, dear, he had not taken too kindly to being lied to, she observed, as he favoured her with a superior look from down his lofty nose. Swiftly she turned back to her sister, who was her more immediate concern, and from somewhere she found a light-hearted tone in which to enquire, 'Would you excuse us, Josy? Um, Latham and I——'

'Of course,' Josy butted in, with such obvious relief that she did not need to hear any reason why she was being excluded. Her manners, however, were such that she stayed to greet their caller. 'Good morning, Mr Tavenner,' she bade him, and was all ready to take flight as he answered her pleasantly,

'Good morning, Josy.'

As her sister went kitchenwards, Belvia made enormous efforts to get herself more of one piece. 'Shall we go to the sitting-room?' She addressed Latham over her shoulder, knowing that so much as to glance his way until she was more in control would negate all her efforts in that department.

She was still wondering why had he called. What, if he did not want to see her sister—as he had claimed—was he doing there? Why, she was agitating as he followed her into the tastefully furnished sitting-room, did he want to see *her*?

He closed the door behind him, and she turned, looked at his dear face—and knew, as her heart renewed its fluttering, that to do so was a mistake. For he was staring directly at her, scrutinising her face, taking in her jeans and T-shirt-clad figure, her long legs and slender shape. She wanted to speak, but found her throat drier than ever, and doubted that anything at all lucid she might be able to find to say would be audible anyway.

Latham, however, chose that moment to save her the trouble. 'I thought,' he began as a cool opener, 'given the power there seems to be between us to stir each other—sexually——' He broke off as her eyes widened and pink tinged her cheeks. Trust him not to balk from straight talking!

She could have done without such straight talking, especially on such a subject. She was just not used to it. 'Go on,' she invited bravely.

'Taking that into account——' he took her up on her offer '—I decided it better that I come here for the discussion you wanted with me the other evening.'

'About Josy?' He nodded, and her heart leapt. He really was not anywhere near as black-hearted as she would have had him painted. 'Take a seat,' she suggested, never loving him more than at that moment when, not waiting any longer for her to phone him, he had obviated the need for her to come to his flat—where the physical chemistry between them seemed to ignite—by deciding instead to come to her home. 'Can I get you coffee?'

'No, thanks,' he declined, and if he was in a hurry in his busy day appeared to convey the opposite as, clearly waiting for her to be seated first, he went and stood by a well-padded couch.

Belvia opted to sit in a matching well-padded chair and, as he sat down too and glanced over to her, she realised that the floor was all hers and he was waiting for her to get on with it.

She took a shaky breath. 'Josy's very shy,' she stated, starting to feel agitated again.

'So you said.'

'Extremely shy.'

'You said that too.'

Belvia took another glance at him. He was sitting there cool and calm and, since this was a meeting she had wanted, manifestly waiting for her to get on with it. That irked her and, as ever where he was concerned, she was glad to feel nettled; it made her feel less all over the place about him.

And suddenly she was erupting. 'I just can't believe you're truly serious in your pursuit of her!'

'Why can't you?' he questioned, quick as a flash.

'Because—well, because...' Damn him! He *knew* why! But he was waiting, watching and waiting. 'Because...'

'So tell me?'

'You know... The way you—um—sexually...'

'For you, you mean?' he queried, as she knew full well *he* had known full well all along.

'That's *exactly* what I mean!' she flared, her cheeks starting to colour again. Oh, devil take it, she fumed. She would get nowhere by being angry—not that Latham looked as though he would lose any sleep over that. But he was looking at her rather intently again, and she would have given anything to know what he was thinking.

If asked, she would have said he had his mind on the person under discussion—Josy. Which was why Belvia stared at him open-mouthed when bluntly, and quite out of the blue, he questioned toughly, 'Just how sexually active *have* you been in your life?'

'I—I...' she stammered, her thoughts leaping everywhere in an effort to get on to his wavelength. She was not sure what to make of his unexpected question. Was it that he had remembered the way she had blushed when she had opened the door and seen him standing there, and...? But he was waiting. She opted to give him the truth. 'I—haven't been...er...' Grief, this straight talking was nowhere near as easy for her as it was for him. 'You're the closest I've come...' she tried again—only to have her Latham Tavenner-thumping desires on the loose again.

For, clearly no more ready to believe her now than he had been before, Latham threw her a furious look and, as if unable to remain still, he was off the couch and standing by the fireplace. 'Don't give me that rot!' he barked, his chin jutting at an aggressive angle. 'I want the truth from you, woman, nothing less!' he snarled.

Damn you, she fumed inwardly, on the instant as furious as he. He would not believe her when she told him the truth, so to hell with him. She swallowed hard on her fury and, ready now to lie her head off if need be, agreed, 'Very well.' Though what her sexual activity had to do with what they were discussing, she failed to see. Who was she? Merely the——

'So, go on.' Apparently he felt he had waited long enough for her to begin speaking truthfully about anything.

'What about?'

His eyes narrowed, and she guessed from that narrow-eyed look that he suspected she was messing him about—and was not prepared to put up with too much more of it. 'About,' he clipped, 'your sister.'

Belvia hesitated. 'I'm—not sure...' she began.

'Get on with it!' he ordered, giving her an impatient look. And Belvia knew then that, if she did not soon start talking, any minute now Latham would be striding out of the room and would almost immediately renew his pursuit of Josy.

'Can—can I trust you?' Belvia asked, knowing that she had to tell him more than that her sister was extremely shy, but not wanting to tell him anything.

'More than I can trust you, I'd say!' he rapped.

'Damn you!' she erupted, and felt so het-up suddenly that she could not bear to be seated either. Since, however, he was occupying the floor-space over by the fireplace, she opted to go and stand looking out of the window. Though as she weighed up just how much she should tell him, and centred her thoughts on Josy and the dreadful time the dear love was going through, to her horror, she felt the prickle of tears in her eyes.

Appalled, she wanted to escape, to get herself under control. But she gulped down tears, and realised she could not escape—could not, because Latham had moved and had come to stand close by, and she dared not so much as turn to glance his way.

And then she had no need to, for Latham was right behind her. 'You're distressed!' he exclaimed. She shook her head to deny any such thing. But all at once she felt his hands on her arms, turning her to face him, and never had she heard his voice so kind, so gentle, as when, his hands falling from her arms, he placed sensitive fingers under her chin and tilted her head so she should look at him as he asked, 'What is it, Belvia?'

She looked at him, looked into warm grey eyes, and felt in that moment that she could tell him anything. 'Josy,' she choked. 'She's a rare person, a precious person.' She was still striving for control as she added, 'She hasn't an evil thought in her head, an ill deed in her body.'

'So?'

'So—I don't want her hurt.'

Quietly Latham studied her. 'I won't hurt her,' he stated equally quietly.

'But you are hurting her,' Belvia told him urgently. 'Just by asking her out, you're hurting her.'

'She's that sensitive?' he questioned disbelievingly.

'It isn't just that——' She broke off—there was no more she could add.

But Latham seemed to think that there was. 'Tell me about it?' he requested, looking at her levelly.

Staring into his eyes, she saw nothing but encouragement there. But still she hesitated. 'I... I'm...'

'Afraid?' he guessed. Wordlessly she nodded. 'Don't be,' he murmured. 'You can trust me, I promise you.'

Oh, Latham, she inwardly cried, in turmoil within herself. Josy wanted nothing but to be left alone—yet

Belvia had a feeling that nothing would make this man back off from what he was going after—unless he knew of a very good reason why he should do so. She stared into his eyes again, into his face, and saw nothing but understanding there, a willingness to understand.

She turned from him and his hand dropped from her. She stared unseeingly out of the window, still in turmoil, but heard every word when Latham asked, 'Tell me why, when other men must want to date your sister, I should not.' A knife turned in her and added to Belvia's torment—it hurt that Latham wanted to date Josy and not her. 'She must have been out with other men,' he added.

Belvia buried her own pain, but somehow then felt strangely that she could trust him with absolutely anything. 'Only one—and he was very special to her,' she heard her own voice answer.

'Was?' he picked up.

Belvia bit her lip. They did not come any sharper than Latham Tavenner. 'He—died.'

'Recently?'

'Not four months ago.'

Latham was silent for a moment or two, and again she would have given anything to know what he was thinking. 'Why didn't your father say?' he asked, and from that Belvia guessed that Latham would have soft-pedalled a bit had he known. A warmth for the man she loved washed over her and she moved from the window to her chair, afraid this time that some of her warmth of feeling for him might show.

Latham returned to his seat on the couch, but when he looked at her, just sat and looked at her without saying a word, she knew that he was silently reminding her that there was an answer outstanding.

'My father... he knows next to nothing about it,' she had to confess.

'He doesn't know your sister had someone very special in her life—and lost him?' Latham questioned, keeping any incredulity that he might feel out of his voice, but his enquiry nevertheless telling Belvia that, having got her to open up, he would insist on knowing all that there was to know—that he wanted every i dotted and every t crossed.

'Josy—didn't want him to know,' Belvia found herself telling him.

'So you kept quiet about it too?'

'Josy asked me not to say anything,' she replied—and soon had any hopes that that might be the end of his questioning dashed.

For, 'Why?' he asked.

'Why?' she repeated, and saw from his face that he knew she was playing for time—and was insisting on an answer. 'Why, because... Well, as you know...' She looked at him and saw there was no let-up in his want-to-know-everything expression. 'Well,' she set off again, 'as you know, my sister is painfully shy—always has been with strangers.'

'Yes, I know that,' he agreed quietly, and there was something in his voice which seemed to Belvia just then to be totally sensitive to what she was saying.

She looked across at him, saw the hint of an encouraging smile on his face, and loved him—and found she was going on to reveal, 'But while she has always been shy with humans, Josy has always been in her element with animals—horses in particular.'

. 'She owns a horse, I believe.'

Belvia nodded, warming to him for his kind tone. 'We inherited some money from our mother when we were twenty-one, eighteen months ago, and Josy bought Hetty with some of her money, and——'

'What did you do with yours?'

Belvia blinked. His question was unexpected; they had been talking about Josy. 'Oh, I threw in the job I was doing at the time and went into training for something I really wanted to do,' she replied with a smile. She saw his serious glance seem to pause a moment, then move to her curving mouth, and a flutter of emotion washed over her just at being in the same room with him. 'Er—anyhow, it was a lovely time for us both. I was doing something I enjoyed, and Josy had Hetty. We haven't room for stabling ourselves,' she went on, 'but that was no problem because there's a riding-stables a couple of miles from here and Josy arranged to have Hetty stabled there.'

'Presumably she went to see her horse every day?'

'Oh, she did. It was such a happy time for her,' Belvia replied, remembering how it had been. 'As soon as she had her chores for the day done she would be up at the stables, Saturday, Sunday, rain or shine. Over a period of time, though,' she continued, her voice starting to dip as she remembered, 'the more she went to the stables, the more she began to relax with a man who was a groom there. Then one day she confided to me about Marc...' Her voice faded, Josy's pain her pain.

'She had fallen in love?' Latham queried gently.

Belvia nodded, too full of emotion to speak. She made a coughing sound to clear her constricted throat, and was remembering it as it had been when she went on to reveal, 'It was a very big moment for her on the day she asked Father if she could invite Marc home to introduce him.'

'Your father was not too pleased with the idea.'

'How did you...?' Her voice tailed off. Good grief, where was her brain? Her father was trying to impress Latham, yet here she was within an ace of revealing what an out-and-out snob her father was! 'My father wants only what's best for Josy. For me too,' she added hastily, in her hope to make him see her father in a better light.

'But you didn't want to marry a groom,' Latham pointed out, and she wished she had not included herself in this. Neither she nor anything to do with her was why he was here.

'How did you know that Josy wanted to marry Marc?' She opted for diversionary tactics.

'It's obvious.'

She realised it probably was, and her glance slid from him. 'I suppose it is,' she agreed.

'But your father said no, that he didn't wish your sister to marry her love.'

'Josy didn't ask for either his blessing or consent.'

'Didn't she, now?'

Belvia shook her head. 'No,' she replied, and knew he wanted more, but she could not tell him more.

That was, she was certain she could not tell him more while he was seated on the couch. But when suddenly, although completely without haste, he left his seat and came and sat on the arm of her chair, her certainty became clouded by confusion. He was close, too close; his nearness was making a nonsense of her. When he bent down and gently took her hands in his, and queried softly, 'So?' Belvia had the hardest work in the world to hide from him her innermost feelings for him.

'So she married, without telling him,' she replied—and was aghast at what she had just said. 'I . . .'

'Your father didn't know one of his daughters got married?' Latham asked, his surprise evident.

'He—he still doesn't know,' she stammered in a rush, as, appalled by what she had revealed, she hastened to repair what she had done—for Josy's sake she had to get Latham to promise not to say a word to her father. 'Josy proved stronger and more spirited than I'd have thought when she decided to marry Marc and tell Father after the honeymoon. But . . .'

'Was that when Marc died, on their honeymoon?' Latham asked.

Belvia realised that, since she had said Josy had been going to tell their father after her honeymoon, it was not so very difficult to work out that a tragedy had befallen Marc before the honeymoon was over.

'Yes,' she confirmed. 'Josy told father she was going away for a few days—which stretched. I was at the wedding. Just me and another witness. I cried buckets, I was so happy for her,' she inserted, but went swiftly on, anxious, now that she had said so much, to get it all said. 'They went away to Marc's people in France, to tell them of their marriage and to honeymoon there. But only the next day Josy phoned from France to say Marc was dead.'

'You flew at once to her,' Latham stated, as if he knew it for a fact.

'That's about it. I took a few minutes out to leave a message with my father's secretary to the effect that I'd decided to take a short holiday too—and went. Josy was in shock—we flew back after the funeral.'

'And you *still* didn't tell your father what had happened?' Latham queried, his incredulity straining at the leash.

'It's the way Josy wants it,' Belvia replied, clamping her lips firmly shut on words such as: who could blame her sister after the way their father had been about Marc?

'You're reiterating that your father knows nothing of your sister's marriage?'

'I am.'

'That he has no idea that she's a widow?'

'He doesn't,' she answered, adding quickly, 'And I'd ask you to respect what I've told you. Give me your w——'

'Didn't your father notice she was in a state of shock?' Latham cut through what she was saying to question her.

'Josy's always been incapacitated by shyness.'

'Within her own family?' he asked, an eyebrow arching in surprise.

'No, of course not. But she's always been quiet, so— Well, my father's a busy man—he probably wouldn't notice if she was a little more quiet than usual, and anyhow...' Her voice tailed off, but he would not allow her to leave it there.

'Anyhow—what?' he pressed.

She shrugged. 'Anyhow, I covered for her every time she dashed from the room to howl somewhere in private.'

Momentarily she felt the grip he still had on her hands tighten. Then he abruptly let go and, getting up from the arm of her chair, he went and stood again over by the fireplace.

And it was from there that, to her astonishment, he clearly stated, 'All of which goes to show that you're a pretty wonderful sister.'

Her mouth fell open. What had brought that on? They had been talking about Josy, not her. He had made a nonsense of her again—just one compliment from him, that was all it took, and she went weak. But, for Josy's sake, she had to be strong.

That knowledge left her struggling and searching around for some comment which would for a second time take attention away from herself. 'I've heard tell that you're a pretty wonderful brother,' she found out of nowhere, with no idea just then where she'd heard it, and, her head still not together, little more idea about anything else either.

Her comment had the desired effect, however, in that Latham threw her a far from complimentary look and scowled at her, as if being reminded of his sister had brought to mind some unpleasant memory. Was he perhaps not such good friends with his sister as she had believed? she wondered.

Whatever the case, Belvia saw, as he drummed his fingers on the mantelpiece while, deep in thought, he stared hostilely at her, that his mood had undergone a sudden change.

Nor was it for the better, she discovered, when, all sign of gentleness and understanding gone, he asked harshly, 'Bearing in mind your mammoth propensity for telling lies—how much of what you've just told me should I believe?'

The swine! To get her talking—and then to turn on her! In the next moment she was on her feet, facing him, staring him straight in the eye. 'Everything I've told you about my sister is true!' she snapped. She was starting to shake inside but did not know whether it was from anger, or just from an emotional reaction to him; all she knew then was that, before he left her home, she wanted his word that he would repeat none of what she had told him. 'And,' she went on hurriedly, 'I'd like your promise that you won't say anything to my father of what I've told you.'

For an answer he favoured her with an arrogant stare. 'Is that all?' he questioned curtly.

He was annoying her again—an indulgence she could not afford. To hide her annoyance she wandered to the back of the couch when she thought she had got herself sufficiently under control to answer his question. 'As a matter of fact, no,' she replied. Raising her head, her eyes, she looked at him. God, he looked tough. 'I should also like your promise that you'll back off,' she made herself go on.

'Back off?'

Ooh, what she would not give to have another crack at him. The baiting brute, he knew damn well what she was talking about. 'Josy,' she stated succinctly. 'My sister. Will you leave her alone?' Confound it, what was this man doing to her? A moment ago she had been more or less demanding that he leave Josy alone, yet now, in less than five seconds, she was almost pleading with him to leave her alone. 'It can't be that you l-love her, can it?' she asked, and did not know, as she waited for him to answer, how she would be able to take it if he answered that he did love her sister.

But he did not answer and, even while her heart beat anxiously, Belvia began to hate him because, without

saying a word, he could—because of force of circumstances—make her go from demanding to pleading.

'Please,' she requested, and was left having to ask,
'Please tell me what you intend to do.'

Latham moved away from the fireplace, and as he
came nearer so her heart beat the faster. But the couch
was still between them when, after studying her earnest
expression for a few moments more, he began, 'I'll...'
He paused. 'Let you know.'

'Oh, please!' she cried—really, this just was not good
enough.

But he was already on his way to the door, and the
only promise she got was the, 'I'll be in touch,' which
he threw over his shoulder on his way out.

CHAPTER SIX

BELVIA spent the following hours in an agony of anguish, and that anguish was still with her when she awoke on Thursday morning. No sooner had Latham departed the day before than she had realised that, by telling him all she had about Josy, he could have her jumping through hoops! If he so desired he could make her do anything he wanted and—if she was to protect her sister from him—there was not a thing she could do about it. She was at his mercy whatever he, with his 'I'll be in touch,' decided.

She knew why she had told him so much, of course. From the love she bore him, she had felt she could trust him. That he had seemed sensitive and understanding had gone a long way towards that trust, but it was of no help to her now. And while it was unfortunately true that the love that had grown in her for him—which had come unannounced and unwanted—was of such strength that she thought that there was nothing she would not do for him, the wealth of love she had for her still-vulnerable sister meant that she would do all in her power to protect her.

Belvia got out of bed wondering when Latham would be 'in touch'. She had half expected him to ring last night, and had half jumped out of her skin when the phone had rung. But the call had not been for her but for her father, in connection with a golf tournament Fereday Products were co-sponsoring on Sunday. How, when Fereday Products were next door to broke, they could co-sponsor anything, defeated her. Though, according to her father, to be *seen* to be prosperous was everything.

She pushed Latham out of her head and went downstairs, starting to hope that today she might not have to resort to lying her head off.

She had had little compunction in telling a whole string of whoppers to the man she loved, but liked less having to lie to her sister. Yet she had been totally stumped yesterday, when no sooner had he gone, Josy had sought her out and asked anxiously, 'What did he want?' The truth, that Latham was still after Josy, had had to be avoided at all costs.

'Oh, nothing too important,' she had replied, while her thoughts had gone scurrying to come up with a reason that had nothing to do with Josy, nor Latham either. 'We—er—— You know that concert thing I went to with him the other Monday,' she had pulled out of an unknown somewhere.

'Yes,' Josy had replied, giving Belvia another second to get her powers of super-invention into gear.

'Well, that night——'

'You were all right? You weren't harmed in any way?' Josy had cut in in utmost concern, giving her not only another couple of seconds but the gleam of an idea.

'No, I told you, Latham's manners were impeccable,' she had smiled. 'But during the evening I met a man called Rodney Phillips who works for Latham.' And it was here that the truth had started to stretch. 'Anyhow, Rodney Phillips asked Latham for my phone number, apparently, and it was only after he'd given it to him that his PA told him that Rodney has a terrible reputation for being rather unpleasant with women when he's had a drink or two. Latham was more or less passing our door when he felt he was morally bound to come and pass on what his PA had said, because he feels sure that Rodney Phillips might phone and ask me out.'

'That was very decent of him,' Josy had opined—and had left Belvia feeling a trifle stunned at her unexpected powers of invention, and sending a silent apology to Rodney Phillips, whom she had judged to be totally harmless.

And the phone stayed silent. Belvia went to bed on Thursday night feeling het-up and angry. She hated this waiting game, this guarding the telephone, this going out only to exercise Hetty and dashing back fearful that Latham might have phoned in her absence.

'Fancy coming to the supermarket with me?' Josy asked her just after eleven on Friday morning.

There and back, with shopping in between, the supermarket was a two-hour trip. 'Do you mind if I don't? I promised myself I'd do a wardrobe clear-out today, and if I don't soon get started I'll——'

'If you're throwing out your green two-piece, put my name on it,' Josy butted in—and Belvia could not have been better pleased. Not because her sister had taken her excuse without offence, but because this was the first time in an age that she had shown the smallest interest in clothes. Was she starting to recover? Oh, she did so hope so. It was only a small step, Belvia knew that, but it was a step in the right direction.

Josy had been gone only about fifteen minutes when the doorbell sounded, and Belvia's stomach tightened in knots. It would not be him, it could not be him, she told herself as she went to answer it. What busy man of business could afford to take time out of his schedule twice in one week for something that had nothing to do with business?

Nervously she put her hand on the door-catch, and had to take a deep and steadying breath before she opened it—and it was him. And her heart sang and danced just to see him—casually clothed, even though this was the middle of a business day.

In return Latham was eyeing her, taking in her tailored trousers with crisp shirt tucked into the waistband. What he was thinking she could not tell, for his expression told her nothing. 'Me—or Josy?' she asked, as she attempted to steady her heartbeat by reminding herself that his visit might bode nothing good for her sister.

Latham eyed her unblinkingly for a few seconds longer. Then, clearly remembering their exchange the last time she had opened the door to him, when she had said that Josy was not in and he had replied that it was not Josy he had come to see, 'You,' he clipped.

Belvia did not make the mistake of offering him coffee this time. This man, for all his casual air, meant business. She remembered how she had realised that, having handed him all the aces, so to speak, she had placed herself entirely at his mercy—and tried not to panic.

'We'll go to the sitting-room,' she stated, and led the way. He followed without saying another word, and in the sitting-room Belvia pointed to the chair she had sat in on Wednesday while she went over to the couch. They were both seated when, perhaps hoping to defer what she guessed in advance might be something not too pleasant, 'Josy really is out today,' she commented.

'Somewhere interesting?'

'Only the supermarket,' she replied, and suddenly wanted it all said and done so that she would know the worst.

As too did Latham apparently want it all said, for, his tone crisp, he asked, 'Is Josy well enough for you to leave her for a few days?'

Belvia shot him a wary look. In point of fact, while returning her affection, Josy enjoyed solitude sometimes and, if her comment about the green two-piece was anything to go by, had made a start on recovery.

But Belvia had no intention of telling him that—she had been far too open before. 'What do you have in mind?' she hedged, and found she was looking into a pair of cool grey eyes which never flinched.

'I've a country retreat in Wiltshire where I occasionally spend a weekend. I'm on my way there now, as a matter of fact.'

'Oh, yes?' she queried politely.

'I've invited some people down tomorrow, a married couple. They'll stay overnight, and,' he added, 'I'd like you to come with me, and be there too.'

For a moment, as what he said penetrated, her thoughts went haywire. The thought of spending the whole of today with him, of being with him for the whole weekend, albeit with other people as from tomorrow, sounded like absolute bliss. Suddenly, though, she crashed down back to earth. It was not as simple as that—he did not love her—and there were strings.

'Why?' she asked shortly.

Latham shrugged. 'While you may not be such a good housekeeper as your sister, I'm sure you'd be able to cope in the kitchen.'

So he wanted her to cook for him and his guests. Belvia could not see that as any problem, but—she had trusted him without thinking on Wednesday, and had regretted it ever since.

'What's this got to do with Josy?' she asked—the question which was at the basis of her knowing him.

'The decision is yours. Come with me—and your sister will not be bothered by me ever again.'

Belvia's breath caught. Surely for him to be able to state that so categorically had to mean that he was not in love with Josy, didn't it? Oh, how wonderful! Suddenly her heart was singing. Man-like, Latham had only been interested in her sister because she was unattainable, but he had no deep love for her.

Suddenly Belvia realised she was going off into orbit in her relief—and so fought hard to counteract it. Why should she go and be his skivvy? she made herself think belligerently—only to be tripped up by thoughts of not only her sister but her father also. And—oh, grief—her father would only have to hear the merest whisper of what had gone on and without question, if he knew she had refused, should Latham so request her sister the next time, he would put pressure on Josy to go.

Abruptly a stray strand of caution came to Belvia, which blotted out all other thoughts and, before she knew it, she was blurting out shortly, 'I'd have a room to myself?'

Of course she would, she realised on the next moment, and, feeling dreadfully embarrassed all at once, she wished she had stayed quiet. Though she was not at all sure about the mild-mannered smile that came to Latham's expression as he scrutinised her anxious face for a few seconds. She did not trust that mild-mannered smile.

Then she found that she had indeed worried unnecessarily, for, not missing that she had just as good as told him she would go with him, he replied, 'The property is a three-bedroom cottage.' Relief rushed in that of course she was to have her own room. But, as Latham's mild-mannered smile took on a silky edge, Belvia began to grow wary again, and was soon learning that her relief had been premature. As too had any thought that she had worried unnecessarily because, without so much as a change in tone, Latham went on, 'Unfortunately, I've had the middle bedroom converted into two *en suite* bathrooms.'

Her throat dried, but she would not swallow and show him how this news was affecting her nerves—she would not. 'So—your cottage is now a two-bedroom cottage?' Bother his wanting every i dotted, every t crossed. Before she so much as set foot outside her home, she wanted every fact established.

'Your training in accountancy is standing you in good stead,' he murmured sardonically, and again she wanted to hit him—it did not require a calculator to subtract one from three to make it two.

'So,' she pressed doggedly on, 'where would I sleep.'

'Oh, I wouldn't dream of allowing you to sleep anywhere but in a bedroom,' he answered pleasantly, adding, 'And to save your next question—I've no intention of dossing down on the sitting-room sofa, either.'

Belvia swallowed then, despite her determination not to; she just could not help it. But she was still as dogged as ever to find out at the outset just what went on here.

'You're not suggesting for a moment, I suppose, that I share a room with your female guest while you...?' He was shaking his head long before she could finish.

'Not for a moment,' he agreed casually.

God, how she hated, loved, hated him! 'You're saying that, when your guests arrive tomorrow, I'm to sleep in the same room as you?' she insisted on knowing.

He smiled a smile of pure mockery. 'There, I *was* right,' he drawled. 'You are bright.'

Oh, how she wanted to wipe all that mockery from his face. Failing that, she threw him a cutting look that did not even dent him, and fought a panicky but losing battle within herself. She would not go, most definitely she would not go, was her first thought. Then she thought of Josy—and knew without a single doubt that if she did not go, then he would feel free to renew his pursuit of her sister.

Nerves were most definitely starting to bite when Belvia stared at him hostilely, and demanded, 'You'd expect me to sleep in your bed?'

His mouth twitched and, at the thought that he must find it amusing that she could be so hostile and yet ask such a question, she again wanted to hit him. 'If you absolutely can't resist it,' he mocked, and veritable sparks of outrage and impotent fury flashed in her eyes.

The pig! The arrant swine! The diabolical rat! He damn well knew what he could do to her! Damn him to hell. 'What about my reputation?' she erupted, that appearing to be about her only defence. Stuff his bed— she'd sleep on the floor sooner!

'Ye gods!' he exclaimed. 'She's gone old-fashioned on me!' Belvia shot out of her chair, too furious to sit. She stormed over to the window—if she went anywhere near him she would hammer his head in. She was not looking at him, but knew he was on his feet too—and a harshness had entered his tones when he grated, 'What reputation?'

She guessed she had rather walked into that. Though if he thought she was having an affair with a married man he was not taking into account that she might have something better to do with her weekend than go off somewhere with him. Not, on second thoughts, that what she wanted was of the slightest importance to him.

She turned to look at him standing by the mantelpiece and gave him a withering look, which bounced off him. 'What if I don't come and—for the want of a better word—housekeep for——?'

'Hostess,' Latham cut in coolly, and as coolly and effectively answered the question she had not finished asking by querying, 'When will your sister be back?'

Which as good as told her it was her—or Josy. 'You're bluffing!' Belvia challenged, somehow unable to believe she could have fallen in love with a man who, after all she had revealed of her sister's widowhood, could be so hard.

His answer was to stride to the door without further comment. Her bluff called, Belvia was galvanised into action and reached the door at the same time as he did. 'You win!' she gasped, with no doubt in her mind then that if she allowed Latham to go from the room he would waste no more time with her, but would relentlessly go after her sister. She stared up at him from wide brown eyes, loved him and felt defeated, but knew that it was not over yet. 'Have I your promise that, if I do share a room with you, you won't—er—come over all—er—amorous?' she asked quietly.

His answer was at first to stare down into her eyes with a look so bordering on gentleness that her heartbeat suddenly started to race. She felt he was on the point of telling her to forget the whole thing. But then suddenly something seemed to come over him, and all at once that gentle look had hardened, and then had changed again, and a look of utter wickedness was on his face when he mocked, 'What about *my* virtue?'

How she kept her hand off him then, she did not know—but she had only one more question to ask. 'If I do this—you'll leave my sister alone?'

He looked at her seriously for long, long moments, and then it was that he told her what she wanted to hear. 'You have my word,' he said quietly.

Belvia looked at him for perhaps a second longer and, the die cast, she took a shaky breath. 'I should like to leave before Josy comes back,' she decided.

His reply was to open the door. 'It shouldn't take more than a few minutes for you to throw a few things into a weekend case,' he decreed.

Without a word Belvia went past him and up the stairs to her room. Now that she accepted that she had no choice but to go, her head started to spin with unanswerable questions. Why her? He did not like her. Certainly did not love her. Her heart lightened slightly at the certainty that Latham did not love Josy either. But she had not thought the soup she had made for dinner that time had been so great that he would think of her when, despite his 'hostess' comment, he wanted a housekeeper for the weekend.

Although, on reflection, since he had only two bedrooms, perhaps that was the reason. She got out a suitcase, and began to see that of course it was the reason. He needed someone to cook for him and his guests this weekend and, since he had nowhere to sleep a cook, on the strength of her soup she had been elected.

Any further thoughts she might have had on the subject were cut short when just then, and without so much as a knock or a by-your-leave, Latham Tavenner opened her bedroom door and walked straight in.

'I could have been changing!' she protested, and was made to weather his look that said, I've seen you half undressed before, so why the noise?

She clamped her lips together and watched astonished as he moved over to her bedroom window and glanced out. 'I thought I'd carry your case down,' he remarked, his back to her as he looked out at the view below.

Ever the gent! 'I've barely started packing yet!' she complained.

'I'll wait.' There was no end to his sauce, she fumed to herself. 'Do you do any of the garden?' he enquired conversationally.

Belvia threw him a withering look which, since he had his back to her, was wasted. 'Josy does most of it,' she replied coldly, opening drawers and throwing underwear and nightwear into her case, and darting into the bathroom for some toiletries before going smartly to the wardrobe and, concerned to get out of there before her sister returned, taking out the first things she touched. 'I'll have to write a note to Josy,' she informed the straight back of the man in her room as she snapped her case shut. 'And I'll have to make a phone call before I...'

The rest of it died in her throat when Latham left his contemplation of the garden to shoot round, and his conversational tone abruptly vanished. 'Who to?' he demanded aggressively.

'My stars!' she exploded. 'You're never the same two minutes together!'

'It's part of my charm. Who to?' he insisted.

She tossed him an irritated look and would have ignored him, but he left his place over by the window and somehow, as he came nearer, she began to feel threatened—not by him, but by what his nearness could do to her. If he touched her, laid so much as a finger on her arm... 'Oh, this is ridiculous!' she erupted. 'I merely have to ring the stables to——' Anger pure and simple caused her to break off. Since it did not look as though he intended to leave her room until she did, then he was going to overhear her conversation anyway.

To hell with him, she railed inwardly and, going over to the phone by her bed, refused to say another word to him, but dialled the number of the stables and was fortunate enough to find the person she wanted to speak to near at hand.

Once her phone call was made, she went to her writing-desk and, finding it impossible to ignore Latham, did her best anyway, only to find he was looking over her shoulder, reading everything she wrote, as she penned her note.

'Dear Josy,
Kate rang—in something of a state. After-retirement blues, I think. I've said I'll go and stay with her for a few days. Rang Tracey, by the way. She'll exercise Hetty till I get back. See you some time Sunday.
Love, Belvia.'

'Who's Kate?' Latham wanted to know.

'My God—don't tell me you missed something!' Belvia exclaimed waspishly—and knew she was very definitely going light-headed when he laughed, and she discovered that she wanted to join in. 'Kate's someone I used to work with,' she told him belligerently—anything rather than let him see that they shared the same perverse sense of humour.

Belvia left the note to her sister propped up on the hall table and went from the house, to discover that Latham had dispensed with a chauffeur's services and was driving himself that Friday.

She told herself as they drove along that she was not going to enjoy one single solitary moment of the next two days—but could not deny that her emotions were confused and all over the place just to be seated in his car with him, a whole weekend in his company stretching before her.

Latham had chosen to take the scenic route rather than the motorway, and it was nearing one when he pulled up at a pleasant-looking hotel. 'We'll lunch here,' he decided.

She loved him; it was weakening her. 'I'm not to begin my skivvying straight away, then?' she queried tartly.

'You're priceless,' he answered good-humouredly, and Belvia just did not know what to make of him. An hour earlier he'd been tough, unyielding, giving her little choice but to agree with what he wanted. Yet now, for all there had been sparse conversation between them, he was behaving most amiably and, as he came round and opened her door for her, being well-mannered to boot.

Lunch went better than she had expected, given the circumstances. It had crossed her mind that, with the two of them being scratchy with each other, she would not be able to eat a thing. But, as before, she found his manners were immaculate in company and, as she was being treated with every courtesy, it somehow rubbed off on to her, so that her own innate good manners soon surfaced. So much so that they were at the pudding stage before she realised it, the whole of the lunchtime going splendidly.

He had even made her laugh over some small incident to do with his work, but as she looked across the table at him she immediately sobered. She loved him—was that why she felt so relaxed, so utterly at one with him?

'Something wrong?' he enquired, and seemed so much at one with her too, so much in tune—instantly aware of her smallest change of mood—that her heart jerked.

She shook her head, fully aware that only a short while ago she would have replied with some tart answer. Aware too that, because of the love she had for him, she was imagining a 'togetherness' that just was not there. But even so, she loved him so much that she suddenly did not want to be the instigator of hostility. What she wanted, for just a few hours, if the gods were kind, was a pleasant time to remember. She had no idea how the rest of the weekend might go—indeed, she was doing her darnedest not to think about it but to enjoy only the present. The weekend would be over soon enough and, with Latham's word given that he would not pursue Josy, Belvia realised she would never see him after that.

She smiled at him over her coffee-cup, saw his glance at her still, and quickly veiled her eyes, lest he see anything in them of how she truly felt about him.

They were both in quiet mood, it seemed, when they went out to his car. They were later driving through a small town when, out of the blue, Latham remarked,

'Talking of supermarkets...' and, as amusement pulled the corners of her lovely mouth upwards, he glanced her way, before turning his attention to a supermarket car-park.

'This is one way to spend a Friday afternoon,' she remarked drily as, trolley in grip, they entered the mêlée.

'Is it always like this?'

'I expect so.' She laughed, loved him, and had never found supermarket-shopping so exciting. 'What do you want?'

His eyes strayed to her mouth, then slowly, as if having to drag his gaze away, up to her eyes. 'What do you suggest?'

'Me?' she queried. 'It's your shopping-trolley!'

'You're the cook,' he reminded her—but so charmingly she didn't have a chance to get uptight about her enforced role.

'I expect you've got a fridge?'

'Must have.'

She wanted to laugh again, so turned away and headed for the fresh vegetables section.

They reached Rose Cottage around five o'clock. 'This is a *cottage*?' she asked as she stood on the drive and studied the detached building, in its own grounds with not a sign of another property thereabouts.

'Like it?'

She did, given that she was starting to feel a shade nervous. She knew that in other circumstances she could be totally relaxed and happy here. 'It's lovely! How did you find it?'

'Through a friend of a friend.'

Jealousy bit, and she did not like it. Was the friend a lady-friend? She did not want to know. She turned her back on the virile look of him. 'We'd better get the shopping in.'

The inside of the cottage was everything a weekend retreat should be, she felt. A cosy, carpeted sitting-room housed a couple of padded chairs, a three-seater settee and a small table. The dining-room was much smaller, with room only for a table and four chairs, and with the kitchen leading off, of about equal size.

She helped Latham put away the food they had purchased, but was far more interested in doing a reconnoitre of the bedrooms. She had her chance when Latham decided to go outside.

Her weekend case was at the bottom of the stairs, she noted as she left the kitchen. She picked it up and, case in hand, she went up the stairs. As he had said, there were two bedrooms, separated by *en suite* bathrooms. In one of the bedrooms there were twin beds, and in the other only one—a double. Next Belvia checked the airing-cupboard. Good, there was plenty of bedlinen.

She gathered up an armful of it and set to work. First she made up the double bed. It was where she would sleep tonight. She would change the sheets for his guests in the morning. Then she went into the other bedroom. Before she started work in there, however, she took a glance out of the bedroom window, from which she could see fields and hedgerows and, just below, the side of the cottage where Latham had parked his car.

She was just about to come away from the window when a movement from within the car caught her attention. She stayed where she was, and a moment later realised that Latham was inside his car using his car phone. Only then did she realise that she had not seen a telephone inside the cottage—perfect for a weekend away from it all. Though it rather spoilt the whole idea if one then brought a phone with one, she thought. And, while hating it like blazes if Latham was on the phone to some female of his acquaintance, making social arrangements for the week to come, she pondered on whether she should telephone her sister to check that all was well.

On the basis that to do so might cause her to have to tell yet more lies, Belvia decided against it, and came away from the window to busy herself making up the two beds. Besides, as she had told Latham, Josy quite liked her own company sometimes.

Belvia was just smoothing the fresh duvet-cover on the second of the twin beds when she heard Latham enter the cottage. The following sound she heard was his footsteps as he came up the stairs—and she froze.

She straightened when, hold-all in hand, he came directly to the room she was in. Oh, thank heaven! This room must be his; she was not going to have to share the room with the double bed with him.

'I th-thought this would be your room,' she commented quickly, only her initial stammer giving away her nervousness—perhaps he had not noticed it. 'I've made up these beds and the one in the other room. I thought that——'

'Slow down,' he suggested with a calm smile.

She supposed she had rather been gabbling on like some express train in her attempt to get it all said. She smiled—had to. She still loved him. 'I thought I'd sleep in the double bed tonight—by myself,' she added quickly, in case he thought differently. 'I can change the bedding in the morning.'

Latham, his eyes holding hers, dropped his hold-all down by his feet and came over to her; wonderfully, magically, his arms came out to her, and gently, tenderly, he gathered her to him. And for a while, held gently against him, she felt at peace. Oddly, she had the most uncanny feeling, when he seemed in no hurry to let her go, that he felt some sort of comfort to have her in his arms.

But then, to show just how crazy being in love with him had made her, Latham pushed her gently away from his entirely undemanding embrace and, to send her heart soaring, dropped a breeze of a kiss on the side of her face and demanded lightly, 'What are you going to cook me for my supper, woman?'

She took a step back from him, and a side-step in the direction of the door. 'You've only just had your lunch!' she laughed.

'What's that got to do with anything?' he wanted to know—and she got out of there quickly. She felt in danger of throwing herself back into his arms.

Dinner was an uncomplicated affair of tinned soup, salmon pasta and salad, with an option of chocolate gâteau or cheese and biscuits. They both elected to have cheese.

'I'll make the coffee,' Latham volunteered.

'Why not?' Belvia replied cheerfully, and cleared some of the meal-time debris away while he attended to the coffee.

They returned to the dining-room to take their coffee, and Belvia gave herself the sternest lecture on keeping a check on her cheerfulness, her smiles, if he were not to discern that, for her, the sun rose and set with him.

'Have you had this cottage long?' she enquired, and could have groaned aloud—he'd think she was a property freak or something. Hadn't she asked him one time how long he had lived in his London flat?

'Not so long,' he replied amiably, but before she could draw another breath he was preferring to go off on a tack of his own. 'You accused me today of having missed something—what else have I missed about you, I wonder?'

Belvia looked at him and felt quite weak inside about him. Which of course called for the sternest measures. 'I shall lie if I have to,' she told him, knowing from experience that he would not leave it there.

'I don't doubt it,' he grinned. And, as if recalling that morning in her home when, after he had read her note to her sister, she had said, 'Don't tell me you missed something,' he went on to refer to her note again by asking, 'Do I gather from your note, from your phone call to Tracey at the stables, that you've only been riding your sister's horse because she feels unable to do so herself—and not, as you allowed me to believe, from selfish motives only?'

'Hey, steady there, Mr Tavenner—go on like that and you'll be finding out I'm not so very terrible after all,' she warned, her insides playing havoc with her at the warm look that came to his eyes. It was time, she felt, to talk of something else. 'Do you ride?' she asked. 'But of course you do.'

'Do I?'

'You wanted Josy's opinion about a horse you were thinking of buying one time,' she reminded him, certain now, as she had been then, that he'd had no such intention.

'So I did,' he replied, but the devilish look in his eyes told its own story.

'And you've no doubt that *I'm* a liar?'

He gazed at her steadily for some moments before going back to the subject that had been under discussion. 'So, the moment you heard your sister's calamitous news, you took over the exercising of her horse and——' He broke off, and then, not a glimmer of a smile about him, 'When did you give up your job?' he asked suddenly, sharply.

'Three or four months ago,' she replied honestly, her thoughts too startled at this change of tack for her to think of disguising that fact, or even to wonder why she should.

'Three or four months ago!' he repeated. 'That was when your sister's husband was killed. That was the time when your sister needed you.' Belvia tried to think up a trite answer, but there wasn't one. 'For your sister, you gave up all hope of the career that you so dearly wanted,' he stated softly, 'and it wasn't from boredom with the work—as your father said.'

Oh, grief, Belvia panicked. She so wanted Latham's good opinion of her—yet if he thought for a single moment that her father had lied to him then, dealing in a world where a man's word was everything, she knew her father would not stand a chance of obtaining the huge finance he was after.

'I—er—thought it best to tell him I was bored with the job—otherwise he might have tried to persuade me to change my mind,' she invented, and, suddenly discovering that she was finding it harder and harder to lie to Latham, she sought desperately to think of something with which to change the subject. She found it in a question that had been in and out of her head several times that day. 'Oh, by the way, I never thought to ask——' she made her voice casual '—but who are your guests tomorrow?'

At once any sign of a warm light in his eyes vanished, and she almost wished she had kept her question to herself. Latham plainly did not care for her asking about his guests—and that annoyed her. For heaven's sake, she would know who they were tomorrow—she was going to have to cook for them, *and* play hostess!

She got to her feet and went to the kitchen, carrying her used coffee-cup and saucer with her, and consequently had her back to Latham when he followed her. She ignored him, and could see no earthly reason why she should speak to him.

Then she found, when he moved and took the cup and saucer out of her hand and placed them on the draining-board, that he had moved to face her. And, what was more, he was making her look at him when, in curt and clipped tones, he informed her, 'My guests tomorrow will be my sister Caroline, and her husband, Graeme Astill.'

Graeme Astill! That name rang a clear and very unpleasant bell with her. 'Oh—I know him!' she exclaimed jerkily, before she could stop herself—remembering Graeme Astill for the womaniser he was. She had been at a party, not a year ago, and he had been there—his wife not with him—acting in a very unmarried manner. She was faintly staggered to hear Latham say he was married to his sister.

'You have a problem with that?' Latham demanded grimly, the jerkiness of her exclamation not lost on him.

The fact that tomorrow she would share a bedroom with Latham, and could not see his brother-in-law keeping quiet about it at the next party he went to, made her feel uncomfortable. Some of her friends could quite easily be there too! 'And if I do?' she challenged sharply.

He looked at her grimly, a murderous light in his eyes. 'Tough,' he rapped, and, making her absolutely furious, 'You're far too free with your favours!' he added.

How she stopped herself from hitting him Belvia never knew. But, too furious to pause and analyse that remark, she somehow managed to hang on to a thread of dignity, though feeling that if she stayed near him another minute she would end up assaulting him. 'Thanks!' she snapped, and, as a red mist of rage came before her eyes, 'You're so good at making coffee—you can try your hand at washing-up!' she spat—and escaped quickly up to bed before that last thread of self-control split asunder.

CHAPTER SEVEN

BELVIA had thought she would not sleep a wink that night, but proof that she had slept was there in the fact that, having taken an age to drop off, she overslept, and was awakened by a voice in the region of the bedroom door asking sardonically, 'Do you intend to get up today?'

He sounded no more pleasant this morning than he had when, without a word of goodnight, she had left him with the washing-up. She eyed him acrimoniously— even as her heart accelerated its beat just to see him she determined that she did not like him very much that morning. 'Thanks for the tea!' she snapped sarcastically, and hated him when he favoured her with a disagreeable look and went out.

Swine, she dubbed him afresh, sat up in bed—and suddenly loved him with her whole heart. Because there reposing on the bedside table was a cup and saucer which hadn't been there when she had lain down last night. He *had* brought her a cup of tea.

What was more, when bathed and dressed she went down to the kitchen, she discovered that he had also tried his hand at washing-up because there was not a used utensil or piece of unwashed china to be seen.

At that moment the back door opened and Latham came in. 'Thanks for the tea,' she said a shade more civilly. He did not answer but, on thinking about it, there was not a lot he could say in reply. 'Have you had

breakfast?' she enquired, hating herself for wanting to
be pleasant to him but seeming unable to be any other
way. After tomorrow she would never see him again.

'About an hour ago,' he replied and, sensing censure,
Belvia gave up all half-formed thoughts of parting
friends. To the devil with it, she thought crossly, and
made breakfast for one.

After toast and coffee she went upstairs and stripped
the bed she had used and remade it with fresh bedlinen,
tidied and dusted and set about removing all traces of
her own occupation from the bedroom and bathroom.
Having placed all her belongings on the landing outside,
all she had to do was take her weekend case and im-
pedimenta to the other bedroom and bathroom.

She opened the door of the bedroom which Latham
had used last night, though as she stood and stared in
there was no sign that he had been there at all. Both
beds were made, so he must have made his.

Belvia went into the room, and pulling back the duvet
of the nearest bed, she saw that it had not been slept in.
Fine. She slipped her nightdress beneath the pillow, took
her toilet-bag into the bathroom and went to put the rest
of her belongings away. In all it took her about ten
minutes. But at the end of those ten minutes the fact
that she would be sleeping that night in this room, she
in one bed, Latham in the other, started to get to her.

In something of a hurry she left the room and went
downstairs, her feelings towards her host none too sweet.
He was in the kitchen having a cup of coffee, she observed, and she was then a mixture of regret that she
had not offered him one when she had made her own,
and of why the dickens should she? She had not asked

to be brought away from the safety of her own home. Let him make his own coffee—he was big enough!

She went over to the sink just as he stood up. 'We'll go for a walk,' he announced, sounding for all the world as if he felt caged in.

What a pity! she thought scratchily, and found the sweetest pleasure in replying, 'You go for a walk! *I'm* cleaning vegetables.'

He gave her a long-suffering look—though what he thought he had to be long-suffering about she did not know—and, having apparently changed his mind about going for a walk, went and found himself something to do outside.

Good, she fumed, and missed him, and wanted him back, and wanted to go for a walk with him—but peeled potatoes and parsnips and attended to beans and broccoli, and mixed the batter for a Yorkshire pudding.

Because she had to know, and because it was just too ridiculous not to ask, she went outside to find him once the chores she had set herself were completed. Though she did not have to look very far and he, if anything, more or less found her. Because if he had been listening for the sound of her leaving the house—and possibly decamping—he could not have appeared more quickly.

'Going somewhere?' he grated.

How could she go anywhere when, until tomorrow, Josy's peace of mind was still under threat? 'Just say the word!' she offered, weathered his arrogant look, and snapped, 'What time are your guests arriving?'

'Anxious to see them?' he snarled.

'You should go back to bed and get out the other side!' she erupted, suddenly felt panicky inside, and wished she had not mentioned that word 'bed'. 'Look here,

Tavenner,' she went on crossly, 'if I'm to be cook, then I need to know what time you need feeding.'

He surveyed her angry, mutinous expression with cool detachment for some seconds. 'We'll eat this evening,' he then announced, and, as she turned about, 'For now I'll make do with a sandwich.'

What did your last servant die of? she fumed inwardly as she did an about-turn and went back inside the cottage—and then wondered, how could she? How could she think and behave like that when she loved him so much?

She could, she realised only a minute later as she got out the makings of a sandwich, because while she might love him, he did not love her. And that, without him knowing it, was painful to bear. She wanted only to store up memories, happy memories of this short time with him. But there was little chance of that. Tomorrow it would be all over and their paths would never cross again, and while she wanted only to be loving and giving to him, she could not be, because whatever happened he must never know of her love for him.

'My sister will be here around three,' Latham announced while he ate his sandwich.

He sounded affable. 'Isn't your brother-in-law coming after all?' she asked.

His affability was an illusion. 'Does that worry you?' he snarled.

Belvia stared at him. 'God, somebody should have sorted you out when you were a child!' she flared.

'Fancy trying it?' he rapped, his jaw jutting at an aggressive angle.

'I haven't got that long!' she hissed—and suddenly, against all odds, while they were glaring angrily at each other, as his lips started to twitch, so hers did the same, and all at once they both burst out laughing. But she did not need to see him laughing and amused: their sense of humour melded as one, and... Oh, grief, she thought as he stopped and stared at her, and all she could think of to do was to order him to clear off. And, as if he was more or less thinking something of the same—he went.

Graeme Astill did arrive with his wife, but Belvia did not like him any better on meeting him for a second time than she had on the first. But good manners prevailed. She took an instant liking to Latham's sister who, in her opinion, was much too good for her husband.

'I wasn't sure what we were doing for a meal this evening.' Caroline, a tall blonde of about twenty-eight, smiled as she went into the kitchen with Belvia. 'If we're going out, fine, but if not, I've brought an apple pie— a favourite of Latham's—as my contribution.'

Belvia could have stayed listening to Caroline talk of her brother's likes and dislikes for the rest of the afternoon, but Caroline had nothing to add, and she realised that to ask anything would only show an interest in him which she would rather no one knew about. Though what did either of the Astills think she was doing there with him that weekend if she was not interested in him? Sharing a bedroom with him... Belvia blanked her mind off, and was glad that it was Latham who showed his sister and brother-in-law to their room.

Jealousy then started to nip when, with neither Caroline nor Graeme raising so much as half an eyebrow to see her there, she began to wonder if Latham was forever bringing some female away for a weekend in the country. Again she blanked her mind off, deciding that she would much rather not know.

It niggled away at her, however, and when Latham left his sister and brother-in-law upstairs and came out to the kitchen words she had not meant to say spilled from her tongue as if of their own volition. 'I expect you bring all your lady-friends here?' she questioned, and was instantly appalled, not only at her question but at the tart way she had asked it. And, even as she saw Latham halt, an alert look coming to his eyes followed by long moments of speculation, so she was searching frantically for something to add which would show that she was not the least bit interested.

He gazed at her intently, but replied tautly, 'If it worries you, apart from Caroline, you are the only female I've invited here.'

At once her jealous soul was eased. 'It doesn't worry me in the slightest!' she scorned, and, so that he should know the subject was done with, and not after all worth a mention, added, 'Caroline kindly brought an apple pie, so I won't have to bother making a pudding for afters.' He did not care a light. Since, however, he had brought her there for the sole purpose of cooking for his guests, she trotted out sarcastically, 'That is, unless you insist on my making something.'

He gave her a venomous look and she guessed he was finding her tedious. And that suited her fine. Though she began to wonder just what in creation went on in his head when, as afternoon gave way to early evening, he seemed to grow quieter and quieter.

Was it her imagination, or was he brooding about something? Was it just that, because of her love for him, she was over-sensitive where he was concerned? Was she,

in her love for him, her unrequited love for him, picking
up vibes which simply were not there?

She did not think so, but as she and Caroline served
dinner she watched him. He, she realised with something of a jolt as her glance caught his several times,
was watching her!

Heavens above, she was getting paranoid, she realised,
and determined as the fish starter gave way to sorbet,
which was followed by the main course, that she would
buck her ideas up. Since she had nothing she wished to
discuss with Latham, and had no wish whatever to
engage Graeme Astill in conversation, she was left
chatting with Caroline. Which, she discovered, was not
the smallest hardship. As she liked Caroline, so Caroline
seemed to like her.

Latham, as host, started the ball rolling, however, by
acquainting his sister with the fact that, like herself,
Belvia rode most days. He dropped out of the conversation while she and Belvia discussed the various merits
of their mounts. From there, although there was no connection, they seemed to slip naturally into a conversation on the latest fashions and, as the conversation
changed again and Latham entered it briefly, their chat
moved on and Belvia discovered that Caroline was quite
a good golfer.

'Do you play?' Caroline asked.

Belvia shook her head. 'Afraid not,' she smiled, but
was able to converse for a few more minutes on the golf
tournament her father was co-sponsoring the next day,
and then hear how Caroline had played that particular
course and thought it a good one.

Then she and Caroline cleared the used dishes away
and brought in the apple pie, which was delicious, and
Belvia said so.

'A small thing after that lovely meal you put together!' Caroline exclaimed. 'Did you bring everything with you, or did you buy locally?'

'Belvia and I raided a supermarket on the way down yesterday,' Latham cut in, and while Belvia's heart fluttered at how close his words seemed to make them—not that he meant it to be taken that way, of course—his sister looked at him in some astoundment.

'*You*—in a supermarket!' she exclaimed.

'Given a couple of cracked ankles from the occasional wayward trolley, I quite enjoyed the experience,' he replied, and Belvia so hoped he was speaking the truth, because she had loved it.

They adjourned to the sitting-room for coffee, where she was pleased to notice that Latham's brooding look had gone. Pleased, too, that she somehow found she was seated next to him on the settee, Caroline and Graeme in the two chairs at either side of the settee. Belvia owned to feeling all over the place to have Latham this near but, since she did not have to look at him unless she was speaking directly to him, she knew he would not discern any of what she was feeling.

Conversation over coffee was fairly general, but when after a while Latham got to his feet and said that he thought, in the circumstance of the two females having fed them, that the two males should do the washing-up, she thought it a brilliant idea. With luck, and remembering the mountain of washing-up out there, she might be fast asleep by the time Latham came up to share the bedroom.

'If no one minds, I think I'll go to bed,' she said as casually as she could. 'This country air...'

'I think I'll go up too,' Caroline chimed in, and Belvia could have hugged her.

'How kind!' her husband muttered—and Belvia realised that he was not too thrilled to be roped in to help with the dish-washing. But she was not concerned with his problems just then. In her view her problems were much more important than Latham's brother-in-law's—and he was a man she just could not take to.

'Night!' she murmured generally, and without so much as a flick of a glance to Latham she headed for the stairs—Caroline following.

They parted at the top of the stairs where Belvia, seemingly still casual, ambled to the room she would share with Latham. Once inside, however, the door closed to the outside world, she tore around—cleaning her teeth, taking the quickest shower on record and donning her nightdress.

Well within fifteen minutes, she would have sworn, she was in bed and ready to snick off the bedside light. She listened, but could hear no movement on or near the stairs. Good. Latham was still on kitchen fatigue and, if this morning was anything to go by, he liked to finish any job he started, and would use more time in putting all the saucepans and dishes away.

She put out the light, pulled the covers up way past her ears and tried desperately hard to fall asleep. She wanted to be sound asleep when Latham came up. She wanted to sleep solidly through the night and not to wake until Latham had left his bed in the morning.

But she could not fall asleep. What seemed like an hour later she opened her eyes, and found the room flooded with moonlight. Oh, heck—in her rush she had forgotten to close the curtains.

Belvia was on the point of getting out of bed to remedy that error when she heard a footfall on the stairs, and she stiffened and stayed still—she was not going anywhere.

By her calculations there were two pairs of feet coming up the stairs. She pulled the duvet closer around her ears and closed her eyes fast, while at the same time she aimed for rhythmic breathing.

Her rhythmic breathing fractured slightly when she heard the bedroom door open, and heard Latham come quietly into the room. He did not put on the light, and she concentrated hard on her breathing. Time seemed to crawl along agonisingly slowly for the next ten or twenty minutes as she lay listening to sounds that told her that Latham was in the habit of showering last thing at night too.

Then she heard the bathroom door close, heard Latham come and, it seemed, stand by the side of her bed—she was not going to open her eyes to find out. She was tense, and had the devil's own work to keep her breathing regular, and still could not relax when she heard the sound of the other bed taking his weight.

Annoyingly, and in no time flat, she heard the rhythm of his regular breathing. A moment later, though, and she knew that she should be glad that he had gone out like a light. Because it was not him she was afraid of, but herself. Had he touched her, given her so much as a peck on the cheek, she was so aware of him that she doubted she would have been able to hold back from wanting more. She loved him, was in love with him, and wanted, oh, so badly to be held in his arms.

For a further age she lay there listening to his even-paced breathing, loving him with all her heart, yet

knowing that in less than twenty-four hours it would be
all over, that she would never see him again. The thought
of never seeing him again was suddenly so dreadful that
she did not know how she could take it.

How long she lay awake being torn apart by thoughts
of never seeing Latham again, Belvia never knew. But
eventually a welcome sleep came to give her rest.

Though it seemed to her that one minute she was ready
to break her heart over Latham—and the next the bedside
lamp was on and he was sitting on her bed bending over
her, his hands on her upper arms as he called her name.

'Belvia, you're dreaming, wake up,' he was saying.

'What...?' She opened her eyes, took a shocked
breath. 'What...?' she gasped again, looking up into
his concerned face as she tried to take in where they were
and tried to get a grasp on reality.

'You were creating murder in your sleep,' he explained gently. 'Don't be alarmed, you're all right.'

'Oh, Latham!' she sighed, struggling to sit up. 'Was
I shouting?'

'So you do it often?' he asked, a hint of teasing
humour in his voice.

'Sometimes,' she smiled. 'When I'm disturbed about
something, usually—school exams, that sort of thing.'

'You're disturbed now, tonight?' he enquired, his
amusement fading.

But she wanted his amusement back—she did not want
to part with him on bad terms. 'Don't be cross,' she
pleaded, and could no more help it than fly: not wanting
to see his eyes grow cold, she leaned forward and rested
her head on his chest.

She felt him go rigid, knew that he was going to push
her away, but wanted just a few more moments. Then,

his voice more of a growl than anything, he grated, 'Damn it, Belvia—what do you think I'm made of?' and, as if he could not stop himself, his hands came to her arms again.

But instead of pushing her away, as she had been sure was in his mind, his grip on her arms became firmer. She pulled her head back and looked into his eyes. They were not cold, but warm.

Gently, their lips met. 'Oh, Latham,' she sighed.

'You're awake?' he growled. 'Am *I* the one who's dreaming?'

She loved him; she almost told him so. 'Kiss me,' she whispered, and he did, gathering her up in his arms, and it was beautiful. She moved closer to him.

She felt his mouth gentle on hers, then, as the pressure increased, her lips parted, and Latham pulled her closer to him. 'My dear,' he breathed, and she was in a transport of wonder that his endearment for her sounded so natural on his lips.

He kissed her again, gathering her yet closer to him, and as her arms went around him she suddenly became aware that his body was naked. 'Latham!' she gasped, vaguely realising that he must have shot out of bed without thought on hearing her yelling in her sleep.

'Belvia,' he murmured.

Oh, how she loved him; she could feel his body-heat through the thinness of her nightie, and it was, oh, so wonderful to be this close to him. She kissed him, was kissed in return, and adored him when he traced tender kisses down her throat, felt her heart pound when his hands caressed her back, and felt a fierce fire of need ignite in her when gently his fingers caressed their way to her breasts. With each swollen globe captive in his hold, she had not the smallest protest to make, but wanted to cry out his name again and again. Love me, she wanted to cry, and loved him.

Again they kissed, his hands caressing to her waist, and she was on fire for him. She pressed herself to him, and wanted to be closer still, and sighed with utter content when he pushed the duvet on to the floor and, reaching for her, lay down with her, their closeness assured because the width of the bed was meant only for one.

She moved herself joyously to him, heard him groan with desire, and felt only the merest hint of shyness when, finding that her nightdress had ridden up, he took hold of the hem. 'Do you really need this?' he breathed.

'N-No,' she replied jerkily, and kept close into him so that he should not see her body when, in next to no time, they were both kneeling on the bed while he divested her of her only piece of clothing and her nightdress joined the duvet on the floor. 'C-can you...? Would you—p-put the light out?' she asked into his shoulder.

'You're—embarrassed by your body?' he questioned into her ear, a most wonderful teasing note there in his voice, holding her close against him as he reached for the light switch.

She nodded. Then corrected, 'Not embarrassed, exactly. Shy, I think.'

'Shy?'

She wanted to tell him that she had never been naked with a man before—but she knew he would not believe her, and she was afraid that it would change his mood and he would take this wonderful time away from her. So she kissed him, and pressed her naked breasts against him, and heard him groan again—and knew that he had forgotten that he had asked a question.

Gently then he eased her body from him, and in the glow of the full moon his gaze embraced her. 'Your face is beautiful—and so is your body,' he murmured and, as if to salute her beauty, he placed a gentle kiss on her mouth—and bent his head to kiss each throbbing, hardened crown of her breasts. 'My darling,' he breathed, and she was enraptured.

Tenderly he laid her down on the mattress and leaned over her, tracing wonderful, mind-bending kisses on her mouth, her breasts, her belly and her thighs.

'Oh, Latham, darling,' she breathed shyly, 'I want you so much.'

'Sweet love,' he breathed, his voice thick in his throat, and gently eased his body over hers.

Belvia put her arms around him and held him to her tightly, her mouth dry at the feel of his all-maleness against her skin, a hint of panic whispering through her aching need for him.

'Oh, now, please,' she begged on a moment of courage.

'Soon, my dear,' he promised, and moved her, stroked her thighs and kissed her. Her body seemed to answer all the signals, for, as a few more minutes passed, the time seemed to be just right when Latham kissed her and placed himself where it seemed so right to her that he should be.

'Latham!' She called his name, and it was as if hearing his name on her lips was what he needed to hear, for, a moment later, he joined her to start the ultimate part of their lovemaking. But as he moved to her, she moved to him—and felt pain, which she had been too needful of him to think of. And, 'No!' she cried—and he stilled. In the next instant, so rapidly that she could not so quickly take it in, Latham had jerked from her as if shot, and was sitting stunned, staring at her in traumatised disbelief.

'You're—a virgin!' he croaked, and shook his head as if still not believing it.

With panicking hands she reached out and caught hold of his arms. He couldn't go away from her, not now. I love you, I love you, she wanted to tell him. 'Please, please don't be angry with me,' she pleaded. 'I did try to tell you before, only...'

'Only I wouldn't listen,' he answered and, seeming to make great strides to cope with his shock, went on, 'Hell's teeth, I'm not angry with you, my love—but myself. Oh, God,' he groaned, 'I must have terrified you!'

'No, you haven't,' she denied, ready then to deny she had ever known so much as a moment's panic.

'I should have guessed, should have seen. Your shyness, your...'

It was then that Belvia began to see just how sensitive the man she was in love with was. And she leaned forward and kissed him, cutting off his words, hoping to make him see that he had nothing to hate himself for.

'I'm sorry I said no,' she whispered, putting her arms around him, holding him close. 'I didn't mean, no, I didn't want to,' she hurriedly went on to explain. 'I think it was more—I hadn't realised there would be pain. I mean, I suppose I must have known, but...' Oh, heck, she was getting herself so tangled up in knots. She just left her explanation hanging there, and said instead, 'Please make love to me.' And again she kissed him, and while she kissed him her hands caressed his back. She pressed her breasts against him, heard a desperate kind of sound and took her mouth from his to kiss his chest, and moulded herself against him.

And at last, 'Dear love,' he breathed. 'You're sure this is right for you?'

'Oh, Latham, my darling,' she cried. 'I've never been more sure about anything. I need you, I want you so badly.' She kissed him again, and against his mouth she begged, 'Please, Latham.' And she felt him respond, his arms coming around her as he took over.

This time, though, in his awareness of her virginity, Latham put a rein on his passion. She was aware of it in the slow, delicate way he brought her to new heights, teasing her breasts to wanting peaks, caressing those swollen globes with his mouth, his tongue, gently, tenderly stroking her belly, her thighs.

'Oh, Latham,' she sighed, having no idea that she could feel like this, hoping with all she had that it was the same for him. She stroked his body too.

And at last, tenderly, gently, Latham returned to her, and this time she did not cry out. For, with a wealth of consideration for the pain he must cause her, Latham moved with her in restrained passion. Moved and checked and moved, and stayed with her until he had made her totally his.

Later Latham cradled her in his arms to sleep and Belvia just could not get over it. He was wonderful—kind, gentle and overwhelmingly sensitive. She lay for some while with her eyes closed, sleep starting to tiptoe in. She felt Latham place a light kiss on her hair, and knew contentment and nothing more, until she opened her eyes again and discovered that it was daylight.

Contentment had caused her to have her best night's sleep—or what had been left of the night—since she had first met Latham. Her mental anguish seemed to have flown, for surely no man could be so gentle, so considerate, so tenderly loving if he did not feel some kind of regard for her?

She stirred in her bed and knew that, at some time while she slept, Latham must have gone to sleep in the other bed. She smiled a loving smile. Poor darling, he had waited until she had gone to sleep but must have been cramped beyond enduring while he waited for sleep to claim her.

Simply because she had to look at him she eased herself over to face the other bed and, feeling dreadfully shy suddenly—he could be awake too—she had to take another second or two before she could look across the yard or so of carpet that separated the two beds. She raised her eyes—but the other bed was empty.

For about a minute more she lay there, realising that he must be an early riser and, seeing that she was still sound asleep, must have moved especially quietly so as not to wake her. A smile touched her mouth again at his thoughtfulness. But all at once she was realising that when she went downstairs she was going to have to greet him in front of his sister and her husband.

That thought prompted her into speedy action to get bathed and dressed. While she did not doubt that Latham was sophisticated enough for him to greet her without any outward show of the closeness they had shared, she recalled her latent inclination to blush when he was around—and that was before they had lain naked with each other. By that scale of reckoning, the least she could expect was that she would go a brilliant crimson the next time she saw him.

Her hope, as she hurried down the stairs to greet Latham in private, was doomed the moment she reached the kitchen. 'I'm just making coffee—fancy one?' Caroline Astill asked her with the cheeriest of smiles.

'Love one,' Belvia responded, unable to see any sign of Latham as she busied herself getting a couple of cups and saucers out of a cupboard. And, not asking the question she wanted to ask—did Caroline know where Latham was?—she instead queried casually, 'Graeme not down yet?'

'He's gone,' Caroline informed her, something in her voice alerting Belvia to the fact that he was not merely out walking.

'Gone—where?' she enquired carefully.

'I don't know,' Caroline replied, but added, almost to herself, and as though it was a matter of some great relief, 'And I've only just realised I don't really care.'

'You—don't care?'

'I did, very much. To start with I was so much in love with him that I put up with his inconstant love.'

'Oh,' Belvia murmured. Poor Caroline. It sounded as if she knew of her husband's affairs with other women.

'Oh, indeed,' Caroline commented and, bringing two cups of coffee over to the kitchen table, she sat down and, as Belvia followed suit continued, 'Up until this morning, when I came down and saw him fall unconscious to the floor, I'd thought I was still in love with him, but——' She broke off when she observed Belvia's amazed expression.

'Graeme was unconscious? He'd been drinking...?'

Caroline shook her head. 'Latham flattened him!'

'Latham did?' Belvia was astounded. 'He hit him?'

'Knocked him clean out,' Caroline answered, and confided, 'He'd been asking for it for years, and it was beautiful to see—which is how I suddenly knew that the love I'd had for him all these years was dead. That he was a habit, and that I no longer needed him.'

There did not seem any appropriate remark to make to that, and as all that Caroline had said started to settle in her mind, so Belvia more urgently than ever wanted to know where Latham was. Had he been very upset? Must have been, she supposed. You could not knock someone out stone-cold without being furious about something. Oh, poor darling Latham. He had probably hit him from anger at the way he treated his sister. She recalled then that, while observing such courtesies as having him for a house-guest demanded, Latham had not been over-affable with him yesterday.

'Is Latham out walking?' she asked, realising that he could well have gone for a walk to cool down after flooring his brother-in-law. She was left gaping at Caroline's reply.

'He's gone back to London,' she informed her, and, catching Belvia's open-mouthed look, 'I'm sorry, didn't he say?'

'I—um—overslept.' Belvia's pride came to her aid. Her hopes, her dreams, might be fracturing about her, but she was the only one who was going to know it. 'I expect he would have said had I not been such a sleepy-head.'

'He said something about having some business to attend to. It must have been important business too——' Caroline smiled '—or he'd never have gone.' Belvia smiled back to show that it did not hurt and, seeing her smile, Caroline tacked on, 'He barely waited to blow on his knuckles after decking Graeme, then he was off.'

'That's the way it is in business,' Belvia replied and, borrowing some of Caroline's cheerfulness, she got up from the table, consulting her watch without seeing the dial. 'I suppose I'd better do something about getting back to London myself.'

'I'm returning to London myself shortly—I'll give you a lift, if you like,' Caroline offered in a friendly way.

'Didn't Graeme take the car?' Belvia paused to ask.

'It's my car, and I have the keys. With luck we might see him hitching it if we hurry. We'll give him a toot,' she added with happy maliciousness.

Belvia had to smile—but up in the room she had shared with Latham, she felt more like breaking her heart. Oh, how could she have been so unutterably foolish? The realisation that there had been nothing special for him in their lovemaking last night, nothing special at all—and that she was no more to him than some cheap, one-night fling—was crucifying.

It did not take her long to gather her belongings and to pack them, but she was so churned up inside that her hands were shaking as she fastened the catches on her case, and she just had to take a few minutes more in trying to calm herself.

Latham had been so wonderful, so sensitive with her last night, she could not help recalling, and then found that tears were streaming down her face. Oh, damn him, damn him to hell. No one had the right to make anyone feel the way she was feeling now.

Belvia dried her eyes and checked that there was no sign of her tears, then took her case downstairs. She left Caroline to lock up and did not know if she was glad or sorry that Caroline, after her initial confidence, was fairly silent on the journey back to London. She, too, plainly had a lot on her mind.

With too much time to think, Belvia tried to concentrate her thoughts during the journey on anything but Latham. But again and again he was there in her head. She recalled, painfully, how it had not been her he was interested in at all anyway, but Josy. He had done the gentlemanly thing and backed off when she had explained about her sister's recent bereavement—though it was she who'd had to pay the price.

Belvia quickly cancelled that last thought. She had no idea why he had taken her in exchange for her sister, so to speak—and she certainly was not going to ring him up and ask him. But she had no reason to complain. He had wanted a cook, and she had cooked. But it was she who had wanted him to make love to her, and he had. They had made beautiful love, but not before—at his first knowledge that she was a virgin—he had broken from her. She had urged him to stay—she had been a more than willing partner.

Caroline dropped her off at her home, apologising for not being very good company. 'It's just dawning on me that I've no one to please but myself—I think I'm going to enjoy it,' she grinned, and Belvia saw so much of Latham in his sister's grin that she could barely speak.

'Have fun!' she smiled, added her thanks for the lift and an invitation to come in for coffee and, when Caroline suggested another time, went indoors, to find Josy looking more alive than she had for a long time.

'How's Kate?' Josy asked, before Belvia could ask if anything had happened to put that light of interest in her sister's eyes.

'K——?' Belvia bucked her ideas up to remember that she had used Kate as an excuse for being away for the weekend. She evaded another outright lie. 'Anything happening here I should know about?' she enquired.

'Several things, actually,' Josy replied. 'Er—shall I make some coffee while you take your case upstairs?'

Belvia went upstairs, washed her hands and ran a comb through her hair, and caught a defeated look in the wide brown eyes that looked back at her. Since she and Josy were often so attuned to each other's smallest upset, she knew that she was going to have to guard with all she had against Josy seeing how emotionally shattered she felt.

She put her own haunted feelings to the back of her mind and returned downstairs to find that Josy had brought a tray of coffee into the sitting-room. 'So,' she encouraged, recollecting that Josy had said several things had happened, 'what happened first?'

Josy carefully poured her a cup of coffee and passed it over. 'Well, to begin with, I've been having quite a lot of private battles with myself just lately, in connection with Hetty.'

'Hetty?'

'Mm,' Josy confirmed. 'It seemed to me that I just wasn't being fair expecting you to exercise her for me the whole time.'

'Oh, love, I don't mind,' Belvia exclaimed at once.

'I know you don't—you've been marvellous. Anyhow, that hasn't stopped me from being unhappy about not exercising her myself. Anyway, I was feeling doubly guilty on Friday when I read your note and knew you'd had to consider me and Hetty before you could go to stay with Kate for the weekend.'

'Go on,' Belvia urged quickly, not needing to add guilt for telling lies to the rest of her unhappiness.

'Well,' Josy continued, 'it bothered me the whole of Friday, but I did nothing about it. I don't know now if I actually would have done anything about it if...' Her voice tailed off, and Belvia looked at her with renewed interest, sensing that something pretty gigantic had taken place in her absence.

'If?' she prompted.

'If Marc's cousin had not called in.'

'Marc's cousin—from France?'

'You've never met him. I only met him the one time myself—the day Marc and I arrived in France. He wasn't at Marc's funeral, but he's in England on some business or other,' Josy explained. 'Anyhow, I gave him coffee, and somehow, probably because Marc and I met at a stables, we seemed to naturally get round to talking about horses. Somehow, too, he began to tell me how he had a couple of mounts but how, with him being away so much, he needed someone reliable to look after them.' She took a hard swallow, and then said, 'Suddenly, as we were speaking, he all at once stopped, and then said, "I don't suppose you'd be interested in the job?" going on to tell me that he thought it might be a shade too quiet for me because he lived in an isolated spot with not too many people around.'

'You didn't say yes?' Belvia stared at her in disbelief.

'No. I said no straight away. But, since he had offered me the job, I felt that a straight no was a bit blunt, so I qualified it by telling him that I hadn't had anything to do with horses since Marc died—and he just looked at me and said, "Don't you think that you should," and talked quietly to me for quite some while—with the end result being that he wanted to see where Marc worked, and...'

'You've been up to the stables!'

'And ridden Hetty,' Josy replied to her amazement. 'And...' She got up out of her chair and seemed the same nervous Josy she had been before Belvia went away as she went over to the window and straightened two folds in the curtains before she went on. 'And before he left he asked me to consider most carefully taking on the job, to consider going to France, be it only for six months.'

'And—you have?' Belvia queried, trying to keep her astonishment hidden. This had to be Josy's decision. She must not attempt to influence her in any way. While it seemed to her, bearing in mind Josy's shy temperament, to be too tremendous a step for her to take, Belvia recalled how Josy seemed to have a penchant for occasionally surprising her and doing something entirely out of character. Look at how, when Belvia would have said the odds were more for her remaining forever a spinster, she had taken that other tremendous step and had got married.

'I'm—still thinking about it,' Josy confessed. 'But— what about Father?'

'What about him?'

'He'll hit the roof if I suggest I won't be here to housekeep for him.'

'Let him pay for a housekeeper. If he can afford to part-sponsor a golf tournament, he can afford that expense.'

'Oh, Bel, I'm so glad you're back,' Josy cried, as if Belvia had killed off some of her dragons, and then, her attention arrested by something the other side of the

window, her tone quickened. 'If I did go to France for
a while, though, I'd have no need to worry about Latham
Tavenner, would I?' she exclaimed.

Belvia's breath caught at just the sound of his name—
oh, how she wished that she could hate him. 'You don't
have to worry about him any more,' she assured her
quietly, and, not wanting Josy to be upset ever again,
she told her that which she knew to be fact. 'I promise
you, Jo, you'll never see him again.'

It was she who was the more upset of the two this
time, however, because, to show just how very much she
had got that wrong, Josy replied, 'I will. He's just pulled
up on the drive!'

For all of ten seconds Belvia went through the gamut
of emotions, so that she was incapable of coherent
thinking. Then, even while her brain-patterns were all
over the place, she started to grow angry. How dared he
come here and badger Josy? How dared he, after...

Suddenly she caught her sister's worried look on her.
'I'll deal with him,' she stated, wanting to run a mile
and crown him, all at the same time. 'How about you
go into the kitchen and see about making Father's
favourite pudding? It might sweeten him up if you decide
you have anything you want to tell him.'

Josy did not hang about but, expertly scooping up
cups and saucers on to the tray as she went, carried the
tray out from the sitting-room and, as the doorbell
sounded, went kitchenwards.

Belvia waited until her sister was clear of the hallway,
then went to the front door. But, with her legs suddenly
feeling like so much jelly, she had to lean against the
stout oak door for quite some seconds. Then, impatiently, the doorbell sounded again—and Belvia,

striving all the time for control, put her hand to the handle. For her own sake, for the sake of her pride—and he had left her with little enough of that—she had to be strong. He might have taken her to bed, but it was Josy he was after.

CHAPTER EIGHT

BELVIA kept her eyes lowered as she pulled back the front door but, as her gaze travelled up the long length of him, she at last had to look at him. And, as she had known she would, she blushed a furious crimson.

'My——' he began, his eyes on her face, her colour.

But she did not need any sarcastic comments from him—even if his expression did not seem to be particularly sarcastic—and from somewhere she found the acid she needed to snap tartly, 'I thought you promised to keep away from my sister!'

'You don't seriously still believe——' He broke off, seemed oddly at a loss for words, but then took what seemed to her to be a long breath, as though groping for self-control—though what he needed self-control for, she failed to see. But it appeared he had the control he needed, for his voice was even, stern almost, when he continued, 'It seems I've more explaining to do than I realised—are you going to let me come in?'

Oh, why did he have to come here? She wanted to see him, of course she did, but all she had been to him was a one-night indulgence and that did not need *any* explaining!

'Come in—if you must.' She denied her fast-beating heart even as she hated herself for her weakness. Any explaining he wanted to do could be done in two minutes on the doorstep, surely?

Having been weak enough to accede to his request, however, she turned about, leaving him to follow her into the sitting-room. Once there, though, she was undecided whether to sit down as her shaky limbs required or, since this could not possibly take very long, remain standing.

The matter was settled for her when Latham closed the sitting-room door and went over to the couch and waited, clearly asking her permission to be seated. By that time she was afraid to speak in case she gave away, by word or look, a hint of how she felt about him.

She went over to one of the easy chairs and, by taking possession of it, let her action speak for her. Latham followed suit and, seated on the couch, turned to face her. Oh, Lord, how dear he was to her!

She lowered her eyes, studied his shoes without really seeing them—but suddenly started to grow angry. Who the devil did he think he was that he could be the way he had been with her last night and then, without so much as a word, troll off this morning when business beckoned—and then come calling at her home, as casual as you like? Dammit, what the devil did he think *she* was!

'I'm surprised you expected to find me here!' she snapped tartly, raising her eyes to give him the full benefit of her hostility.

'I knew you'd be here,' he replied calmly, bearing her hostility very well.

'You knew!' She added lying to his list of crimes. 'How could you know? You left me stranded at...' Her voice tailed off. Oh, what a fool she was—she had not meant to refer to that wonderful, sublime time in Wiltshire.

'It wasn't my intention to leave you stranded,' Latham assured her, and when she stared at him, not ready to believe a word of it, went on, 'I went back to Rose Cottage for you, only——'

'You've been back to Rose Cottage!'

'Of course I have!' he confirmed straight away. 'Leave aside my feelings when I got there and found the place locked up.' *He* had feelings! Before her startled thoughts could sort themselves out, though, he was going on. 'The obvious thing to do was to ring Caroline to enquire if she'd seen anything of you.'

'She told you she'd given me a lift.'

He nodded, and added with bone-melting gentleness, 'I wish you had waited.'

Oh, no, please don't, the weakness in her for him implored, 'You know, somehow I just knew that I'd end up being the one in the wrong!' Her mouth overrode her weakness.

'Oh, love——' he smiled '—I deserve everything you throw at me.'

She wanted neither his endearments nor that wonderful, quite marvellous, twitch of his lips. She looked at her watch without the least interest in what time of day it was. 'If I could ask you to finish your explanation,' she suggested pointedly. 'My father will expect his lunch on the table at one o'clock sharp, and Josy likes me to—um—mix the Yorkshire pudding.' Why should Latham Tavenner have the prerogative of lying?

'Your father's part-sponsoring a golf tournament today,' Latham replied with a level look.

She knew that, but she had not expected him to remember. 'So he is, but that doesn't mean that he has to personally attend. He will, of course, later—to present some of the prizes.' Having started to lie, she found herself in too deep not to continue. 'But he always has liked his Sunday lunch at home.'

'He hasn't been to the tournament yet, then?'

'Not yet,' she confirmed. 'So if——' She broke off. Latham was looking at her with a look on his face which she found hard to distinguish. It seemed to fall midway between amusement and—affection!

Affection! scoffed her head, but she was all ears when Latham asked, 'Did I once say you were priceless?' And then, causing her heart to race feverishly, 'You, my dear,' he added, 'are above price.'

Much more of this and she would be forgetting about pride, forgetting that she had to live with herself once he had gone. 'Now what did I do?' she questioned snappily.

'Blatantly lied, for a start,' he replied urbanely.

'You can talk!' she retorted—but couldn't resist asking, 'How did I lie? When did I lie—er—recently?'

'Recently, not five minutes ago.'

'You're suggesting my father is not at home——?'

'I'm not merely suggesting, I'm stating it for a fact,' he cut in unequivocally. And, even as her mouth started to form the word 'how', he was metaphorically pulling the rug from under her feet by adding, 'He was at the golf tournament when I went to see him first thing this morning.'

'You've been to see my father?' she questioned in astonishment, the fact that she had been found out in her 'blatant' lie not seeming to be of importance just then.

'I have,' he agreed.

'But—but...' she spluttered—and got a few more words together to accuse hostilely, 'You didn't think to

mention at any time yesterday that you were going to
see him this morning!'

'I didn't mention it because I didn't know then,' he
replied.

Which left her without argument. She gave what she
hoped looked like a careless shrug. 'I confess your way
of doing business seems a little haphazard, but——'

'I didn't go to see your father on a business matter,'
Latham stated before she could finish.

Her eyes shot wide—he'd gone to see her father on a
personal matter! Her foolish heart started to race—and
then she remembered, and something inside her froze.
'Josy,' she said, and that was all. But Latham
understood.

Why, then, he shook his head she could not tell. Nor
could she believe it when, his eyes steady on hers, he
told her categorically, 'I was never, at any time, interested
in Josy.'

Not for one single solitary moment could she believe
it. 'I should thank God your name's not Pinocchio, if
I were you—otherwise the length of your nose would hit
the other side of this room.'

She stood up, impatient with him that he could tell
such lies, and impatient with herself that there was
something in her that wanted to believe him, whatever
outrageous lie he uttered.

She presented him with her back, loving him even while
she hated him—and knew herself for a fool once more
when, leaving the couch, he came and stood behind her,
placing his hands in a gentle hold on her upper arms.
She should have moved away, but she felt helpless to do
so. She wanted him to hold her. He had held her oh, so
gently last night.

She tried to banish such reminders, and then Latham was speaking again, and was saying, 'My dear, I don't want to hurt you but, in order to clear away all lies and deceits between us, hurt you I'm afraid I must,' and her mouth went dry. His tone, those words 'between us', as if 'us' mattered, made her want to hear every word he had to say. Made her want to stay and listen to what he had to explain—no matter how hurt it sounded as if she might be in the process.

'It—concerns me, then?' she asked chokily, and did not know where to look when Latham turned her round to face him.

'You're trembling,' he murmured.

'It's the weather,' she replied, and nearly died when he brushed a feather-light kiss on her brow.

'Come and sit down,' he urged, and led her not back to the chair she had occupied but to the couch. And it did nothing to quiet her trembling when he sat down on the couch beside her.

'So,' she said as she strove desperately to get herself back together, 'You went to see my father—on a personal matter, you said?'

'That's right,' he agreed, but added very carefully, 'Though, at the beginning, before you and I had met, it was your father who came to see me.'

'Ah!' Belvia exclaimed, and only then realised that, when so much had taken place between her and Latham, she was going to have to remember at all times that her father still wanted him to invest in Fereday Products. 'Hmm—my father came to see you about some business, I expect?' she queried.

But to her astoundment Latham replied, 'No,' going on, 'And if I could spare telling you what I have to, I

would. But I insist you know the truth before...' He
checked, took a deep and steadying breath, and seemed
to change direction when he went on quietly, 'Perhaps,
to save you from tying yourself in knots in trying to
make me think well of your father, I should state that
I now know everything there is to know about him—
including the fact that he's anxious for my company to
invest in his.'

'Oh!' Belvia exclaimed, not certain she did not grow
a little pink about the cheeks.

'Don't be embarrassed,' Latham smiled, watching her,
and nearly sank her yet again when, seeming sensitive
to her every thought, he carefully stated, 'What lies between you and me has nothing to do with money.'

She stared at him for long seconds and knew then that,
whatever it was he had to explain, she wanted to hear
every word. More, as her intelligence started to function
again, she wanted to know, since Latham was again referring to their two selves, what in heaven's name her
father had to do with any of it. She thought it was time
she began to find out.

'You—um—suggested that the first time my father
came to see you—it was not about business.'

'It seemed not—though it's only today that I found
out that that was just a ploy.' Oh, grief! She wanted the
floor to open up and swallow her. Latham too, by the
sound of it, had now learned just how devious her father
could be for his own ends.

'He—er—didn't ask you to invest straight away?'

'Business was never mentioned,' Latham replied and,
making her head all haywire again, he took a gentle hold
of both her hands and held them firmly in his. He seemed
reluctant as he added, 'What your father came to see

me about was the——' his grip tightened '—the affair which he knew you were having with my brother-in-law.'

'The aff——' Witlessly, she stared at him. '*Me*!' she exclaimed, her tone shocked. 'But—but I never——'

'Don't you think I *know* that?' Latham cut in. 'My dear, don't I know, more than anyone, that you've never had an affair in your life?' Warm colour stained her skin again, and suddenly Latham let go of one of her hands and placed an arm about her shoulders. 'Sweet Belvia,' he entreated, 'can you not see how it was with me? How I couldn't rest until I had everything sorted out?'

She was still striving to recover from hearing that her father had gone to him with some tale that she was having an affair with Caroline's husband. But at what Latham had just said her hopes started to rise. 'Is—is that why you—um—rushed off this morning?' Had he gone from her because he thought her—important?

'It was more than time somebody started to be fair to you,' he replied, and Belvia looked at him, loved him, and knew she was never going to be able to concentrate—not while he had his arm about her.

She moved a few inches from him, pulling out of his arm, pulling her hand from his hold. 'Perhaps you'd better start at the very beginning,' she requested, as evenly as she could.

Latham studied every detail of her face. 'It won't be pleasant,' he warned, and she could not help thinking, as he continued to watch her, that should any of what he had to say seem too much for her he would stop immediately—which was enough for her to determine to mask her emotions as much as possible. She wanted, needed, to hear all that there was to hear.

'Caroline told me over the phone,' he began, 'that because of an empathy she immediately felt with you, she found herself telling you of her husband's unfaithfulness to her.'

'I knew beforehand,' Belvia admitted. 'He was at a party I was at this past year. We were introduced and someone told me he was married—but you'd never have known it from the way he was behaving. Caroline's well rid of him.'

'I couldn't agree more. She's had far more to put up with than any woman should.' He paused, and quietly added, 'He's in the middle of some affair right now.'

Belvia stared at him. 'And you thought, because of what my father said, that I was the woman he was having an affair with?'

'I didn't just take your father's word for it,' he replied. 'To tell it as it is, Caroline has been married to Astill for five years, and in those five years for my sister's happiness—since she stated she still wanted him— I've bought off as many women. When some months ago I recognised that look in her eyes that said she was hurting again, I employed a top-class private investigatory firm I'd used before to find out who the current woman was.'

'Good heavens!' Belvia exclaimed, this being a whole new world to her. 'You bought that woman off too?'

But Latham shook his head. 'This time Astill was playing it very cagily, and the investigators, although still on to it, were coming up with nothing.'

'You're sure he was having an affair?'

'That was beyond doubt. Who with, however, was what I needed to know, for my sister's sake.'

'Graeme Astill must have known about the private detectives you'd put on to him before.'

'Caroline, in a weak moment of their last reconciliation, told him of it.'

'I see,' Belvia commented, realising that Graeme Astill, as Latham had said, had been playing this one cagily rather than have his brother-in-law spoil his fun for him. 'But...' She stopped, unable to see any tie-in here with her father. Even while she felt bruised that her father could apparently go to a stranger and say that she was the one Graeme Astill was having an affair with, questions suddenly started queuing up to be answered.

'I don't understand any of this,' she admitted helplessly. 'Why would my father tell you I was having an affair with Caroline's husband when I wasn't? What good...? And how did my father know he was having an affair anyway? And...' Her voice faded as her intelligence really got to work. 'I didn't know my father even knew Graeme Astill!'

'He doesn't,' Latham replied, adding swiftly, 'According to your father, when I insisted this morning on knowing everything there was to know, he'd listened in to an intimate phone conversation his secretary had with Astill some weeks ago.'

Even while Belvia felt slightly sickened—any other person accidentally happening on an intimate conversation would drop the phone like a hot coal, but not her father—she was gasping, 'Vanessa Stanley! Is she the one...?'

'There was not the slightest doubt, your father said, that the two were having an affair. Just as there was no doubt—my name coming up, apparently, and the fact that I was furious to know who the woman was—that they were taking every precaution to prevent me from finding out.'

'Your brother-in-law didn't want you buying Vanessa off?' Belvia queried as she quickly digested that indeed Vanessa Stanley was the one.

'I doubt very much that he mentioned she might be rewarded to give him up, but he no doubt fed her some plausible line about why their affair must remain most secret.'

'But...' She was starting to grow a touch confused, so sought to pin her thoughts on the most basic knowledge. 'So—while my father knew about their affair, neither Vanessa nor your brother-in-law was aware that anyone else knew.'

'They thought they had been much too clever—and but for that phone call, they had,' Latham agreed.

'Yes, but I still don't see——' She broke off. Knowing her devious father well, all at once, with a clarity that was nauseating, she did begin to see. And—while she could hardly credit that her father would use her so— she was quietly stating, 'My father thought that, if he came to you with this piece of information, you'd be so pleased you would look favourably on his request—at some future date naturally——' he could be both devious and wily, her father '—for investment...'

'Had he been speaking the truth, I should, of course, have felt very much indebted to him.'

'But you didn't know he wasn't speaking the truth until...' Oh, grief! It was only last night that he had found out... She flicked a glance at Latham; he looked warmly back at her and reached for her hands. But she took them out of his range. She needed a clear head— even his warm look was devastating, without the feel of his skin against hers. 'So—my father came to you and said that I was the woman your brother-in-law was having an affair with,' she went on, striving desperately hard to keep her head straight.

'Your father's much more subtle than that, Belvia,' Latham replied gently. 'At first he wouldn't tell me anything, but said that he needed to contact my brother-in-law quite urgently—and did I know where he could be found? I suggested he rang him at home, but in the ensuing conversation gathered that he wanted to contact him without my sister knowing.'

'Ah! That was when your protective antennae for your sister went on red alert?'

'Antennae for our sisters we share, you and I,' Latham commented softly, and her heart raced, and her insides fluttered at his tone—and Belvia had to try harder than ever to keep her head straight.

'What happened then?' she asked firmly.

'The upshot was,' Latham answered, seeming now to want it all said and done with quickly, 'what with my refusing to say where he might find my brother-in-law until he told me more, your father had to "reluctantly" confess that Astill was having an affair with his daughter, and that he wanted it stopped.'

Belvia looked away from him, embarrassed that her father could have gone to him with such a tale, embarrassed that Latham should know that her father cared so little for her.

She swallowed hard when she felt Latham take her hands in his warm clasp, and she had never loved him more when he said, as though seeing her embarrassment, as if trying to ease it and her hurt, 'His business is in sorry trouble, my darling.'

Oh, Latham, she thought in panic, her embarrassment and pain swiftly sent on their way by that utterly unbelievable 'my darling'. Perhaps he always calls every woman he has made love to 'my darling', she made herself think—anything rather than believe, because she loved him so, what her heart wanted to believe—that his 'my darling' meant that he had a little caring for her.

'Having learned who "the woman" was, having believed my father, you told him to leave it with you—that you would stop it for him?' Belvia questioned, as coolly as she was able.

'I saw no reason to disbelieve him,' Latham owned. 'Though naturally I went and saw Astill and confronted him with the fact that I knew your name.'

'He didn't deny it?' she questioned, startled.

'He looked astonished when I trotted out your name—as well he might,' Latham replied. 'Only I thought his astonishment stemmed from the fact that I'd found out what he was trying to keep a closely guarded secret. But he recovered fast and, as quick-thinking and as devious as your father, must have realised that if I thought you were the one it would give him more freedom with the Stanley woman. And I was left in the frustrating position of being unable to lay a fist on him—because Caroline still wanted him and because of the promise I'd made to her—and, because your father had said you had money of your own, of being unable to attempt to buy you off.'

'Why didn't you come and ask me about it?' she asked, entirely unthinkingly, then halted in her tracks. 'You would never have believed any denial I made, anyway, would you?'

'For my sins—I confess, no. Though not without cause,' he added.

'What cause...?' she began, then remembered. 'I confirmed it for you myself, didn't I?—that night we met, that night when you came to dinner and...'

'And you went out, tossing into the room those immortal words, "After dinner is the only time he can get away from his wife".'

'No wonder you looked furious!'

'Furious, and more determined than ever to put a stop to it. By that time I'd reasoned that either you were as brazen as hell, or that Astill, rather than have you warned off, had kept it to himself that I knew you were his mistress. I realised too that, as we'd agreed, your father had said nothing to you about the fact that I knew.'

'Why would he say anything?' Belvia put in, not liking her father very much just then.

'Try not to be upset,' Latham pressed. 'The whole thing's a mess, a nightmare. But once we've got it all unravelled...' That warm look was in his eyes again—and suddenly Belvia found herself in a state of not knowing what to believe in any more, and looked quickly away.

'Why did you accept my father's invitation to dinner that night?' she asked, again hoping that if she went back to the beginning it might be of some help.

'Your father had stressed that, while your sister would do anything he asked of her, you were as intractable as the devil. But, to my mind, while you plainly did not hold the sanctity of marriage in the same high regard that he did, I felt that, intractable or no, you must have a weak spot somewhere. I needed to see you, preferably over a meal, where you'd be forced to spend more than a few minutes in my company.'

'Did you find it—my weak spot?'

'Astonishingly quickly. No sooner had I seen the way you were hovering protectively over your sister while your father introduced Josy and me than I knew that there were no lengths you wouldn't go to for her. That protection of Josy was further endorsed, should I have needed it endorsing, when each time I tried to engage her in conversation you answered for her.'

Belvia realised that, since he was so protective of his own sister, that same trait in her must have been easily recognisable. She let go a long-drawn breath as she suddenly recalled how he had categorically stated that he had never at any time been interested in Josy. 'You decided to try to get through to intractable me by using my sister?' she asked.

'I'd never seen anything so clear-cut, so evident,' he replied. 'I saw at once that I had only to make the smallest play for your shy sister—and you would be in there protecting her like a shot.'

'You thought to ask me to give up your brother-in-law in exchange for not pursuing Josy?'

'That was perhaps the obvious thing to do. But, discussing that solution with your father—and we've been in frequent touch throughout,' he inserted, 'he—who knew you better than me, remember—felt you would verbally agree to give up Astill but would continue with your clandestine meetings and tell Astill, who would only become more cagey than ever. Which left me deciding that, to limit your time with your lover, I would, for a start, take you on myself.'

'You were so certain I would go out with you? That Josy would go out with you?'

'Josy, so your father said—and, remember, I'd no idea of what little game he was playing in the background— would agree if he mentioned that it would please him if she would do so. But you, love, as I recall, I didn't have to invite out at all those first couple of times—you just turned up.'

'But—you weren't expecting me, that first time. That time I arrived in the car you sent you were expecting Josy.'

'I was expecting none other than you, believe me,' Latham corrected her quietly. 'I knew before I rang Josy on Monday that your father had that morning spoken with her on the subject of her being more friendly to his guests in future. Just as I knew that she would come looking for you the moment after she'd agreed to come out with me that evening.'

'You probably also knew that I'd try to phone you to say she couldn't come,' Belvia suggested, and he smiled, and her heart fluttered crazily.

'Your father rang to tip me off about ten seconds before you rang,' he owned. 'Just enough time for me to instruct my PA that I was out of town should any Miss Belvia Fereday ring.'

'But—you say you were expecting none other than me,' Belvia reminded him and, as she remembered, 'You looked amazed to see me—as if you couldn't believe...!'

'If I stared at you when you got out of that car, my dear, it was not from amazement,' he interrupted, 'but because I was stunned.'

'Stunned?'

Latham nodded. 'Quite simply, I thought you the most lovely creature I'd ever seen.'

'You d-did?' she croaked.

'Oh, yes,' he breathed. 'And that was when everything started to go wrong.'

'Wrong?'

He smiled. 'Wrong, right—I soon didn't know where the hell I was,' he revealed. 'All I knew for sure was that if by any small chance Josy had turned up that evening, then I'd have taken every care of her.'

Her heart warmed some more to him that, having seen how dreadfully shy her sister was, he would have afforded her some of the same regard he gave his own sister. 'But it wasn't Josy who turned up—but me.'

'Indeed it was you,' he agreed. 'And I looked at you, sat beside you in the theatre, and life was never the same again. I had to leave you in the interval to go and try to get my head back together.'

Belvia shot him a startled look. 'Y-You're saying I—um—affected you in some...? That you were aware of me during the——'

'I'm saying all of that,' Latham continued. 'I'm saying that while I wanted you there, where photographers were, where there was every chance Astill would see a picture of you with me, I at the same time felt the stirrings of jealousy when I returned to find Rodney Phillips sitting in my seat—taking up my space with you.'

'Oh, heavens,' she whispered shakily, any intelligence she might have been blessed with suddenly deserting her—what did he mean?

'"Oh, heavens," it was, little one,' Latham stated gently. 'There was I, when I'd had no such intention, taking you on to dinner—and there you were—an entirely new experience for me—walking out on me when dinner had barely got started.'

'I—um—told your chauffeur that you wouldn't need him again that night,' she confessed, her brain-power still scattered.

'I know—he told me the next morning. I knew I was in trouble when I found myself laughing at your sauce.'

'You were—in trouble?'

'What would you call it when the next time I saw you—you again turning up in your sister's place—chemistry should rear its head and I should start to desire you?'

Some of her intelligence stirred—from what she could remember, that desire had not been one-sided. 'I've—never felt like that before,' she owned shakily.

'Now, I know it—then, I didn't. Are you going to forgive me?' he asked.

She felt on shaky ground again. 'Should I?'

'Oh, sweet love,' he groaned and, as if he could not take much more of her sitting even that little bit away, he put his arm about her, and she did not pull away, but went willingly. Latham held her quietly to him for several seconds, before going on to tell her, 'Your father had worked it all out very carefully. He did not rush into it but—he told me this morning—spent several days going over his plan to put me in his debt—to owe him a favour. He believed he had all the angles covered. He'd asked me not to mention to you that I knew you were having an affair with my brother-in-law—because he knew you would deny it. He had also calculated that I might go and see Astill and give him the name of his lady-love, but, by the very nature of Astill wanting to keep his real lady-love's name a secret, he reckoned—as in fact did happen—that Astill would let me go on believing his mistress was you—or anyone else, for that matter. Provided I didn't come up with the name Vanessa Stanley he'd got nothing to worry about.'

'Did Caroline think I was——?'

'No,' Latham answered before she could finish. 'She knew he was having an affair, of course, but she still doesn't know who with. And now, thank the Lord, she no longer cares. But, on the subject of caring, your father thought he had it all meticulously worked out before he came to see me.' He paused, and then, his eyes watchful on her, he went on carefully, 'What he had not taken into account, though, was that having met you I should start to care—about you.'

Her eyes went huge in her face, and her throat dried again. 'C-Care...?' It was as much as she could manage.

Latham looked tenderly down at her and smiled. 'Oh, yes, sweet love, care,' he breathed. 'From your father's viewpoint, once he'd got the investment he needed signed and sealed by my company, you need never have been any the wiser. He'd planned to tell me you had dropped Astill—and he could hardly be blamed if Astill subsequently took up with his secretary.' Devious, Belvia realised, was hardly a strong enough word for her father. 'In his opinion, whether I thought Astill would have told you of my knowing you were the one was immaterial. And you, in your ignorance of what was going on, were hardly likely to mention his name either. So far as your father was concerned, I could think you as brazen about it as I liked. But, while everything began the way he calculated it might, what he did not know was that I soon started to love your spirit, to care about your vulnerability.' She stared at him transfixed, and was barely breathing when, cupping the side of her face with one hand, he breathed oh, so tenderly, 'In fact, my darling, he had not calculated that I should start to fall in love with you.'

'You—love me?' she choked huskily.

'So very much,' he replied softly, and placed the tenderest of kisses on her slightly parted lips. 'I've known it, even as I've tried to deny it, from that night you came to my apartment to explain about Josy—only never got round to it. I followed you to the kitchen and I wanted you as you wanted me, but you said you were confused. And it was then that, as I recognised your vulnerability, as I held you, I knew confusion too. Because it wasn't just desire I felt for you—and it wasn't supposed to be like that. You were a hard case, you weren't supposed to be vulnerable—yet you were. But as we started to make love it was wonderful, different—head-swimmingly different—not like the time before, when I'd jeered at you for sleeping around and you nearly fractured my cheekbone for my trouble. This time you were putting a stop to our lovemaking, and daring to tell me that it wasn't right.'

'I'm sorry.'

'*You're* apologising?'

'I wanted to... That night I wanted...' Her voice started to fracture. 'Only, that first time, my—er—first time, I wanted it to be with someone who loved me.'

Latham pulled back and looked deeply into her beautiful eyes. 'Are you saying what I think you're saying, my shy darling?' he asked gently, yet with a hint of strain there in his voice too. 'Are you saying what every instinct, what everything I've learned—not been told—about you is saying? That—that night—you were in love—with me?'

'I—couldn't believe it. But it was true,' she replied on a low whisper.

'That you love me?' It seemed, with all the evidence there, that he still needed to hear it.

She smiled and, when an hour ago wild horses would not have dragged that truthful confession from her, 'I do love you,' she shyly agreed.

'Sweet love,' he groaned, and gathered her close up to him, saying not another word for long, long minutes. Not even kissing her but, as though he had been through great, great torment and had a need to hold her—hold her knowing that she loved no one but him—just holding her close up against his heart.

Then, gently, he kissed her and pulled back, as if hoping to see the confirmation of her words in her eyes. And it was there.

'Oh, I adore you!' he breathed, and kissed her and held her and kissed her some more—before pulling back, and, as if striving hard to get his head together, saying, 'This can't be, I've been so foul to you—I don't deserve that you should love me.'

'True,' she laughed, for just then she was so full of emotion it was that or tears.

'Oh, I love you, I love you, I love you,' he stated throatily, and kissed her and went on, as if searching for words of comfort for any hurt she felt, 'In your father's favour, he told me that had he known I intended taking you away for the weekend he would have found some way of preventing you from going.'

'Most likely because he felt his plan was at risk—I expect you'd have said that your brother-in-law would be there too.' Suddenly she could not weigh that up at all, and just had to say, 'I don't understand why Graeme

Astill accepted your invitation if he knew that I'd be th...' Her voice faded, realisation coming to her. 'You didn't tell him I'd be there, did you?'

'What a mess has been created!' Latham replied. 'But, since I want you to know absolutely everything, I have to confess that, apart from alerting Caroline to keep the weekend free and to make sure her husband was available, I'd not issued any invitation to Rose Cottage when I came to see you on Friday.'

'You hadn't? But...' She stared at him. 'But you said...'

'Lies, all round, have been flying about like confetti,' Latham confirmed. 'I lied to you when I said on Friday morning that I'd invited people down to Wiltshire. But, in my defence, sweet love, I'd come to see you on Wednesday purely because I felt such a need to see you, to hear you.'

'I'd asked if I could ring you...'

'Exactly—but you hadn't, and thoughts of you were driving me insane. I decided to come and see you and play it by ear. You then told me of the dreadful time Josy was going through and how she was a rare and precious person—and all I could think was that you were a rare and precious person too, and how your pain was my pain, but how I was going to have to hurt you and soon—because I just couldn't take much more.'

'Oh, my love!' Belvia exclaimed, the endearment slipping out purely because she could not stop it.

'Oh, that was worth waiting to hear,' he murmured, and gently kissed her—but then manfully resumed. 'So, there was I, falling deeper and deeper in love with you and wanting only to protect you, while at the same time determined to break this affair you were having, and soon. By Friday, after two nights of torment, I knew I couldn't take any more.'

'So you came here and told me a pack of lies,' she teased lovingly.

'Oh, God—you're marvellous,' he groaned, kissed her, and scraped together some more determination to continue. 'With everything erupting in my head, all I could do was concentrate on the facts as I knew them and—in danger of losing my grip on logic too—try to think logically. I knew Astill and his mistress had discussed me, and could only calculate that, if anything, you'd have told him I was after your sister.'

'Because it was Josy you had invited to the theatre and to dinner at your flat?'

Latham nodded. 'It also seemed safe to assume that—forgive me, love—because of the way you responded to me when I held you in my arms, you were unlikely to have told him about that.'

'A fair assumption,' she mumbled, going a little pink about the cheeks.

'You're adorable!' Latham exclaimed, and had to kiss her once more.

'And . . .' she prompted.

He gave her a loving look, but went on, 'Which in turn gave me the idea for this weekend.'

'You thought to put us all together?'

'While part of me was all against the thought of having him and you together at Rose Cottage—I needed it all settled. I've no time whatsoever for Astill but, from what I knew of him, I just couldn't see him taking his mistress sleeping with another man under the same roof—and not ending the affair. The result would be, I thought, that my sister would have what she wanted and, more importantly to me now, you too would be free. All I had to do was to ensure Astill didn't hear a whisper of it from you, before I'd got you incommunicado.'

'Incommunicado?' she queried—and then light dawned. 'You followed me up to my room, ostensibly to carry my case down, but really...'

'To make sure you didn't phone him,' Latham finished for her.

'You read my note to Josy too, in——'

'In case it was a note to your lover—and never loved you more when I realised that for Josy to believe what you'd written about going to stay with your retired friend who was feeling low, it must be the kind of typical thing you would do. Just as it was typical of you that you'd arrange for someone to exercise her horse while you were away.'

'Actually, Josy very bravely managed to exercise Hetty herself,' Belvia replied, and, her happiness brimming over, 'Oh, I do love you, Mr Tavenner.'

'Kiss me when you say that, woman,' he growled, and she did, and it was quite some minutes later that they breathlessly broke apart. Looking down into her slightly flushed face, he said, 'That, I think, was what helped me to keep going.'

'A kiss?' She was too bemused to think straight and, his eyes caressing her, he gave her an adoring smile.

'How could you be in love with him, or anyone else, yet respond so ardently to me? I was in love with you and didn't want to look at another woman, much less return an embrace.'

'Oh, tell me more!' she cried.

'Minx,' he laughed, and she loved him.

'So—um . . .' She tried to get her head back together. 'So what made you think I'd go away with you in the first place?' She managed to get a question together.

'Was there any doubt, sweetheart?' he asked gently.

She remembered his threat to Josy. 'No, I suppose not,' she smiled.

'And you don't hate me?'

'How could I?'

'How could you not? Though, if it's any consolation, I nearly blew it when you looked up at me, all big brown eyes, and asked for my promise not to come over all amorous. That was when I wanted to hold you safe in my arms, to protect you, and to tell you everything was all right.'

'But everything was not all right, was it?'

'Very far from being all right,' he agreed. 'So off we went, and I so enjoyed being with you, just the two of us—lunch—the supermarket—it was all wonderful; you were wonderful. We reached Rose Cottage and I began to hate like hell that I was going to have to get on the phone to my sister and invite her and her husband down.'

'Oh, darling,' she sighed—but then cried, suddenly remembering, 'You phoned Caroline from your car-phone!'

'I did,' he confirmed. 'I had to. I had to kill whatever it was between you and Astill dead.'

'You were beginning to doubt I was having an affair with him?' she questioned, thinking that was what he meant. But he shook his head.

'The evidence was too strong. And yet you seemed oddly nervous when I came into the bedroom while you were bed-making. Something wasn't right—I knew it.'

'You held me in your arms,' she recalled.

'And that *did* seem right,' he smiled. 'It felt as though that was where you belonged—it felt right for me, so it had to be right for you too, didn't it?'

'Oh, it was,' she beamed.

'Oh, love,' he murmured, and held her close. 'I must have been blind. Everything was adding up to you being a totally different woman from the one I'd been led to believe you were—yet still I was ready to believe the worst.'

'You were determined to believe I was having an affair with your brother-in-law?'

'I did ask you on Friday night if you had a problem with it when you admitted that you knew him.'

'I only met him the one time—at that party. But that was long enough to realise he has a loose mouth, and would see no need to keep from any mutual acquaintances, friends, that I'd been rooming with you...'

'Oh, dear love—that was what you meant. I thought...'

'I see now what you thought,' she laughed. 'You thought I was saying I had a problem because if I was rooming with anyone, it should be him.'

'You've so much to forgive me for. I only began to realise just how much when last night I held you sleeping in my arms.'

'Oh, Latham,' she cried. 'I tried so hard to be asleep before you came up the stairs.' She smiled as she told him, 'Brute that you are, I was wide awake—and you came up and went out like a light.'

'No way!'

Startled, she stared at him. 'You didn't? But—your breathing was...'

'The same as yours.' His smile matched hers. 'We were both pretending like hell. For my part I was in torment, wanting to come to you, while at the same time knowing that I wanted more from you than just one night.'

'Oh, darling,' she sighed, all her fears about how little he must think of her gone forever.

'Sweet love, I wanted your affair with Astill over, ended, out of the way, before I claimed you. Then your breathing really did relax and I knew you *were* asleep. But just as I'd started to grow calmer, so you suddenly started yelling. I was out of bed, had to wake you. Yet while I was desperately trying to be strong you suddenly leaned against me and—I was lost.'

'Blaming me again?' she teased lightly.

'Never again,' he murmured, and laid his lips on her hair, and after a minute or so of just holding her quietly he told her how it had been with him. 'At first I just couldn't get over this stupendous loving we had shared, couldn't get over the wonderful and astonishing discovery I'd made about you. I couldn't believe it, and but for the fact that you were sleeping naked in my arms, I might well have believed I was dreaming after all. And then, as daylight started to enter our room, I began to grow angry.'

'Angry? With me?' she asked, looking at him wide-eyed.

'Not with you—never again with you, sweet love. Though at first I was tempted to wake you so you might answer some of the questions that were spinning furiously through my mind.'

'Why didn't you—wake me, I mean?'

Latham smiled tenderly down at her. 'The reason, lovely Belvia, being that as I looked at you my heart

was so filled with love for you that I wanted to shower
you with kisses. And yet, should I have kissed you gently
awake, then I could not be certain that I wouldn't be
lost again, that I wouldn't make love to you again.'

'You didn't want to?' she asked, unaware of her
naïveté.

'Sweet innocent,' Latham crooned, 'I have so much
to teach you. But not then. Then I owed you more than
that I should again make you mine. First I wanted
answers—not from you, I realised. You, my darling,
owed me nothing. But somebody did.'

'My father?'

'He'd come to me, seemingly worried to death that
you were having an affair with my brother-in-law. You'd
confirmed you had a married man-friend. My brother-
in-law himself, when challenged, admitted he was the
one—a smoke-screen to stop me finding out who he was
really seeing, I now realise. As I also realised, as you
lay sleeping, that your unfortunate remark stemmed
purely from the fact that you were too spirited to be put
down by my clear dislike of what I thought you to be.'
He kissed the tip of her nose lest that comment in any
way bruised her.

'To be honest, I was feeling most awkward at the start
of the evening that my father was entertaining you purely
for his own ends. Though, as the evening went on,' she
felt she should confess, 'I couldn't help thinking that
perhaps you and my father deserved each other.'

Latham smiled, as if in agreement. But his smile had
gone when he revealed, 'I thought back to that time when
this morning I set about looking for answers. I've met
all types through my business but didn't know what to
believe about Edwin Fereday. I wanted to declare my

love—dared to hope that the hint of jealousy I'd hoped I'd heard in your voice when you'd asked about the lady-friends I'd brought down to Rose Cottage might mean you cared just a little. I'd had to dismiss it at the time, but resurrected it again when I realised Astill was nothing to you. I added that hope to the wonderful way you had given yourself to me—and, hardly daring to breathe for fear of waking you, I took my clothes out to the landing and got dressed.'

'You got dressed out . . .'

'I didn't want to disturb you. From the very beginning you had not been treated right. You owed neither me nor anyone else a thing—but I was owed! From the beginning I'd been misled. It was time I collected a few answers.'

'You went to see my father?'

'By a stroke of luck Astill was wandering about downstairs, looking for aspirins.'

'You asked him first . . .'

'It didn't get as far as that. Before I could grab him by the throat and tell him to start talking he had the temerity to ask—the implication obvious—if I'd had a good night. Sorry, my darling, but there are types like him around.'

'Obviously you didn't reply.'

'He was measuring his length on the floor before I could speak—it was truly one of the most satisfying experiences of my life. But, before I could stand him up and repeat the pleasure, Caroline was standing there, witness to how I was too enraged to remember my promise never to hit him. I couldn't regret what I'd done, but was glad to hear her say thanks, and add as she stepped over him and came out to my car with me that she intended to divorce him. Which, my darling, left me with just one more person to see before I came back to claim you.'

Oh, how wonderful that sounded. And oh, how she wished that she had dumped her pride and waited at Rose Cottage. 'Oh, if only I'd known you intended to come back.'

'You'd have saved me going half demented, hope fading with every mile, when I left Rose Cottage for a second time today—this time in search of you.'

'Oh, Latham!' she cried, and leaned forward and kissed him. Then she pulled back and, her brain-patterns all haywire, from somewhere found enough intelligence to suggest, 'The—um—first time you left was to go in search of my father?'

'And did he have a tale to tell!'

'A believable one?'

'At first, no. Only when I told him I knew absolutely everything, and he slipped up to the small extent that he revealed he was considering—only considering, mind—approaching my company for some capital, did I get an inkling of what he was really about. How, incredibly, he was prepared to use both you and your sister, and anybody else he had to; to keep Fereday Products in business. He wriggled like hell, but at last I got the whole of it out of him.'

'H-How did you leave things?' Belvia asked, aware that she loved her parent but not feeling she owed him anything.

'I said something to the effect that I'd be in touch, and raced off to Wiltshire.'

Gently their lips met, and for a while Belvia was oblivious to everything save that she loved Latham and that he, unbelievably, loved her. Then, his look tender, Latham was pulling back.

'You're heady stuff, Miss Fereday,' he stated, his voice thick in his throat. 'I'm trying like hell to remember that it's Sunday morning, I'm in the sitting-room in your home, and that your sister could come in at any moment.'

'I don't think she will,' Belvia smiled, knowing it for a fact. But then, trying to get her head together after the nonsense he had made of it, she asked, 'Um—er—will you be in touch with my father about his business, do you suppose? Er—will you invest in his company, do you——?' She broke off. Latham was looking at her with a most serious look in his eyes. 'What...?' she questioned chokily, and felt one of his hands come up again to the side of her face.

'What do you think, my sweet love? Should I let him have the investment he needs—send in my own men to ride shotgun? He won't like it—but he won't get a better offer. Or——' his arm about her shoulders tightened '—should I let my father-in-law's firm go under?'

'Father-in-law?' she croaked.

'In case you haven't realised it, dearest love, that's what he'll be to me when, as soon as I can arrange it, you become my wife.'

'Oh!' she gasped, pink tingeing her cheeks, her heart racing fit to burst—and Latham started to look anxious.

'You *are* going to marry me, aren't you?' he demanded sharply. 'Hell's teeth! God knows I don't deserve you, but——'

'I'd like very much to marry you,' Belvia cut in quickly, her voice little above a whisper.

He checked. 'What did you say?' he asked urgently.

'I'd like to be Mrs Latham Tavenner as soon as you can arrange it, please,' she said, and heard his small sound of utter delight—and the next she knew she was crushed up against his heart—where she wanted to be.

*　　*　　*

Cathy Williams is Trinidadian and was brought up on the twin islands of Trinidad and Tobago. She was awarded a scholarship to study in Britain, and came to Exeter University in 1975 to continue her studies into the great loves of her life: languages and literature. It was there that Cathy met her husband, Richard. Since they married Cathy has lived in England, originally in the Thames Valley but now in the Midlands. Cathy and Richard have three small daughters. Cathy had her first book published by Mills & Boon® in 1991 and she has since had more than 20 novels distributed worldwide.

CHARADE OF THE HEART
by
CATHY WILLIAMS

CHAPTER ONE

BETH looked carefully at her sister and counted to ten. It was difficult, but she wanted to find exactly the right words to explain, without resorting to downright exasperation, that there was absolutely no way she was even going to contemplate taking part in this juvenile scheme.

They had reached an age when these sorts of escapades should long have been left behind. When on earth was Laura ever going to grow up? It was tiring always being the one to frown and nod sagely and act reasonable.

'Well?' Laura prompted. 'What do you think?'

Have you got a few days to spare? Beth asked herself. She looked at her sister's flushed face, framed by the tangle of long auburn hair, and sighed.

'It's the craziest idea you've ever come up with,' she said, with what she considered a huge amount of restraint, 'and there's no chance that you're going to get me involved with it. I would rather spend the rest of my life in a snake pit. So you can wipe that grin off your face and leave my lunch alone.'

They were sitting in her kitchen, a cosy yellow room with pale, speckled wallpaper and matching curtains which had taken Beth ages to make. She tapped her sister's hand, which had been making surreptitious inroads into her plate of salad, and considered the matter resolutely closed.

'Oh, Beth.' Laura slipped out of her chair and went around to her sister, folding her arms around her neck.

5

'It's not that crazy, really it isn't, not when you think about it. And it's the only thing I can think of.' Beth could hear the tears in her sister's voice and hardened her heart. Laura had the knack of turning the tears on with alarming ease and she wasn't going to fall for it. Not this time.

She bit into a lettuce leaf liberally soaked with salad cream and didn't say a word.

'You're mad,' she muttered finally, disengaging herself from her sister's stranglehold and clearing away the table.

Laura followed her to the kitchen sink and dipped her finger into the basin of soapy water, trailing it into circular patterns, her long hair hanging forward and hiding her face.

'You're so unsympathetic,' she muttered. 'Here I am, in the worst fix in my life, and you're not prepared to do anything at all to help. I was counting on you, Beth. Why do you think I drove all the way up here in this weather? If I had known that you wouldn't give me the time of day, then I'd have stayed at home and...and...' Her voice trembled, and Beth sighed again.

'I'm not unsympathetic,' she said gently. 'Stunned perhaps, but not unsympathetic. I mean, how on earth could you have let yourself become pregnant? Don't tell me that it just slipped your mind that there are about a million types of contraceptives available.'

She eyed the half-completed washing-up with resignation and led her sister into the lounge.

Like the kitchen, it was small, but imaginatively furnished. Beth's job as secretary-cum-book-keeper in a small electronics company didn't pay that much. It was all she could do to meet the mortgage on her tiny two-bedroomed flat. But it was hers and she had decorated it as tastefully as she could on a minuscule budget.

Whenever she felt like giving up, she told herself that things would improve as soon as she had completed her accountancy course and could find herself a better job. All that studying she had to do in her free time would pay dividends.

By nature she was an optimist. Didn't they say that every cloud had a silver lining?

Laura had collapsed on to one of the chairs and was hugging a cushion. A picture of misery. Beth looked at her doubtfully. This didn't seem like any act, although it was hard to tell. Laura had the ability to look woebegone if the weather report began with showers and light snow.

'Look,' Beth said calmly, 'there's no point weeping and wailing. You're pregnant, with no chance of marrying the father of the child. You'll just have to do what anyone else in your situation would do. Work for as long as you can and then leave. You've said that you can't go back to the job as you haven't been there long enough to qualify for maternity leave. So what? It's hardly the end of the world.'

She bit back the temptation to lecture on the sheer insanity of becoming involved with a married man, not to mention becoming pregnant by him. Her sister had enough problems on her plate without that.

From the sound of it, though, Beth could think of a thousand better places to put her loyalty than with a creep who had knowingly involved himself with Laura when his responsibilities lay elsewhere. He didn't know about the pregnancy but she seriously doubted that that would have influenced his actions. He had left her sister high and dry after a three-month fling. A baby on the way was hardly likely to have changed that.

Couldn't Laura have suspected the sort of man he was?

'It's the end of the world for me,' Laura said, in between sobs. Beth handed her a box of tissues. 'Jobs like mine don't grow on trees, you know. I love it there. It pays more than I could ever hope to get in a lifetime of doing secretarial work.'

'Then you should have thought about all that before you got yourself into this situation.'

'How was I to know that David...' there was another onslaught of weeping and she blew her nose noisily into a tissue '...that David was married? He didn't tell me until he decided to walk out. And by then it was too late. I was already pregnant. And I'm still in love with him,' she finished miserably.

'Surely not,' Beth said, aghast.

'I knew you wouldn't understand.' There was an edge of accusation in Laura's voice now. 'You've never been in love. Not even with Craig. It's easy for you to sit there and sound horrified just because I haven't had the common sense to have acted the way you would have done! You don't know what it's like! You've always been so sensible. When Dad died, you were the one who was strong enough to support Mum, and when she remarried you were the one who told me not to cry because that would only make her unhappy, and, when they both went to Australia to live last year, you were the one who waved them off at the airport and told me that life had to go on!'

Beth felt the prick of tears behind her eyes. Laura had managed to make her sound like a monster, but she was practical, that was all. Was that some sort of crime? As for Craig...she preferred not to dwell on that and pushed it to the back of her mind. Easy enough to do. Laura was right about that, at any rate. She hadn't been in love with him, had felt no fireworks. When he had broken off their relationship she had been upset, but not distraught, had picked up the pieces and carried on. It was the only way, wasn't it?

Now her sister had sprung this latest escapade on her, and had expected . . . what?

She had spent a lifetime reacting in the only way she had known how to her sister's recklessness. Now that control, that inability to become involved, had become as much part of her as the colour of her hair or the shape of her nose.

'You're being unfair!' she protested uncomfortably.

'No, I'm not. You don't want to understand. In a minute you'll start telling me to pull myself together.'

'I just don't know what to do,' Beth objected. 'I'm not some sort of miracle-worker. I understand, honestly, and I'll help in whatever way I can, you know that. I'll baby-sit, I'll buy things for it, as much as I can afford, I'll even sell my flat and move up to London to be closer to you. What more do you want me to say?'

Silly question. Beth waited for the inevitable response.

'You know how you can help me, if you really want to,' Laura insisted stubbornly. There were smudges on her face from where the tears had dried, giving her a fragile, pathetic appearance.

'It wouldn't work,' Beth said helplessly, but there was less determination in her voice now, and Laura sensed it, moving in like a shark that had scented blood and was homing in for the kill.

'It could work,' she said earnestly, moving forward closer, impatiently sweeping her hair away from her face. 'Come with me, I'll show you.'

She stood up and held out her hand. Beth reluctantly took it, allowing herself to be led into the bedroom. Like a lamb to the slaughter.

Laura guided her to the tall mirror that stood next to the dressing-table in the bedroom.

Outside the wind was fierce and relentless, rattling the window-panes ever so slightly. It was a perfectly dark night, the moon obscured by the dense layers of cloud that had hung over the country for the past few days.

Inside, the bedside lamps threw patterns of light and shadow across the room and the overhead light with its pretty apricot shade picked out the figures of the sisters, illuminating them.

Beth looked silently at their reflections, seeing them through Laura's eyes and reluctantly understanding what had inspired her sister's hare-brained plan.

Two women, both the same height, both the same shape, both with the same oval faces and luminous green eyes. Identical twins.

She was the first to look away, throwing herself on to the bed and staring sightlessly up at the ceiling.

Trading places. It had been a ridiculous game when they were children, but they weren't children now. They were women in their early twenties, and surely the time for ridiculous games was over?

Laura sat on the bed, her knees pulled up to her chin.

'Please, Beth, do it for me. It can work. I'm sure of it. Would I jeopardise my whole life if I didn't believe that?'

You're mad enough, Beth felt tempted to say.

'My boss would never notice,' she continued persuasively. 'He's hardly ever there. He owns a string of hotels worldwide, not to mention enough other business interests that keep him out of the country for weeks on end. My orders tend to come by phone or fax. And when he is around he's always far too busy to notice me other than in the capacity of the secretary who follows his dictates.'

'Sounds a treasure,' Beth said drily.

'You know what I mean. He breathes, eats and sleeps work. No, maybe not sleeps. He has enough women around to fulfil him on that score.'

'Charming.'

'But what I'm saying to you is this: we don't have the sort of close working relationship that would make him notice any difference if you replaced me. He probably wouldn't even see that our hairstyles were different and, if he did, you could tell him that you had had your hair cut.'

'And you like working for this man?' Beth sat up, propping her head on her elbow and staring curiously at her sister. The man hardly sounded like a comfortable type to be around.

'I love it. I've never had so much responsibility in a job in my life before. That's why I'm so desperate to hang on to it. As far as I'm concerned, working for Marcos Adrino is the best thing that ever happened to me. That——' she patted her stomach '—and the baby. It's all I have left of David, and I'm happy with that.'

'Oh, yes, the baby. So I'm to cunningly replace you at the Adrino corporation, not arousing so much as a whisker of suspicion, while you move into my flat and temp until the baby's born, and then what?'

'And then,' Laura elaborated, her eyes positively gleaming now that victory was tantalisingly within reach, 'and then I move back up to London and take up where you left off. My friend Katie is a professional child-minder. She's already promised to look after it.'

'Convenient.'

'Yes, it is,' Laura agreed, unaware of the oblique sarcasm in her sister's voice.

'And how do I cope with all those little details like knowing the layout of the office? The filing system?' Why, Beth wondered, am I actually allowing my curiosity to encourage Laura in her mad ideas?

'I'll fill you in on that. It all runs remarkably smoothly. Marcos told me when I first applied for the job that the secret of a successful office lay in its simplicity. Everything documented and on computer so that no one was indispensable to the company.'

'Except him, of course.'

'Right.' Laura's voice was full of awe.

The man obviously had something, Beth thought, although from where she was sitting that something sounded very much like a healthy dose of arrogance.

'And don't you think that other people might notice our little swap?'

'Not likely. Marcos's office occupies the top floor of the building, and there are only a handful of people there. The two vice-presidents who work for him, and their secretaries, whom I have very little to do with.'

She rattled off their names and Beth held up her hand to staunch the flow of information.

'And what about my job?' she asked. 'Do I just tell them that I'm taking seven months' leave to help my sister out in a scheme that could have come straight out of a third-rate movie, but to hang on, I'll be back?'

'You quit.'

'I quit.'

'Sure. Why not? You know that you're only there because it's convenient and because it helps pay the mortgage. I can get a temp job somewhere and pay your mortgage, and you can use my huge salary for the next seven months to build up that little nest-egg you're always telling me you wish you had.'

'I see.'

Beth could hardly credit her sister with the fore-thought she had taken in preparing the ground plan of all this. For every question, she had an answer, and all of the answers were logical in a bizarre way.

'Besides,' Laura continued, 'you told me how much you'd like to get out of here for a bit, to put a little distance between you and Craig. Here's your chance.'

'It was wishful thinking!' Beth objected weakly. 'Be-sides, I've got over all that.'

'Have you?'

Beth looked at her sister and sighed. She knew what lay behind this piercing concern for her emotional well-being. It had little to do with the state of her heart and much more to do with the fact that it would fit in very nicely with her plans, thank you very much.

'Yes,' she said firmly, 'I have. I don't look like someone on the verge of a nervous breakdown, do I? I'm quite grateful to him in a way; he taught me a valuable lesson about the male species. They're best left alone.'

She had enjoyed an undemanding relationship with Craig for seven months before he'd left her for someone else. Men like that, she had decided, instilled caution when it came to the rest of their sex. She wouldn't be getting involved with another man for a very long time indeed, and she could have told her sister that dragging up that unfortunate episode and tacking it on to her ar-guments was useless.

She didn't, though. Talking about Craig still made her feel vaguely disillusioned, and Beth preferred not to dwell on anything that served no purpose other than to depress her.

Instead she offered her own counter-argument. 'And Mum? Do you think that Mum will give this little venture her blessing?'

Laura sat upright and adopted a complacent expression which sent chills down Beth's spine. It was the same expression she had seen whenever her sister was about to confront a problem with an irrefutably foolproof answer.

'That's the beauty of it,' she said smugly. 'You know how Mum's always spent her life tearing her hair over me. In fact, she still does that now, even if it is only by letter. Well, I won't tell her about the pregnancy just yet. I'll fill her in just before the baby's due, and by the time she arrives the swap will be accomplished, and I'll be back in my job. Easy.'

Beth shook her head wonderingly. 'Is it all worth it?' she asked.

'For me, yes. I know you're content to stay in the hicks here, studying by night, working by day to pay the bills, but it's not for me. I love London. I love my job. I don't want to own a cosy little place. Not yet.'

Beth groaned.

'And when the baby arrives?' she asked. 'You're going to have to settle down, Laura. Babies and the wild single life don't exactly go hand in hand.'

Laura's eyes shifted away from her sister's face. 'Time enough to think about that.'

What other answer had she seriously expected? Beth thought. Laura had always lived on the premise that the future was a bridge to be crossed when you came to it. While *she* had worked hard towards building something for herself, Laura had run through a series of unsatisfactory jobs, never thinking of tomorrow.

'The wonderful thing is,' Laura was saying, her voice low and urgent, 'I've been at the Adrino corporation for six months now. Long enough to know that it's the only job for me, but not so long that I know too much for you to catch up on. Right now, I'm doing pretty routine work, even if I do have the freedom to prioritise it the way I want, and you would be able to slot in with no trouble at all. And if you don't understand anything, no one will be too surprised if you ask questions.'

'Including your boss?'

'Just so long as you only ask the question once,' Laura replied truthfully. 'He has the sort of brilliant mind that grasps things immediately, and he expects everyone who works for him to do the same.'

This sounded worse and worse. The man was an ogre. Beth could picture him without too much trouble. An arrogant tycoon, someone with a receding hairline and a bit of a paunch, testimony to stress and business lunches, but with enough money to attract whatever bimbo his heart desired.

'Please,' Laura wheedled, creeping up the bed to hold her sister's hand. 'If you hate it there, I promise I'll do what you want. I'll admit that I'm pregnant and I'll work my notice and then leave. What have you got to lose?'

Beth hesitated, and Laura immediately seized the opportunity.

'And the rest up here will do me good,' she said fervently. 'I'll be able to do some thinking, and I'll get away from London for a while. There are too many memories for me in London. We could both do with swapping places for our health.'

'That's emotional blackmail,' Beth pointed out wearily.

But the battle was over, and by the time they finally switched off the lights she was already coming to terms with the fact that she was either as crazy as her sister or else so lacking in will-power that she had allowed herself to agree with something which bore all the resemblance of a jaunt in a minefield.

Laura had taken a week off work, and they spent the time laboriously going over the routines in the Adrino corporation. She had brought one of the company magazines with her, and she pointed out all the faces of the people Beth would meet and would have to recognise.

They weren't that many, mostly the people who worked in the higher echelons of the company. It was a fortunate coincidence that her sister had not been in London long enough to acquire her usual following of male admirers. Her closest friend was Katie, who was aware of the plan.

David, she assured Beth with a note of bitterness, although he worked in the company, which was where she had met him, had applied and got a transfer abroad.

'Running as far away as he could from me,' she said with an attempt at bravado.

'Isn't that easier than if he had been around?' Beth enquired mildly, and her sister shrugged agreement.

By the end of the week, Laura had managed to find herself a temp job, but her work at the Adrino corporation had obviously spoiled her. She rattled off what she would have to do now and was clearly appalled by the prospect.

Beth tactfully refrained from another lecture on it all being her fault, and that as she had made her bed, so would she have to lie on it.

She herself had successfully managed to resign from her job without having to give the obligatory one-month notice. She had pleaded an unfortunate family matter and tactfully left it to her boss to decipher whatever he wanted from that obscure statement.

It had hurt a lot less than she had expected. Had she really spent so much time in a job that she had shed without too many tears? Or maybe it was the stirrings of what was awaiting her.

Laura had made the whole scheme sound like a marvellous adventure, but the following Monday morning, as Beth stood outside the impressive Adrino building, she felt far from adventurous.

She felt an impostor, dressed in her sister's jade-green suit. Was there a law against this sort of thing? she wondered.

She smoothed her hair back nervously and chewed on her lip. All around her people rushed past, lots of little soldier ants hurrying to their jobs.

A dull sun was attempting to break the stranglehold of grey clouds but it was easy to see that it was a losing battle.

She felt a light spitting of rain and merged into the line of soldier ants, finding herself swept into the massive building.

If I don't look at anyone, she thought, then I won't risk ignoring any recognisable faces.

But she was perspiring with nerves as the lift whooshed up to the top floor, disgorging her into the plushest set of offices she had ever seen in her life before.

The carpet was of muted grey-blue and thick enough to make footsteps soundless. The offices lay behind smoke-coloured glass.

One of the secretaries looked up as she walked past and waved, and Beth waved back. Marian, secretary to Ron Wood, the financial director.

'Nice week off?' Marian asked, stopping her in her tracks, and Beth smiled and nodded.

'A little eventful,' she said, inwardly grinning at the accuracy of the description, 'but relaxing on the whole.'

'Good. I wish I had a week off coming up. I'm up to my ears in it. You've had your hair cut?'

Beth ran her fingers self-consciously through her bob. 'Spur-of-the-moment,' she said vaguely.

'Suits you. Makes you look more businesslike. Not,' Marian continued hurriedly, 'that you didn't look great with long hair.'

Beth accepted the compliment with a smile. She liked Marian straight away. She was in her middle thirties, tending towards plumpness and quite plain to look at with her short wavy brown hair and spectacles, until she smiled. Then her face lit up and was really very attractive.

'See you later, anyway,' she said with another wave, and Beth nodded, walking confidently towards her office which she knew was at the end of the corridor.

First hurdle, she thought, successfully manoeuvred and out of the way. It surely couldn't be as simple as this. Life was never that simple. It always insisted on throwing in a few complications to making the going more interesting.

But right now her self-confidence was a notch higher.

There would be a stack of typing awaiting her—she knew that from what Laura had explained—but that would be no problem. She had spent a long time working with the same computer system.

She pushed open the door to her office and gasped.

It was a large room, carpeted in the same shade of muted grey, but the walls were covered by an elegant dove-grey wallpaper. Her desk was an impressive mahogany affair, and the filing cabinets, also in mahogany, were stacked neatly against the wall.

Opposite, a large abstract painting dominated the wall. It wasn't the sort of thing she would have chosen herself, but she decided that she rather liked it. It was soothing.

Marcos Adrino had probably hand-picked it. She had had to revise some of her ideas on his appearance. From the picture in the company magazine, he was younger than she had originally thought, but she had no doubt that the paunch was still there. The handful of wealthy men she had met had all seemed to be slightly overweight. Products of too much access to rich food.

She hung her coat on the coat-stand and settled comfortably into her chair, browsing through the pile of letters, most of which she could tell at a glance, from experience, simply needed filing. Faxed letters from the boss were awaiting typing.

Beth looked at the strong, aggressive handwriting and felt a twinge of relief that he wasn't around. She could do with a few days breaking in before she faced him.

She switched on the computer terminal and was about to begin working on the first letter when the door behind her opened.

She heard his voice before she saw him. It was deep, and right now tinged with enough hardness to freeze her to the spot.

'Here at last. In my office. Now.'

She swivelled around to see him vanishing back into his room, and her head began to throb with nerves.

One day into this, and already things weren't going to plan. He was not supposed to be here today. He was supposed to spend most of his time out of the country. In fact, from what Laura had told her, he was supposed to be in Paris and Geneva until the end of the week. At least. So what on earth was he doing here?

She licked her lips nervously and wished that she had listened to her good sense and laughed her sister right out of town.

He was standing by the window waiting for her, his body negligently leaning against the sill, one hand thrust into his trouser-pocket.

The difference between the man in front of her and the one she had conjured up was so vast that she looked away in confusion.

Marcos Adrino was tall and, far from having a paunch, he had not a spare ounce of fat to be seen. In fact, he had the body of a superbly tuned athlete, broad-shouldered and lean-hipped. A body that looked powerful, even though it was covered by an expensively tailored charcoal-grey suit.

Beth cleared her throat and looked at him, taking in the hard, clever lines of his face, the black hair, the dark, penetrating eyes, the curve of his mouth.

Pull yourself together, girl, she told herself. You're the sensible one, remember?

He was staring at her through narrowed eyes.

'Sit down,' he ordered abruptly.

Beth edged over to the chair and sat down, lowering her eyes to her shorthand pad, making an effort to steady her hand.

It wouldn't do to look ill-at-ease. She got the feeling that this man picked up things like that, processed them through his shrewd brain, and always came up with the right answer.

He remained standing where he was and she looked up at him with a bright smile.

'I didn't expect you,' she said in a businesslike voice.

'I dare say you didn't,' he drawled.

'Successful trip?'

'It would have been, if I hadn't been privy to certain rumours circulating.'

'Rumours?'

She managed a weak smile.

'Rumour number one has it that you've been shirking your responsibilities here,' he said coldly. 'I don't pay you to waltz into this office any time you feel like it.'

Beth gathered her wits together. This wasn't a dictating session at all. She should have guessed that the minute she saw that forbidding expression on his face.

'I didn't realise that I had been,' she ventured.

'Really.' He moved over to his chair and sat in it, inclining back, his hands clasped behind his head. 'In that case, you don't seem to be aware of the time you're supposed to get here. I can assure you that it's not ten o'clock.'

His voice was smooth and razor-sharp, and Beth looked at him with dislike. She had been spot-on when she had read arrogance behind her sister's description of her boss. It was stamped all over him, but she was damned if he was going to stamp it all over her.

'If I've been late on a couple of occasions,' she said coolly, 'then I apologise. It won't happen again.'

'It had better not. You've exhausted your first chance with me. Next time it happens and you don't provide an acceptable excuse, you're out. Understand?'

Beth swallowed her anger.

'And what excuse would you consider acceptable?' she asked with interest, forgetting that she was supposed to be holding on to her sister's job and not kissing it sweet goodbye through the window. 'Death, perhaps?'

Marcos's mouth narrowed to a thin line.

'Nor do I pay you to give me lip, is that clear?' He stared at her and Beth defiantly met his gaze.

'I'm sorry,' she muttered, fiddling with her pad.

This man was more than merely uncomfortable to be around. He was unbearable, and if Laura had been around she would quite happily have strangled her on the spot.

'Have you prepared the groundwork on the St Lucian project?' he asked, changing the subject.

He was trying to catch her out. Beth could sense it instinctively and she thanked her lucky stars that Laura had filled her in on all the details of the major jobs he was working on.

The St Lucian project involved an immense lot of work concerning the construction of an exclusive complex in St Lucia, the sort of complex that catered for the sort of people who never associated holidays with cost.

'Yes,' she responded calmly. 'The groundwork's all been covered and an appointment with the Minister of Tourism is scheduled for next week.'

It felt good to reel off the right answer. Marcos Adrino would have had no hesitation in reducing her to the size of a pea had she not been able to meet his question with an adequate response.

She got the feeling that he had no compunction when it came to eliminating dead wood from his company. Or, for that matter, from his life. She considered what her sister had told her about his private affairs, about the women who were drawn to him like iron filings to a magnet. Now, seeing him, she realised that he was the kind of man who treated women as disposable playthings. Men, she thought, she could well do without, and this breed of man was particularly on the objectionable list.

'I do feel, however,' she said, throwing in her own opinion on what Laura had told her about the project, 'that more care should be taken to involve the visitors into the island life. A fabulous complex is one thing, but it can be enhanced by easy access to the local customs.'

'You have opinions now, have you?' he asked softly. 'And since when has your efficiency extended beyond my orders?'

Beth didn't answer. She would have to remember to act in character, and Laura would never have volunteered such an observation without being asked.

'Is that all?' she murmured, preparing to leave. 'Sir?'

'The name is Marcos,' he answered easily, 'use it. You always have. And no, as a matter of fact, that's not all. Not by a long shot.'

Beth waited and the silence built around her like an electric field.

He had something else to say, and, from the sound of this particular brand of silence, whatever it was it wasn't pleasant.

CHAPTER TWO

NEVER in her entire life had Beth felt so acutely ill at ease. And the worst part was, Marcos Adrino wasn't at all embarrassed at her discomfort. He continued to stare at her, those black eyes taking in absolutely everything, until she felt like jumping up from the chair and begging for forgiveness for whatever the hell it was she was supposed to have done, because he still hadn't said.

He would have made a great interrogator, she thought. He certainly had the ability to fill his silences with unspoken threat.

'I've been hearing other, slightly more distasteful rumours about you,' he broke the silence, but there was still a dangerous softness to his voice. He idly picked up the silver letter-opener from his desk, running the edge along his finger with caressing delicacy.

Did he have to do that? Beth wondered nervously. Was he doing it on purpose? She didn't think so. There was something absent-minded about his action, but even so, it was menacing.

No wonder, when Laura had spoken about him, her voice had been filled with awe.

Of course, she decided, falling back on her good, old-fashioned sense of practicality, any awe Laura felt towards him was totally misplaced. All that forbidding arrogance didn't intimidate her at all. Well, not now anyway. Maybe to start with, but she had got the measure of him now, she decided.

He had something unpleasant to say to her and, instead of just coming right out with it, which was what any normal boss would have done, he was playing a cat-and-mouse game with her. Creating a shroud of tension around her, waiting for her to snap, at which point he would no doubt find the whole scenario hugely entertaining.

'Oh, yes?' Beth asked politely.

His mouth hardened. Any minute now, she thought, and he'll tell me that I have an attitude problem. But she was damned if she was going to let Marcos Adrino walk all over her. He might treat the rest of the human race like that, but not her. Not if she had any say in the matter.

She fleetingly thought that she was supposed to be impersonating her sister and that Laura would never have dreamt of answering back to him, and promptly pushed the thought aside for future reference.

'You don't seem overly concerned,' he said, dropping the letter-knife and standing up.

Beth followed his movements warily as he walked around the desk to perch on it directly in front of her.

Another little ploy, she told herself. Designed to make the guilty party feel inferior and vulnerable. It won't work.

Her green eyes serenely met his, and she saw an expression of what? Puzzlement? Almost as though he was trying to figure something out. Then it was gone and he was looking at her with cold disapproval.

'Of course I'm interested in whatever rumours you've heard,' Beth agreed with the same level of controlled politeness in her voice. 'Not that rumours are always based on fact.'

'Your week off certainly seems to have turned you into a little philosopher,' Marcos observed coolly. 'I don't remember you being so opinionated before. Who did you spend the time with?'

'No one,' Beth said hurriedly.

'Not even David Ryan?'

So this is it, she thought, I might have guessed. Her face reddened and then just as quickly drained of all colour.

'I see that's managed to crack that controlled little façade of yours.'

'May I ask who has been spreading these...rumours?' she asked. Not that I'll be able to deny them. Laura, she groaned inwardly, why on earth did you have to fool around with someone in the company? Why couldn't you have contented yourself with any one of the hundreds of other men in London who had nothing at all to do with the Adrino corporation?

Marcos smiled coldly. 'I really don't think that's relevant, do you?'

'I suppose not,' Beth said dully.

'The fact is that you and Ryan have been sleeping together, haven't you?'

'I didn't realise that what I did outside of company time——'

'You know damn well that it's not allowed. You're my secretary and Ryan isn't just one of the junior members of staff. He's one of our directors.'

'He is?' She hadn't thought to ask Laura what David's status in the company was, and Laura had, naturally, tactfully omitted to mention it.

'Don't try and plead ignorance,' Marcos bit out. 'It won't work. I had noticed that his work was becoming sloppy. Is that why he requested a transfer to Paris?'

'I don't know. You'll have to ask him,' Beth hedged, looking away.

'I'm asking you. But don't worry, your face says it all for you. No doubt you drove the poor fellow into a corner and he fled from the country to get away from you.'

'I resent that!' she exclaimed hotly, standing up. It was on the tip of her tongue to inform him that she wasn't paid to sit in his office and be systematically insulted. That he could expect her resignation first thing in the morning. But, of course, she couldn't. Laura would never have forgiven her if their convoluted efforts to secure her job had lasted precisely two hours and had resulted in Beth walking out.

She bit back her words and rearranged her features into what she hoped was an expression of subdued apology.

'Sit back down,' Marcos commanded abruptly. 'You'll leave when I'm finished with you. You've been playing with Ryan, and who else? Is he one of a succession of men you've been sleeping with in my company?'

'No, of course not.'

'Because I won't have it. I can do without being known as someone who has a tramp for a secretary.'

'I am not a tramp!' Two bright patches of colour had appeared on her cheeks, and she realised that she was perspiring all over.

'I needn't tell you that rumours of your affair with Ryan could very quickly spread into rumours of an affair with me.'

The black eyes glinted cynically at her. She wondered briefly whether that wasn't bothering him as much as Laura's love-affair with David. After all, it was easy for a boss to lose credibility with his staff if it was rumoured that he was sleeping with his secretary.

And that would be quite an easy assumption to make. He was attractive, she supposed, if you liked that sort of ruthless appeal, and he was aware enough of his own sexuality to realise that women were drawn to him.

'I can assure you that you don't need to fear anything on that score,' she informed him stiffly.

'No?' He raised one eyebrow, and this time there was a distinct gleam of lazy amusement in his eyes.

It altered the hard contours of his face totally, and she caught a swift, disturbing glimpse of the sort of self-assured charm that could knock any defenceless woman for six.

But she was far from defenceless. Oh, no. She had always been a controlled person, and since Craig she had erected a good many barriers to protect her from ever again being taken in by a few charming smiles and some well-rehearsed chat-up lines. That glimpse of raw sex appeal, she firmly told herself, stood no chance.

'No,' she told him.

'You mean you're not attracted to me?' There was slightly more amusement in his eyes now, and it made Beth angry. There had been nothing amusing in his accusations a minute ago and, if he thought that he could dictate her responses to him by turning on a bit of masculine charm, then he was in for an unpleasant surprise.

'That's right.' She stood up and smoothed her skirt, then she bent to retrieve the shorthand pad and her pencil. And not once did she even glance in his direction. 'Is that all, now?'

'That's all.' He moved across to the window and stood staring broodingly out. The fine drizzle that had started earlier in the morning had not let up. She could see the persistent wetness clinging to the window-pane, as though the top of the building were stuck in the middle of a cloud.

She turned to go and halted at the door when she heard the deep timbre of his voice behind her.

'Just so long as we understand each other,' he said silkily. He had turned to face her, and Beth's mouth suddenly went dry. No wonder this man had such a high opinion of himself. He was clever, that much was apparent in his eyes, and he knew it. He was powerful, and he knew it. And he was sexy, and that he was certainly aware of.

But he wasn't perfect. If he were he would be able to see the stubborn hostility in her face.

'I think we do, Mr Adrino.'

'Marcos. I told you when you first got this job that everyone in the company was on a first-name basis.'

'So you did,' Beth murmured, unable to resist a smile as she thought that they had done it. They had really managed to pull the wool over Marcos Adrino's sharp eyes. They had fooled him. He didn't have a clue that the woman standing in front of him had never been interviewed by him for any job.

'Care to tell me what that smile on your face is all about?' he drawled. 'I can't imagine that the past hour has exactly filled you with a warm glow.'

You'd be surprised, Beth wanted to retort, still highly amused at the thought that she had fooled the infallible Marcos Adrino.

Her smile widened. 'Just looking forward to my day's work,' she said blandly. 'Job satisfaction is a wonderful thing.'

'Isn't it? And by the way,' he added, as she opened the door, 'what have you done to your hair?'

'Oh, I had it cut,' Beth said cautiously. Had her triumph been short-lived? 'I fancied a change,' she mumbled vaguely when he didn't say anything.

'You've succeeded,' he said, sticking his hands into his pockets. 'From where I'm standing, you've succeeded very well indeed.'

Beth stepped out of the office and shut the door firmly behind her. His words were ominously perspicacious. She really would have to remember that she couldn't give in to the temptation to react in the way she customarily would have done. That she and Laura, identical twins though they were, were very different as two individuals.

She almost fell into her chair with the relief of no longer being in Marcos's presence.

It hadn't just been his relentless accusations, she thought suddenly, as she logged into the computer and ran her eyes briefly over the huge store of files, realising that she would have to work a lot of overtime to really understand Laura's job fully.

There was something alarming about him. Maybe it was just that she was not accustomed to being confronted by a man who acted as though the whole world was designed to fall in with his orders.

Her little job in Cambridge had certainly not prepared her for this particular breed of man. Her own boss had been quite mild-mannered. A sympathetic middle-aged man with three children, all girls, who wore a look of perpetual harassment on his face. Whenever anyone joked to him about it, he would laugh and reply, what do you expect, living with four women?

Beth couldn't imagine that Marcos Adrino had ever been mild-mannered. He had probably been born arrogant. She tried to imagine him as a baby and found that she couldn't. The only image she could conjure up was that dark, devilish, ruthlessly handsome face.

She stuck a couple of horns and a tail on her mental image, chuckled and then settled into the laborious task of catching up with the outstanding workload of typing.

When Marcos next strode out of his office, he glanced across at her with surprise.

'Dieting?' he drawled, slinging on his coat and pausing to stand over her.

Immediately Beth felt her pulses begin to race.

'Pardon?'

'It's nearly two o'clock,' he told her, and she returned his curious stare with surprise.

'Is it?' she asked, consulting her watch and feeling unnervingly gauche and idiotic. 'Oh, yes, so it is. I must have become a bit involved.'

'So I see. Keep it up and you won't feel the sting of my disapproval again.'

'Yes, sir,' she replied tartly, wanting to hit him, and his lips curved into a small smile.

'I won't be back until tomorrow afternoon. I have two meetings tomorrow at Harlow and Ridgewood's. Last-minute arrangements; they probably won't be in your diary. Finish compiling the research into Santo Domingo, will you? I want to get all that off the ground by the end of the month. Latest. I take it you won't object to doing a bit of overtime to get it all cleared?'

'Of course not.' Had he really expected any other answer? The question had been phrased in such a way as to negate any other reply. Not that she had any objection to overtime anyway. For the salary that Laura was being paid, working long hours was more or less expected.

Not, she thought, that her sister had allowed that line of reasoning to enter her mind from what Marcos had told her. She would have to confront Laura with that.

He strode towards the door, and Beth subconsciously thought how graceful his movements were for someone of his height and powerful build. Stealthy, she corrected herself. Like a jungle animal. He probably slept with one eye open as well.

He paused just as he was about to leave and threw over his shoulder, 'By the way, if Angela calls, make some excuse. She's being a bit of a nuisance.'

With that he clicked the door behind him and Beth frowned. Angela? Who on earth was Angela? She was obviously meant to know who Angela was and was expected to dispatch her efficiently out of his life. Was this all in the line of duty? Ha!

She spent the remainder of the afternoon ploughing through the stack of dictated tapes and messages in her tray, occasionally breaking off to take phone calls and to rummage through the computer files, gradually building up a picture of Marcos's extensive business involvements.

There was much more to it than hotels, although they were by far the bulk of his business. Hotels spread across the world, from New York to Tokyo.

In addition he had investments in several electronics firms and software companies.

Had he built all this from nothing? Even if he had not, the man was clearly a dynamo in the concrete jungle.

When she next looked at her watch, it had gone seven o'clock and she hastily packed up. This, she reminded herself, was only a temporary excursion into the Adrino corporation. Filling in time until Laura could take over. It wouldn't do to start becoming too involved.

Now she understood why her sister had been so keen to keep her feet in the company.

She made her way back on the Underground to Laura's flat, which was in Swiss Cottage. It was a rented apartment. Very comfortable and large enough really for two people, but lacking in character. Nothing like her little place, but then you never had the incentive to do anything with property that did not belong to you, she supposed.

Laura, anyway, had never been terribly houseproud. While she could spend hours browsing in an antique shop, Laura had always been more than happy to flit from boutique to boutique, spending all her money on clothes.

And it showed, Beth thought wryly, as she prepared herself a light meal of tuna and French bread. Her sister's wardrobe was about five times the size of hers and the clothes were way out of her price range.

As soon as she had eaten, she telephoned her sister, waiting in frustration as she heard the flat ringing tone. Surely Laura wouldn't be out living it up, for heaven's sake? She hardly knew a soul in Cambridge. Beth herself only had a handful of good friends there. She had told them that she was going to be away for a while and that her sister would be looking after her flat, but none of them knew any of the details and she didn't care for the thought of Laura spilling them unwittingly.

Her train of thought was broken by Laura's voice at the end of the line.

'Beth,' she heard the voice distantly, and felt a sudden pang of longing to be back in her flat in Cambridge and far away from this dreadful affair. 'How was your first day at work?' There was a brief pause, then she continued anxiously, 'You made out all right, didn't you?'

'Oh, none of your colleagues recognised anything amiss,' Beth began. 'They commented on the change of hairstyle but that was about all, and I've been doing a lot of work getting myself up to the mark on your work.'

'You will remember that it's not permanent, won't you?'

Beth smiled. 'Of course I will. Believe me, working for Marcos Adrino, invigorating though the work might be, isn't my cup of tea.'

She heard her sister gasp down the line and her smile broadened. She could imagine Laura's expression of horror that she had been plunged into the deep end so suddenly.

'But he's not back in England until the end of the week,' she wailed.

'Well, then, he's obviously more unpredictable than you thought. He was there when I got in, and I don't have to tell you that I almost had a heart attack when I heard his voice from behind me.' She shivered involuntarily.

'What did you do? What did you say? You didn't give the game away, did you?' Laura's voice had risen to a panicky squeak.

'No, and don't get so excited, for heaven's sake. Not in your condition.' She sat down on the sofa, curling her legs underneath her, her eyes absent-mindedly wandering over the television which she had switched on earlier, having turned down the volume to make the phone call. It was a cheap thriller of some sort, and the entire cast seemed to be wearing expressions of either bewilderment or guilt.

'Well? Tell me all the details. Hang on, I'll just settle down here. Your cushions are so delicate. You need some great big ones on the floor.'

'Thanks, but try not to give in to the urge to redecorate my flat. You've done quite enough at the moment, what with redecorating my life.'

'So spill the beans. Tell all.'

'Laura,' Beth said bluntly, 'what the hell has been going on in that office with you?'

'What do you mean?'

'I mean the man laid into me the minute I was in his office. He said that you had been shirking your job, coming in late.'

'Oh.' There was a sheepish silence at the other end, then Laura burst out defensively, 'It only happened a couple of times.'

'A couple?'

'Well, four or five.'

Beth sighed. 'Well, he found out about the four or five times and he was livid.'

'Oh, dear. I wonder who told him? I had morning sickness. Honestly, Beth, I just couldn't drag myself into work on time, and I could hardly tell anyone, could I? I'm sorry. Although it's kind of a relief that you were there to handle him. I've heard that he can be positively scary when he's crossed. I would have just burst into tears, I know it. I've been very emotional since I got pregnant.'

'Thanks,' Beth commented wryly. 'But I can tell you I wished I'd never been talked into this insanity.'

'You're not going to back out, are you?' There was a hint of tears already in Laura's voice.

'No, but I want some honesty from you. This David character. Was he the only one? I mean...'

'Beth! How could you even imply...!'

'You can be a bit of a flirt,' she stated flatly, 'so don't play the innocent with me, my girl. Don't forget, I know you better than anyone else in the world. You've spent a lifetime mastering the art of getting yourself into scrapes with men, so don't act as though you're shocked by the question.'

'I haven't been sleeping around, if you must know,' Laura said with asperity. 'The minute I met David, that was it.'

'Good.' At least that was one less problem to worry about, Beth thought. She couldn't have coped with an entourage of men beating a path to the top floor whenever the coast was clear.

'What do you think of Marcos?' She heard her sister's voice and it was brimming over with curiosity.

'I've met more pleasant people in my time,' Beth answered firmly. 'He's every bit as arrogant as I expected him to be.'

'But attractive, wouldn't you say?'

'I suppose so,' Beth confessed grudgingly, remembering the feeling of hostility he had evoked in her, 'though not my type. He's too self-confident for his own good and he acts as though when he says jump he really expects the rest of the world to obey.'

'Oh, they do.'

I can believe it, Beth thought. She changed the topic. She didn't like talking about Marcos Adrino. It made her think of him, and thinking of him made her skin begin to prickle.

They chatted about what the weather was doing, Beth reminded Laura not to forget to water her plants and to collect a dress from the dry cleaners down the road, and it was only as she got into bed that she suddenly remembered Angela.

She had completely forgotten to ask Laura who the hell Angela was, and how she was supposed to handle her.

Then she decided that she didn't care anyway. As far as she could see, it wasn't part of her job description, or rather her sister's, to deal with Marcos's personal life, and if he didn't like it, then he could lump it.

She put it to the back of her mind and there it remained the following morning as she busied herself with her twin tasks of briefing herself on the company, including the project in Santo Domingo, and typing up the reports that had been left on her desk after she had gone home.

Marcos had obviously put in an appearance at the company, and it must have been late because he had been nowhere to be seen when she had left. He must run on overdrive, she thought.

She was relaxing over her fifteen-minute lunch break comprised of a cup of black coffee and an apple, when the door to her office was flung open and Marcos swept in, bringing with him that feeling of restless energy that she had seen the day before.

'I'll have one of those,' he said without stopping at her desk, 'in my office.'

He strode into his office, slamming the door behind him and Beth winced. A very good afternoon to you too, she mouthed, gulping down her last bite of apple and moving over to the percolator.

He was poring over some paperwork at his desk and he barely glanced up when she entered.

'Your coffee?' she reminded him of her presence.

He stared at the cup, then he stared at her. 'What the hell is that?'

'It's a cup of coffee,' she answered. What else could it be? A jug of orange juice?

'I don't take my coffee black. I take it white, with one teaspoon of sugar.' He leant back in his chair and scrutinised her. 'Surely you should know that by now?' he asked softly. 'You've really changed, and more than just your hairstyle. Am I missing something here? Am I being a bit dense?'

Beth retrieved the cup from the desk, steadying her nerves. She had automatically poured him the same coffee as she had herself. Stupid. Little oversights like this made this dangerous game as glaringly obvious as if she had committed some larger, more noticeable mistake.

'I'm sorry. My mind must have been elsewhere.'

'Either that, or you left it behind in Cambridge.'

'What?' Beth asked sharply, smiling to hide the sudden tension she felt.

'You went to stay with your sister, didn't you? Jane told me.'

'My sister?' Her mind was working furiously. Who, she wondered, was Jane? The office spy from the sounds of it, and office spies could be extremely dangerous.

'Something wrong with your hearing today, Laura?' he asked, his eyes narrowing suspiciously.

Beth smiled again. 'Of course I went to stay with my sister. In Cambridge.' She gave a little laugh. 'I would have gone somewhere more glamorous, but my funds were a little low at the time.' She would have to stop being so jumpy every time she thought that he was edging towards the truth. After all, there was no way that he could even suspect that Laura was miles away in her little flat, while she was here pretending to be someone she was not.

'Where would you have gone?' he asked curiously. 'I would have associated you a few weeks ago with somewhere on the French Riviera, close to a few nightclubs, but perhaps I misread you completely.'

Beth shrugged non-committally. She didn't like this sudden digression on to personal topics. There could be a lot of unexpected traps here. For a start, she didn't know what Laura had told him about herself, if anything, and he wasn't likely to dismiss another slip-up like the coffee. He was altogether too shrewd. His clever, calculating mind probably stored information that most normal people would forget within seconds. Stored it and had it quite handy to recall at a moment's notice.

'I've never been to the French Riviera,' Beth finally volunteered, as he continued to look at her from under his dark lashes. 'And I've never felt any particular wish to go, if you must know. In fact, I haven't done a great deal of travelling at all.'

'But you'd like to?' he prompted.

Beth fidgeted uncomfortably. She didn't like this. She was sure that he couldn't give two hoots whether she hated the idea of planes, or else saved madly to go on one. Laura had said that he barely noticed her except in her capacity as secretary. So why the sudden interest now? She wondered whether he suspected something odd, a little thought hovering somewhere at the back of his mind. A little thought that he was beginning to explore.

'Wouldn't everyone?' she answered distantly.

'No. I personally have seen enough of airports to last me a lifetime. Hotel life, you know, outstays its welcome very quickly.'

'Does it? I wouldn't know. Anyway, I'll make you a fresh cup of coffee now, if you like.'

'Why,' he drawled, 'do I get the impression that you're eager to get out of my company?'

His words, for reasons that she couldn't fathom, sent a hot flood of colour to her cheeks. Or maybe it was the way he had spoken them, in that lazy, slightly speculative voice.

Whatever, there was no answer to that question and she left the office quickly, only realising how tense she had been when she exhaled her breath deeply in the safety of her own room.

By the time she re-entered his office she was perfectly in control of her senses once again, and the cup of coffee was precisely how he liked it.

He began to talk to her about work and she breathed a sigh of relief. When he talked about work, she was on relatively safe ground.

As she was leaving his office, she turned around and said on the spur of the moment, 'Do you remember what you said to me about getting bored of hotel life very quickly?'

He looked up from his paperwork and nodded.

'Well,' Beth continued awkwardly, 'it's just a thought, but these projects in St Lucia and Santo Domingo—you could try and make them places that would never outstay their welcome.'

He looked at her assessingly.

'Any suggestions?'

Beth laughed genuinely. 'None at all. Don't forget I'm inexperienced enough to find any sort of hotel life quite a novelty.'

He looked as though he was about to say something, but when he finally did it was only to inform her briskly that she could apply herself to giving the matter some thought, then he returned to his paperwork.

Effective dismissal, Beth thought, letting herself out, but she felt suddenly invigorated.

She was absorbed in reading one of the folders on St Lucia when the outside door to her office opened. But it wasn't Marian, who normally peeped in with files or reports for Marcos.

This woman she had never seen before.

'Can I help you?' Beth asked, wondering how she had managed to bypass the usual security checks and make her way successfully to the top floor.

'Is Marcos around?' The woman smiled politely. She was very poised, every strand of blonde hair neatly tucked into a sophisticated chignon at the back of her neck.

'Who may I say is asking?'

'Oh, don't bother to announce me,' she said quickly, 'I'll let myself in.'

Before Beth could do anything to stop her, the woman had made her way to the connecting door, and Beth could just see Marcos's dark head look up, then the door was very firmly closed.

She returned to her work, but her mind was seething with questions.

Finally, and with a feeling of ridiculous surreptitiousness, she called Laura at her workplace, and said without preamble, 'A blonde woman just walked into Marcos's office. She didn't tell me who she was. Am I supposed to know?'

'Blonde?' Laura asked. 'Very leggy and very glamorous? Probably wearing silk or cashmere?'

'That's the one.' The woman had been dressed in a pale pink cashmere suit with a strand of pearls around her neck, and they didn't look like the synthetic stuff either.

'Remember I told you that Marcos is quite something with the women?'

'Yes,' Beth answered.

'Well, that's one of them. Angela Fordyce.' She groaned down the phone. 'He finished with her about three weeks ago, and under no circumstances were you supposed to let her in to see him!'

CHAPTER THREE

BETH tried to summon up the feeling of bravado she had had the previous day when she had resolutely decided that Marcos could handle his own damned personal life.

But sitting here, in front of her computer, her eyes flitting warily across to the connecting door, it was difficult.

She had already been subjected to his cold anger and it was something she had no desire to experience again.

She frowned at the file she had been poring over a minute before, but the words were just a jumble of black and white. Eventually she gave up.

She could, she thought, leave for home. It was already half-past five. She chewed her lip, glanced across at the door again and remained undecidedly rooted to her chair for another half an hour.

This is ridiculous, she finally decided. Hovering about here like some sort of criminal waiting to stand before the judge.

She stacked her papers away and unhooked her coat from the coat-stand. Now that she had decided to leave, her feet couldn't move fast enough, and by the time she made it to the ground floor she was positively churning with tension.

She only managed to regain some of her equilibrium on the Underground back to the flat, but even when she was safely indoors she found that she was plagued by the same sense of apprehension.

More alarmingly, her mind was fizzing over with questions that she knew shouldn't concern her at all.

Was that the type of woman he fancied? Tall and blonde and with the sort of impeccable good looks that spoke of hours painstakingly spent in front of the mirror? Angela Fordyce, she found herself thinking uncharitably, didn't look as though her brain had ever taxed itself with anything more complicated than whether her colour scheme for the day matched.

Not that it was any concern of hers anyway. The man was infinitely dislikeable, someone who constantly seemed to rub her up the wrong way. He was welcome to his following of leggy blondes. Peculiar though it might seen, they probably suited him. Men whose work lives ran on constant pressure no doubt found the company of brainless bimbos relaxing. They could unwind without the tiring obligation of actually having to respond to any manner of intelligent conversation.

She switched on the television, laughing at her line of thought. Am I really so bitchy? she wondered. She had never been before.

She had changed into a pair of tight jeans and a loose sweater and she had a sudden, unwelcome image of herself standing next to Angela Fordyce, her short bob hardly the most glamorous hairstyle in the world, her face bereft of any make-up, her feet inelegantly clad in a pair of thick woollen socks to stave off the cold.

With a little frown she shoved the image to the back of her mind and settled down to follow the detective movie. She liked detective movies. Something about them appealed to the logical processes in her brain. That was probably why she enjoyed the mathematical precision of her accountancy course. There was no room for emotive flights in an accountancy course. Things made sense with it. Two and two always added up to four.

Her mother once told her that it was a trait that she must have inherited from her father. He had possessed a fine mind, a mind that had enjoyed the precision of logic.

Laura, she had said, took after her. They were both volatile and emotional. Two and two, with a generous helping of imagination, sometimes added up to five.

Why, Beth thought pensively, had she suddenly remembered that? Was it because her cool, reasonable approach to life had recently been less reliable? Odd.

She refocused her attention on the small screen and was once again absorbed in various permutations of theory being volunteered by the chief detective, when there was a sharp knocking on the door.

She reluctantly got up, wondering who on earth it could be. Were there such things as door-to-door salesmen in London? Or maybe it was Katie. She had been meaning to get in touch with Katie, but hadn't found the time so far.

She pulled open the door and her body tensed immediately.

'Oh,' she said, simply because she couldn't find anything better to say, 'it's you.'

'Surprised?' Marcos walked past her into the small lounge, making no apology for his appearance even though it was after ten o'clock.

He stood in the centre of the room and stared with blatant curiosity around him.

Beth felt her hackles begin to rise.

'I thought only doctors paid home visits,' she said pointedly, shutting the door behind her. She would have preferred to leave it open, so that he could get the message that she really didn't want him in the flat, but it was simply too cold outside for that.

Now that the door was shut, she had a sudden feeling of choking claustrophobia.

'Funny,' he mused, 'I would have expected your flat to have more of an imprint of your personality on it. It looks as though you only use it as a place to sleep.'

'Have you come here for something specific?' Beth asked, reasserting her presence. She moved to the chair furthest away from him and sat primly on it, leaning forward slightly, her arms folded across her chest.

She was aware of her heart beating quickly and heavily. What was he doing here? He had obviously just come from work, he was still wearing his suit, although that didn't exactly speak volumes, did it? She had left him at the office with Angela; who knows what they had got up to? He might have finished with her, but men, she knew, were very susceptible to a beautiful and willing woman, even a beautiful and willing woman who had gone past her sell-by date.

'Why did you let her into the office?' He looked at her through half-closed eyes.

'What?'

'You heard. Angela. Why did you let her into my office when I expressly told you not to?'

Oh, so this is it, she thought. He couldn't even have the courtesy to wait until the morning before venting his anger.

She felt a stab of indignation. Some of that bravado that had eluded her earlier on was returning.

'I could hardly put her under civil arrest just because she wanted to see you, could I?'

'You could have told her that I was out,' he said forcefully. 'Or ill, or in a meeting. The list of excuses is endless. You've always managed to handle that sort of situation before.'

'Have I indeed?' So it was one of her unofficial duties, and one which her sister had happily complied with. Well, she had no intention of following suit.

'Yes, you damn well have,' he snapped.

'Well, as a matter of fact,' Beth informed him calmly, 'I don't see why I have to handle your personal life for you.'

'What?' he roared. He stood up and began pacing the room, running his fingers through his hair. Beth watched him without moving, fascinated. It was an effort to finally drag her eyes away and sternly remind herself of all those qualities he possessed which she thoroughly disliked.

'I said——'

'I heard what you said the first time.'

'Then, there's no problem, is there?'

'There damn well is! I don't like the implied criticism in your voice one bit! Have you forgotten that you're my secretary?'

This was quite a different sort of anger from the icy anger he had shown her when she had first arrived at the office. This was more like a thunderous rage.

Beth didn't see any reason why she should bend under its impact when he was exercising it in her flat. Or rather her sister's flat. Whatever.

'I've decided that my duties stop with my work,' she stated in a voice that was far more controlled than she actually felt.

'Oh, you've decided, have you?' Marcos asked smoothly. 'And since when? Since that overhaul you had on your week off? That damn sister of yours has a lot to answer for.'

Doesn't she just? Beth thought.

He paced across to where she was sitting, and before she could take defensive measures leaned over her, his hands gripping either side of her chair.

Beth felt herself automatically flinch back. This was way too close for comfort. He was making her giddy; something about his nearness overwhelmed her. It was almost an effort to breathe normally.

'I...' she began, then her mouth seemed to dry up and she found that she couldn't complete the sentence.

'I know what you think,' he said grimly, overriding anything she might have had to say. 'You've suddenly decided that it's all right to start passing moral judgements on my personal life.'

'I haven't decided any such thing,' she muttered weakly. She just wanted him to go away, now, even if it was only to another part of the room. He was too close, his arms only inches away from her breasts.

'You damn well have,' he shot back, his eyes glinting. 'As far as I'm concerned this little self-righteous act of yours doesn't cut any ice with me whatsoever. You're hardly eligible for the horrified virgin act, are you?'

His words were carefully placed. Without thinking, Beth raised her hand and slapped him angrily across the cheek, watching in horror as his face swivelled under the impact.

The hooded black eyes met hers with a gleam.

'That certainly hit home, didn't it?' he said softly.

'You're despicable.'

'At least I don't pretend to be what I'm not.'

His words, unthinkingly, were so accurate that Beth felt her face blanch.

'You've been sleeping around with Ryan and God knows how many other men, and you actually have the nerve to silently criticise me!'

There was no answer to that one.

'Moreover,' he continued, still leaning over her, stifling her with his proximity, 'I damn well ought to give you the sack for what you've just done.'

'Why don't you?' Beth challenged, throwing caution to the winds.

'God knows,' he muttered, standing up. She released her breath slowly as he moved away to stand next to the window.

She had saved Laura's job, if only by the skin of her teeth, and the thought should have made her feel elated, but it didn't. Something had changed, her control had slipped and that made her uneasy and a little bit frightened.

This was poetic justice, she thought, for having been stupid enough to take part in this monumental piece of deception in the first place.

'The fact is——' Marcos turned to face her '—I didn't really come here to talk about Angela in the first place. She's no longer part of my life anyway. No, I came here to ask you whether your passport's in order.'

'Pardon?' Beth's eyes opened wide. Things were moving way too fast for her liking.

'Your passport—is it in order?'

She nodded. 'Why do you ask?'

'Because you're coming to St Lucia with me.'

'I am?' she squeaked, suddenly realising that for some reason she couldn't fathom she didn't want to do that at all.

'You can book the flights tomorrow, and we'll fly on Thursday morning. I have a meeting arranged with my man over there that evening.'

'Thursday? This Thursday morning?' She knew that she must sound like a parrot, repeating everything he said, but their conversation was beginning to have an air of unreality about it.

'You really should have that hearing problem seen to,' he said sarcastically. 'This Thursday. Yes. You should be able to make all the arrangements in a day. I'll be out of the office.' He paused significantly. 'You said you wanted to travel, didn't you?' he drawled.

'Yes, but...' But not with you, she finished silently.

He was staring at her and he must have been reading her mind, because his next words were, 'You can relax. You won't be alone with me, not that I would have thought that you were intimidated by being thrown together with a member of the opposite sex. No, Jane will be coming with us.'

'Jane?' She decided to ignore his sarcastic remark at her expense. He could think what he liked of her from now on; she didn't care.

'Yes, Jane Morris,' he said impatiently. 'Marketing manager?'

'Of course. Jane.' The name rang a vague bell in her head now that she heard the surname. It must have been one of the names that Laura had mentioned when she had been filling her in on the company personnel.

'And in case you get any ideas,' he said, resuming his unnerving prowling around the room, 'this is a business trip. I don't intend to have to keep my eye on you.'

'Why would you have to do that?' Beth asked with genuine curiosity.

'Because,' he said, stopping to look down at her, 'from what I've heard you're not against, shall we say, promoting yourself at the first available opportunity?'

He smiled cynically and she had an irresistible urge to repeat her slap, but she controlled it. Instead she stared down at her fingers, not trusting herself to answer.

'Not going to see me to the door?' he asked, throwing his scarf around his neck.

Beth got up reluctantly, following him to the front door and keeping just enough distance between them so that her nervous system didn't start doing funny things again.

'You know something?' he said in a lazy voice, as he was about to leave. 'Out of work clothes, you're not at all what I had expected.' His eyes scanned her briefly, but Beth had the oddest sensation of having been stripped of her clothing. 'My character assessment of you was obviously wildly misplaced.'

With that parting shot, she watched him as he stepped quickly across to his car, a sleek Jaguar which had been slotted in between two contraptions that looked as though they had seen action in the First World War.

She waited until the car had sped off and was out of sight, then she slowly let herself back into the flat, shivering from the night air.

Her movements were leisurely as she cleared away her coffee-cup, undressed, slipped into her pyjamas, but her thoughts were tripping over each other.

An all-expenses-paid trip to the Caribbean should have sent her spirits zooming on to Cloud Nine, but she considered the prospect with growing apprehension.

Working with him was bad enough, but in St Lucia she would be in his presence without respite. Almost without respite, she amended. There was Jane Morris, whoever she might be.

She glanced at the bedside clock, wondering whether it was too late to telephone her sister and decided that pregnant women would definitely be a little put out by a phone call in the middle of the night.

Instead she flung open the wardrobe drawers and inspected Laura's supply of clothing.

At least, she thought wryly, she wouldn't have to rush out in her lunch hour and purchase a set of summer clothes. There were T-shirts of every hue, light dresses, shorts and swimsuits. She picked them up slowly. All bikinis. And the sort of bikinis that left very little to the imagination. Not a one-piece in sight. Well, it was too late to remedy that. They would have to do.

By the time she finally got into bed it was well into the early hours of the morning and she awakened six hours later feeling totally unrefreshed.

Outside, the sunshine had resolutely lost the battle it had been fighting for the past day or so, and it was raining furiously.

Lucky me. Tomorrow I'll be out of all this, she thought brightly, wishing she could feel slightly more enthusiastic.

Her thoughts were even gloomier one hour later when she arrived at the office.

She had spoken to Laura, had had to endure at least fifteen minutes of her shrieks of envy, and had then been informed that Jane Morris was not exactly the most congenial companion to be stuck with for a few days.

'She doesn't like me,' Laura had said emphatically. 'She's never liked me. I'm surprised she hasn't put in an appearance in Marcos's office as yet. She's always hovering around, like a bad smell, just itching to make some snide little dig at my expense. Maybe she got eaten up by her workload.'

'She can't be that bad,' Beth had protested in dismay, only to be informed that she was worse.

'She thinks I sleep around,' Laura had said casually, and Beth got the distinct impression that this little titbit had been deliberately saved until she was well and truly ensconced down here.

'Which you don't,' she had said wearily.

'Certainly not! I have to admit that I became quite friendly with some of the guys in the office, you know, had a few drinks now and then after work, but that was as far as it went. And once David came along, well...'

Quite friendly? A few drinks? Oh, God. Beth hadn't wanted to hear any more. She had rested her head on her hand, feeling like an unwary climber who had suddenly stumbled into thick fog.

Was it any wonder that there was just the tiniest whiff of a reputation surrounding her sister? Couldn't Laura ever handle herself with a bit of moderation?

And Fate didn't even have the compassion to comply with her plea that the plane be already fully booked.

She phoned through with the dates, her fingers crossed that the last-minute booking would ensure no seats, only to be told that she was very fortunate as they were travelling out of the tourist season so that there was no problem with the flight. Especially in the first class section. He quoted her a price and Beth gulped in shock.

'Can't take any more of this dreary English weather, eh?' the girl's voice down the other end joked.

'I can,' Beth replied seriously, 'but it's the boss's orders.'

'Would you like to swap jobs?'

Quicker than you can imagine, she thought.

At least she had been granted one day's reprieve from Marcos. She wouldn't be seeing him until the following morning at Gatwick Airport, nor, she was relieved to find, would she have to make the trip up with Jane. There was a memo waiting for her on the desk when she arrived to work that bluntly informed her that Jane would be overnighting in Reigate, so that Laura would have to find her own way to the airport.

During her lunch-hour, Beth darted out to the chemist's and bought herself some suntan oil and moisturising cream, and then spent the rest of the day trying to concentrate on her workload.

For once she left on the dot of five. There was packing to do, even though they would only be away for four days, and in between she fitted in her overdue telephone call to Katie.

She was astonished to discover what a relief it was to chat to someone who was aware of her true identity. In the background she could hear the sound of screaming children, and she grinned. Laura was in for a shock when she discovered that her bundle of joy was also a bundle of hard work.

But there was one thing to be grateful for. Katie sounded like a pleasant, down-to-earth person. They both amicably grumbled that taking part in Laura's scheme had been temporary insanity.

'She can be very persuasive,' Katie sighed.

Beth laughed. 'It's called nagging and it's an art she mastered long ago. She can coerce her way into anything. She just switches on that pleading look and then talks until you give up out of sheer weariness.'

Katie chuckled. 'But don't you love it?'

'Unfortunately.'

She had an early night, for the first time since she had arrived in London, and only felt a renewed onslaught of nerves when she arrived at the airport.

There was no Marcos around, and no one had tapped her on her shoulder, so she presumed that the unpleasant Jane had not arrived either.

Laura had described her to Beth, so hopefully she would be able to recognise the woman without too much difficulty.

She did. Jane was waiting in the roomy lounge upstairs reserved for the first class travellers, and Beth approached her cautiously.

'You've had your hair cut,' Jane greeted her, not bothering to stand up. 'Not trying to cultivate an impression of efficiency, by any chance?'

Beth sat down next to her and realised that her sister had not exaggerated. Jane did not like Laura. It was there in the tone of her voice and in the sharp look in her eyes.

She was a plain woman, somewhere in her mid-thirties, Beth reckoned, with close-cropped mousy brown hair, a pear-shaped figure that looked as though it would run to fat the minute one chocolate bar too many was consumed, and cold pale blue eyes.

The pale blue eyes were fixed maliciously on her now.

'How did you manage to talk your way into going on this trip with Marcos?' she asked. 'He never usually takes you anywhere with him.'

Beth shrugged and fished out a magazine from her bag. 'Maybe he's decided that my horizons need enlarging,' she suggested blandly.

Jane's thin lips compressed. 'I doubt that. You're only a secretary, after all.'

'How nice of you to remind me.'

She could tell that her composure was beginning to annoy the other woman. Perhaps Laura had not been quite so outspoken with her. Knowing her sister, she had probably taken the easier route of avoidance.

'Or maybe you talked your way into it. We all know about you.'

Beth lowered the magazine she had been about to read and looked coolly at the other woman.

'And what precisely do you know?'

Jane smiled, but her eyes were gleaming with malevolence. 'Oh, your reputation precedes you. David Ryan, for instance?'

So I was right, she thought. This was the informer.

'You were the one who told Marcos about...'

'Who else?' She smoothed her skirt, dusting a few invisible flecks from it. 'I thought it was my duty to do so. After all, it's not exactly professional to be conducting an affair with one of the directors, is it?'

'Of course not,' Beth gushed sarcastically. 'I can only thank you for the interest you've shown in the company, and in me too, because I'm sure you only had my welfare at heart.'

Jane looked at her with hatred. 'Anyway, that's put paid to any little ideas you might have had of sleeping with Marcos. I'm sure he's not the kind of man to fraternise with tarts.'

Beth took a deep breath. What she really wanted to do was jump to her feet and bring her magazine resoundingly down on Jane's head, but she had no intention of giving in to any such impulse. She knew instinctively that composure was the only way to deal with this level of dislike.

'I'm sure you're right,' she said placidly, opening the magazine and turning the pages with interest. She could feel the other woman simmering beside her, waiting for an opportunity to continue the conversation.

It was almost laughable, she thought. And of course blatantly transparent. Jane Morris had done everything in her power to blacken Laura's name, because of the little green monster.

It accounted for Marcos's insinuations that Laura was a practised temptress and Laura's own declarations that she might have joked around with some of the men in the office before David appeared on the scene, but that it had got no further than that.

She began reading one of the articles, ignoring Jane's presence, only glancing up when the Tannoy informed them that it was time to board. There was still no sign of Marcos anywhere, and Beth had a sudden, awful thought. What if he had been delayed somehow? Four days with Jane was a fate worse than death.

'I hope,' Jane said with an insincere little snicker, 'that you won't let anything I've just told you get in the way of work.'

Beth looked at her pityingly. 'Why should I? Don't you know that there's nothing you could tell me that would have an effect on me whatsoever?'

They boarded the plane in frozen silence. She was almost glad to see Marcos finally arrive. He gave her a brief smile and a nod.

'Marcos?' Jane beckoned with a saccharine smile. She patted the seat next to her. 'I've brought my papers with me; I thought we might go over some of them on the way over.'

He slid his long body next to her, and Beth continued where she had left off with her magazine, listening to their low murmur on her left with irritation.

There was a reason behind Jane's jealousy of Laura, Beth realised. It wasn't simply that Jane was painfully unglamorous, though too vain ever to see herself in that light, and Laura was not.

No, Jane was infatuated with Marcos. It was apparent in the semi-flirtatious expression she wore whenever she looked at him.

And there were a lot of those. During the nine-hour flight, Beth caught herself glancing surreptitiously at them, noticing the way Jane touched him lightly ever so often, her hand lingering on his arm as they pored over some piece of paper. Always making sure that any conversation he began with Beth was instantly diverted back to herself.

And Marcos, she was amazed to see, wasn't aware of it at all.

But then, she thought acidly, why should he be? If she was right, and his type was along the lines of Angela Fordyce, then poor Jane wouldn't enter his scope at all. He saw her strictly as a working companion and was totally oblivious to any provocation behind her movements.

She was almost tempted to tell Jane that she had nothing to fear from her. Marcos Adrino was anything but sexy as far as she was concerned.

'Enjoyed the flight?' he asked, leaning over to her, as the plane descended towards Hewanorra International Airport.

'Luxurious,' Beth averred. 'A great way to travel for my first trip abroad.'

'First trip?' Jane piped up, inclining her body so that she could see Beth more clearly. 'Surely not. And I always thought that you would be the well-travelled sort.' She said it in a tone of voice that suggested an insult, and Beth stiffened.

'I'm not,' she said shortly, thankful that the roar of the engine as the plane landed made any further conversation impossible.

'You don't mind if I grip your hand, Marcos?' she heard Jane asking. 'I'm ever so nervous about landings.' She giggled coyly. 'I have a very sensitive disposition, you know. I can be as hard as nails when I'm in the office, but this sort of thing brings out the little girl in me.'

Marcos looked faintly startled, but acquiesced politely, and Beth watched Jane's fingers curl around his brown wrist.

She felt her stomach plummet as the plane bumped over the tarmac and then braked to a halt, slowly turning until it had finally stopped, and the passengers began to stand up, stretching and reaching for their bags in the overhead lockers.

They moved swiftly through customs. Beth could see some of the other passengers, mostly women, glancing furtively across at Marcos, wondering whether they should recognise him.

And, she admitted grudgingly, he certainly had an air about him. He was dressed casually in a pair of light grey trousers and an off-white shirt carelessly rolled to the elbows. An outfit that somehow managed to do much more for him than it would have done for anyone else.

His arms were strong and sprinkled with fine dark hair, and he moved with the easy grace of someone born to be in command. Jane was clearly in her element, and Beth thought with self-disgust that she was almost as bad, staring at him as though she had never seen a member of the male sex before.

Had she forgotten that she was here to work, as he had put it in no uncertain terms? More importantly, had she forgotten that men were not conducive to peace of mind, least of all men like him?

She wondered how he could have actually listened to anything Jane had had to say about Laura, and then realised that her sister, with her flamboyantly tousled hair streaming down her back, and that vivacious glint in her eyes, didn't exactly encourage the image of a shy, reserved individual.

She grinned to herself. He must have thought he was going mad when he had been confronted with her, same green eyes, but with a far more sober expression in them, and a neat little bob.

Outside the sun was brilliant, and Beth stood still for a moment, her eyes taking in the sharp azure of the skies, the vivid green of the foliage here and there.

It was everything she had imagined, and more. There was something steamy and untamed about this tropical island.

His contact was waiting for them at the airport. He was a young man with fresh good looks and a crisp English accent. He led them to the car, chatting to Marcos about his ideas for the hotel, but it didn't escape Beth that he had shown more than just friendly interest in her.

Nor had it escaped Jane, but Beth didn't care. It felt so good to be in the warmth, her light cotton dress blowing gently around her legs, that she didn't care about anything at all.

They were staying at one of the hotels to the very north of the island, relatively close to where Marcos had earmarked the site for his own development, and Beth relaxed in the air-conditioned car, silently appreciating the scenery as they headed off.

It really was a breathtakingly beautiful island. Roger, who was driving the car, explained for her benefit bits and pieces of the island's history, pointing out the huge banana plantations as they drove through. In the rear-view mirror she caught his eyes and smiled, listening in rapt silence as around them the dense, bright greenery of the plantation flashed past.

It was mountainous and lush, its hidden depths speaking to them with the noises of animals and insects.

They emerged from the hills into Castries and then further north where the houses seemed to be flattened against the hillside and framed by a wild green backdrop studded with the vivid colours of the bougainvillaea plants.

Too soon they had arrived at their hotel, a large place overlooking Reduit Bay with its white sand and shimmering water in the distance.

Beth got out of the car and stretched her legs, temporarily oblivious to everyone else as she stared around her.

Only Roger's voice at her side brought her back to reality.

'Stunning, isn't it?' he asked, his handsome, boyish face breaking into a grin.

Beth grinned back stupidly. 'And some.'

'I know you're here to work,' he said, glancing across to where Marcos was standing with Jane, involved in some discussion, 'but maybe we could get together for some drinks a bit later?'

'Maybe,' Beth said vaguely.

She could well do without the unexpected complication of Roger, however nice he was, but she knew that an outright refusal would have offended him, and anyway, what was the harm in a few drinks?

She turned towards the hotel to see Marcos looking at her through narrowed eyes. Jane shot her a triumphant glance and whispered something to him.

This, Beth thought wearily, was going to be a long four days, however splendid the scenery was.

CHAPTER FOUR

Roger followed them into the hotel, and then told Marcos that he had set up the meeting with the various local dignitaries and Herb Brewster, the Caribbean national manager of the Adrino chain, for eight that evening.

'I don't know whether you'll need me around at this stage of the discussions?' he asked, glancing involuntarily to where Beth was standing, idly perusing some of the hotel's promotional literature.

Marcos followed the line of his gaze expressionlessly, and Beth looked up in time to see Jane smiling craftily at her.

She gave them all a large, guileless smile and Roger's grin grew broader.

She sincerely hoped that Roger would not prove to be the persistent type. She abhorred the idea of leading men on—not that there had exactly been a series of them cluttering up her life anyway.

Craig had been the only one in as long as she could remember who had managed to break through the glaring hands-off signals she gave off.

She had watched Laura's constant entourage of men with amusement, but that sort of thing was not for her, she had decided a long time ago. But Craig had persisted, growing first piqued, then bored, then angry at her refusal to sleep with him. He had eventually left, leaving her to wonder whether it had all been worth it.

Could a man never enjoy a relationship without assuming that sex would be the inevitable outcome?

Marcos was frowning slightly at her, but Roger either did not notice or else saw nothing sinister in it. He sidled across to her and whispered, 'Tonight? How about a drink? I'm staying at one of the other hotels and the bigwigs will be having their meeting. So say I pick you up here around nine o'clock?'

The question hung in the air, and out of the corner of her eye she could see Marcos looking at her, his face grim.

'Why not?' she replied on impulse. If Marcos thought the worse of her, then that was his affair. She surely wouldn't be required to do any work on her first evening in St Lucia?

As soon as Roger had left, Jane approached her and said in a voice loud enough for Marcos to hear, 'My, you do establish your... contacts quickly.'

Beth bit back the retort. 'You're quite welcome to join us.'

'I wouldn't dream of it,' Jane said loudly. 'You know what they say about two's company. Anyway, I have some homework to catch up on later. I do envy you just being a secretary. Personally speaking, I don't think I'll have the time to enjoy this lovely island.'

Shame, Beth thought to herself, you must be very stupid to pass up the opportunity of seeing this wonderful place simply in an effort to impress Marcos Adrino.

She watched as Jane left for her room with an airy wave, preceded by the porter carrying her luggage, and was about to do the same when she felt Marcos's hand close around her arm.

'Not so fast,' he drawled.

Beth stopped in her tracks and turned to face him, staring pointedly down at where he was gripping her arm. It was lost on him. He continued to grasp her, leading her across to one of the bars.

'Care for a drink?' he asked.

'No. Thank you.'

'What will it be? Something long and cold?'

Beth shrugged and tried to ignore the sensation of his fingers on her bare flesh. His hand was warm on her skin and sent a little *frisson* of awareness through her body.

'I'll have a grapefruit juice,' she said finally, realising that any attempt to get to her room was futile. This man was not accustomed to having his implicit orders countermanded, and he wasn't about to change now.

'Fine.' He ordered drinks for them both, and ushered her across to a chair.

'What do you think of St Lucia so far?' he asked, his dark eyes meeting hers directly.

Beth's gaze shifted away from him. Whenever he looked at her so intently, she immediately began to feel nervous and self-conscious.

'It's beautiful.'

'I hope it doesn't go to your head.'

'Meaning?'

'Meaning that you seem to have forgotten my little warning to you.'

'I haven't.' Why pretend that she didn't know what he was talking about?

'And it still didn't stop you from making arrangements to see Roger Drew tonight?' he asked softly.

Beth's eyes flashed. 'I didn't think that all my time here was answerable to you!'

'It is if I tell you so.'

'Don't you think that that's a little autocratic?' she asked sweetly, stifling her anger at his attitude. She had never met someone so arrogant in her life before. Was it really any wonder that she disliked him so much?

'You're not here on a goddammed holiday.'

'I realise that. And I wouldn't have made arrangements to see anyone if I knew that there was work to be done. But, unlike Jane,' she couldn't resist adding, even though she could hear the childish edge in her voice, 'I don't have a workload to take to bed.'

'So you've decided to replace it with something else? Or, should I say, someone else?'

'How dare you?'

'I dare because you work for me. A little detail that you seem to have conveniently put to the back of your mind.' He sipped from his drink, and continued to stare at her from under his long lashes.

Beth wanted to tell him that it was none of his business what she did with Roger Drew, but sensed instinctively that such a remark would be akin to playing dangerously close to a fire.

She had already come close to losing her sister's job for her. There was no point in pushing her luck.

If only, she thought. If only it were *my* job, then I'd tell him exactly what he could do with it. She tried to think of the bliss of never having to set eyes on that devilishly handsome face in her life again, but her mind refused to co-operate. Had he got so much under her skin? she wondered uneasily.

'Something about you doesn't add up,' he said lazily, not taking his eyes off her. 'I don't know if it's the impression you're trying to make, but with that new hairdo you seem to be trying to give off different signals. Now, though, I can see that it was just my mind playing tricks on me. I mean, you seem to have forgotten Ryan with the greatest of ease, don't you?'

Beth fidgeted in her chair, her face burning. She hated mention of David Ryan's name. He was the man who had betrayed her sister, and anyway, she was hardly qualified to talk about him.

But Marcos obviously expected some kind of answer.

'I haven't forgotten him,' she said, lowering her eyes.

'Trying to, then?' he prompted, his eyes hard. 'Trying to drown your lovesick blues in another man?'

'No! I'm not trying to do any such thing!'

'Then what? Don't tell me that you still feel anything for him.'

'Yes, I do!' She remembered her sister's words, her pathetic expressions of love. 'I still love him!' It was out before she could help herself, and she saw an icy shutter clamp down over his eyes.

'Love?' he scorned. 'Is that how you express your love? By leading on Drew?' He sat forward and, his action too quick to be avoidable, took her face between his hands, forcing her to look at him.

Beth had the buckling sensation of going under.

'I won't allow it!' he asserted.

'It's none of your business,' she exploded, her anger partly aimed at herself for having expressed an opinion that she was really not qualified to speak on. How could she have let this stupid charade overcome her natural sense of discretion? How could she have let slip anything about David, when, whether Marcos knew it or not, it had nothing to do with her personally?

She hated this deceit. Not for the first time, she wished desperately that she had stuck to her guns and refused to give in to her sister.

'It damned well is! Have you forgotten that he's a member of my company? Have you forgotten that I don't need my secretary to shout her indiscretions from the roof-tops?'

'I'm doing nothing of the sort!' she protested feebly. But she could see all too clearly how she must appear in his eyes. A woman who had slept with one man, in fact still professed to love him, yet was not against making a rendezvous with another the minute the opportunity arose.

There was blatant scorn on his face. It was this contempt that made her burst out vehemently, 'I don't lecture to you on how you conduct your personal life!' She held her breath, waiting for the inevitable fury, but none came.

Instead, he relaxed back in his chair. 'Would you like to?' he asked with lazy interest.

'Would I like to what?' She still felt dazed at this abrupt departure from what she had expected.

'Lecture to me on my personal life. I know you've got a bagful of opinions on it, even though it's clear to the both of us that you have no right. So come on, tell me what you think. No one ever has before. It might make an amusing change.'

There was silence. Was this yet another game he was playing with her? she wondered. He seemed to be waiting for her answer, mildly curious, his long fingers stroking the side of his glass absent-mindedly.

'I really don't think that we ought to be having this conversation,' she ventured awkwardly. 'I am only your secretary, after all.'

'You mean if we had slept together, you might have had more of a right to tell me what you thought?'

His voice was tantalisingly soft and it sent an excited shiver through her.

Unbidden, a thousand thoughts sprang into her head. Slept with him. If she had slept with him. What would it be like?

She suddenly felt so strong a yearning to find out that she gasped in shock.

Those long, clever fingers, what would it be like to feel them exploring her body, to feel his mouth moving restlessly against hers?

My God, she thought with a flood of panic, get a grip on yourself! You've been disillusioned once before, remember? He's not your type, remember?

'It's not my place to volunteer any information like that,' she whispered huskily, not daring to look at him fully in the face, concentrating on the potted plant just to the right of him. A magnificent dwarf palm that would never have survived in England.

'It's not stopped you before. In fact, until recently, I assumed that you didn't have any opinions on my private life one way or another, but now—well, tell me. It's an order.'

'If you really want to know,' Beth began hesitatingly, her body rigid with tension, 'from what I've seen, you don't mind using women for your own ends. You take them and, as soon as they stop amusing you, you have no qualms in dropping them. Like a child that suddenly loses interest in a plaything. Don't you care that they might be more involved with you than you are with them?'

She thought of Angela Fordyce, desperate enough to accost him in his office even though he had finished with her. She looked like a woman who had always pulled the strings, except with Marcos.

'Why do you object to that? Aren't you the same?'

Beth's automatic response was to deny the accusation, but how could she?

'Besides,' he continued when she remained silent, 'I never give promises I can't keep. True enough, I wine, dine and bed them, but I play fairly. I never let them think that the relationship stretches beyond those parameters.'

'You make sure that they don't get their feet into the front door.'

'That's right,' he drawled. 'I never was interested in playing house—not as a little boy, and not now. Marriage is one institution I don't intend to succumb to. From what I've seen, the attractions are invariably short-lived.'

Beth swallowed some of the fruit juice. She felt as though they were entirely alone, swept up into some terribly intimate vortex.

'I see,' she said.

'I'm sure you do.' The knowing criticism behind his words snapped her back to reality.

For a second she had an insane desire to confess everything to him, but of course it was insane. She was in too deep now to fall victim to any such impulse.

All she could do was ride with the tide and hope that it brought her to safe shores eventually.

'What time do we start work tomorrow?' she asked, her voice still unsteady. She had to bring this conversation back to a manageable level. At all costs.

Marcos shot her a lazy, assessing look. 'Nine. I have a meeting with some planners. I'll want you there to take notes and you can type up the necessary report in the afternoon. I've instructed the hotel to have a typewriter installed in your bedroom. Not as advanced as the computer, but it'll have to do.'

'Certainly.' Her voice was definitely more controlled now. She risked a glance at him and felt another strange quiver shoot through her.

'I think I'll leave now,' she muttered, standing up, eager to escape his company. 'I need a bath, and I have unpacking to do...' Her voice tapered out.

'Have a nice night out. With Roger. And take this as a warning: keep your hands off him. You can bed-hop with anyone else, just so long as he doesn't work for me.'

He meant it too. Every word. The threat lay there in those black eyes and in the grim lines of his mouth.

Beth walked away quickly, her heart beating so loudly that it hurt. She barely noticed her surroundings as she followed the porter to her bedroom, anxious for him to leave so that she could release her body from its heightened tension in privacy.

As soon as he had gone, she felt herself go limp. She ran a bath, settling comfortably into it and wished that her thoughts were as comfortable.

But they weren't. They were chaotic, mad, teasing little shadows that fluttered away the minute she tried to control them.

If only she could stand back from Marcos, but something inside her refused to oblige. She felt like a moth, lured by a bright light, but bright lights, she reminded herself, could be fatal to unsuspecting moths.

She had a light supper in her room, excusing herself to Jane on the weak grounds that she wanted to get some rest before she went out that evening.

'Fine,' Jane agreed coolly, 'as I told you, I have a lot of reading to do anyway. Where are you and Roger going?' There was a tinge of envy in her voice which

Beth ignored. She felt sorry for Jane. The other woman was obviously lonely and loneliness often bred spite.

'I don't know,' Beth said pleasantly. 'We'll probably just stay here for a drink. I want an early night.'

'Really?' She said that in a tone that implied disbelief. 'Well, have a good time.'

'Thank you,' Beth replied politely.

Actually the last thing she needed was an evening of stilted conversation with someone she didn't know from Adam, but it would have been churlish to have now given him some excuse, having promised earlier to meet him.

She had a quick nap, and then dressed hurriedly in a pair of lilac culottes and a matching flowered blouse.

Roger was waiting downstairs for her. He ran his eyes approvingly over her slim body and ushered her out to where the car was waiting.

'But I thought we could stay here,' Beth protested.

'I know a nice little place. Much cosier than here.' He smiled warmly at her. 'Don't worry about my keeping you out too late. I have orders to collect the master at a specific time.'

'The master?' She giggled, relaxing. 'Is that how you refer to Marcos?'

Roger grinned at her, opening the car door for her to enter. 'Don't you think that it's an apt description?'

'It has a ring about it,' she agreed, staring out of the window as the car pulled out of the confines of the hotel.

She had rolled the window down, and the sultry breeze blew lazily over her, whipping her hair around her face.

The darkness around them was alive with night sounds, the peaceful calling of insects. It filled the air, a constant reminder that there, in the shadows, life on a different level was throbbing and alive.

They drove to a charming bar, all verandas and gables, and Beth happily allowed Roger to lead the conversation for the evening, relishing the warmth and enjoying his amusing anecdotes.

She liked Roger. He was relaxing. Nothing about him taxed her, or set her on edge. In fact, he was as diametrically opposed to Marcos as anyone could be.

She had two piña coladas, and found that she was laughing a lot and really rather enjoying herself.

'Can we do this again?' Roger asked when they were back at the hotel.

'Who knows?' Beth replied evasively. 'It was fun, but I have an awful lot of work to get through while I'm here.' And besides, she added to herself, Marcos is watching me, and for some ridiculous reason I care what he thinks.

'Is that a polite brush-off?' His voice was light-heartedly resigned rather than mortally offended, and for that she was glad.

'I don't want involvement,' she said truthfully.

'Does that just apply to me, or is the rest of the male species included?'

'Oh, the latter.' She laughed, and had another, unexpectedly vivid image of Marcos's cynical face, then she blinked and the vision vanished.

'Why not?'

'I like my life the way it is at the moment,' she responded, hearing a shade of doubt in her voice. She always had liked the simplicity of her life, its untroubled predictability. Craig had temporarily ruffled the calm surface, but afterwards the ripples had gradually smoothed over and things had returned to what they had been. She had seen it as a salutary experience. So why was she beginning to feel dissatisfied now?

'So we part as platonic friends?' Roger asked lightly, and she nodded. 'Platonic friends can still have drinks together, you know. Or do you have a rule against that as well?'

'No rule.'

'Then if the opportunity arises?'

'Sure. A platonic drink would be very enjoyable.' They smiled at one another, and then he bent forwards, brushing his lips against hers, deepening his kiss until she pulled away.

'That,' he informed her ruefully, 'was just my way of saying goodbye to what might have been. And now I'll leave you in peace. The Prince of Darkness summons.' They laughed, and Beth made her way back to the bedroom. The two piña coladas had made her feel pleasantly fuzzy, and Roger's company had been a welcome change from the confused tension which she always felt in Marcos's presence.

Not, she thought the following morning, that there was an opportunity to feel anything except exhausted. The meeting was hard, and she sat alongside Marcos, barely finding the time to look up, her hand flying over her pad as she took notes of everything that was being said. Jane made sure that she contributed her fair share to what was being discussed, glancing across every so often at Beth, reminding her of their different responsibilities.

'There's no need to lock yourself away and type all this up,' Marcos told her, as the meeting dispersed. 'It seems a shame to waste this weather. Why don't you go down to the beach?'

Jane had edged towards them. She fluttered her lashes in Marcos's direction. 'I will, even if Beth doesn't,' she said. 'I need a tan, don't you think? Are you coming down? I'd feel much safer with a man around. The sea can be a scary place to a city gal like me.'

'I hardly think there's anything to fear if you stay close to the shore,' he said drily, glancing at her.

Beth could almost feel Jane vibrating under his dark gaze.

'Get your swimsuit,' he told Beth, turning to face her, and she replied tartly,

'Is that another order?'

'You're beginning to catch on.'

Jane was watching this interchange suspiciously. 'Perhaps Roger would like to tag along?' she interjected. 'By the way, did you have a good time last night?'

Marcos's expression changed imperceptibly. 'Drew's tied up for the whole of today,' he informed Beth, his voice hard.

'What a shame,' a little stab of mischief prompted her to reply. 'And yes,' she added, looking at Jane, 'we had a lovely time last night.'

Marcos's face grew grimmer. 'I'll see you two on the beach in ten minutes. We can have lunch there.'

'Promise?' Jane's lips pouted, but Marcos wasn't looking at her at all. He was looking at Beth, his eyes silently reminding her of his warning, and she smiled innocently back at him.

She refused to be daunted on a day like this. When the sky was so perfectly blue, and in the distance she could see the silvery sparkle of the water, crystal-clear and invitingly warm.

'I'll see you both on the beach, then,' she affirmed cheerily, and pranced back to the bedroom, dumping her stack of notes on the bed, and quickly changing into her swimming costume.

It really was a minuscule affair. Jade-green and designed to attract attention. Typical of her sister.

She modestly covered herself with a loose-fitting T-shirt, but the minute she removed it she realised exactly how revealing the bikini was by the heads that swivelled around as she walked past.

Jane's mouth fell open, but it was Marcos's reaction which made her face turn red. He was staring at her through narrowed eyes, and she felt suddenly and powerfully aware of just how much of her breasts was exposed.

Jane looked at them both and broke the silence. 'The sea looks great, doesn't it, Marcos?' It worked. His attention reluctantly shifted away from Beth and he began chatting to Jane.

Beth took the opportunity to stretch out her beach towel, a little distance away from theirs, and she lay down on it, diligently applying the suntan oil over her body.

Nevertheless she was frighteningly aware of Marcos next to her, his body lean and mesmerising, clad only in his swimming trunks. He certainly didn't look as though he needed a tan at all. It wasn't fair. Couldn't he have one little bit of physical imperfection?

Even relaxing as he was now, there was something aggressive about him. Maybe it had something to do with his physique. It struck her forcibly just how devastatingly attractive he was and she stopped herself before she was besieged by any more unwelcome thoughts.

Instead, she looked around her. Reduit Beach was most people's idea of paradise. It stretched away into the distance, a seemingly never-ending expanse of soft white sand leading down to turquoise waters.

It was fairly uncrowded, freckled with holiday makers, some of whom looked as though they were applying the same precision to their tanning as they would have done to their jobs. Half an hour on the front, half an hour on the back, a quick dip in the sea, then starting all over again.

Laura would have loved this, Beth thought wistfully. Neither of them had ever travelled very much. There had simply not been enough money to stretch to such luxuries when they were growing up. Their holidays had mostly been spent at beaches in England, and there was no comparison.

Jane had managed to persuade Marcos to accompany her into the sea, and Beth idly watched as their figures were swallowed by the water.

Marcos immediately began swimming out to sea, his strokes strong and assured, while Jane paddled about close to the shore and hungrily followed his progress.

When he was safely in the distance, Beth made her way to the water, submerging herself, her body temperature adjusting remarkably quickly to the temperature of the water. She made desultory conversation with Jane, finding her continual barbed comments more of an irritation than an insult, and when she could stand no more she began swimming out.

It was wonderfully liberating being surrounded only by water, water so clear that she could easily see down to the sandy bottom.

She was about to begin the haul back to shore when a sudden pain shot through her calf and she yelped in agony, spluttering as she frantically made an effort to keep above the surface of the water.

She could barely move her leg and she floundered, desperately trying to massage it back into life while not drowning in the process.

Of course she wouldn't drown; she had only to holler for help. Nevertheless, she was relieved when she felt arms around her, supporting her body at the waist.

'Thanks,' she murmured sheepishly, twisting to see her rescuer, then the smile froze on her lips.

Why Marcos? Why, when there were other people in the water, did it have to be Marcos who was now helping her back to land, his arms sending prickles of heat through her?

'What happened?' Jane asked, only to be abruptly told by Marcos that there was no need for her to accompany them.

'Cramp,' Beth explained and Jane's mouth tightened.

He helped her back to her towel and sat her down gently.

'Suffer often with this?' he asked, squatting next to her. He began kneading her foot and Beth instinctively pulled away. 'Don't act like a child,' he said tersely. She relaxed reluctantly, letting him massage her calf, the rhythmic movements of his hands gradually easing the painful knot.

'It's fine now,' she said, as soon as she possibly could. She flexed her ankle tentatively, then with more confidence as the pain faded. 'I'm all right.'

'Don't I deserve a thank-you?'

'Thank you,' she murmured obediently, wishing that he would vanish back into the water and leave her alone.

She lay down flat on the towel and squinted against the sun, but was uncomfortably aware that he had not budged.

'There's no need for you to baby-sit me, you know,' she hinted.

'I'm not.'

'Then why don't you go back into the water?' she asked, abandoning any pretence of subtlety.

'Because the view from here is infinitely more satisfying,' he said. He leaned over her so that he blocked out the sun and the warmth in his eyes made the blood rush madly to her head.

She couldn't think straight. She couldn't even seem to move her limbs because a strange torpor had settled over them, and they felt like lead weights.

'I don't think I've ever seen quite such a small bikini before,' he murmured. 'I can't imagine why you don't dispense with it altogether.'

Laura, she thought desperately, this is your fault. My modest one-piece is languishing back in Cambridge and here I am, decked out in this tiny green thing that leaves nothing to the imagination.

There was no response to that remark, none that she could think of anyway. She smiled weakly and hoped that he couldn't hear the thudding of her heart under her ribcage.

'I don't appear to have noticed before,' he was saying, his eyes straying over her body, 'but you really are remarkably attractive. But you know that already, don't you?'

'Do I?' Beth squeaked.

'No one who wears a bikini like that is unaware of the effect she has on men.'

It's not my bikini, she wanted to wail. His observations were a curious blend of perceptiveness and misjudgements, as though he could see into her depths but was constantly being fooled by surface appearance. Hardly surprising when she was masquerading under a false identity.

'Isn't it nearly time for lunch?' she questioned in a feeble attempt to change the conversation.

He was not to be so easily diverted.

'In fact, right now, I could be sorely tempted to break my own rules about non-involvement between members of staff.'

Beth's body froze as she felt his finger trail a path along her collarbone, down to the inviting valley between her breasts, which were aching as though in anticipation of forbidden delights.

She wondered where Jane was. Still obeying orders and splashing about in the water?

She could hardly breathe. His finger finished its delicate exploration of her cleavage, then moved up the swell of her breast until she felt it circle the hardened tip of her nipple, rubbing it gently till she was drowning under a barrage of new and overpowering sensations.

She had never been touched by a man before, not like this. Marcos made her whole body pulse with response, electrified her until she was filled with a need that frightened her with its intensity.

'Please,' she uttered, 'no.'

'You don't like it?' His voice was rough and as unsteady as her own. He moved his finger to her other waiting nipple, and it swelled under his touch.

'Does Ryan make you feel like this?'

Beth's half-closed eyes shot open, and her brain cleared instantly. What the hell was she doing? Had she completely taken leave of her senses?

She sat up and pulled her T-shirt over her.

'Get away from me,' she said numbly.

'Why? Don't tell me that your thoughts were on Ryan, because I won't believe you. Can you really try and convince me that you love another man when I can feel you opening up under my fingers like a flower?'

'I don't have to tell you anything at all.'

'And you don't object to whatever conclusions I draw?' he asked tightly.

'Please, just leave me alone.'

'My pleasure.' The contempt was back in his eyes as he looked at her and she wanted the ground to open up and swallow her.

She was still trembling when he walked away.

CHAPTER FIVE

BETH was hardly aware of what they ate for lunch. She knew from the menu that it was typical local fare—crab-back with cheesy christophene and salad—and normally she would have savoured every mouthful, but it tasted like cardboard.

She couldn't even summon up the energy to respond to Jane's slyly caustic comments, although she was aware of the other girl watching her suspiciously out of the corner of her eye.

She was still too shocked by what had happened on the beach. Marcos had touched her and all of a sudden her world had shifted on its axis. Her careful, neat little arrangement of emotions had been shattered, and what had been exposed was a primitive yearning that she had not even known she possessed. Nothing she had felt for Craig had prepared her for this.

The sheer force of it had knocked her for six.

Around her, Marcos and Jane conversed politely, and she joined in when it was necessary, her mouth finding the right responses though her mind was miles away.

What a fool she had been. What a silly, gullible little fool.

Marcos didn't look as though he had been in the slightest bit affected by what had happened between them. But then, she thought bitterly, why should he? He had only, after all, used her to satisfy his curiosity. For a while, she had turned him on, and he had reacted. The fact that she had responded to him only proved his point that she had no scruples.

She had never before in her life felt so helpless.

She was relieved when he politely excused himself, saying that he had an appointment to view his potential site. She barely noticed that Jane had remained where she was, sipping her fruit juice, until she spoke.

'How's your leg feeling?'

Beth looked at her warily. It was an inoffensive enough question, but she knew from experience that very few of Jane's remarks to her were ever devoid of some undertone of malice.

'Much better, thank you.'

'I suppose you think you're clever, don't you?' she asked conversationally, rolling her glass in between her fingers so that the ice cubes clinked together.

'I have no idea what you're talking about.' Beth glanced at her. Her face was beginning to show the hall-marks of too much sun. Her nose was tinged red, as were her cheeks, and her hair, without the aid of a brush as they had lunched straight from the beach, hung in short, uneven strands around her face. She was wearing a white T-shirt, an unflattering colour on her without the benefit of a tan.

Beth sighed. Right now, she just wasn't up to a bout of verbal warfare, but she had a feeling that that was just what she was in for.

'Don't think that I didn't see through that phoney cramp routine,' she bit out without preamble.

'It wasn't phoney!'

She carried on as though Beth had not spoken. 'Don't think that I don't know that you'd do anything to get Marcos's attention.'

'And how was I supposed to know that he would be the one to come to my aid?' Beth enquired logically, holding on to her calm with great difficulty. 'Believe it or not, I don't have eyes in the back of my head!'

As a matter of fact, he was the last person she had wanted around, but she wasn't going to say that.

'Look,' she said wearily, 'can't we stop all this and at least be civil towards one another? I have no axe to grind with you, and we are going to be here for another two days. We could at least call a temporary truce.' She ventured a smile but met with no response.

'I would if I could see anything likeable about you. Ever since you joined the company, you've rubbed me up the wrong way. Preening and posing and acting as though you're God's gift to men.'

Had Laura acted like that? Beth doubted it. Her sister was vivacious and bubbly, like a glass of champagne, but she was not the kind of girl ever to court disfavour with anyone, and she certainly didn't preen and pose.

'I think that remark is totally uncalled for,' she snapped.

'I don't care what you think! I can only repeat what I've said before. You're wasting your time with Marcos. Men like him don't need women like you. They can have anyone they want. Do you really think that he would find anything about you appealing?'

'You're wasting your time, and mine, Jane. I'm not interested in him.'

'Doesn't look that way to me.'

Her eyes were chips of ice in a face distorted by anger.

'In case you didn't know, inter-company relationships are strictly forbidden . . .' Beth began appeasingly.

'Not that you would ever let that stand in your way.'

There was a heavy silence and Beth wondered what she could say to pour oil on these waters. Nothing, she decided. She had no reason to justify herself.

At the back of her mind, though, a little nagging thought began to spout. What if, without wanting it, she was attracted to Marcos? Of course she couldn't be, but then again, she had reacted to him in a way that was totally uncharacteristic and uncontrolled.

Maybe Jane had picked up her unconscious response. And if Jane had picked it up, who was to say that Marcos hadn't as well?

The thought made her go cold.

'Why do you care what I think of Marcos anyway?' she asked eventually.

Jane reddened.

'Look,' Beth said, feeling a surge of pity for the other woman, 'he goes in for beautiful blondes. You're right. He's a man who can pick and choose, and those are the types he chooses. Surely there are lots of men out there; you're not unattractive...' Her voice faltered as the embarrassment on Jane's face gave way to fury.

Too late, Beth realised that she had chosen the wrong words to express her sympathy. Jane would not want to be told that Marcos was as out of her reach as a shooting star.

'This is silly,' she began, hastily trying to retrace her steps. 'Marcos is not interested in either of us...'

Oh, lord, she groaned inwardly. How much more tactless can I get?

'Don't patronise me,' Jane hissed furiously. 'I may not be tall and blonde——'

'I didn't mean it in that——'

'—but I know one thing for sure. If I can't have Marcos, then you certainly won't!'

She stood up and swept away, her head held high.

Beth remained where she was, ordering a cup of tea, even though the weather was so hot, thoughtfully taking small sips out of it. Tea was a great soother, a lovely British habit that never failed her.

What a mess, she thought. Not only had Marcos Adrino shown her that she was far more of a vulnerable fool than she had ever suspected, but from the look of it he had managed to turn Jane's world upside-down as well. How long had the poor woman been nurturing her dreams? Had her obsession with him crept up on her insidiously, like some dreadful illness, only becoming apparent when it was too late to take preventative measures?

Men like him, she thought angrily, ought to have a health warning on them. It was at least a small blessing that Laura had remained untouched by his charm. She preferred the adoring kind of man, and Beth somehow could never see Marcos in that role.

No, he had been brutally honest with her when he had told her that commitment was not for him. He preferred the excitement of the chase, the sweet short period of possession, and then the freedom to discard.

If I had read his character reference on paper, Beth decided, I would have disliked him on the spot.

She wandered up to her room for a short siesta and gloomily contemplated the remainder of the day.

They were due to accompany him on a sightseeing tour of the island, to get the feel of the community, he had told them earlier on. Just the three of them. It had the makings of a nightmare.

Outside the sun poured through the window. She could imagine the sizzling heat, even though it was beautifully cool inside the bedroom with the air-conditioning on.

She tried to doze, but every time she felt herself sinking into sleep some new disturbing thought would flash through her mind, and finally she gave up altogether.

On top of everything else, she thought, that damned man has succeeded in throwing my sleeping pattern out of joint. If I develop insomnia I'll damn well charge the sleeping tablets to his account.

Poor Jane, she thought sympathetically, at least he only invades my thoughts because I dislike him. Imagine how awful to be infatuated with him, to be haunted by his image, like something tauntingly close and yet inaccessible. Despite the madness of her response to him on the beach, it at least had the saving grace of only being a hiccup in her self-control, and one which would not recur.

At three o'clock she got dressed, putting on a pair of green culottes and a tan sleeveless shirt. He was waiting for her in the foyer, staring outside, half turned away, and she took the opportunity to look at him with unashamed openness.

His strong hands were thrust into the pockets of his shorts, and even thinking himself unobserved he still had something watchful and alert about him. What was going on in that mind of his? He had obviously just had a shower. His hair was still damp and was combed away from his face, emphasising the hard, ruthless stamp of his features.

He turned suddenly, catching her observation, and his expression changed to one of amusement.

Beth pursed her lips and walked towards him.

'Where's Jane?' she asked, looking around for the other girl.

'She's not coming,' Marcos responded flatly, 'something about a headache.'

'A headache?' Beth looked at him, dismay clouding her face. Simple arithmetic meant that that left only the two of them on this marvellous sightseeing tour. 'Couldn't she have taken a couple of aspirin? Doesn't she know that the fresh air will do her good?' Doesn't she know that she just can't leave me stranded like this? Her prickly nature might be irritating, but it was nothing compared to what Marcos aroused in her.

He shrugged indolently. 'It appears not. Why are you so concerned? I didn't sense that there was a great deal of love lost between the two of you.'

He began walking out of the foyer towards the car and Beth followed helplessly, half running to keep up with him.

Once outside the confines of the hotel, with its central air-conditioning system, the heat wrapped around her lovingly. There was enough of a breeze to temper the warmth and she tossed her hair back.

'Perhaps she's feeling a bit better,' she offered hopefully, as he unlocked her car door.

'Perhaps,' Marcos replied drily, 'you're scared of being alone with me.'

Beth jumped into the car and slammed the door behind her.

'Well?' he prompted softly as the car throbbed into life. 'Have I hit the nail on the head?'

'Certainly not!' she denied hotly, but as he drove out he was whistling, as though the thought was affording him a great deal of amusement.

'So tell me something about yourself,' he said, driving fairly slowly over the bumpy road. He shot her a swift glance and grinned.

'You're in a sparkling mood,' Beth muttered.

'I guess I am. Things are going well with the project.'

‘They are?’ She relaxed a bit as curiosity got the better of her. That, and the fact that Marcos Adrino could be disarmingly charming at times. ‘Did you look around the site?’

‘I did, and it’s just what I had in mind. Close to the sea, but without any other hotels nudging it from the sides. And an untamed, lush backdrop that looks as though it’s stepped straight out of a postcard.’

‘The sort of place that encourages people to lose track of time?’ Beth volunteered, her mind captivated by the image.

Marcos darted her another appraising look. ‘Precisely. You have a knack with words, has anyone ever told you that?’

Beth laughed. ‘No one that I can remember offhand.’

They were driving through dense landscape now, a carpet of banana trees, their wide leaves dancing in the breeze. Marcos pointed out a turning to Marigot Bay and Hurricane Hole, a smooth sheet of water where yachts bobbed gracefully on the currents.

Beth watched, fascinated, listening to his descriptions and immersed in the splendid scenery. It was like driving through a rain forest. She had never before seen such an abundance of flora and fauna, and then suddenly the view became dominated by the startling sight of the Pitons, twin peaks, soaring proudly upwards.

She gasped in pleasure.

‘Stunning, isn’t it?’ Marcos said, appreciating her response. ‘You should see them from the sea. Quite amazing. The sort of unforgettable sight that lives in your imagination long after you’ve left the island.’

‘You sound quite poetic,’ she teased.

'It's easy to be poetic about nature,' Marcos said semi-seriously, 'it's only slightly more difficult when you try to apply it to the human race.'

Beth looked at him, startled. 'Surely you don't believe that!'

'When you live in the concrete jungle, you see enough deception to jaundice any finer emotions you might have for the rest of your life.'

He began talking about where they were going, down towards Soufrière, the small town that lent its name to the Soufrière volcano, and Beth was relieved that the subject had been changed.

Any talk of deception was a bit too close to the bone for her liking. She suddenly pictured how Marcos would react to the deception being perpetrated on his own doorstep, and she felt her blood run cold.

He would not be amused. He certainly would not wave it aside as a childish prank. She found that she was perspiring slightly, and focused her attention on the scenery, losing herself temporarily in it.

The Soufrière volcano, Marcos assured her, had not seen activity since the eighteenth century.

'Oh, good,' Beth said with a grin, 'it's nice to know that we're not being suicidal in coming here.'

He laughed and together they looked at the sunken crater in silence, a dead grey pool that seemed curiously lifeless amid the fertile growth.

'Back north?' he asked, and she nodded, surprised at the length of time that had elapsed. And not a moment's discomfort with him. When they hadn't been absorbed in the panoramic view, they had amicably chatted about any and everything. He had a dry sense of humour and appeared to be able to talk on any subject with ease. He seemed to know as much about music and the theatre as he did about the financial market and the economy.

'You never answered my original question,' he reminded her, as they retraced their tracks in the car, only now driving with dusk fast on their heels, instead of in blistering sunshine.

'What original question?' Beth asked, puzzled.

'The one about yourself.'

'Oh, that one. Not much to answer. I have a sister, a mother, a stepfather and no pets.'

He grinned, and the twilight lent his face a magnetic sensuality. Beth slapped down her reaction and told herself that, however pleasant he could be, he was still dangerous. It wouldn't do to let that slip her mind even for a moment.

'Sounds about right,' he murmured, driving more carefully now as the light faded.

'You have a sister, a mother, a stepfather and no pets as well?' she asked with interest, just in case he began quizzing her on Laura.

'No,' Marcos said evenly, the humour no longer apparent in his voice. 'I have none of those. My mother died when I was three and my father followed suit ten years later. He died bankrupt.'

'I'm sorry.' And she was, instinctively so. She wanted to reach out and touch him, but that was impossible. She twined her fingers together uselessly on her lap.

'Are you? So am I. I watched my father die, and I can tell you that bankruptcy is not very dignified. It's degrading and it's pathetic, especially to a man as fiercely proud as my father was.' He could not conceal his bitterness, and, as though disliking the turn in the conversation, abruptly switched the topic.

But his remarks, surely unintentional, had shown Beth a side to him that she would never have known existed. Not, she admitted, that she had given a great deal of thought to his parents and whether they were still alive, or what they did for a living.

Was that why he had had the ruthless drive to make himself a fortune? Children, she knew, often felt the compulsion to avoid the errors of their parents. She had been lucky. Her parents had had a warm and happy marriage, and she and Laura had grown up with the comforting thought that nothing was impossible.

Maybe, she thought wryly, that was why she was in this situation now.

He was talking to her about a party being given the next evening, their last evening on the island.

'A few of the local people and members of staff who have been helping with this project.'

'Where?' Beth asked.

'One of the bars in the hotel. We've rented it for the night. Should be right up your alley.'

'Meaning?'

'Don't you like dancing?'

'Oh.' Beth blushed. She had assumed the worst behind his statement. 'I suppose so, yes. Though I haven't done any of that for quite a while.'

'Now isn't that curious?' Marcos said, as the car slotted neatly into one of the vacant spaces in the hotel car park. He switched off the engine and stared at her. 'From what I gathered, you did a lot of that with Ryan.'

Beth floundered for words, finally managing to say stiltedly, 'Yes, of course. I guess I thought you were referring to the singles scene.'

Didn't that just go to prove it? she thought, angry with herself. It was too damned easy to let her guard fall when Marcos turned on the charm. When he was snarling, she made sure that all her defences were properly in place, but when he smiled she forgot all about her sense of caution, and that was a sure way to court disaster.

And he had smiled too much this afternoon for her own good. She realised that she had found herself liking him. Liking him! The thought made her suddenly uneasy, and she snapped open her door, frantic now to escape his presence.

'I'm out tonight,' he said, catching up with her easily. 'But do you fancy a drink now?'

'No,' she replied sharply, 'I mean, no, thank you. I...I think I'll pop in and make sure that Jane's all right.'

'Of course,' Marcos drawled laconically, sensing her change of mood. 'I forgot that Jane's welfare is close to your heart.'

He looked down at her, his hair tousled from the drive, and she felt a pulse begin to beat steadily in her temple.

She felt... What did she feel? My God, I want him to touch me. The yearning was so powerful that she wanted to faint from it.

She spun around on her heels and without a backward glance dashed towards the sanctuary of her bedroom, only releasing a long breath once she was inside.

As an afterthought, she dialled through to Jane's room and a drowsy voice answered.

'I just wanted to find out how you were feeling,' Beth said. She couldn't say why she was bothering to be a good Samaritan, when the girl had had nothing pleasant to say to her from day one.

'Much better, thank you.' Jane's voice sank a few degrees cooler as soon as she recognised the person at the other end, and Beth sighed. 'How was your afternoon with Marcos?'

'St Lucia is beautiful,' she replied, skirting around the question. 'We drove south towards Soufrière and then came back. It's a great place to build a hotel.'

'I don't suppose either of you even missed my company.' Jane's voice was sullen and short-tempered and Beth could well imagine the downturned mouth.

'More than you think,' she answered honestly. Face it, if Jane had been there, she would not be going through this turmoil because she would still have been cocooned in her convenient line of thinking that Marcos was an arrogant bastard.

'Oh, yes,' Jane taunted down the line, 'like a hole in the head.'

'Look,' Beth said, her patience wearing thin, 'I didn't telephone you to argue.'

'No, you telephoned me because you felt sorry for me.'

'Yes. No! What I mean is...'

'I know what you mean! Thanks for the concern, but no, thanks.'

There was the dead tone as the receiver was replaced and Beth scowled at it. Poor Laura. Little wonder that she had hoped that Jane had been eaten by her workload.

She knew that she had infinitely more patience than her sister, and when it came to Jane even her supply was wearing at the edges.

And it was non-existent in the case of Marcos. He could antagonise her beyond endurance. But, a little voice whispered, he can also make you laugh more than anyone else ever has. She ignored the little voice.

But she was extra-careful now. Throughout the following day, she kept a low profile, sheltering behind

Jane, grateful for her presence even though it could be trying most of the time.

In the afternoon, they visited the marketplace in Castries, an enchanting scene, bustling with people and jammed with all sorts of things for sale, from straw hats and bags to vegetables.

Beth conveniently detached herself from Jane and Marcos, and strolled around it at leisure, buying a couple of souvenirs to take back for Laura.

By the time they were back in the hotel, she was exhausted from the sun and the walking. The heat, she found, sapped her energy and left her ready for bed at a surprisingly early hour.

Maybe, she thought optimistically, she could creep away from the party without anyone noticing and catch up on her sleep.

And if she couldn't, then at least Roger was going to be there. She could relax with him and with any luck avoid Marcos completely. Because she had found, much to her annoyance, that her eyes still insisted on sneaking to observe him, even though her brain was firmly against any such temptation.

She dressed carefully for the party. Her sister's choice in evening wear was as flamboyant as her choice in swimsuits. If only she had thought ahead, she would have brought some of her own modest clothes down from Cambridge, but she had brought only a few working clothes and her jeans and jumpers. How was she to know that within a few days of working there she would be asked to go to St Lucia?

The black jersey dress which she chose was flattering, but extrovertly so. It was cut off the shoulder, following the curve of her breasts lovingly, falling from her waist in rich folds to mid-calf.

She applied a minimum of make-up and brushed her hair until it gleamed. Then she waited until she was perfectly sure that everyone else had arrived.

She was not into making grand entrances, and she certainly didn't intend to start now.

She knew, without conceit, that she was attractive, but she had always been more than happy to play it down, preferring to look cool and sensible rather than sexy. Her sister, with those long rippling locks and extravagant gestures, was sexy. And Beth had always chosen the other route.

She wondered whether it was because they were identical twins. Their mother had never dressed them in the same clothes, and they had been encouraged to assert their individuality from an early age.

She could remember, quite clearly, when they were only children, going to a birthday party with Laura. The hostess had exclaimed to her father how different they were, even though they looked exactly alike, feature for feature. Her father had pulled Beth on to his lap and laughed.

'This one,' he had said, tapping her nose affectionately, 'is my practical, serious little baby. Quite different from her sister, but still two sides of the same coin.'

I miss my father, she thought. The previous day, when they had been sightseeing, during one of the comfortable lulls between them, Marcos had asked her about her parents, and she had found herself confiding in him, talking about her father, saying things that had surprised her. He had managed to stir up a nest of bittersweet memories inside her.

The man, she thought now, regarding her reflection sombrely, had a talent for drawing people out, hearing their confidences. The sign of the inveterate charmer.

The man who listened was halfway to winning a woman's heart.

It was just a good job that she was clever enough to spot the danger. Not that he had any interest in winning her heart. Oh, no. That sort of thing came naturally to him. He could bowl a woman over while remaining immune to the situation.

The room was already crowded by the time she finally made it down.

There were the local people, some four or five in total, who had also brought their other halves. One had brought his two teenage daughters who wore on their pretty olive-skinned faces a mixture of shyness and delight. Then there were the company members, including Roger. He spotted her immediately and waved, moving over to take her by her arm.

'You might be late,' he informed her wolfishly, 'but you're well worth the wait.'

Beth laughed, accepting the drink that he had brought over to her, her eyes involuntarily skirting around the room, settling briefly on Marcos until she felt that familiar quickening of her pulses. Then she looked away.

He was talking to two men, dominating the conversation, while Jane hovered on the sidelines, nodding vigorously to everything he said.

He had not even seen her enter the room, and for that she was grateful. Better to be ignored than confronted by him.

She began chatting to Roger, telling him about what she had seen of the island, genuinely envious when he told her that he would be there for at least another week.

'Doing all the groundwork. The Prince of Darkness has no qualms about delegation, and actually I don't mind, because I know that he could do it all himself if he had the time or really wanted to. That's the difference between a good boss and a bad one. The bad ones give orders but half the time they don't know what they're talking about.'

'Very philosophical.' Beth grinned. 'Sounds as if the Prince of Darkness has a fan club in you.'

Roger shrugged. 'He's bloody clever, and he's fair. He's had to work his way up from nothing, you know.'

'I know.'

Roger looked at her in surprise. 'You know? He told you?'

She nodded and he whistled under his breath. 'I only know that on hearsay. From what I gather, the great man never discusses anything personal, with anyone. How on earth did you manage to get on his list of confidantes?'

'I'm not!' Beth protested, her face pink. But throughout the meal she knew that her admission had given him food for speculation. She had connived to sit as far away from Marcos as she feasibly could, in between Roger and a charming St Lucian gentleman, the father of the teenage girls. Nevertheless, it was impossible to miss the strains of his deep voice. Whatever was being discussed at that end of the table, it was obvious that he controlled it. As he seemed to do with everything else.

As the dessert dishes were being cleared away, she glanced across at him and for a minute their eyes locked. He looked quickly at Roger and then back to her, and this time there was a shade of mockery in his expression.

Beth hurriedly diverted her attention to the St Lucian gentleman and drowned her confusion in another gulp of her peach daiquiri.

She decided that if she kept her eyes focused away from Marcos, then the evening really was quite enjoyable. Despite Marcos's predictions, there wasn't any dancing—and for that she heaved a sigh of relief. That might have brought her in dangerous proximity to him. There was very little shop talk, and what there was was interesting.

As the first of the guests began drifting away, she had a smug feeling of having done quite well, thank you very much.

Roger was among the last to leave, and he drew her aside surreptitiously.

'Can I look you up back in London?' he whispered.

'Sure,' Beth agreed whole-heartedly.

'Just so long as I don't mind sticking to the rules of the game.'

She blushed and her face grew even redder when he placed a discreet kiss on her lips before leaving. A kiss that expressed affection rather than passion.

Even so, Marcos's voice behind her made her jump,

'Not a painful farewell, I hope?'

Beth turned towards him, too relaxed from her small share of daiquiris to work up the enthusiasm for an argument.

'Farewells are always painful when they're with someone you like,' she said lightly.

Wrong figure of speech. His eyes darkened. 'I wouldn't know,' he said silkily. Jane was lurking in the background, and he bade her goodnight in a voice that immediately hastened her departure.

She threw Beth a venomous glance and left.

'Perhaps,' Beth said, edging away, 'you don't like anyone.'

'On the contrary. I like a lot of people.'

'But not enough?'

He lounged against the door-frame and surveyed her thoroughly through half-closed eyes.

'Depends on your definition of enough, doesn't it?'

'I think,' she said hastily, before she found herself treading deep waters once again, 'it's my bedtime.'

Marcos took her by her elbow, his touch sending shivers along her spine.

'I'll see you up.'

Oh, God, Beth thought desperately, this is playing with fire; please don't let me get burnt.

If only her damned body would listen to her.

CHAPTER SIX

THEY walked back to Beth's room in silence. She felt as though she were a piece of elastic, her nerves being stretched further and further with each step she took. At least they got her there in one piece, for which she was immeasurably grateful, although by the time she stood outside the door they were feeling distinctly wobbly.

She had already fished out her key from her bag, ready to make a quick getaway.

'Well,' she said, in a high, nervous voice which she tried to conceal with a little laugh, 'thanks for the lift—walk.' She fumbled with the key and felt him remove it from her fingers.

'Allow me,' he murmured, opening the door in one swift movement.

Beth stepped inside and then turned to face him, blocking his entry. If it was one place she did not want Marcos Adrino, it was within the confines of her bedroom.

She reached out for the key, mumbling a polite, Goodbye and wasn't it a pleasant evening? but instead of handing it to her he side-stepped her into the room and carelessly tossed them on to the small table by the bed.

Beth watched in dismay as he proceeded to prowl through the room, before finally stopping by the window and perching indolently against it, his arms folded across his chest.

This was not going to plan at all. She had not expected him to walk with her to her room, and she had even less expected him to barge in and install himself by the window.

She remained uncertainly by the door, not daring to take a step further, unsure what she should do now.

'You can close the door behind you,' he drawled, taking the decision out of her hands. There was a small smile on his lips, as though he could read exactly what she was thinking.

Indecision turned to anger and she slammed the door behind her, moving across to the sanctuary of one of the wicker chairs.

She had not bothered to draw the curtains before she had left earlier on, and outside the black sky was studded with stars. The silence between them was broken only by the background noise of the air-conditioning.

Beth looked at him, his dark eyes hypnotising her, blotting out her thought processes, making her mouth go suddenly dry.

'I'm awfully tired,' she ventured. 'It's been a long day. I really would like to get to bed now.'

'Feel free.'

'Without unwelcome spectators in the room!'

Her brief flirtation with anger was immediately quelled as he walked towards her, to be replaced by something that felt strangely like vertigo.

'This dress,' he murmured, standing in front of her, 'becomes you.' His finger slowly traced the outline of her exposed shoulders and her hair stood on end.

'Thank you,' Beth whispered hoarsely, edging away slightly.

'They say that you can tell a woman's personality by her wardrobe.'

'Do they?' She tried a nonchalant smile that immediately died on her lips.

'Mm. This dress, your bikini yesterday—they speak of quite an extrovert, daring personality. Are you?'

His hooded eyes bored into her. Something about his voice was like a low, seductive caress, and Beth fought it as hard as she could. She wasn't born yesterday. He was bored and, even though her morals left him cold, she attracted him.

Like a lot of men, she suspected that he had two standards. While it was all right for him to explore womankind, it was not nearly so acceptable for a woman to do likewise.

No, she was not his sort at all, but still he fancied her.

It was a purely physical thing. He specialised in that, didn't he? He used his sheer animal magnetism ruthlessly to get what he wanted, and who he wanted, and no doubt he saw her as easy game. After all, hadn't she, as far as he was concerned, slept with David Ryan and who knew how many others?

'It really is very late,' she said in a firmer voice, slipping away from him to stand pointedly by the door. 'Tomorrow we fly back, and I know I won't get a minute's sleep on the plane. I didn't on the way across. Maybe I'm allergic to travel. When I was young, I would always get car sick.' She was babbling. They both knew it.

He gave her a slow, predatory smile.

'You don't look terribly sleepy to me.'

'Don't I?' Of course I don't. With my cheeks all flushed, I know what I look. I look excited.

And she was. Her heart was beating quickly and she knew that if he laid another finger on her she would explode.

Had Laura felt like this with David? For the first time she could understand what had prompted her sister to sleep with him, disobeying company etiquette.

But wasn't that different? She was in love with him. Her mind suddenly shifted into overdrive and a wave of panic gripped her as she realised that what she felt for Marcos wasn't simply lust. It ran deeper than that. She was in love with him. She had flouted all her principles, all her well-meaning intentions, and fallen in love with him!

When did this happen? she thought desperately, staring at him with wide eyes. He had found cracks in her, insinuated himself, and now the realisation made her feel like a piece of driftwood being carried along by a torrent of water from which all escape was barred.

That was why, when he had touched her on the beach, her body had been set alight with desire. That was why she followed him with her eyes, and, when he wasn't around, with her mind.

'Please,' she whispered, 'please go.'

'Or else what?' he asked, moving towards her.

He rested his hand on the nape of her neck, caressing it in slow movements.

'Haven't you forgotten your company policy about relationships?' Beth asked weakly.

Her reminder had no effect on him at all. He didn't smack his forehead with his hand and smile apologetically, he didn't turn away from her brusquely. In fact he didn't do anything at all.

'I own the company,' he said huskily. 'I have my own set of rules.'

He raised his other hand to her head, tilting it upwards, then he kissed her eyes, his lips barely touching her skin, but nevertheless sending sweet electrical charges through her body.

'No,' Beth moaned, already regretting what had not yet taken place between them. 'You must go. Now.'

'Because you're attracted to me?'

She didn't answer.

'Don't try and kid me that you're not,' he murmured, taking her silence for denial. 'I know you are. I can feel it, but I want to hear you say it. Tell me that you want me.'

'You're very attractive, Marcos...'

'Tell me!'

'Yes!' she bit out. 'I want you. Now are you satisfied?'

'I will be.'

He brought his lips to hers, his mouth moving unhurriedly over hers, his tongue exploring the moistness of her mouth.

Beth shuddered, and then, in a gesture of defeat, brought her arms around him, curling her fingers in his hair.

Marcos gave a stifled moan and began to kiss her harder, until she heard herself whimpering against him, unable to stem the tide of passion welling inside.

She was hardly aware of him lifting her off her feet and carrying her towards the bed.

He lay her down, staring at her while he undressed, tugging off his shirt with impatient hands. Beth followed each movement hungrily.

'Now you,' he said, the bed sinking slightly as he lowered his body on to it. 'I want to undress you slowly. I want to touch every bit of you until I can't stand the agony of wanting any longer.'

He ran his hands along her thighs, gently pulling down her lacy briefs. Beth's legs parted. Her eyes were half closed now, her breath coming in quick little spurts.

She was moist and ready when his fingers began to explore the secret depths of her womanhood. The pleasure was intense.

Then he freed her of her dress, kissing the flat planes of her stomach, moving lower until she squirmed against him.

He was taking his time, inching her along bit by bit, so that the ecstasy was almost painful.

He trailed kisses along her stomach and then carefully unhooked her bra, exposing one full breast, the nipple hard with arousal.

His tongue flicked against it, and then, as though he couldn't himself stand the agony, sucked harder.

Beth felt as though she was burning up. She stroked his back roughly, arching as he kissed her neck.

'It's still a woman's prerogative to change her mind,' he murmured into her ear.

If only, Beth thought. In fact, if only this woman had had a shred of common sense in the first place.

'I would if I could,' she replied honestly, her eyes drowsy with passion.

'Good, because I don't think I would have been able to let you.'

He cupped her breast with his hand, massaging it, rolling the nipple between his fingers.

'Touch me too,' he ordered roughly, guiding her hand, and she felt a surge of power as she heard him moan.

She had never been touched by a man before, had never touched one, but her responses were not unsure. She was too feverish with desire, too caught up with the emotions coursing through her body, to feel anything but a desperate need for him.

She tensed slightly as he slid into her, and he stopped, frowning.

'I'm not hurting you, am I?'

'Of course not,' Beth replied. Not, anyway, in the way that you think.

He moved against her, fierce and assured, bringing her to a shuddering climax.

I had to lose my virginity one day, she thought sadly. What better way to lose it than to the man I'm in love with?

She tentatively stroked his stomach and he smiled.

'Don't. You might find that I have far more stamina than you think.'

'How modest of you.'

He chuckled and turned to face her.

'That's one thing I like about you,' he said, 'your sense of humour.'

'That and my body.'

'You're right, two things.'

Beth felt a surge of tears and blinked them away furiously. Hadn't she known that she would regret it? His lovemaking had demolished the last vestiges of her defences, leaving her vulnerable and exposed.

She had walked into it with her eyes wide open. Deep down, she must have known that he would have left if she had only said so. He was not the sort of man to force himself on a woman. He had no need. The world, she considered bitterly, could provide an endless supply for his taking.

He touched her cheek and she sighed.

'What was that for?' he asked curiously.

'What happened between us——' she hesitated '—what happened between us shouldn't have happened.'

'Didn't you enjoy it?' He kissed her ear, holding her hair in his fingers, and then blew gently into it.

'That's not the point,' she said, but already her arguments were weakening. He kissed the nape of her neck, his hand straying to her breast, and she relaxed against him.

'Then what is?' he asked huskily.

'There are things,' Beth said falteringly, 'things that you don't know about me.'

'And there are things that you don't know about me,' he pointed out. 'Why don't we just let nature take its course?' He caressed her thighs, parting her legs with his hands until she felt a feverish limpness invade her.

'It's not as simple as that,' she said. Half of her wanted badly to tell him the truth, but the other half informed her coldly that to reveal the truth would put paid to Laura's job and she would never again feel the sensuous delight that he aroused. He would turn his back on her in rage, she knew that, and now that he had opened this world to her, how on earth was she going to survive without it?

Sooner or later the truth would come out—that was as sure as the sun rose and set—but at least she could enjoy their temporary relationship and then, when the time came, she could make the inevitable departure.

Because inevitable it would be, whether or not this masquerade was happening. He was a man born to move on; why not take what she could, while she could? She would have a lifetime to recuperate, wouldn't she?

'I can't remember the last time a woman turned me on the way you do,' he murmured. 'I feel as though I can't have enough of you. Isn't that strange, all this time you've been working for me, and only now this is happening?'

'Strange,' Beth repeated faintly.

He was as aroused as she was, and this time their love-making was fiercer and harder.

Even in the air-conditioned room she could feel his body perspiring next to hers, and as he lay down beside her she traced her fingers along his stomach, feeling its dampness.

'Tell me,' he said, 'about Ryan. What do you feel for him now?'

He turned on his side to face her.

'I'd rather not talk about him,' Beth said quickly.

'Why not?' Marcos's eyes narrowed on her face. 'Does he still mean something to you?'

'Honestly,' she pleaded, 'can we drop the subject?'

'You're my woman now,' he said grimly. 'I want your thoughts to be on me and me alone.'

Fat chance, Beth thought despairingly, of their being anywhere else.

But the possessive arrogance in his voice stirred something in her, made her feel warm and heady.

'If we carry on this ... this affair, could we still work together?'

'I could always fire you.'

'No! Don't do that!'

'You mean you value your job more than you do me?' he teased.

'Jobs are hard to come by these days.'

'And men aren't?'

'You're playing with words now.'

'So I am,' Marcos agreed silkily. 'I studied law at university. The habit of exploiting the English language has never quite deserted me.'

'That's terrible!' Beth joked, kissing him lightly, relishing her ability to arouse him. 'It means that you're never sincere.'

'I sincerely want to bed you over and over again,' he mocked, a lazy smile on his lips.

'You did mention your stamina...' She lay back on the bed, tempting him with her nudity, watching desire flare in his dark eyes.

'You wanton,' he moaned, bending his head to take her nipple into his mouth. Beth wriggled against him, urging his hands to explore other parts of her body that were also aching to be touched.

He was right, she was a wanton with him, totally lacking in inhibitions. She should be ashamed, but somehow when he touched her there was no room left for anything like that. He filled her horizons with his presence, he made a laughing-stock of all her moral guidelines. Most of all, he made her helpless.

If she weren't so damned helpless, then, she thought, she could tell him what needed to be told, she could find the strength to take the consequences.

Love more than hurt, it was agony—but it was irresistible.

As they boarded the plane the following day, Beth took one last lingering look at the timeless beauty around her and thought that St Lucia would always have a special place in her heart. It was there that she was found and lost.

They were discreet, but it was impossible to hide from Jane the fact that something had happened between them. There was a familiarity between them that hadn't been there before, and Jane's sharp eyes absorbed it all.

'You've slept with him, haven't you?' she accused acidly, when Marcos had left his seat for a few minutes.

Beth didn't answer. She didn't have to; the tell-tale flush on her cheeks said it all for her.

'Well, you got what you wanted,' Jane muttered, her eyes daggers. 'You bedded the boss. What were you hoping for? A pay rise?' She laughed shortly, 'Because he won't marry you, you know.'

The venom in her voice spurred Beth into self-defence. 'Nor would I expect him to!' she lied.

'Ha! Crack another one! All women hope for marriage, even someone like you. Not that you've had much luck. I mean, first David, now Marcos.'

Beth gritted her teeth together. Jane's words stung, because they were true. Admit it or not, she wanted Marcos Adrino for herself—not just for a week, or a month, or even a year, but for a lifetime.

'And what about you?' Beth asked quietly. 'Don't you want to get married?'

Jane flushed suddenly. 'Sure, but I don't intend to play the field until it happens.'

Beth didn't bother to object.

'Look,' she said earnestly, leaning across the aisle, 'maybe you're right. Marcos is inaccessible, and I'm a fool. But you don't have to be. You could find someone, someone to share things with. Isn't that better than clinging to a wild dream?'

It was a baldly honest statement, and Jane's face looked first surprised, then angry.

'You'll be sorry you ever got involved with him,' she promised. 'I'll...'

What she intended to do was lost on Beth, because at that moment Marcos reappeared, his eyes not taking in Jane at all, but hungrily dwelling on Beth until a surge of colour flooded her cheeks.

He slipped into the seat next to her and murmured, 'I don't think I've ever enjoyed a plane flight as much as this. Right now, I could take you. Maybe we could explore the more private regions of this plane together?'

'Not on your life!' Beth looked at him, horrified, and then burst into helpless giggling. The thought of finding somewhere on a plane private enough in which to make love was wildly amusing.

'What about if we spread a blanket discreetly over ourselves ...?'

'Somehow,' Beth informed him drily, 'I think we might be noticed. There are other people in this compartment, not least Jane.'

'Jane?'

'Your employee sitting across the aisle.'

'Oh, Jane. She won't notice a thing. Besides, she's glued to a magazine.'

A casual dismissal. Was this how he would speak about her once their affair was over? It was a fair chance that that would happen even before she had a chance to tell him who she really was, because she would tell him. Just as soon as she found the courage.

They chatted throughout the flight, but under the easy conversation his eyes were burning, devouring her. He touched her lightly, but just a fraction of a second longer than was necessary, so that she knew what was going through his head.

And she felt like a teenager, as though loving him had stripped her of her years and turned her into the vulnerable girl she had once been.

When they finally arrived back in London, it was an effort to drag herself away from him. Suddenly Laura's flat seemed like an exercise in isolation.

But Jane had resolutely hovered, determined to stay until she saw them leave on their separate ways.

Beth caught a taxi back to Swiss Cottage, dumping her suitcases on to the ground and heading for the telephone.

The time had come to put a stop to their little game.

Laura picked up the phone almost instantly, and Beth smiled.

'You weren't sitting on the phone, were you?' she asked lightly.

'Of course I was. Waiting for your call. How was it? Was it very hot?'

'Very,' Beth agreed. 'Hot and beautiful. Paradise, in fact. I could have stayed longer.'

'Well, I'm glad you didn't,' Laura said petulantly. 'I've been eaten with envy ever since you left. If you'd stayed any longer, you would have found my corpse in your flat.'

Beth laughed loudly. 'You eat too much to ever waste away from anything, including envy!'

'I could waste away from love,' Laura said seriously. 'I've tried, but I can't get David out of my mind. I just want to see him so badly... And especially now that I'm beginning to show.' There was a wistful sigh on the line.

'Laura, I've been thinking,' Beth said slowly. 'This won't work. I mean, my being here, pretending to be you. It was silly. No, more than that, it was reckless. We have to come clean, and then maybe you should get in touch with David, tell him about the baby; he has a right to know.'

'Never!'

'But...'

'Please, Beth, for me. Whatever you think of all this, you're in it now, and neither of us can back down.'

'Things have changed, Laura.'

'What?'

I'm in love with your boss, she had meant to say, but now she found that she couldn't admit it, not even to her sister. It was something she wanted to keep to herself for a while.

'I don't feel comfortable with this deception.'

'Please, for me.' She started to cry and Beth clicked her tongue impatiently.

'Don't,' she said sharply. 'All right, I'll keep silent for the time being, but I can't promise that I'll be able to stick it out.'

'Fair enough,' Laura conceded quickly, and Beth could see what was running through her sister's mind as clearly as if it had been written up in bold letters on a notice board. Laura hoped that she could persuade her to keep going, knowing, as Beth did, that the longer the charade continued, the more difficult it would be to confess.

Half an hour later, Beth hung up with the uneasy feeling that nothing had been resolved.

And something would have to be done. Things couldn't continue the way they were. Now that Marcos wasn't around, she could think more clearly, and she knew that she would have to gamble her temporary happiness on his understanding.

She unpacked lethargically and had a bath, afterwards standing for ages by the window and staring out, comparing the grey mournful skies outside with the brilliantly blue ones in St Lucia.

Had the sunshine gone to their heads? she wondered. Maybe it had addled them both, released some hidden spring, which would now slot back into place back in grim old England.

She tried to imagine life without Marcos and couldn't. It was just physically impossible to get him out of her head.

But the following day was work, and maybe the change of climate had already cleared her out of his system.

The thought continued to haunt her, right through the night, and on the journey in the following morning.

She told herself to be prepared, but by the time she let herself into the office her skin was already tingling with apprehension.

He was already in; his coat was slung over the coat-stand.

Beth slowly hung hers next to it, and blindly glanced down at the masses of post that had arrived in their absence.

Letters from abroad, inter-company memos, copies of engineering reports on some of their planned sites. She sat down and began sorting them out, half her mind on Marcos, just yards away from her behind his closed door.

When he finally buzzed her to bring him in a cup of coffee and to come with her shorthand pad, she heard herself replying in a crisp, distant voice. Not the voice of a lover. She had no intention of acting like a lovesick teenager, especially when there was a good chance that he had now relegated her to the category of the 'Brief Fling'.

He glanced up when she entered, then leaned back in his chair and surveyed her more thoroughly.

Beth absolutely refused to act coy. It was not her style anyway. She had always been a direct person; now she stared directly into his eyes and then sat down, her hand poised to take the dictation.

'Had a good night?' he asked softly.

'Fine,' Beth mumbled. 'I was pretty tired, though. How was yours?'

'Awful.'

She looked hesitantly at him, a flicker of delight coursing through her. 'Yes?'

'And you needn't look so smug.'

Beth controlled her expression, but she felt light-headed with joy.

'I didn't think I was.'

'I spent the entire night thinking about you, wanting you. In fact I was very nearly tempted to pay you a surprise visit.'

'Were you?'

'Is that all you can say?' But he shot her a sudden, charming smile that made her blood turn to water.

'No, there's an awful lot more I can say,' she informed him sincerely.

'Good, then you can say it tonight. I'll pick you up at eight.'

He returned to his work, quickly flicking through some folders on his desk, rattling off orders for her with his usual staccato rapidity, until she was happily lost in a whirlwind of work.

That was one thing about working for him; there was no time to daydream. He did not spare himself, and he did not expect his employees to do so, either.

Nor did he make any further allusions that day to the fact that their relationship was no longer the boss-secretary relationship. She didn't think that he really cared whether anyone knew about them or not, but on the other hand he had no intention of broadcasting it. And neither had she.

She was not given to sharing confidences by nature, and anyway her conscience wouldn't have allowed it.

As she dressed for dinner that evening, she felt the worry nagging away at the back of her mind. This charade had started out as a temporary game, a gamble to help her thoughtless sister out of a difficult situation and herself out of an unenviable rut after her own unsuccessful fling with Craig. Now it was much more. It had become a dangerous masquerade, with much more to lose than a job with a good salary.

Wilful Cupid had catapulted her into a dreadful no-win situation. To confess would be to lose Marcos, but to keep silent was only a cowardly way of buying time.

Her eyes flicked nervously as the doorbell rang, and she opened the door to see Marcos standing there, casually dressed, his black hair severely combed away from his face, a Harrods bag in his hand.

'I thought we were going to eat out,' Beth said, surprised, warming as he smiled at her slowly.

'Everything I want to eat is right here,' he drawled, shutting the door behind him. 'Cheese, salmon, salad and champagne. Courtesy of that fine department store.'

Beth grinned. 'How thoughtful of you.'

'And of course,' he murmured, coiling his long fingers into her hair and upturning her face to his, 'there's you. The most edible thing on the menu.'

His lips explored hers with leisurely sensuality, nibbling and teasing until she was gasping for breath. He pulled away eventually and said huskily, 'I've been waiting to do that all day.'

'That has a clichéd ring about it,' Beth said, but she was laughing, the nagging doubts conveniently put into temporary storage. She took the bag from him and they went into the cramped kitchen, his arms around her, his teeth gently nipping her neck while she chopped the lettuce and tomatoes.

'I'll never get this done!' she protested. 'Are you normally such a pest in the kitchen?'

'I'm hardly ever in one,' he said, picking up one of the kitchen implements and twirling it around as though it were some strange apparatus which he had never laid eyes on before.

'Haven't any of your girlfriends had them?' Beth asked curiously, averting her eyes because the desire to find out was stronger than she would have imagined.

Marcos shrugged. 'I expect so. I rarely ventured inside.'

'You surely didn't wine and dine them all of the time!' She thought of the elegant Angela Fordyce. No, she couldn't picture her in a kitchen at all. Maybe they liked a constant round of restaurants. As far as she was concerned, though, that thought held little appeal.

'Isn't that the standard courtship game?' he said flatly. 'I had no interest in the architecture of their houses apart from the obvious, and I certainly didn't want any of them cluttering up my apartment.' He had opened the bottle of chilled champagne and handed her a glass.

Beth regarded him soberly over the rim. Unintentionally, he was telling her what she already knew. That he was not a man for commitment. He liked change, and when the time came for her to confess all he would toss her out like useless rubbish. Except with me, she thought uneasily, it'll be far worse because his pride will have been affronted. God, why am I in this mess? But even as she asked the question the answer provided itself. She was in love with him, and doesn't love make cowards of us all? she thought. Wasn't it an addiction that made a fool out of good sense?

'Why not?' she asked, walking into the lounge. 'Don't you believe in love and marriage?'

'Do you?' The dark eyes scrutinised her face. 'Was that what you wanted out of Ryan?' His voice was hard.

'Marriage isn't on my agenda,' she said, avoiding the question.

'Then we see eye-to-eye.' He came and sat next to her, lightly tracing the contour of her body through her dress. 'Because I don't believe in marriage at all. All that stuff about love is so much hot air. I've seen enough failed marriages around me to last a lifetime. No, the only certainty is with yourself.'

'You mean your career,' Beth amended. He was at least being honest, but honesty hurt.

'I guess I do,' he said lazily. 'Women come and go, but without a career——' He shrugged. 'I've seen first-hand what happens, and that's not the way I intend to go.'

'And how long do you give us?' she asked, noticing that her hand trembled as she took a sip of the champagne. 'A week? A month? Three months maybe?'

'Who knows? Does it matter to you?'

'Oh, no,' she said bitterly, 'but if I knew, maybe I could plan my diary accordingly.'

He laughed at that, but she wasn't laughing at all. She wished she had never given him the opportunity for truth. Truth had a curious way of backfiring.

'You make me laugh,' he said, his eyes feverish as they swept possessively over her body, 'and that's a first for any woman. I'm prepared to live dangerously. Are you?' His hand cupped her breast, and under the thin cotton of her dress she felt her body hot with arousal.

Oh, yes, she thought, I'm living dangerously all right. More dangerously than you could ever imagine. Right now I feel as though I'm walking on a knife-edge, with two very sheer drops on either side. But until then . . .

She lay back on the sofa, breathing quickly as he unbuttoned the front of her dress, exposing her nudity to his hungry gaze, closing her eyes as his mouth found the hardened tips of her breasts.

Until then, I'll fill myself with you, my love, because it'll have to last a lifetime.

CHAPTER SEVEN

GRADUALLY Beth's life slotted into a pattern of love-making by night, while during the day no one would guess that there was anything between her and Marcos at all.

And every day she fell a little deeper in love with him. But that didn't stop the worry nagging away at the back of her mind. Every morning she woke up and thought, Today's the day, today I'll confess everything; but the thought of the immense void that his absence in her life would bring always made her good intentions die on her lips. So she kept silent, hating her cowardice, torn between the ecstasy of being with him and the agony of knowing that every minute brought her closer to the end.

And at work Jane continued to be a malicious threat hovering in the background, yapping at her heels like a little terrier that wanted to bite but found it maddeningly impossible.

She was in the office now, an irritating presence which Beth attempted to ignore by concentrating on her word-processor. Eventually Jane gave up her round of antagonistic questions and sullenly flopped into the chair facing Beth.

'I'm about to go to lunch,' Beth said pointedly.

'I didn't realise you ever went to lunch,' Jane said with staged incredulity. 'I thought you just stayed up here working and building up brownie points with Marcos.'

'I'll make sure that he gets those files you brought,' Beth said politely, changing the subject with accustomed swiftness. Jane insisted on angling every conversation back to Marcos, and particularly this morning Beth was not in the mood for it. She had too much on her mind.

'Still sleeping with the boss?' Jane enquired idly, juggling the plastic container with the pens so that they rattled irritatingly.

It was the very first time she had brought this out in the open, and Beth stared at her aghast.

'I beg your pardon?'

'You heard.'

'I thought I must have been mistaken.' There was a tremor in her voice which Jane seized upon with malicious glee.

'Would you like me to repeat the question?'

Beth snatched the irritating pen container out of Jane's hand and dumped it unceremoniously on the far side of the desk. 'There's no need,' she said tightly, 'because my answer's going to be the same anyway. It's none of your business. It never has been and it isn't now. So if you don't mind...' She began slipping on her cardigan, a rose-coloured one that matched her skirt and picked up the floral colours in her short-sleeved jumper.

'Marcos has changed, you know,' Jane said, an element of bitterness in her voice. 'He's not as caustic as he used to be, and he never, ever flirts any more. It's all your fault.'

Beth's mouth dropped open. 'I hadn't noticed any change in him,' she said without thinking.

'Well, he has, and it's all your fault. I suppose it's what you've been working towards, domesticating him.' Her tone was acidly accusatory.

'I really don't know what you're talking about.'

'You mean you don't want to know what I'm talking about. I——'

She was cut off in mid-sentence as the telephone began to ring, and Beth picked up the receiver with gratitude.

She didn't want to argue with Jane, she didn't want to be rude, but she knew that she would be if she remained a second more in the office.

Right now, her nerves were near to breaking and an unprovoked argument would just be the final straw.

'Good afternoon, Adrino corporation, how may I help you?'

She had hoped that Jane would vanish but she remained where she was, tapping her fingers lightly on the desk and staring around her. Waiting to resume her attack, Beth thought wearily.

There was a pause down the other end, then a man's voice whispered huskily, 'Darling.'

'Hello?' Beth asked, bewildered.

'My darling, don't you recognise me?'

'I think you must have the wrong number,' Beth said courteously.

Jane was staring at her now, intrigued no doubt by the one-sided conversation she was hearing.

'Laura, darling, it's me.'

At this Beth felt her body freeze. This was no wrong number. Whoever the caller was, he knew her sister, and the realisation of who it was struck her just as the man identified himself.

'Laura, it's me, David.'

'Oh.' Her voice had sunk to a whisper, and the colour had drained from her face.

She needed to sit down. She looked across and saw Jane looking at her with undisguised interest now.

Quite purposefully, she turned her back towards the girl, knowing that her action would probably only increase her curiosity, but determined that this conversation should not be overheard.

'You,' she said into the mouthpiece, 'what do you want?'

'Laura, darling...'

'Don't call me that,' Beth said sharply.

'Why?' David demanded. 'You still are. Despite everything. Look, we need to talk.'

'No!' There was definite panic in her voice now.

'Yes!' he spoke urgently. 'We need to talk! I'm in England...'

'Oh, God.' Hysteria was grabbing her by the throat. She didn't need this further complication in her life, not now. It was complicated enough already.

'I want to see you, Laura. I need to. Tonight. I'll come around to your place...'

'No!' She rested her forehead on the palm of her hand to stop it from trembling.

'Please, Laura. I have a lot of explaining to do.' Some of the urgency had left his voice now. He was pleading. She didn't want him to plead with her. She wanted him to go away.

But, she thought despairingly, it was not her place to send him away without a hearing. Laura would have to do that. Much as she hated it, she would have to agree to see him, and somehow get her sister down to London as quickly as she could.

Out of the corner of her eye she could see Jane avidly listening to as much as she possibly could, and she groaned inwardly.

There was a time when her life had been so simple, so uncomplicated. Now she felt as though she was walking a minefield.

'All right,' she agreed finally, 'tonight. At eight o'clock.'

Without giving him a chance to prolong the conversation, she hung up and swivelled around in the chair to see Jane smiling nastily at her.

'Who was that?' she asked casually, standing up.

'A girlfriend,' Beth lied coolly. 'Now, if you don't mind, I really would like to go to lunch. I'll see that Marcos looks at the files as soon as he's in.'

'Sure.' Jane smiled again, looking very much like a cat that had found some unexpected cream.

Beth didn't care any more. She just wanted to find some very dark, very private place, preferably on another planet, and leave all these problems behind her.

She spent the remainder of the day attempting to plough through her work, but her concentration was weak. Several times she found herself staring vacantly at the computer, her mind absorbed in her own problems.

Laura, as luck would have it, was uncontactable.

'She's gone to the doctor,' one of her colleagues informed Beth in a voice that implied that she was the unfortunate one who had got lumbered with the extra workload.

Beth knew what that meant. Trips to the doctor, as Laura had grumpily told her a few weeks ago, invariably meant a wait of anything between half an hour and two hours.

And then, after that, there was no guarantee that her sister would immediately return to the flat.

In fact, when she phoned at five-thirty, there was still no answer.

Weren't twins supposed to have some kind of uncanny telepathy? she wondered. If so, the invisible communication lines had definitely broken down in their case.

At least Marcos had not been in. He had flown to Paris for a breakfast meeting, and without him around she had had the freedom to give full rein to her dreadful foreboding.

She'd been a fool, she decided, as she travelled back to the flat that evening, for once oblivious to the chaotic crush of bodies against hers. She should have arranged to see him some other day, any other day. Jane, she thought miserably, hovering in the background, had not been conducive to rational thought at the time.

Anyway, there was no point debating the issue now. She had no idea where David was staying, so she couldn't cancel at the last minute.

She had just enough time, when she got back to the flat, to half-heartedly eat a bowl of pasta and have a quick bath when there was a sharp ring on the doorbell.

She jumped up from where she was sitting with a last, desperate wish that all this was some awful nightmare, and slowly opened the door.

During all the conversations she had had with Laura, her sister had only sketchily described what David looked like.

The man standing in front of her more or less fitted the description. Medium height, brown hair, blue eyes, and a face that looked as though it was on the point of smiling.

A nice face. Nothing like what she had expected. Men with nice faces, she thought, shouldn't behave like bastards. At least with Marcos you knew where you stood.

One look at that cold, arrogant, sexy face left you in no doubt that he could be a bastard if crossed.

Not so David. He was smiling now, extending a large bunch of flowers at her.

'Thank you,' Beth muttered uncomfortably, letting him into the flat with a sinking feeling of finality.

He brushed past her and then turned around, his blue eyes crinkling at the corners.

'You've had your hair cut,' he said, and she got the impression that he was as temporarily lost for words as she was, though for completely different reasons.

'I have a different hairstyle, yes,' Beth answered carefully.

She hoped that he would not do anything stupid, like try to kiss her, but, just in case, she walked away in search of a vase, dumping the flowers unceremoniously into it.

When she returned, she saw that he had taken off his jacket, which was damp, and had slung it over one of the chairs.

'You're wet,' she said bluntly.

'It's been raining. Hadn't you noticed?'

'No. It was fine when I left work earlier on.'

There was an awkward silence and Beth looked away.

'You don't seem terribly pleased to see me,' he said quietly, stepping towards her.

Beth efficiently stepped backwards. 'David, there's something that I need to tell you,' she blurted out in a rush, waiting for him to interrupt, but he didn't. He waited patiently and she thought again what a nice face he had. The sort of face that had, she reminded herself, seduced her sister into thinking that it matched the rest of him.

She took a deep breath, and began the tortuous explanation which she had always thought would have been directed at Marcos. The bizarreness of the whole situation rang in her ears as she heard herself trying to rationalise it, and when she had finished she didn't feel in the slightest cleansed by the confession. But then, she thought, she wasn't confessing to a man who held her life in his hands.

'But why?' was his only response, bewilderment creasing his forehead.

'That,' Beth said, 'has to come from Laura.' She stood up and began restlessly pacing the room. 'I'll phone and see whether she's in as yet, and get her to come down here as soon as she can.'

There was, she was pleased and relieved to see, no outburst of fury. His astonishment had swiftly been followed by calm acceptance. He obviously knew that there was a hell of a lot of explaining to be done, but he was prepared to wait for it.

She had no idea how she got through the next three hours. Laura, thank heaven, had been in at last, and had agreed to come down at once, her voice full of mingled anticipation and apprehension. Beth fixed David a light supper and stiltedly conversed with him from the opposite side of the room, unwilling to like him after what he had put Laura through, but finding it difficult to resist his easygoing good nature.

All the time she kept one eye on the clock. When the doorbell finally went, she rushed to her feet, pulling open the door, a smile of relief on her face. The smile froze on her lips.

Marcos was standing outside, still in his suit, although he had discarded the tie and undone the top button, and he wasn't smiling.

'Hello,' Beth said uncertainly, not moving from her position by the door.

'Surprised to see me?' he asked tightly, and without waiting for an answer pushed her aside and strode into the room.

Beth rushed behind him in dismay, standing still when she saw him stop in the middle of the room to stare at David.

'Ryan,' he said grimly.

David stood up, his only sign of embarrassment the reddish flush on his face.

'Marcos,' he said, 'I didn't expect you...'

'No, I'm sure you didn't. I'm sure neither of you did.'

He spun around to face Beth, his eyes narrowed with anger.

'I can explain...' Beth whispered miserably. But she couldn't. Not yet.

'Really,' he said icily. 'I'm sure you can think up something very interesting, but I'm not in the mood for fairy-tales right now.'

David's expression of bewilderment was growing by the minute.

'Marcos...' Beth began unsteadily, as he turned to leave.

Before she could complete the sentence, she felt his iron grip on her arm and she raised her eyes to his, inwardly cringing at the frozen black depths.

'You bitch,' he bit out softly. 'You bloody little bitch.'

'You're hurting me!' She tried to wriggle free of his grip, but he tightened his hand on her arm and she winced in pain.

'I could hurt you a whole lot more than this, the way I feel at the moment,' he said through gritted teeth, 'but you don't even deserve my anger.' With that he released her, and she staggered backwards.

The front door slammed behind him and she shot David a panic-stricken look.

'I'll be back in a while,' she whispered, grabbing her jacket and racing out of the flat before he could say a word. 'Laura will be here soon,' she threw over her shoulder.

Marcos was walking quickly towards his car, and even from a distance Beth could feel the rage emanating from him like something tangible.

She couldn't allow him to leave like this, not without any word of explanation.

She ran behind him, and he swung around to face her, the darkness of the night lending a frightening fury to his features.

She had never seen him like this before. She had seen his cold anger on that first day, and she had seen contempt, but she had never witnessed this chilling anger.

'Marcos,' she pleaded, her hand instinctively reaching out to him.

He thrust it aside, and stared down at her.

'How could you?' he asked, his face tight.

'It's not what you think,' Beth said, her face red with the misery of being in an impossible situation.

'No?' he jeered. 'You and he were just having a friendly chat, were you? Two ex-lovers discussing the weather and catching up on old news? Is that the line you're going to feed me?'

'Yes, as a matter of fact, we were just chatting, as it happens!'

'How cosy.'

'I had no idea that he was in England until today!' Beth said in a high, desperate voice. 'You have to believe me! He telephoned out of the blue and invited himself over!'

'And of course the word "no" doesn't exist in your vocabulary?'

Tears were blurring her eyes, making it impossible for her to speak.

'Lost for words, are you, darling?'

'Why won't you believe me? We haven't slept together. This is all a huge mistake. Who told you that he was here, anyway?'

'No, the only mistakes are the ones I've been blind enough to make.' Now he sounded as furious with himself as he was with her. She knew what he must be thinking. That he had been made to look a fool. 'And, if you must know, Jane told me what was going on.'

'Jane, of course.'

'I didn't want to believe her, but I had to find out, and it's just as well I came over, isn't it? Found out for myself just what type of woman you were. Tell me, would you have ... continued to entertain us both? Or would you just have satisfied Ryan while he was over here? For old times' sake?'

She slapped his face at that, hard, the ringing sound creating a dreadful silence.

For a second, she thought that he was going to slap her back, but he didn't. Hadn't he said that she wasn't worth his anger?

His black eyes glittered.

'You're way off target!' she whispered urgently. 'You don't understand.'

'So where's the explanation, sweetheart? Make me understand. Isn't that why you rushed out here? To present me with some imaginative little story? Well, I'm listening: where is it?'

Beth looked at him in silence. Behind her she heard a taxi pull up outside the flat, and knew instinctively that it was Laura.

'You'll have to see for yourself,' she said. 'Please, Marcos. Please come with me.' Her voice broke, and, much as she hated it, she felt the tears streaming down her face, and she wiped them away with the back of her closed fist.

He remained as rigid as a rock, and she held her breath, waiting for him to tell her to go to hell, but he finally said coolly, 'Why not? Perhaps an amusing little story from you is just what I need. But it had better be amusing, sweetheart, or you'll find out just what it means to cross me.'

They walked back to the flat in silence and heard excited voices coming from within even before they had entered.

Beth slowly opened the door, watching as Laura and David disengaged from each other's arms, feeling Marcos's breath warm on her neck behind her.

'Here's your explanation,' she said with a sweeping gesture. Her eyes were still red from crying and she could hear her voice, laced with misery.

Laura's eyes widened as Marcos entered, but Beth hardly noticed. She was concentrating too intensely on Marcos's reaction to notice much else.

The shock registered on his face for what must only have been a matter of seconds, then it was replaced by cold inscrutability.

'Meet my twin,' Beth whispered. 'Laura. Your ex-secretary. I'm Beth, her sister.'

He caught on quickly, very quickly, but Beth was hardly surprised. His mental agility had amazed her in the past but she had slowly grown accustomed to it. He had a mind like a knife, able to cut through the unimportant to the heart of the problem.

Now his brain clicked into gear, and threw up the correct conclusion with astonishing speed.

He slowly turned to her, seeing her as though for the first time.

'A game,' he said with freezing stiffness, 'you two have been playing a little game at my expense. One pregnant sister decides to have her twin stand in so that she doesn't lose her job, is that right? Am I heading in more or less the right direction?'

Beth nodded mutely.

'I didn't want to——' she began, but he cut her short.

'Spare me your excuses,' he said coldly. 'Only a coward attempts to hide behind them.'

'She means it, Marcos,' Laura burst out. 'She never wanted to do this at all. I persuaded her, I used everything, even emotional blackmail. If you want someone to blame, blame me!'

One look from Marcos silenced her, then he returned his attention to Beth.

'Enjoyed it, did you?' he asked softly, with a twisted smile. 'Enjoyed taking me for a ride? Did you see it as a perverse kind of challenge? How long you could carry on the charade?'

'You're so wrong,' she murmured. Her misery had given way to a numbness, as though she had temporarily stepped outside her body, and was observing events from a distance. Even in her state she recognised the reaction as a kind of self-defence mechanism.

'A liar,' he drawled, 'a cheap little liar.'

There was a hush. Laura and David had retired to some other part of the flat, obviously knowing that what was happening between Beth and Marcos was not for their ears.

'I know what you must be thinking, and you're right. I lied to you, but only about my identity.'

She lifted her chin defiantly and he gave a short, cynical laugh.

'Only. Lucky old me. Well, you had your fun, and now I think I can find better things to amuse me.'

He turned to go and Beth caught hold of his arm, releasing it when he looked down at her hand distastefully.

There was so much more to say, but she knew with despairing certainty that none of it would get said now. He had made his mind up and who could blame him? How could he know that she had fallen head over heels in love with him?

'You don't want to try and understand, do you?' she asked. 'It's so much easier for you to believe the worst!'

'The facts speak for themselves, darling.'

'All right. I made a mistake. I should have told you, but I never found the opportunity.'

'Oh, no. There were no opportunities during all those times we were in bed together, were there?'

'How could I?'

He shot her a contemptuous smile. 'You're right. It would hardly have been an aphrodisiac, would it?'

'Stop acting as though your life has been unblemished!' Beth shouted, her misery giving way to anger. 'Stop acting as though you have the final word on everything that's sunshine and light! Are you going to try and tell me that you've treated the opposite sex with scrupulous fairness? That you've never made mistakes?'

'At least women knew where they stood with me. I didn't resort to the comfort of lies.'

'I had to think about Laura!'

'You had to think about yourself, you mean. You were here for a short stint. Why blow it when sleeping with the boss was so convenient?'

'You're acting as though I have no morals.'

'Well, from where I'm standing, they're not exactly shouting at me.'

Their eyes clashed and she was the first to look away, unable to find anything that would make him understand.

'And you would know all about morals, I suppose,' Beth intoned bitterly. 'Are you going to tell me that you weren't quite prepared to hand me my walking papers the minute I outstayed my welcome in your life?'

'Don't try and twist things round to suit your argument.' The dark eyes raked mercilessly over her face. 'Your behaviour was despicable.'

She stared mutely at him. 'I'm still the same person,' she said defiantly. 'Only my name's different.'

'You don't really expect me to buy that, do you?' he asked icily. 'You led me up the garden path. You conveniently avoided telling me the truth because, oh, dear, the opportunity never seemed to arise, and you stand there expecting me to forgive and forget?'

'No,' she muttered into the developing silence, 'I don't suppose I do. I know you well enough to realise that you don't forgive mistakes, even mistakes of the innocent variety.'

'You're damn right,' he said, his eyes knifing into her. 'And I don't forget, either.'

'That's nothing to be proud of,' Beth informed him dully.

'From where you're standing, I don't really think you can afford to say much on that subject, do you?' he asked with a contemptuous sneer. 'No, if I were you, I'd take a long, hard look at myself and then ask whether I'm qualified to give advice to anyone on morality.'

She looked at him, flinching at the glittering hardness she saw in his eyes. This was so much worse than she had ever expected. Had there been a ray of hope lurking in her subconscious that he might forgive her her sin of omission? If so, she was in no doubt now that any such hope had been sadly misguided.

'Do you want me to return to work?' she asked inconsequentially, realising that there was nothing to gain by prolonging their conversation. Nothing she could say would ever wipe the disdain from his face. No one liked being deceived, least of all someone like Marcos Adrino.

He smiled again, cruelly. 'Oh, yes. You'll continue until I can find a suitable replacement, and you should count yourself lucky that I don't take legal steps to make you pay for what you did. You'll work for me, all right, and actually it might even be salutary for me to be forced to view my stupidity on a daily basis. They say that you learn from your mistakes; well, what better way for me to learn than to have my mistake staring me in the face every day of the week?'

This time he did not slam the front door, and Beth didn't follow him. There was no point. There was nothing left to be said.

CHAPTER EIGHT

BETH had no idea how she got through what little remained of the night. She blindly washed up the few dirty plates in the kitchen and then busied herself with tidying up the lounge, only looking up when Laura bounced into the room, full of life, her face wreathed in smiles.

Things, it transpired, had been sorted out between the two of them. Life was rosy and full of promise and her sister, true to form, was regaling her with her new-found happiness, thoughtless of the fact that all Beth wanted to do was find a dark corner and cry her eyes out.

Laura had never been good at facing other people's distress and, Beth noted wryly, she certainly hadn't changed in that respect.

She was on top of the world. David, Beth learned, had been miserable in Paris, had pined for her. And, more to the point, had no wife.

'He told me he was married,' Laura announced gleefully, 'he left the country, because he was afraid that he was getting too involved with me and he had never envisaged his life with a wife before. It daunted him. He didn't want to hurt me and he said he needed time to think, to put things in perspective. He's told me that if Marcos says anything about us he's quite prepared to quit his job and find another, anywhere I want him to.'

'So all's well that ends well.'

'You don't mind, do you?'

'Of course not!' Beth exclaimed sincerely. 'Why should I mind? I'm happy for you.'

'And you're all right?'

'Fine.' She managed a smile. Out of habit, she found herself sparing Laura her own misery, knowing that it would burst her bubble of joy, and wouldn't serve any purpose anyway.

Come what may, she had to carry on. Much as she wanted to, she couldn't take refuge in her room and weep until there were no tears left because that would be the pattern of her life for the rest of her days. She had to face the world bravely, even though she was cracking up inside.

Marcos, she told herself philosophically as she later stared at her bedside clock and tried to court sleep, was not designed to be hemmed in by a committed relationship. He was too much of a predator. She had known that all along. Surely that knowledge must make her burden easier to bear? If it did, it certainly didn't feel like it at the moment, though.

Right now she felt utterly hopeless.

She only wished that she didn't have to face him for the next couple of weeks, but perhaps it would strengthen her.

To her relief, he wasn't around when she arrived at work the following morning. She busied herself at the computer, but her mind was on the door, waiting for it to open, and, when it finally did, she felt her stomach constrict into a tight knot.

Marcos looked at her with a flat, unreadable expression and nodded coolly.

It was as though she were a complete stranger, and one with whom he did not particularly wish to acquaint himself.

He vanished into his office, buzzing her towards lunchtime.

Beth faced him across his desk with trepidation, wanting to see something on his face, some indication that she was on his mind, even if only in a negative aspect. But there was nothing and she realised that there would be no post-mortems on their failed relationship, no questions asked about her deception, no interest in anything she did.

When he spoke, it was about work and his manner was crisp and businesslike. He had told her that she didn't deserve his anger, and now she could see that as far as he was concerned she didn't deserve his contempt either. It was as though she didn't exist as a person at all.

It hurt. Underneath her bland exterior, as she carried on with her work, she was hurting more than she dreamed possible.

By five-thirty she felt as though she had undergone several years in a torture chamber.

She hesitated as she slipped on her cardigan, and then took her courage into her hands and knocked on his door. She just couldn't leave in this atmosphere of silence. She would prefer him to get angry with her, to rant and rave, anything rather than this.

He was studying some files on his desk when she entered, and he barely glanced up at her.

'I'm just off,' Beth said nervously, one hand still on the door. She felt as though she would physically crumble if she released it.

'Fine,' Marcos said politely. He raised his eyes to hers but the expression on his face didn't change.

Beth looked at him, trying desperately to see the man behind the mask. Her eyes followed the line of his powerful arms, arms that had held her, the curve of his mouth that had covered her body with kisses, the black eyes that had burnt with feverish passion.

'Is there anything you want before I leave?' Her words sounded embarrassingly provocative, even though they were not meant to be, and she carried on hastily, 'I've prepared all the information on those two hotels in North America. It's on my desk...' Her voice trailed off.

'No, you can go now.' He looked back down at the files on his desk and she felt a spurt of anger. All right, so she had been wrong, but how could he act as though they had shared nothing? He had not even seen fit to listen to what she had to say.

'Marcos...' she began.

He looked up at her and this time his eyes were hard. 'I told you to leave. Do I have to remind you that you take orders from me? The door is behind you.'

They stared at each other in silence, and Beth was the first to look away.

'Yes,' she mumbled, 'I'll see you tomorrow.'

'Goodnight.'

Beth had never known that she could miss anyone as she missed Marcos, but she did. She realised very quickly the following day that he had no intention of treating her in any way other than that of the polite, distant boss. Emotionally, he had dismissed her from his life, and his attitude rammed home the point far more forcefully than if he had sat her down and told her so himself.

On top of that there was the trauma of now sharing the flat with two other people, and, much as she loved her sister, she found that she preferred the privacy of being on her own.

To be fair, they were very easygoing. And blissfully in love. David had enthusiastically entered into the spirit of impending fatherhood, and they were both happily planning what they should buy, and when.

It was only when she returned to the flat after another endlessly long day at work that he informed her that he had lost his job.

Beth was staggered. More staggered than he appeared to be.

She stormed into work the following day, itching for Marcos to come back from his all-day meeting in Norwich, and when he did she quietly asked if she could have a few words with him.

'I have a lot to do,' he said, frowning, glancing at his watch, but she resolutely held her ground.

'This won't take long.' She met his eyes with that bland, icy expression which she had developed over the past two days, and he nodded curtly, preceding her into his office.

'Well,' he said, moving to sit behind his desk, 'what is it?'

'It's about David.' There was not a flicker of emotion in the black eyes, and some of her courage faltered. 'He's told me that he's been sacked.'

Marcos stifled a yawn, as though to imply that this subject could hardly qualify as being worth his valuable time.

'I'm sorry the whole thing bores you,' Beth said stiffly, 'but I don't think it's particularly fair to sack someone simply because of what's happened between us.'

'I did not sack David,' he informed her coldly. 'We mutually agreed that it was best for him to leave——'

'You sacked him.'

'And,' he continued, ignoring her interruption, 'if you think that this has anything to do with you, then you flatter yourself.'

Beth turned bright red. She could feel her nails biting into the soft flesh of her upper arms.

'Are you telling me that I meant nothing to you?' she bit out, unable to prevent herself.

He leaned back, folding his arms across his chest, and surveyed her without interest.

'I have no desire to discuss what...happened between us.'

'I can't agree to that!' Beth threw at him. 'Not when it affects someone else! Because I don't believe that David's dismissal had nothing to do with us!'

'I don't give a damn what you believe,' Marcos said in a courteous, conversational tone of voice, as though they were discussing the weather or the state of the economy. 'And as for your original question——' he picked up his fountain pen and tapped it lightly on the desk '—you meant to me what every other woman has meant to me. A brief liaison. Except,' he added, his eyes flint-hard, 'I don't normally part company with my women with quite such a sour aftertaste in my mouth.'

There was a heavy silence.

'No,' she pointed out bitterly, 'you prefer your women to have the sour aftertaste.'

'Is that what you have?'

He stood up and walked across to the window, staring outside, his back to her.

'Yes,' she admitted quietly. 'I have the sour aftertaste of someone whose side of the story hasn't really been heard.'

Marcos gave a dry laugh. 'And I thought that I'd heard all there was to hear on that little matter. Enough, at any rate, to last a lifetime.' He turned to face her, staring at her as though she had suddenly metamorphosed into some curiously disgusting specimen.

'I love my sister! That was the reason I agreed to the whole damn thing in the first place. I had no idea that I would become involved with you.'

'Oh,' he said sarcastically, 'you expect me to buy that, do you? You did it out of love. Well, heaven preserve me from that particular emotion if that's the sort of thing it inspires.'

His words cut her to the quick, but she would not show him that. If he wanted to treat her like a stranger, then two could play at that game.

'Yes, silly, isn't it?' she said coldly. 'Love can make us do all sorts of things that are totally out of character.'

'I wouldn't know. I have no siblings. As for love for someone of the opposite sex—well, that's unexplored territory, and will stay that way as far as I am concerned. Now, is that all? Or have you something else to get off your chest? If you have——' he looked at his watch '—you'd better do so quickly, because I have an appointment.'

'Far be it from me to stand in the way of your appointments,' Beth retorted.

She swung around to leave and saw the outer door open to admit Angela.

Beth stared at her, quickly covering up her reaction with an expression of coolness. But she was far from feeling cool inside. Her heart had flipped over in her chest, and she felt as though she could hardly breathe.

So this was his appointment. Some appointment. Why didn't he just say bed companion?

I really mean nothing to him, she thought with agony. As far as he is concerned, it's out with the old and in with the new.

Angela was smiling at her, although her eyes were all for Marcos.

She was a vision in pale turquoise, her hair loose this time and flowing over her shoulders. She looked as though she had been poured into her dress, an impression which even the casual jacket thrown over could not quite conceal.

'Ready, darling?' she asked Marcos. He nodded, his eyes flitting past her to where Beth was at her desk, her eyes averted, fumbling with her handbag.

She turned to face them, and as she did so she watched in horror as Angela lifted her face to his, and his dark head swept downwards to kiss her lingeringly.

Then he put his hand around her waist and addressed Beth with mild surprise.

'Oh, are you still here?'

No, she wanted to yell, this is just a figment of your imagination. 'I'm just leaving,' she said blandly. 'Have a pleasant evening.'

'Oh, we will,' Marcos promised softly. 'A meal, the opera, and then, who knows?'

At his side, Angela giggled coyly, her full lips forming into an instinctive pout.

Beth had the insane desire to strangle her. Instead she yanked open the door and walked quickly to the lift, hurrying just in case she was forced to share it with them. That would have been the last straw. It had been bad enough watching them drool all over each other in the office, but to have to witness similar displays of affection in the lift would have been unbearable.

She didn't go straight back to the flat. Instead, she walked through Knightsbridge, where the shops were all still open, browsing in front of the elegant store fronts, while her mind chewed over the image of Marcos and Angela like a dog with a bone.

Had he contacted her as soon as he had walked out of her life? The tears prickled behind her eyes and she blinked them away. She refused to spend her life weeping over a man who had told her in no uncertain terms precisely what she meant to him. And, as if that wasn't enough, had shown her.

'A meal, the opera, and then, who knows?' The words rang in her head relentlessly. Who knows indeed? From what she had seen, she knew exactly what they would be getting up to later on in the evening, and it certainly wasn't witty repartee and intellectual discussion.

When she had exhausted herself walking around the shops, she went to Covent Garden, where she found a little place to have a cup of coffee.

It was teeming with tourists. All full of life and going somewhere. Unlike her. Where was she going? Her life lacked direction, like a boat without a rudder on stormy seas. She was drifting in a world of pain.

It was after eight by the time she finally made it back to Swiss Cottage, and she breathed a sigh of relief when she found that Laura and David had taken themselves off for the evening.

She had no desire to speak to anyone at all, and rather than risk it she retired to bed early, and made a half-hearted attempt to read her book to sleep.

It was pointless. Her brain continued to worry the question of Marcos and Angela. She found herself looking at the clock, wondering what they were doing now, and it was only in the early hours of the morning that she finally drifted into a restless sleep.

She awakened the following morning, her body aching as though she was in for an attack of the flu, her eyes heavy.

The reflection that stared back at her in the mirror made her grimace. She looked as if she hadn't slept in a week.

She tried to hide it with some light make-up, and dressed carefully in her most sober lightweight suit.

She had gradually bought herself a wardrobe of clothes and was no longer dependent on Laura's, a fact which had made her smile, since her sister had no need of her own clothes now.

'You look dreadful,' Laura greeted her brightly when she finally emerged from her bedroom. David had already gone to an interview for a job in the city.

'You're so kind,' Beth replied.

'What's the matter with you?'

'What do you think?' Beth poured herself a cup of coffee, unable to face anything else.

'Marcos.'

'He's already found my replacement,' she said lightly. 'An older model but still in very good shape.'

'Why don't you leave?' Laura asked. 'You could return to Cambridge, you might even be able to go back to your old job.'

'And what about working my notice?' Beth asked. 'The last thing I need is to be given a bad reference.'

'He wouldn't do that! Don't be ridiculous. In fact——' she wrinkled her nose expressively '—I'm surprised that he's making you work there at all, given everything that's happened.'

'I'm not.' Beth drained her cup and reached out for her bag. 'I think he enjoys my discomfort.'

'Sadistic monster.'

Beth nodded and headed off. He's a sadistic monster, she told herself, so it should be easy to face him. After all, who goes weak at the knees when they're confronted by a sadistic monster?

He was already in when she arrived, and, for the first time in days, was whistling softly under his breath.

She sat down and he leant next to her, running through some of her day's workload, his arm very nearly brushing against hers.

Their proximity didn't seem to affect him at all, but it affected her. It was as if she was being subjected to some electrical charge which made her hairs stand on end.

'You seem in a happy mood,' she said icily, edging away from him, loading the paper tray with headed paper.

'Oh, yes.' He perched for a moment on the edge of the desk and Beth averted her eyes. 'Certain activities are so good for... relaxation.'

Beth's blood froze. It was an instantaneous reaction, but she recovered quickly.

'I'm sure.'

'And by the way, I'll be out to lunch. I probably won't be back until about three.'

'You have a meeting with some developers at three-thirty,' she reminded him, consulting the diary.

'I'll try and make it back by then. But if for some reason I'm detained, could you rearrange it for next week some time?'

'Of course,' Beth said stiffly. 'And will you be contactable while you're out of the office?'

He looked at her, his eyes glinting. 'Oh, I think the phone will definitely be off the hook for what I have in mind,' he said softly.

Beth looked at him with burning resentment. 'I already told you that it's not part of my job description to handle your personal life for you. I won't make excuses to your women and I won't make excuses to your clients because you've decided to be unavailable.'

'You'll do as I say,' he grated.

'Or else what?' she threw at him recklessly. 'You'll fire me? Go ahead!'

She had stood up, her cheeks flaming.

'Sit back down,' he bit out coldly, 'and I'll tell you this for free. While you're here, in my office, working for my company, you'll damn well do what I say, and you'll do it with a smile on your face. If you choose not to, well . . . references can be tricky things, can't they?'

'That's unfair,' Beth muttered, trembling.

'That's life.'

He leant across to retrieve a file from her desk, pausing over her with an icy smile. 'And have you finished the work on the St Lucian project?'

Beth shook her head.

'Why not? You've had long enough to do it.'

'I'll try and finish it by this evening.'

'Just so long as you do. Time is money, and I won't tolerate sloppiness in my secretaries.'

'Then why don't you hurry up and find another?' she muttered under her breath, and he cocked his ear as though trying to catch what she was saying.

'I missed that.'

'I said, have you had any luck with finding another secretary?'

'Oh, when I do, you'll be the first to know,' he informed her blandly. 'In the meanwhile, don't forget your instructions.' He threw her a calculatingly cool smile before going back into his office and firmly shutting the door behind him.

Beth wanted to scream. He was doing this on purpose, paying her back in the most effective way possible, and, much as she hated to admit it, it was working. She felt miserable.

He left the office at twelve-thirty promptly, sparing her only a brief nod, and she could quite happily have thrown her cup of coffee at him.

He was despicable, she thought. He was flaunting her replacement in her face and loving every minute of it. She had thought that nothing could hurt more than his cold silence, but now she knew that that was a bed of roses compared to what she was feeling now.

She ate a sandwich for lunch and pulled out a magazine, but the words blurred in front of her eyes, and she found herself thinking about Marcos and Angela with a ferocity that frightened her.

How could he be so cruel? His pride had been hurt by her deception, she knew that, but did he have to extract his pound of flesh in this way?

She could barely muster up the energy to be her usual friendly self on the telephone, and some of the customers with whom she had built up a pleasant chatting relationship over the past months could sense the change in her voice.

'Is there anything wrong?' one of them asked her with concern, and she felt like bursting into tears.

'No,' she said with effort, 'I must be coming down with something.'

'You need a holiday,' he joked.

I need amnesia, she thought miserably, agreeing with him light-heartedly and replacing the telephone.

When the office door opened at two-thirty, her stomach clenched and she waited for his entry. Would there be lipstick stains on his mouth? Maybe his tie would be dishevelled just that little bit, indicating what his lunchtime rendezvous had entailed.

She didn't think that she could bear another minute of this.

But it wasn't Marcos. It was Roger. A little thinner and a little browner, but with the same warm disposition that she had liked when she had first met him. And right now he was just what the doctor ordered.

I won't mention a thing about Marcos, she told herself, I won't say a word, only to find herself pouring her heart out to him five minutes later.

'Poor Roger,' she said shakily, mopping her eyes with the handkerchief he had given her, 'in the wrong place at the wrong time.'

'I don't know,' he said smiling. 'I'm told that I'm quite good at helping women who are carrying the world's problems on their shoulders.'

'Are you really? You own a scaffolding company, do you?' But he had done her a world of good, so when he pulled her to him she rested willingly against his warm frame, enjoying the comfort of his arms more than she would have thought possible.

It had been unbelievably comforting to pour her soul out to another person. True, she had briefly explained the situation to Laura, but her sister had been too wrapped up in her own world to spare her more than the barest cluckings of sympathy.

Roger, on the other hand, had listened. She felt the warm cotton of his shirt under her cheek and had an insane desire to remain where she was until the sharpness of the pain dulled a little.

She was only aware of another presence in the room when he whispered into her ear, 'Don't look now, but I think we've got company.'

She disengaged herself from his arms and saw Marcos staring at them from the door, his black brows meeting in a thunderous frown.

Before she could flee to the sanctuary of her desk, Roger had pulled her back to him, whispering under his breath, 'I think some jealousy might go a long way here.'

Beth cleared her throat meaningfully. Playing any sort of game with Marcos was not something she intended to do, but Roger was ignoring her and there was very little she could say.

'The joyous reunion,' Roger explained to Marcos with such bare-faced cheek that her lips twitched in a reluctant smile.

'I thought you were in the Seychelles,' Marcos said shortly, his eyes avoiding Beth's face. There was a dark flush to his cheeks.

'I was,' Roger said pleasantly enough, 'but something's cropped up and I had to see you personally.'

'In that case you can wait in my office.' His tone of voice implied an order and Roger obediently went through the connecting door, leaving Beth to face Marcos across her desk, oddly defensive.

'No wonder you have so little time to get your work done,' he said with icy hardness. 'You're obviously very easily distracted.'

At least my distractions don't take me out of the office, she wanted to retort.

'We must have been chatting for fifteen minutes before you came in,' she objected.

'I don't pay you to chat.'

Beth looked at the ruthless contours of his face without flinching. 'Shall I fax the information to the relevant offices once I'm finished with the report?' she asked sweetly.

'And you can wipe that smile off your face.'

'What smile?'

'I said that I don't pay you to chat.'

'Which is why I'm discussing the report with you,' she said calmly. 'After all, there's no point both of us wasting our valuable time here chatting, is there?' She stared at him with wide green eyes.

'You're treading a thin line, my girl.'

Beth gazed at him as if she hadn't the faintest idea what he was talking about.

'Were there any messages for me?' he asked curtly, as though her bland expression was beginning to infuriate him, and she smiled briskly.

'Two. I've left them on your desk.'

The look he gave her was sardonic. 'I'm surprised you managed to take any messages when you were so wrapped up in other things.' He looked pointedly at the connecting door to his office and Beth flashed another brisk smile.

Her colour had long returned to normal, and for the first time in days she felt as though she had slightly relieved herself of some of her nightmarish passivity.

'Oh, those calls came before Roger arrived.'

He leaned across to her and she automatically shrank back, not caring for the expression on his face.

'Keep your mind on your work, darling. Just don't forget who pays your salary.'

'How could I do that,' Beth asked with an innocent expression, 'when you won't let me?'

She could see that her control was getting under his skin. He didn't like that one little bit, she thought. He might have seen fit to toss her aside, to remind her with Angela's presence that she meant nothing to him, but that was his way of rubbing salt into an open wound.

He wanted her to respond. What he didn't want was her indifference. She smiled.

'I'd advise you not to keep Roger waiting,' she said blandly. 'You only have half an hour with him, then the rest of the day is booked with appointments.'

'Don't tell me what to do,' he snapped and she smiled again.

'Only doing my secretarial duties,' she murmured tonelessly. 'After all, we can't have any sloppiness, can we?'

He looked as though he could quite easily have hit her and she hurriedly focused her attention on the open file on her desk.

There was no point pushing this temporary triumph too far. But as he strode into his office, slamming the door behind him, she couldn't help thinking that at least the gods had meted out some victory to her, even if it was short-lived and changed nothing at all.

CHAPTER NINE

ROGER did not emerge for another hour and a half, and when he did Beth looked up at him and smiled. He winked back at her and strolled across to her desk.

'So,' he said with no attempt to lower his voice, 'about what we were discussing earlier on. How about it?'

Beth looked at him, bewildered, and he whispered conspiratorially, 'Do try and look as though you know what I'm talking about. I've got my back to Marcos, but I'll bet anything that he's listening to every word we're saying through that open door.'

Beth glanced past Roger, and to her surprise he was right. Not only was Marcos listening to them, he was also staring at them broodingly.

'Well?' he prompted.

'Well, what?'

'How about it?'

'Sure.' She flashed a wide smile, not having the faintest idea what she had agreed to. Lowering her voice, she hissed, 'I don't think this is a very clever idea, really, Roger.'

He ignored her whispered plea. 'So I'll pick you up at eight, then?'

Beth nodded in resignation, and Roger grinned encouragingly. 'Be sure and put on the glad rags, my beautiful; I think we'll paint the town red tonight.'

With that he left the office, a smug smile on his face. Well, he was certainly having fun with his little idea for

154

arousing Marcos's jealousy, but she didn't like it one little bit.

She had had enough schemes to last her a lifetime. Still, it would be nice to go out with Roger for a change, instead of moping around the flat, which seemed to be how she spent most of her leisure time these days.

Marcos's voice, crashing into her introspection, startled her.

'Now that your social gathering has disbanded,' he said in a voice heavy with sarcasm, 'would it be asking too much for you to come in here and apply yourself to a little work?'

Beth obediently trotted into his office and sat down, barely catching her breath before he began barking out his dictation to her, indicating sections on the various reports which she needed to identify, yet giving her hardly enough time to make the necessary notes.

After ten minutes her wrist felt as though it was on the verge of dropping off, and she interrupted him politely, 'Would you mind slowing down a bit?'

Marcos leaned back in his chair and inspected her with infuriating thoroughness.

'Going a bit fast for you, am I?' he asked in a dangerously innocent voice.

Beth recognised the tone instantly. She had heard it used often enough with certain members of staff whose attitude to their work did not happen to conform to his, and it usually preceded one of his bitingly critical attacks.

She eyed him warily, not knowing what sort of response the situation demanded.

'I've reached the bit about the targeted profits,' she began, deciding that she couldn't go too far wrong if she stuck like glue to the subject of work.

'Maybe,' he said in a falsely conciliatory voice as though she hadn't spoken, 'your mind is elsewhere.'

Beth schooled her features into a look of uncomprehending blankness.

'Dear me, have I lost you?'

'My mind wasn't elsewhere,' she objected truthfully, abandoning her stab at pretending that she didn't know what he was talking about.

'Well, you've never had a problem keeping up with me before.' He looked down at the sheafs of paper on his desk and absent-mindedly began leafing through them.

'Still,' he carried on in that voice that was forbidding yet patronising at the same time, 'no doubt you were wrapped up in your plans for this evening with Roger. How exciting for you to be renewing your old friendship.' He uttered the word 'friendship' as though it were one of the seven deadly sins.

He's jealous, she thought suddenly. She felt a brief moment of delight and then just as quickly stifled it. What was there to feel delighted about?

He might be jealous, but it wasn't because he cared two hoots about her. Oh, no. He was jealous because he might no longer want her, but he didn't care for the thought that she might be switching her attentions to someone else. That didn't fit in with his plan to torment her at all. He wanted to have her attention all for himself, so that he could parade Angela in front of her with shameless blatancy.

'Yes, it's very nice seeing Roger after all this time,' Beth responded offhandedly, noticing the grim hardening of his features. 'We got on like a house on fire in St Lucia.'

'Did you really? And now you plan on slotting him into your life on a more...rewarding basis?'

Beth opened her mouth to deny any such thing, and then closed it. Why should she protest her innocence? Why should she give him the satisfaction of suspecting that she had eyes for no one but himself. He probably knew that already anyway, but she damn well wasn't going to confirm it.

She shrugged eloquently and stared at her typing pad.

'I hate to disappoint you,' he ground out, 'but he won't be in the country for more than a week at the most.'

'An awful lot can happen in a week,' Beth pointed out mildly. 'Is there any more dictation or can I return to my desk now?' She smiled at him and he scowled.

'I might have guessed,' he said coolly, 'that you would start playing the field once you had gained a little experience.'

Beth turned white. 'And what exactly is that supposed to mean?'

He shrugged. 'Merely an observation. Women who have spent their lives in physical hibernation often show a tendency to break out once they've tasted what they've missed. And you weren't exactly practised when we first met, were you? Sure, you might have had the odd boyfriend, but none of them did anything for you, did they?' He held his fountain pen up and inspected it. 'In fact, no one did anything for you until I came along.'

There was a thick silence and she wished that the ground would open up and swallow her.

'That's the most arrogant thing I've ever heard in my life,' she muttered in a strangled voice.

'But true, admit it.'

He was staring at her intently, assessing her.

'I don't admit anything of the sort,' Beth threw at him bitterly, 'but maybe you're right about one thing. Maybe I have decided to break out, not that it would be any of your business if I did. As for your generalisations on the female race—well, you should know, shouldn't you? After all, you've slept with enough of them.' And still are, she thought. Or at least with one of them. Angela Fordyce.

'Does that bother you?'

'No!' she lied, snapping shut her typing pad. 'Why should it? And I thought you disapproved of my squandering my working time by chatting? I thought you made it clear that I was paid to come in here and work?' She stared pointedly at her closed typing pad. 'This conversation hardly falls into the category of work, does it?'

He ignored her outburst. 'Roger's not your type.'

'How would you know?' She was beginning to feel hysterical and trapped at this turn in the conversation. How dared he just sit there and act as though he had any kind of control over her life, when he had discarded her without a backward glance? Arrogant, she thought. Hadn't I always known that?

'You'd eat him alive,' Marcos was informing her casually. 'Does he know that underneath that cool little exterior there's a wildcat with a tongue like a razor?'

Beth stood up abruptly. 'I don't have to stay here and listen to any more of this,' she remarked tightly.

Marcos shrugged, his expression unreadable.

'Off you go to do your typing and plan your romantic little evening with him, then. Don't forget, though, that the office party is tomorrow evening, and I'll expect you to be there.'

Beth stared at him blankly. She had forgotten that office party completely. It had been one of those affairs arranged months ago, and with everything that had been going on it had slipped her mind totally.

'So,' he murmured, reading her expression, 'just don't go making any arrangements.'

'I won't,' she snapped, then added with a wicked sense of pleasure, 'Not that it makes much difference. Roger can come to the party with me, can't he?' She flashed him a bright smile. 'So if you'll excuse me I'll just go and start my typing and plan my little romantic evening with him, and, while I'm about it, I'll also plan my romantic little evening tomorrow night as well. After all, office parties can lead to all sorts of things, can't they?'

She turned and walked towards the door, her head held high, half expecting him to summon her back in that peremptory tone of his, but he didn't.

She closed the door quietly behind her and exhaled a long breath.

How much longer could she stand working for him? Just when she thought that things could not get more unbearable they did. I should walk out, she thought, and take the consequences. Except…except life without Marcos around, even a Marcos who could reduce her to tears, was no life at all. Wasn't that why she had been prepared to remain here and work out her notice?

She left work promptly at five-thirty. There had been no more accusations or innuendoes. In fact he had not made any more personal remarks to her for the remainder of the day, his eyes only flicking cursorily over her as she got ready to leave.

She staggered home after delays on the Underground, and spent at least an hour bathing and dressing very carefully. She was determined to have a good time with Roger if it killed her in the process. She was also determined not to think of Marcos at all. In fact, she had devised what she considered a pretty effective way of dealing with the problem. Every time that dark image began creeping into her thoughts, she would immediately focus all her attention on an imaginary scene on a beach somewhere until she felt that the image had safely receded into the background.

It didn't work, of course. Charming though Roger was throughout the evening, her mind insisted on throwing up graphic images of Marcos at the least expected moments, and there was nothing that she could do about it.

Roger, at any rate, had been thoughtful enough not to mention him at all until they had arrived back at her flat.

'Did it work?' he asked curiously and Beth grimaced.

'It was a stupid idea,' she said ruefully, not bothering to feign ignorance.

'Well, there's always tomorrow night.'

'Tomorrow night?'

'The office party.'

'Whoa!' Beth laughed and raised one restraining hand. 'No high jinks at the office party!'

'Would I?' Roger grinned impishly at her and looked offended.

But his little scheme gave her a nervous feeling in the pit of her stomach. He might not realise that playing games with Marcos was a dangerous pastime, but she did. Marcos had a unique set of rules for himself and could be quite ruthless if anyone infringed them.

She spent the next day counting the minutes until it was time to leave, guiltily realising that she was actually looking forward to the party because it meant that she would be provided with an extra opportunity to be in his presence.

With a lot of nagging from Laura, she finally gave in to her sister's choice of dress for the party. A jade-green affair that looked several sizes too small.

'Go to that party and stand out,' her sister had instructed her firmly. 'Make a show of pretending that you're on top of everything.'

Beth had eyed the outfit sceptically. 'In that dress, I'll look as though I want to be on top of *everyone*,' she had commented wryly.

But she had given in, and, she had to admit to herself, it didn't look half bad. It was shoulderless and hugged her body, finishing just above the knees. She stepped into a pair of high-heeled black shoes, brushed her hair until it gleamed in a straight curtain just below her chin, and batted her eyelashes coyly when Laura shrieked in glee at her creation.

Roger was as enthusiastic as well, and by the time they arrived at the London hotel which had been booked for the party Beth was feeling distinctly buoyant.

The place was already teeming with people. Most of the faces she either knew or else recognised, and she happily allowed herself to be absorbed in the throng, conscious of the stares she was receiving from some of her male colleagues.

It was always an eye-opener to see people out of their work clothes, and she knew that some of them were looking at her in a new light, asking themselves whether this was the same soberly dressed, efficient secretary on the top floor. Many of them were new and had only seen Beth, not Laura.

'You're the belle of the ball,' Roger whispered to her when they found themselves alone together by the bar. 'What I want to know is, where is the big man himself?

Shouldn't he be here by now? In fact, he should have been the first person here!'

'Since when has Marcos ever conformed to rules?' Beth asked lightly.

She had already found herself scanning the room for him, much to her irritation, relieved and disappointed at the same time when she did not see him anywhere.

She was about to order a drink at the bar when she heard Roger murmur at her shoulder, 'About time,' and she swung around automatically, spotting him instantly at the door to the salon.

He stood out in any crowd, but tonight he looked superb. He was in evening dress, and the impeccable black cut made him seem taller than usual, his shoulders broader. He was chatting to one of the other managing directors, his eyes cool and watchful even though his lips were curved in a smile at what was being said, and Beth felt her breath catch in her throat.

She watched him compulsively as he turned to the door, obviously waiting for someone else, and she saw Angela Fordyce enter, dressed in a black dress that screamed expense.

'The other woman?' Roger enquired at her shoulder and Beth nodded.

She told herself sternly that she was not in competition, but she felt a thread of jealousy surge through her veins and she had to look away.

'You're far more interesting-looking than she is,' he assured her comfortingly, and Beth laughed.

'That's a questionable compliment, but thank you anyway.'

She gulped down some of her drink, and made a big effort to listen to what Roger was saying to her. She made an even bigger effort not to indulge in her stupid need to scour the room for Marcos's dark, handsome face.

It was difficult but she succeeded. Her natural instinct had always been to keep her emotions to herself, and for once it stood her in good stead. By the end of the evening she could have individually counted Roger's eyelashes, but she didn't mind because she had succeeded in ignoring Marcos's presence completely.

Around her, the music, which had started some while ago, was blaring out. Roger had taken her hand and was leading her to the dance-floor. It was not where she wanted to be. Marcos was there, with Angela, and she wanted to be as far away from them as was physically possible in the room. Annoyed with herself, she eyed them covertly across the shadowy crowds of people. Her eyes locked with Marcos's and she felt her heart skip a beat.

When the music came to an end and she realised that he was walking towards her, her mouth went dry and she turned frantically towards Roger.

'Shall we get ourselves another drink?' she asked, taking him by his elbow.

'You wait here,' he instructed. 'I'll get something for you. What will you have? More of the same?'

'No,' Beth said hurriedly. 'Yes. I mean, I'll come with you.'

Marcos was approaching her and she just wanted to escape, even though she knew that she was reacting like a silly schoolgirl. After all, she could hardly avoid him for the rest of the evening, however much she would have wanted to. It would look highly odd to say the least.

But she couldn't face him. Not yet. Maybe after another drink.

'Don't be silly,' Roger was saying, immune to her pleading look. 'Pointless both of us battling our way through this crowd. No, you save our spot on the dance-floor and I'll only be a minute.'

She watched helplessly as he was eaten up by the people, spinning around when she heard Marcos's voice behind her.

'Care to dance?' he asked softly, as the music began. Another damned slow number, as luck would have it.

Up close he looked even more devastatingly sexy than he had from a distance.

Beth dragged a smile to her lips and shrugged.

'I've had more enthusiastic responses to an invitation to dance,' he drawled, enfolding her in his arms until she felt as though she was going to faint.

She had slept with this man, knew every inch of his body, and, right now, her own body was reacting just as it always had when it was close to his.

Under the stretchy knit of her dress, her breasts felt painfully sore, and she knew that as they rubbed against the stiff material of his dinner-jacket the nipples were hardening in response to his nearness.

'Perhaps you ought to find a more enthusiastic partner,' she replied tightly, and his body stiffened.

'No doubt you can't wait to get back to Roger,' Marcos responded in a hard voice, 'but what would people think if the entire evening passed and the boss didn't once dance with his secretary?'

'Since when have you ever cared what people thought?' Beth pointed out. 'And, since you claim to be so concerned by other people's opinions, what will Angela think?'

He laughed under his breath. 'You're right. I don't care what people think.'

He pressed her harder against him and a quiver of alarm shot through her.

She didn't want him to suspect what kind of response she was having to him. Let him think that she couldn't wait to return to Roger's arms. If he thought that, then it afforded her some protection, because she wouldn't put it past him to play a cruel little game of arousing her, only to smile mockingly and walk away.

'Well, I happen to care a great deal what Roger thinks,' she informed him in as controlled a voice as she could muster. She glanced around for Roger who, as luck would have it, was nowhere to be seen.

'Do you?' Marcos's voice was lazy, but with a edge of something which Beth couldn't quite recognise. 'Why? Have you slept with him?'

'What?' She pulled back and met his black eyes.

'I asked whether you're lovers.'

How nice if I could lie to that one, Beth thought resentfully, but that would have been taking the game one step too far.

'That doesn't deserve an answer,' Beth said tautly.

'You haven't,' Marcos said with a note of satisfaction in his voice, and she could have hit him. He was looking down at her and she stoutly refused to meet those dark, sexy eyes. 'Enjoying the party?' he asked lazily, one hand moving to the nape of her neck, the feel of his fingers making the fine hair stand on end.

'It's very nice,' Beth remarked, holding on to the control in her voice with effort. 'The food was very good, as was the company,' she added pointedly. 'Everyone seems to be having a good time.' That's it, she thought. Keep it polite and you won't run into any difficulties.

'Don't they?' he murmured into her hair. 'And who do you think is going to end up in bed with whom?'

His words brought a heated flush to her cheeks. 'I haven't the faintest idea,' she said evenly.

'Jane and that accountant chap, I think,' Marcos mused. Beth didn't answer, but she inwardly agreed with him. The two had been inseparable since they arrived and it had crossed her mind that at least Jane had had the sense to do what she herself had found so difficult. Namely, cure herself of her addiction to Marcos.

She shrugged. 'Is that the point of office parties?' she eventually asked.

'As you informed me, they can lead to anything,' he said softly, 'but not with you and Roger, I don't think. Even though you've spent the entire evening with him. Don't you know that one of the duties of a good secretary is to socialise at these types of things?'

'Please don't start lecturing to me on the fact that you're paying me to do my duty. I happen to enjoy Roger's company.'

'And I thought that you were avoiding me,' Marcos whispered, amusement in his voice.

What was this all leading to? Beth worried. Had he been drinking?

'You were wrong, then, weren't you?'

'Was I? I've been looking at the two of you. Body language is so interesting, don't you agree? I would have said that, out of this entire lot of people here, you and Roger are the least likely to end up in bed together, however much you try to convince me that it's a possibility. You haven't slept with him, and you won't. And we both know why, don't we?'

The music seemed suddenly very loud and Marcos's grip on her was stifling.

She tried to hang on to her self-control, reassured herself that she could handle whatever little innuendoes he threw at her, but she could feel her heart thudding in her chest and her skin had broken out in a fine perspiration.

'You don't expect an answer to that question, do you?' she asked tightly, when the silence between them threatened to overwhelm her. It infuriated her that he felt himself authorised to make sweeping statements about her sex life. No doubt he wanted her to admit that she was still deeply attracted to him, that no, Roger meant nothing to her. He wanted to hear everything he said confirmed, so that he could torture her with Angela at his leisure, secure in the knowledge that his method of extracting revenge for what she had done was working.

Body language, she thought acidly. Looking at the body language that had been going on between Marcos and Angela left her in no doubt that bed was their final destination.

'No,' he said lazily, 'I don't, as a matter of fact. You would only be confirming the obvious, because it's me you still want. It's written all over you.'

'How dare you?' Beth whispered impotently. The song was drawing to an end, and she pulled away from him, her eyes stinging with anger and humiliation.

Roger was weaving his way back to her, drinks in his hands, and she turned to him with the enormous relief of someone lost at sea who suddenly spied a ship on the horizon.

'Thank you for the dance,' she said through stiff lips, turning away before he could suspect what his amusing little observations had done to her.

She walked blindly towards Roger, her body shaking with emotion.

'What's the matter?' he asked, concerned. He held out the drink for her, but Beth shook her head violently.

She didn't want a drink; that wouldn't cure anything at all. What she wanted was to get away, far away. It dawned on her that there was no point in torturing herself any longer. She would flee back to Cambridge and try to rebuild the shattered pieces of her life. Tomorrow. She would no longer give him the satisfaction of playing his amusing little games at her expense.

'I don't feel terribly well,' she whispered, pulling him a little to one side. 'You stay. I can take a taxi back.'

'I wouldn't dream of it,' he said stoically. 'I'm your escort. Besides, who knows what I would get up to if you weren't chaperoning me?' She could see that he was puzzled at her behaviour, but he wasn't asking any questions, and for that she was grateful.

He took her hand and they threaded their way towards the exit with as little fuss as possible.

In her head she was already wondering what time the earliest train out of London was. Whatever time it was, she would be on it, even if it meant leaving half her clothes unpacked.

They were ready to leave when a soft voice said beside her, 'Going somewhere?'

'Marcos!' Roger grinned and Marcos ignored him, staring at Beth instead. She could almost hear his brain clicking away, working out the reason for her sudden departure.

'Home,' she replied coolly. 'I have a bit of a headache.'

'That was kind of sudden, wasn't it?' Marcos murmured. 'You seemed all right a moment ago when we were dancing.'

'These things do come on suddenly.' Was it her imagination, or was there a hint of smugness in his voice? All of a sudden, she just felt horribly tired.

'Come on, Roger.' She linked her fingers through his and turned to walk away, when Marcos's hand gripped her arm like a vice.

'Not so fast,' he said tautly.

'Let me go!' Beth snapped, furious now at his arrogance. Haven't you had enough of your cat-and-mouse game with me? she wanted to scream.

Roger was looking awkwardly at them both and Marcos turned to him with a snarl.

'Go back to the party, I'll take her back.'

'I do not want to go anywhere with you!' Beth all but shouted. 'Now take your hands off me!'

His fingers were digging into her flesh, making it impossible for her to move. As if suddenly realising that he was hurting her, he relaxed his hold slightly.

'I told you I'll take her back,' he repeated to Roger. 'And that's an order.'

'I'll be fine, Roger,' Beth said, defeated, knowing that he was unsure what to do and not wishing to prolong his embarrassment further.

'Sure?'

'What the hell do you think I'm going to do with her?' Marcos bit out. 'Now clear off!'

He more or less dragged her through the door, collecting her jacket from the cloakroom and tossing it over her shoulders.

'How dare you talk to Roger like that?' Beth asked angrily, as soon as she had recovered her power of speech.

'He works for me!' Marcos thundered, his brows knitted in a dark frown.

'That doesn't give you the right to push him around!' She yanked her arm away from him. 'And I do not want to go anywhere with you!' She began walking quickly towards the taxi rank.

His lean hand shot out, stopping her in her tracks and she raised furious eyes to him. 'Let me go! I'm not going anywhere with you, I told you! I'd rather throw myself under the nearest bus!'

'They don't run at this hour.'

'Hilarious!' she yelled, looking at him. 'What a sense of humour! You missed your calling as a stand-up comedian! Now, if you don't mind, go away.'

'I do mind.' His voice was harsh and it flashed through her mind that he was not nearly as controlled as he seemed to be. Right now, though, the last thing she felt inclined to do was analyse his state of mind. She didn't care what it was. She only cared about reaching the safety of her house, without him.

'Well, isn't that sad?' she bit out. 'But frankly I don't care one way or another.' She wrenched herself free of him and shouted, 'You're a bastard, Marcos Adrino!'

'You made me that way!'

There was a silence and then he reached out, pulling her towards his car, opening the passenger door and pushing her into the seat.

She was hardly inside the car, when he accelerated away from the pavement, tearing along the London streets until they finally pulled up outside Laura's flat.

The journey seemed to have been accomplished in five minutes. One minute they were screeching away from the hotel entrance, the next they were outside the flat, and during that time not one word had passed between them.

Beth had been too caught up in her thoughts, too angry at his arrogance, and he had been wrapped up in his own thoughts as well. She turned to him, her hand on the door-handle.

'Goodbye,' she said stiffly.

She pushed open the car door and she watched in horror as he stepped out of the car, his hands in his pockets, his foot idly kicking the car tyre.

'I can see my way to the front door,' she informed him icily. 'You've done what you set out to do. You've chauffeured me back to my flat; now just go away!'

Their eyes tangled and Beth felt a shiver of panic course through her.

She looked away and he gripped her chin with his fingers, forcing her to look at him. 'Dammit, woman,' he countered furiously, 'look at me! Can't you see what you're doing to me?'

CHAPTER TEN

BETH stared at the commanding dark face reluctantly.

'What do I do to you?' she asked shakily. 'As far as you're concerned, I'm a liar, beyond contempt, and you've made no effort to conceal the fact that as soon as I was out of the way you couldn't wait to...' Her voice felt as though it would break at any moment and she took a deep, steadying breath. 'To jump into bed with someone else.'

She turned away and fumbled with the key, finally managing to insert it into the lock, and with one quick movement she pushed the door open and tried to slip inside. But Marcos prevented her from slamming the door shut behind her, which was what she had in mind, by barging his way in.

Beth watched in growing dismay as he prowled restlessly around the room, finally standing still by the window and turning to face her.

'Where's your sister?'

Beth shrugged, not moving. 'In the bedroom, I expect. Sleeping.' Which, her tone implied, is what I want to be doing right now. Were it not for you.

She gazed miserably at him, drinking in the hard contours of his face, wishing that she could be more in control of her emotions so that she could handle this situation with aplomb.

'I really would appreciate it if you left,' she said finally, when the silence stretching between them was beginning to make her nerves fray even more at the edges than they already were.

Her feet were beginning to tingle with pins and needles from her rigid position by the door and she hesitatingly walked across to one of the chairs, sitting down and staring in alarmed fascination as he approached her. He moved unhurriedly, but even so she felt as though she were in a net, and there was nothing she could do to escape.

Not that she could run and hide anywhere. Where would she go? Into the bathroom? Anyway, hiding wouldn't make him go away. She sensed that instinctively. He would simply wait until she was forced to emerge. In fact, she wouldn't put it past him to use starvation tactics if he felt it would assist his cause.

This, she knew, was an inflammatory situation. The air between them was tense, and whatever he was thinking it was obviously not to his liking, because his face was grim as it surveyed her.

'We need to talk,' he informed her shortly.

'Really?' Beth was rather proud of the fact that her voice did not betray what she was feeling, and she carried on coldly, 'I can't think of anything we could possibly have to talk about. And what about the party? Shouldn't you be getting back there? You're the boss, after all. As you've made clear to me on numerous occasions recently.'

'The party will survive without me,' he said abruptly.

'And Angela? Will she survive without you?' How she loathed that sharp, jealous edge to her voice. So much for her wonderful self-control.

Marcos shrugged carelessly, not taking his eyes off her face. 'She managed well enough before.'

'Good for her, but that won't be necessary because I don't want you here. It would be better if you left and——'

'Better for whom?' he enquired softly. He was standing over her now, and she craned her neck to look at him.

Better for me, she wanted to scream. Better if you just vanished in a puff of smoke and stopped turning my life upside-down whenever it suited you.

'I don't like talking here,' he said abruptly. 'Your sister might hear us, not to mention David, and I don't particularly relish having this conversation overheard.'

'There won't be any conversation,' Beth replied angrily. 'There won't be any conversation because there's nothing left to be said between us. It's all been said and it's pointless discussing any of it further. We had a brief affair, and now it's time we got back to our lives.'

'And what's your life?' Marcos muttered. 'Roger? Are you going to settle for second-best? A man you're not physically attracted to?'

Beth's eyes flashed. What did he want from her? Did he want to break down her defences completely by admitting that she was in love with him so that he could have the final laugh?

'I already told you that what I do is none of your business...'

'Well, it wasn't what I wanted to hear!' With a frighteningly quick movement he took her wrist and pulled her to her feet.

'Too bad!' Beth snapped back, wriggling against him and finally giving up the unequal struggle.

Her cheeks were flushed with confusion and anger, her lips half parted to frame a few more choice words on what he could do with his arrogance, when his head swooped downwards and he kissed her fiercely, his mouth crushing hers.

Beth fought and struggled against him, twisting her head to escape the burning, drugging ferocity of his kiss, but he was stronger than her and he had no intention of letting her go.

His mouth forced hers open and she felt a sickening elation as his tongue found hers, moving moistly against it.

'No!' she protested weakly.

She placed both palms against his chest to push him off, but it was like pushing against a steel barrier.

Finally he released her, and the unexpectedness of it made her sway on her feet. Before she could react, he lifted her up, carrying her across the room to the half-opened door to her bedroom, kicking it and then shutting it behind him. The light had been switched off before she had left for the party earlier on, and the darkness lent a strange intimacy to their situation.

Unable to see him clearly, she became intensely aware of his power. He had lifted her up as though she weighed nothing, and now he deposited her gently on the bed. Immediately she attempted to spring up, but he held her down, waiting until she had regained some of her composure before he spoke.

'We have to talk, Beth. Things can't go on like this. Dammit, woman, I have to know for sure what's going on between the two of you!'

'I thought you claimed to know it all!' There was silence. 'Will you leave if I give you your answer?' she asked desperately. More silence.

Maybe, she thought hopefully, his silence implied that he would. She needed him to. His presence here was like a net around her, making her unable to respond in the way that she knew she must. He had to leave.

She sighed heavily and then spoke. 'Nothing. All right? Is that what you wanted to hear? There's nothing going on between Roger and me. There never has been. He's a friend and that's all.'

This, she thought, was the final humiliation. It was tantamount to confessing that Marcos was the only man who could arouse her.

'Why didn't you tell me that the first time I asked?' he questioned roughly.

'Why should I have? It was none of your business. *I* was none of your business. Did I ask you what was going on between you and Angela?' She could not prevent the bitterness that had crept into her voice. It reverberated in the room, echoing back at her, reminding her how much power lay in Marcos's hands, power to hurt her.

'Nothing,' he said flatly. Suddenly he sounded bemused, as though he had been overtaken by some unexpected turn of event which he couldn't quite fathom.

It was all the more apparent because in every other aspect of his life he was always so much in command. He had an instinctive talent for knowing just how to play a situation, but now he was uncertain, attempting to grapple with a problem which was infinitely more slippery than he had bargained for.

Beth looked at him wide-eyed. Her eyes had adjusted to the darkness in the bedroom, but she could still only discern the shadowy outlines of his features.

'Do you really expect me to believe that?' she asked tightly, forcing herself not to succumb to the thrill of what he had admitted. 'Your idea of nothing going on must be very strange, because you two certainly seemed to have a lot of physical contact considering you claim that it was all a platonic relationship. What was that you said about body language?' God, she thought, her anger directed at herself, there I go again. Acting as though I own him when I know only too well that no one does.

'Dammit, Beth, I'm not lying. I don't understand it myself. No, maybe I do.' He looked away from her uncomfortably and raked his fingers through his hair with a frustrated groan. 'The fact is, nothing has happened between us. Not, I might add, for lack of trying on her part.' He laughed humourlessly. 'I wanted to get you out of my system, and I thought that the most effective way of doing that would be to replace you with another woman, but it didn't work. You see, you must have worked some damn spell on me, because I just couldn't respond to her. Any attraction between us—well, it wasn't there any more and there was no way that I could resurrect it.'

Beth felt a surge of joy rush through her. She smiled, and he must have sensed it because he immediately said, 'I suppose that makes you very happy, does it?'

'I suppose it does,' she agreed.

'Well, I hope that you spent lots of time suffering sleepless nights thinking about it, because that's what you caused me. Ever since everything blew up in my face, dammit. Ever since I walked into that office and saw you with Roger, I've been out of my mind with jealousy. I needed you to tell me that there was nothing between the two of you. God, I needed that more desperately than I wanted to admit to myself.'

He lay down beside her and stroked her hair, his actions gentle. The aggressiveness she had seen in him over the past few days had vanished.

How nice it would be, she thought sadly, to close my eyes and forget everything that has happened between us. To pretend that only the present matters. But she knew that it was an impossible dream. Even if he still desired her, she couldn't pick up the pieces of their affair and carry on.

She knew now with certainty that he meant too much to her. If she had to lose him, then it was better that she lose him now rather than make the same mistake of postponing the inevitable.

'There's no point to this,' she said shakily. 'I can't just hop back into bed with you. Too much has happened.'

'Do you want to hear me apologise for my behaviour?' Marcos asked huskily. 'I do. I was angry with you, I was angry with myself and most of all I was furious because I still wanted you when you should have meant nothing to me. Do you know how much my ego was dented by that charade of yours?' He laughed ruefully. 'I succeeded in a tooth-and-nail world, knew how to deal with the shrewdest of businessmen. No one had ever before pulled the wool over my eyes, yet there you were, calmly confessing to the biggest con I've ever witnessed.'

'I wasn't calm,' Beth pointed out.

'I felt like a complete fool,' Marcos went on. 'I'd met my match in you and I didn't like it.'

He sighed and pulled her against him, and for a minute everything flew out of her head except that peculiar warmth inside her, that stirring of her passions which only he could arouse.

He kissed her eyes, trailing his lips to hers, covering them with exquisite, teasing gentleness, until she thought that she would faint.

It isn't fair, she thought, it just isn't fair that one man can do this to me.

'Marcos,' she began unsteadily, 'I...'

'Don't talk,' he muttered, silencing her with his hand, which had found the zip at the back of her dress and was slowly releasing it, freeing her body from its textured prison.

He slowly pulled the top of her dress down and she wriggled out of it. He owns my body, she thought with sudden clarity. It no longer listens to what I have to say, it listens to his commands.

She had not been wearing a bra, and he caressed her smooth, naked breast with his hand.

'I spent hours imagining him touching you here,' Marcos murmured, his voice as unsteady as hers had been. 'I was tormented by the thought of it. There were times when I felt like I could hunt him down and rip him limb from limb. And enjoy every minute of it. Now do you understand what I meant when I told you that you had made me into a bastard? No woman had ever been able to arouse me to such a pitch of insane jealousy. In fact, no woman had ever come close. But you...'

He rubbed her nipple with his thumb and Beth groaned with excitement.

Somewhere in her mind, some hazy little voice was telling her about her principles, about her decision not to become involved with him again, but, try as she might, she could not summon up enough will-power to listen.

She stroked his face and then coiled her fingers into his hair, urging him to caress with his mouth what his finger had been caressing a moment before.

She felt the wet warmth of his mouth on her breasts, his tongue flicking over the aroused bud, sending darts of ecstasy through her.

He raised himself, and she was dimly aware of him removing his clothing, then he once more bent his head to her breasts, exploring every inch of them with rapturous leisure.

'You have no idea how I've dreamt of this,' he whispered thickly. 'I felt sick with wanting it sometimes. When I saw you at the office, it was all I could do not to grab you and take you to the nearest hotel and make love. I spent hours reminding myself that you had deceived me, fighting that awful, primitive urge that refused to listen to reason.'

He eased her dress off completely, followed by her briefs, and she parted her legs to accommodate his exploring fingers. Her body felt hot and feverish with passion. It was as though she had not made love with him for years.

'I want you, Beth,' he said huskily, kissing her mouth with tiny, hungry kisses. 'I can't tell you how much. More than words could ever express.'

Want, want, want, she thought with icy realisation. The word had dominated his conversation ever since they had returned to the flat. And she had been happy enough to go along with it.

But hadn't she already learnt from one lesson? Did she have to make the same mistake twice to realise that playing with fire entailed burnt fingers?

'I can't,' she whispered, turning away to hide the shine of tears in her eyes.

It took a few seconds for her words to sink in, then his body froze.

'Why not?' he demanded. 'I want you back. I need you to come back to me. Where's the problem?'

'The problem is me,' Beth answered fiercely. 'I know we've slept together, I know we've had our fling, but I can't accept that situation any longer.'

'And what's changed?'

'Nothing and everything.' Her nudity felt uncomfortable now and she drew the quilt around her, protecting her body from his searching eyes. 'I guess I always felt that way, but I was blind before. Now I know that I just can't.'

'After all that I've told you?' Marcos asked roughly.

'What have you told me? That you still want me. It's not enough.'

'Why not?'

She looked at him dumbly, unable to articulate all the myriad reasons why she could no longer be content to be wanted.

'Well, this is it, then.' He got up and slowly began putting on his clothes and Beth watched in silence, afraid to say anything in case she broke down completely.

Besides, there was nothing to say. This time it was final. In the morning she would leave for Cambridge and they would be free of each other. Except, lust was so much easier to surmount. He would recover from his so-called obsession with her in no time at all.

Whereas she... what would she do? Get another job, while away her time decorating her flat and dating pathetic little shadows of him? No man could ever be his equal. She would spend the rest of her years playing an endless game of drawing comparisons.

He began slipping on his shirt, then stopped and sat on the edge of the bed.

'Of course,' he said thoughtfully, 'but no...'

'"Of course but no" what?' Beth asked dully.

'Of course, we could get married.'

There was a long pause and she eyed him warily from under her lashes.

'Don't tease, please,' she whispered finally.

'Who's teasing? Believe me, I wouldn't dream of proposing to anyone unless I meant it.'

'You're proposing to me?' she said in a high voice.

Marcos glanced around the room then his eyes resettled on her face. 'Well, I don't see anyone else in here, do you?'

Beth didn't know whether to laugh or to cry. Neither could express the profound happiness spilling inside of her.

She sat up and flung her arms around his neck, settling for laughing, although her eyes were glistening.

'Does that mean that you accept?' he whispered, and she could hear the smile in his voice.

'What do you think?'

'Think?' Marcos looked down at her strangely. 'I lost the ability to do that competently when I'm with you a long time ago.'

'Good.' She pulled him down beside her and this time she undressed him, loving the feel of his skin under her fingers.

'Of course, you know what this entails. No more Roger.'

'But he's just a friend, and a good one at that!' she protested.

'He might get ideas if he's around you too much,' Marcos grated possessively. 'Maybe I can arrange a few more overseas projects for him.'

'A few more?' Beth raised one questioning eyebrow and he grinned.

'I didn't like him hovering in St Lucia. I think that was when it first hit home with me what you meant. I wanted you all to myself. When you had dinner with him, I spent the entire evening at my meeting over there brooding over what was going on. Whether you were holding hands over the aperitifs and staring romantically at each other over the main course.'

'You did?'

'I did, you little witch.'

Beth giggled with delight. His words filled her with a glow of happiness. 'Why didn't you say?'

Marcos shot her a rueful look. 'And admit that all my single-mindedness, my conviction that marriage was not for me, that women were enjoyable but not strictly essential, was down the drain?'

'You're admitting it now,' she pointed out logically.

'I didn't have much choice,' he muttered. 'Much as I hated it, I was forced to admit to myself that I was in love with you. Madly, blindly and infuriatingly in love with you.'

'What will Angela think?' she teased, nestling against him.

She felt him shrug. 'Oh, she'll get over me. I wasn't the first man she had slept with and I certainly won't be the last. No, women like Angela aren't easily crushed by an unsuccessful romance.' He paused and then asked, 'Were you jealous of her?'

Beth nodded.

'Say it!' he commanded.

'I was jealous of her,' Beth obliged. 'Desperately jealous. Every time I saw you together, something in me seemed to collapse.'

'Good.'

'You know, of course, that there can be no more Angelas.'

Marcos laughed under his breath. 'How could there be?' he asked. 'You've managed to trap me hook, line and sinker. You're the only woman I'm capable of seeing.'

She stroked his stomach and he sighed, covering her hand with his then running his fingers up her arm, trailing them delicately along her collarbone.

Beth closed her eyes, arching back as he kissed the white column of her neck, nibbling her earlobe, enjoying her quick, uneven breathing.

Her breasts pushed against his chest, the friction sending tiny shivers of desire through her.

He lay back, and she slid on top of him and he caressed her breasts with his hands, raising his head slightly to lick them.

Beth groaned. She wanted him; more, it felt, than she had ever wanted him before.

Because now there were no more barriers between them. Before, not even the intensity of their passion could quell the sickening knowledge that she was deceiving him, albeit against her will.

Now there was nothing to hide from him, and that seemed to liberate her, making her responses more abandoned than they had ever been.

'Beth, darling,' he whispered, pulling her down to him, kissing her on her lips, 'I can't hold on for much longer.'

This time she controlled the final rhythm of their lovemaking until their bodies were fused into one and she lost all sense of space and reality.

'My love,' he whispered huskily, turning to face her, 'I want to make you mine as soon as possible. No big white wedding. Something small, and preferably tomorrow.'

'Tomorrow?' she squeaked.

'Or very soon after.'

She looked at him thoughtfully and smiled. 'Well,' she said lazily, 'I suppose it's a good idea to be married quickly. After all, I'd like Laura to be there rather than miles away in a hospital about to give birth. Although, knowing my sister, she's sure to guarantee that things don't run that smoothly.'

She lay against him and thought of how shocked her sister would be when they broke the news to her in the morning. Shocked and delighted. Laura could be thoughtless, but her heart was in the right place, and besides it would be a weight off her mind knowing that Beth was happy, that her impulsive idea had not been an emotional fiasco for her sister.

She would sell her flat in Cambridge. The funny thing was that she had no regrets at the thought of doing so. Wasn't home where the heart was? Cambridge had ceased being her home the minute she'd met Marcos and fallen in love with him.

'You know,' he was musing next to her, 'I never thought Laura would have had the brazenness to concoct that plan of hers.'

'You just didn't know her. Believe me, if there's one person in the world who can concoct a plan like that, it's my sister!'

'Well, I was away for quite a bit of the time that she worked for me. In fact, I barely noticed her there at all. She was efficient, she obeyed my instructions without demur.' He chuckled and stroked her hair away from her face. In the darkness, her eyes met his and the breath caught in her throat as she glimpsed the tenderness in them.

'I should have realised that something was wrong when I first met you. You argued about everything.'

'Not everything!'

'Well, put it this way, you weren't backward at getting your point across, and it didn't seem to bother you in the least that I was your boss.'

'Should it have?'

'Whatever happened to respect?' He grinned with bemused admiration. 'No, I should have put two and two together, and at least suspected that something was wrong. After all, I suddenly began postponing trips away because I actually wanted to be in that damned office with you. Me! A man who had happily roamed the world for years, loving the freedom of having no ties!'

She pulled him towards her and kissed him firmly on the lips, and he stirred against her.

'Suddenly I found myself in a cage, and, worse, liking it!'

'You have the key to your cage,' she said quietly. 'You can leave now if you like.'

'Leave? You might as well tell me that I can fly to the moon, because I can no more leave than I can do that.'

'Poor Marcos.'

'You vixen,' he said fiercely, his leg covering hers, his hand outlining the smooth curves of her body. 'You're dangerous. I could spend a lifetime telling you how dangerous, and not come close to describing it.'

'No more talk,' she murmured. 'We have a lifetime together for that. Right now, let's just enjoy the moment.'

Beth looked at Marcos across the breakfast-table and smiled. The past eight months had been good ones. They had married quietly and honeymooned in Australia, much to her mother's delight.

'You married, and Laura settled with a baby—what a shame I'm not around to interfere,' she had joked.

Marcos looked up, caught Beth's glance and smiled back.

'What a pity I have to go to work,' he said softly, stirring her blood with the warmth of his gaze. Even now, one look from him still had the power to send her thoughts flying.

She no longer worked with him, instead devoting herself to the luxury of completing her book-keeping course, though some of the urgency behind it had been lost.

Laura was amused by it, but not nearly as amused as Beth was by her sister's decision not to return to work after the baby had been born. A bouncing boy who looked like a miniature clone of David.

'It's a pity,' Beth agreed, 'especially since you only have a limited time left with me.'

'What?' Marcos shot her a puzzled look, the dark eyebrows meeting in a frown.

'I mean, you only have a limited time left with me as I am.'

'Darling,' he murmured, coming across to her, kissing her on her lips with infinite care. 'I love you the way you are. There's no need to contemplate plastic surgery. In fact, I forbid it.'

He grinned and she giggled compulsively.

'Isn't it wonderful the way you laugh at my corny jokes?' he teased, caressing her with his eyes. 'It really must be love.'

'Well,' Beth said, sobering up, 'this is no corny joke. You're going to be a father.'

Marcos smiled slowly and shook his head. 'Already?'

'You said often enough that now that the yoke was around you, you might as well enjoy it, offspring and all.'

'So I did,' Marcos murmured, his smile broader now. 'Is that what you meant about no longer looking the same?'

Beth nodded. 'Expanding waistline is on the way,' she said, patting her still flat stomach.

'I've heard it said that pregnant women are very sexy.'

'Have you, now,' she joked.

'Just so long as it's my pregnant woman.' He placed his hand over hers in a gesture that was so painfully tender that it brought a lump to her throat.

'Are you happy?' she whispered.

'Happy?' Marcos chuckled softly. 'You gave me happiness when we met all that time ago, and you haven't stopped. As for going to work...'

He lifted her from the chair and she squealed in mock protestation.

'I think,' he murmured, 'a little celebration is in order.'

And it was.

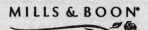

Your Special Christmas Gift

Three romance novels from Mills & Boon® to
unwind with at your leisure—
and a luxurious Le Jardin bath gelée to pamper
you and gently wash your cares away.

for just £5.99

Featuring
Carole Mortimer—Married by Christmas
Betty Neels—A Winter Love Story
Jo Leigh—One Wicked Night

MILLS & BOON®

Makes your Christmas time special

Available from 23rd October 1998

CHRISTMAS

Affairs

MORE THAN JUST KISSES UNDER THE MISTLETOE...

Enjoy three sparkling seasonal romances by your
favourite authors from

MILLS & BOON®
Presents™

HELEN BIANCHIN
For Anique, the season of goodwill has become...
The Seduction Season

SANDRA MARTON
Can Santa weave a spot of Christmas magic for Nick
and Holly in... *A Miracle on Christmas Eve?*

SHARON KENDRICK
Will Aleck and Clemmie have a... *Yuletide Reunion?*

MILLS & BOON®

Makes any time special™

Available from 6th November 1998

HEATHER GRAHAM POZZESSERE

Never Sleep with Strangers

Jon Stuart watched his wife plummet to her death.
Although cleared of any involvement, he endured
years of suspicion. But it was no accident, and he's
now determined to prove it was murder. The prime
suspects are gathered together, and the scene is set
for past and present to collide.

"An incredible story teller!"

—Los Angeles Daily News

MIRA®

1-55166-445-3
**AVAILABLE IN PAPERBACK
FROM NOVEMBER, 1998**

SHANNON OCORK

SECRETS OF THE
TITANIC

The voyage of the century
—where secrets, love and destiny collide.

They were the richest of the rich, Rhode Island's
elite, their glittering jewels and polished manners
hiding tarnished secrets on a voyage that would
change their lives forever.

They had it all and everything to lose.

"Miss OCork is a natural writer and storyteller."
—New York Times Book Review

1-55166-401-1
MIRA Available from October 1998 in paperback

MARGOT DALTON

second thoughts

To Detective Jackie Kaminsky it seemed like a routine
burglary, until she took a second look at the
evidence... The intruder knew his way around
Maribel Lewis's home—yet took nothing.
He *seems* to know Maribel's deepest secret—
and wants payment in blood.

A spellbinding new Kaminsky mystery.

MIRA

1-55166-421-6
AVAILABLE IN PAPERBACK
FROM OCTOBER, 1998

Jennifer
BLAKE

KANE

Down in Louisiana, family comes first.
That's the rule the Benedicts live by.
So when a beautiful redhead starts paying a little
too much attention to Kane Benedict's grandfather,
Kane decides to find out what her *real* motives are.

*"Blake's style is as steamy as a still July night...as overwhelming
hot as Cajun spice."*

—Chicago Times

1-55166-429-1
AVAILABLE IN PAPERBACK
FROM OCTOBER, 1998

MIRA®